SNATCH

by **Gregory Mcdonald**

A HARD CASE CRIME NOVEL

A HARD CASE CRIME BOOK
(HCC-128)
First Hard Case Crime edition: February 2017

Published by

Titan Books
A division of Titan Publishing Group Ltd
144 Southwark Street
London SE1 0UP

in collaboration with Winterfall LLC

Print edition ISBN 978-1-78565-182-3
E-book ISBN 978-1-78565-183-0

Design direction by Max Phillips
www.maxphillips.net

Typeset by Swordsmith Productions

The name "Hard Case Crime" and the Hard Case Crime logo are trademarks of Winterfall LLC. Hard Case Crime books are selected and edited by Charles Ardai.

Printed in the United States of America

Visit us on the web at www.HardCaseCrime.com

SNATCHED

(THE FIRST SNATCH)

Dedicated to several women
I have been lucky to know,
who have taught me from their
courage, strength and wisdom.

One

"Is the Ambassador there?"

"I'm sorry. The Ambassador is in conference."

"This is Mrs. Rinaldi, Sylvia. Calling from California."

"Oh, I'm sorry, Mrs. Rinaldi. One moment."

Across the airport corridor from her was a bookstore. People with luggage at their feet, some with packages under their arms, were browsing. Moving themselves and their luggage a few steps, stopping, taking a book off the rack, looking at it, perhaps keeping it in hand, perhaps putting it back, moving another few steps, sometimes moving back to take a book they had already returned to the rack: they were doing a dance, really, a slow dance with books as partners.

"Christina?"

She turned to face the inside of the phone booth.

"Are you having a good time at your tennis camp? How's your serve coming?"

"Teddy," she said, "What's the change of plans? I'm at the airport in San Francisco now."

"What change of plans?"

"Toby wasn't on the plane."

From behind his desk in his United Nations office, Ambassador Teodoro Rinaldi glanced expressionlessly at the three members of his staff sitting comfortably around the room, notes and note pads on their laps. None looked at him. Unrealistically, politely, they were trying to grant the Ambassador a private conversation with his wife.

In his own head, a distant alarm bell sounded—just once. It was the sound he had been half expecting every moment of his professional life.

Even in front of his own staff he must be careful in what he was to say now.

The Ambassador said to his wife, "Tell me about it."

"Flight 203," she said, "New York to San Francisco, Brandt Airlines, arriving three fifty-three P.M."

"Yes...." he said.

"They were supposed to deliver Toby to the V.I.P. lounge. I was there in plenty of time."

"I see."

"They didn't bring Toby to the lounge. The plane arrived. I watched the electronic board. I waited a half hour, forty minutes, thinking there might be a baggage delay. No Toby. What plane is he on?"

The Ambassador looked at his watch. It was five eighteen in California. His wife's alarm had been growing for almost an hour. She was doing well.

He said, "There had been no change of plans, as far as I know."

"But, Teddy. There must have been."

"What have you done so far?" he asked.

"I explained the situation to the head stewardess in the V.I.P. lounge. She brought me to the manager. The Brandt Airlines manager here. A Mr. Swenson. He was very kind. He was able to tell me Toby's plane reservation was canceled last night. In New York."

"He said what?"

"Why didn't you have someone tell me?"

The Ambassador said, "Hold on one moment." He depressed the intercommunication-system button on his desk and spoke to his secretary: "Sylvia, what plane was my son, Toby, on to California?"

"Brandt Airlines Flight 203," she answered. "Arriving San Francisco International at three fifty-three this afternoon."

"Would you please call Mrs. Brown at the Residence and confirm that Toby got off all right?" From across his office, the Embassy's chief of Public Relations, Ria Marti, looked up at him sharply. The Ambassador said evenly, "There seems to be some delay."

The secretary said, "Yes, sir."

Into the phone the Ambassador said to his wife, "I'm sure there's just some mix-up, Christina. I'm having Sylvia call Mrs. Brown."

"Teddy, Mr. Swenson—the Brandt Airlines manager here—

wasn't able to tell me what plane Toby is on. He said the reservation was simply canceled. He said there is no reservation for Toby Rinaldi on any Brandt Airlines flight today, tomorrow, whenever...."

"The airlines are very careful about these things...." The Ambassador knew that in talking he simply was filling up empty air. He was confronted with two sets of facts that did not jibe. He said, "Hold on." The light of another telephone line on his desk was flashing.

Through the intercom, Sylvia said, "Mrs. Brown is on three, Mr. Ambassador."

"Thank you." The Ambassador put his wife's call on hold and pushed the button for extension 353.

"Mrs. Brown? Did Toby get off all right?"

"Of course."

"You got him to the airport on time?"

"Plenty of time. He even insisted on my sittin' down with a cup of tea. A born diplomat, like his father, sir, I tell you."

"Did someone meet you at the airport?"

"Yes, sir. A young man. From the airlines."

"Did Toby have Mrs. Rinaldi's telephone number at the tennis camp in California?"

"Oh, he had everything, sir. The airlines sent a complete packet, you know, I had to fill out, for sending a child alone on an airplane. Names, addresses, numbers to call, allergies, if any, if the child is a particular eater, please state, Toby's name tag, everything."

"What did the name tag say, Mrs. Brown?"

"It was from the airlines, sir. Well, it said, printed out, you know, I'M BRANDT AIRLINES CAPTAIN and then I had printed in TOBY RINALDI...FLYING FLIGHT 203 TO SAN FRANCISCO and then today's date, sir. It had a picture of an airlines captain's hat in the upper left-hand corner."

"What was the last you saw of Toby?"

"Why, going through the security systems, sir. Toby was real disappointed he couldn't make the warning buzzer go off. Mr. Ambassador, there isn't anything wrong, is there?"

"No," he said too quickly.

"How could there be?" she said. "He was in the charge of airlines people. If they don't know how to put someone on an airplane, I don't know who would. His mother was meeting him in San Francisco."

"Quite right," the Ambassador said. "You haven't heard from the airlines or anyone else since you got home?"

"Well, I did, sir. The carpet-cleaning company. You know, the company that picked up the carpets for cleaning? Their manager called. Fairly choking, he was. He said they could never take responsibility for such priceless carpets. He said we should have told him what they were before they picked them up. He said if we couldn't prove they were heavily insured and—what did he say?—that our insurance policy extended to cover him, he was going to deliver the carpets back to us by five o'clock tonight. Uncleaned. How do you like them green apples, Ambassador? I was about to call you about it."

"I don't know..." he said absently. Without intending to, Mrs. Brown was giving him time to think. He was not thinking well.

"What am I to do about the carpets, Mr. Ambassador?"

"I don't know."

"Well, they'll deliver them back—"

"Fine," he said. "Right."

"Mr. Ambassador, there's nothing wrong, is there?"

"Absolutely not."

"Toby wasn't sick on the plane, or anything? All he had at the airport was orange juice."

"Everything's fine, Mrs. Brown. I expect I'll be in at my usual time."

"Should I try to call Mrs. Rinaldi in California about the carpets?"

"No," the Ambassador said. "Mrs. Rinaldi will be out of touch most of the afternoon."

He pushed the flashing button to extension 351.

"Christina?"

"Teddy? I'm a little worried."

He looked around the office at his staff. Each was quietly

reviewing notes on United Nations Resolution 1176R—the culmination of years of intense diplomatic effort and, finally, negotiation; His Majesty's sole object of desire; a few words, really, that would do more than warships and tanks and planes to keep the Persian Gulf open for the flow of oil to the free world. They were only pretending not to hear his conversation.

Slowly, the Ambassador said to his wife, "I understand."

She said, "You mean there is reason to be worried?"

"Listen, Christina, I suggest you do the obvious, simple things." He had learned the wisdom of keeping people busy in a crisis. "Look around the airport, especially the baggage areas, the snack bars."

She said, "Yes."

"Have Brandt Airlines page Toby. That's simple. The kid knows his own name."

"Teddy, Mr. Svenson said Toby wasn't aboard that airplane. His reservation had been canceled."

He said, "I understand."

"Oh, my God! Teddy!"

Quietly, he said, "That's right."

"Oh, God!"

"Call me back in an hour or so," he said. "I won't leave the office."

He hung up and pushed the intercom button. "Sylvia, call Brandt Airlines and see if that plane Toby was on to California was a through flight. Make sure it didn't stop in Chicago, or wherever."

"It was scheduled as a through flight, Mr. Ambassador. That's why we put Toby on it."

"I see. Nevertheless, make sure the plane didn't land anywhere between here and San Francisco."

"Yes, sir."

The Ambassador sat back in his swivel chair and smiled blankly at his staff.

"Mrs. Brown seems to be having a domestic crisis," he said slowly. "Something about carpets. Getting carpets cleaned."

He blinked at their stares.

"Nevertheless, I think I shall suspend this conference for the moment...."

The three staff members obediently put their papers in order and stood up.

"His Majesty's carpets may seem a small matter next to Resolution 1176R, but they are national treasures."

The Ambassador knew his dissembling was being ignored.

Ria Marti came to his desk and waited until the others had left the office.

She said, "Toby isn't missing, is he?"

He said, "This is about carpets, Ria. Embassy carpets."

"Mr. Ambassador." Ria was scrupulous about using his title in the Embassy offices and almost always at the Residence. "If this is about Toby, you've got to keep me informed from the very beginning. The press would be the hounds of hell on a matter of this sort."

Ambassador Teodoro Rinaldi smiled the smile that he knew had won more negotiations for him than all His Majesty's faith and power.

"Ria," he said, "skies may crumble and mountains tumble, but our young friend Toby will let nothing stand in the way of his trip to Fantazyland."

He saw that using his smile on her had convinced her that something was wrong.

As she was leaving the office, Sylvia's voice came over the intercom. "Mr. Ambassador, I've called Brandt Airlines. They have confirmed their Flight 203 today did not make a stop between New York and San Francisco. The plane landed at San Francisco International a few minutes ahead of schedule."

"Thank you." He kept his finger on the button. "Sylvia, get me His Majesty on the scrambler phone as quickly as possible. This is an emergency."

Two

Christina put her wallet, which had been open to her telephone credit card, into her purse and walked through the cavernous reception hall to the down escalator. In the baggage area, there were three carousels working. Slowly, she walked around each, peering into the crowds.

"Pardon me," she said to a man with an official-looking cap. "Could you tell me if the luggage from the Brandt New York Flight 203 has been picked up?"

The man looked at a wall clock. "That was carousel five. That's long gone, miss."

"Can you tell me if there was any baggage left unclaimed from that flight?"

"I can tell you there wasn't. Only flight we've had today, miss, with unclaimed luggage was from Mexico City. And people from the Bureau of Narcotics picked that up."

"I see. You're sure?"

Looking up over his shoulder, her eyes grew wide. "He's there! On the escalator!"

She sprinted. She jumped the first two steps of the escalator.

"Oh, please," she said to the people on the escalator as she tried to push through them.

"We're all in a hurry, you know," snapped a man with thick glasses.

"My son."

At the top of the escalator, she looked around the airlines' reception area.

A bell rang through the public address system to gain attention for an announcement

She turned.

"Toby!"

His hand was in that of a middle-aged woman who was leading him through glass doors to a parking area.

"Toby!"

She ran through the crowd to him.

Her arm hit the slow-moving automatic door. "Toby, Toby!"

She spun him around by his shoulders.

The child looked terrified.

"Hey!" The middle-aged woman jerked the boy's hand. "Who are you?"

"Oh, I'm sorry!" Christina said. "I'm sorry, I'm sorry."

The woman's pale blue eyes narrowed. "You need help, miss?"

"I'm sorry," Christina said. "My son—wasn't on his plane. I thought…"

The woman said, "I see. It's all right, Peter. The lady didn't mean to frighten you. Peter's my grandson," she said to Christina.

The woman was in pink slacks.

"Yes. I see. I'm sorry, Peter."

"Come on, Peter," the woman said. "We both missed our naps."

They went to the right, along the sidewalk. The boy looked back at Christina.

"I'm sorry," Christina said.

"I'm sorry." She sobbed. "I'm sorry."

Three

"My son appears to be missing."

Ambassador Teodoro Rinaldi had been told His Majesty, the King, was aboard the royal yacht, The Lioness, in the Persian Gulf. Using ship-to-shore, the scrambler system, and trans-world telephone, the Ambassador knew there would be long pauses between their comments to each other and that the King's well-modulated masculine voice would sound like that of Bugs Bunny. A rather slow Bugs Bunny.

"Was he abducted?" the King asked.

"We have no information at this time," the Ambassador said. "We only know that someone interfered in his affairs. Some third, unknown party canceled an airplane reservation in his name. Our housekeeper brought him to the plane. When the plane landed he was to be met by his mother, but he was not aboard the plane."

"Where was he going?"

"From New York to San Francisco," the Ambassador said.

"Why is Christina in San Francisco?" the King asked.

The Ambassador considered the King's ability to cut directly to the heart of a matter. He dreaded it.

"Vacationing. Tennis camp."

The answer seemed inconsequential.

"Why was Toby joining her on the West Coast?"

"Fantazyland. They were going to Fantazyland."

Through his United Nations office window New York had misted. The Ambassador blinked.

"Teddy," the King said. "Are things all right between you and Christina?"

"Yes, sir. She was just run-down and tired. Our efforts have been particularly constant, sustained, lately."

He stopped himself. Belatedly, his diplomatic training told him that the question would have been more convincingly answered with a single word. "Yes." Or "definitely." Or "absolutely."

The King would have realized—as the Ambassador had realized, sitting alone in his office waiting for his call to reach the King—that this was a particularly bad time to have his family away from the protection of the Embassy. He had been unwise—mistaken—in permitting it.

"Teddy. Do you believe Toby has been kidnapped?"

The Ambassador cleared his throat. "We know someone has interfered in his plans. At the moment, we do not know where Toby is. At the risk of causing you pain and anxiety needlessly," the Ambassador said, "I thought it would be best to let you know immediately."

"Teddy, I'm very sorry."

There was no question in the Ambassador's mind that the King's words were sincerely meant.

The King's grandfather had been a merchant. Simply that. A businessman.

A very successful businessman who had gathered unto himself almost every profit-making venture within his reach—banking, agriculture, shipping, oil—as a fat man finishes a bowl of olives put before him, almost not knowing he is doing it. In Italy and Switzerland and Europe at large, Teodoro Rinaldi's great-grandfather had been his contact man, his representative, his interpreter, his doer.

During World War I, the merchant bought himself a uniform (delivered from Switzerland by Rinaldi's great-grandfather) and set out to protect his various business interests in the Persian Gulf. Before the end of World War I, the Allies (persuaded by Rinaldi's great-grandfather) had decided it was in their best interest to draw a line around the merchant-general's various business interests and declare it a friendly nation.

Thus the merchant-general became a King.

And thus the Rinaldi family, originally Italian, subsequently Swiss, became loyal subjects of the King.

The present King, sixteen years older than Teodoro Rinaldi, was a brilliant, handsome man, carefully educated, at Oxford, the Sorbonne, the London School of Economics, to rule.

And Teodoro Rinaldi had been carefully educated, at Harvard College and Georgetown University, to serve his King in the family tradition as foreign representative.

Like few men in the twentieth century, neither considered that life had offered him an alternative.

"Have you informed anyone else that Toby may have been abducted?" the King asked.

"No, sir."

"I assume we're both thinking the same thing," the King said.

"Yes, sir."

"Resolution 1176R."

"Yes."

"But you've had no direct communication from the opposition that they mean to use your son's life as a weapon against you?"

"No, sir."

"You were right to tell me so quickly, Teddy."

"Thank you, Your Highness."

"It's conceivable you will have no direct communication. They might trust you to understand implicitly."

"Yes."

"Sabotage the Resolution or you lose your son."

The Ambassador did not answer.

The King said, "I will have my chief of American Intelligence at the Embassy within the hour."

"Mustafa? Do you mean Mustafa?"

"His name is Turnbull."

"I see." The Ambassador realized he should have known—he should have always realized—that Mustafa, the Embassy's chief of Intelligence—the nice little man with a mustache, very good at reading economic reports and breaking them down to facts relevant to the King, not very good at directing bodyguards, Embassy servants and staff—was not His Majesty's actual chief of Intelligence in the United States.

Before this, the Ambassador had never heard of Turnbull.

Again, he said, "I see."

"He's English trained," the King said. "Been in the United States a long time. You may have complete confidence in him."

"Yes, sir."

"Teddy," the King said, "we will stand together on this?"

It was a question.

Teodoro Rinaldi thought of the King standing over Toby's bassinet the very night he was born. Putting Toby on a polo pony at the age of three. Reading Uncle Whimsy comics to him during long flights in the royal jet. Playing with Toby in the snow at Gstaad.

But he was not Toby's father.

The Ambassador to the United Nations said to the King: "Yes."

"Mr. Ambassador?" Sylvia said. "Mrs. Rinaldi's on 352."

"Thank you." Since talking with the King, Teodoro Rinaldi had sat back from his desk, hands in his lap, motionless, staring at his wastebasket.

"Christina? Any luck?"

"Teddy, I'm scared out of my mind."

Her voice was dry, her tone a little higher than natural, her throat tight.

"Are you still at the airport?"

"Yes."

"What have you done?"

"Everything I can think of. Searched all over this place. Snack bars. Restaurants. Parking lots. Had Toby paged. Checked with the V.I.P. lounge again. Checked Mr. Swenson. There is no un-claimed luggage from that flight."

"Christina, we don't know any more than we did an hour ago."

"Oh." Her voice sounded crushed. It was clear she hadn't been daring to ask. "Have you talked to the boss?"

"The boss" was their name for the King. It came from a ridiculous statement Teddy once made: "I work for a boss like any other boss." The King was not like any other boss. He was a monarch. A dictator. A man with absolute, life-and-death power over his subjects. A power he had never hesitated to use.

"Yes," the Ambassador said. "He sends you his greatest sympathy."

"Stuff that," the wife of the Ambassador said. "What's he doing for us?"

"Sending in the troops."

"What?"

"I'm going back to the Residence right now for a meeting with his top intelligence people."

"Not Mustafa. Oh, my God. Not that nice, little useless man."

"No. Not Mustafa."

"What shall I do? Teddy, I just can't believe Toby is in this airport, or ever was. His reservation was canceled."

"I know."

"Shall I come home? I think I should."

"No. Where does Toby expect you to be?"

"At the airport."

"No. I mean, where does that little packet Mrs. Brown made up for the airlines say you're staying? What was the contact number she gave for you?"

"The tennis camp's. I gave the tennis camp number."

"Then I suggest you go back to the tennis camp. Someone—even Toby—might have tried to call you there."

Then he realized he was giving her reason for false hope. A hope which would doubtlessly be dashed within the hour when she returned to the camp and learned there had been no calls. Her panic, her fear, would begin again.

"But, Teddy, this was my last day there. I'm all packed. Toby and I were going to spend the night in a motel on our way to Fantazyland."

"Does he or anyone else have the telephone number of that motel? I mean, was it listed in the information packet?"

"No."

"Then return to the tennis camp."

"I've checked out. My room is gone."

"I'm sure they can accommodate you somehow. But, Christina—?"

"Yes?"

"For now, tell no one what is going on."

She was silent.

"I mean, don't tell the police. Don't tell the people at the tennis camp."

"I've already told the people at the airlines."

"Don't worry. They won't be the ones to tell either the police or the press. Bad public relations for them. Unless they hear from you again, they'll be quick to assume the problem is solved."

"All right."

"We don't need more pressure on us at this point."

"No," she said, "we don't."

"I suspect there'll be someone out there talking to you before midnight, your time. Someone from our Intelligence Section."

"I don't have anything to tell them. Except that I'm scared to death, Teddy."

"I know. They should be able to help you. You want a doctor? Sedatives? Anything?"

"No," she said quickly. "I want Toby."

"Believe me, Christina, the best brains in the world will be on this. Immediately. You know the boss."

"Yes," she said. "I do. Teddy, there will be no problem about the ransom, will there?"

The question startled him. Ransom. Christina thought Toby had been kidnapped for ransom. An American girl. He had married a young American woman. For nine years she had been the wife of the Ambassador, but she had never really known what that had meant. Constant social engagements. Boring dinners. Quiet talks. Anger at him for staying up late. Not taking vacations. Being nice to people neither of them could stand. Toby had been kidnapped and she had presumed immediately he had been kidnapped for ransom.

It was highly unlikely she was correct.

"Of course not," he answered. "No problem."

"Even if it's millions and millions?"

"The boss will provide."

"I mean, he wouldn't stand back on some damned royal principle, would he?"

She stressed "royal" sardonically. Christina did not think well of the two thousand, five hundred years of fictitious royal lineage the merchant-general-king's descendants had created for themselves. Another example of Christina's inability to understand the nature of power.

"Ransom will be no problem," Teddy said. He was certain the problem of ransom would never arise. Toby was kidnapped for reasons far greater than money.

"Christina? Go back to the tennis camp. We have the number there. I'm sure someone will come to you before midnight. Again, I repeat: tell no one about Toby."

"I won't."

"You'll just have to take this by yourself."

"I understand."

"Trust no one."

"Okay." There was annoyance in her voice.

"Christina, believe me. The longer we keep this quiet, the greater the chance Toby has of surviving."

"Oh, Teddy."

"Sorry, Christina. I had to say that."

Four

"Ambassador Rinaldi, let me get one or two things straight." Turnbull sat forward in the library chair, right forearm resting on his thigh, head angled aggressively toward the Ambassador.

"Your son was traveling alone?"

"Yes."

"And your wife is also traveling alone, on the West Coast?"

"Yes."

The Ambassador stared at His Majesty's chief of Intelligence in the United States. What should he say? That his wife and son were distinctly American in attitudes and found traveling with bodyguards cumbersome and embarrassing? That they all felt that bodyguards only increased the danger to them by drawing attention to them? That they had learned from experience that whatever arrangements the Embassy's Intelligence chief, the benighted Mustafa, made for them would just collapse anyway, causing a great confusion and greater complications?

The Ambassador said, "Let me make this straight to you, Mr. Turnbull—"

"Colonel Turnbull."

Teddy Rinaldi decided to ignore the title, for the moment.

"I am the highest-ranking representative of our nation in this country. I will not accept criticism, personal or professional, from you."

"Admit it, now, Ambassador Rinaldi. You made a mistake."

The Ambassador shrugged. How could he admit that his young American wife finally had rebelled against the tight strictures of Embassy life? Had insisted, reasonably, on getting away by herself for a while? Had insisted upon having a few happy days alone with her son, "play days," she called them, to take Toby to Fantazyland? How could he admit that he felt that if he hadn't agreed…he might have lost both his wife and his son? Immediately, the King had perceived all this: "*Are things all right between you and Christina?*"

"I might have made a more prudent decision," the Ambassador said slowly. "Fantazyland is not perceived as a threatening place."

He had let himself into the Residence—a fourteen-room condominium ten minutes' walk from the United Nations—with his own key and immediately found himself tripping over most of the Residence's carpets rolled up in the foyer. Mrs. Brown appeared, clucking about the carpets, and told him someone was waiting for him in the library.

The Ambassador had closed the library door behind him.

"You've gotten us into one fine mess." Turnbull scratched through his close-cropped, iron-gray hair vigorously enough to change the direction of whatever thoughts lay below the scalp. "Question is: how do I get us out of it?"

"We're talking about my son, Colonel."

"We're talking about Resolution 1176R," Turnbull snapped. "Mr. Ambassador."

"You know about Resolution 1176R?"

"Who do you think has done all the work on it?"

Calmly, the Ambassador said, "I think I have."

Colonel Turnbull glanced at him contemptuously. The Ambassador had observed before that intelligence people were like crows: in announcing the portents of rain they think they are generating a storm.

"Tell me everything you know about this," Turnbull said, sitting back in his chair.

"First, Colonel Turnbull, tell me if you have sent someone to be with my wife."

"I'm going out myself," Turnbull snorted. "Now I want to know two things: what arrangements were made for your son, and who knew about them?"

"Would you like a drink, Colonel?"

"I would not."

"I thought it might be easier…"

Muscles in his jaw flexing, notebook in his lap, pen in hand, Colonel Turnbull waited, saying nothing.

Teddy Rinaldi shrugged and began speaking in a calm, reasonable tone. "As I've said, Colonel, the pressures on my wife have been intense and long sustained. Very long. There has been a constant routine of meetings, lunches, cocktail receptions, dinners, day after day, including weekends, month after month, in our effort to educate other delegates and their governments regarding Resolution 1176R and attract their support and their votes—"

"You've been doin' your job, man. Get on with it."

"My wife was very tired…" The Ambassador hesitated. "…Becoming a little nervous, irritable. You must remember that Christina is born and bred American."

Colonel Turnbull sighed, pointedly.

"There is this tennis camp in California, called The All-Stars', modestly enough, friends had recommended to Christina. She arranged to attend for ten days."

"Were the Embassy's intelligence staff notified of her plans?"

"…Yes." *Poor* Mustafa.

"And no security arrangements were made for her?"

"None in particular, I believe. Embassy car to the airport, first-class flight, a hired limousine and driver meeting her in San Francisco—"

Colonel Turnbull shook his head.

"And your son, Toby?"

"Well…in fact, we haven't been able to see much of Toby lately. He attends boarding school in New Hampshire—"

"Eustace Academy."

"That's right. We thought we'd have some time this last summer, either at the beginning or the end of it, but Resolution 1176R has prevented our even taking a weekend. Toby was at that sailing camp on the Cape. Of course, we did take him to Gstaad for a few days with His Majesty last winter."

"Mr. Ambassador, I'm not looking for diplomatic phrasing. I'm looking for facts."

"All I'm trying to say is that my wife's desire—you might say, demand—to have some play days with our son, Toby, was entirely normal and correct."

"You're trying to excuse yourself for sending your wife and child off, at this point, with absolutely no security."

The Ambassador said, "I suppose I am."

"Give me your son's travel schedule."

"Yesterday afternoon he was driven by school staff to the airport in Boston and put aboard a plane for New York. Mrs. Brown met him at the airport and brought him to the Residence in the Embassy car."

"He spent overnight here at the Residence?"

"Yes."

"Did you see him?"

The Ambassador swallowed hard. "I had a meeting with the French delegation about the Resolution that went on until one thirty in the morning. I was at my desk at the Embassy at seven fifteen in the morning."

"Mr. Ambassador, how many months has it been since you've actually seen your son?"

"I looked in upon him the other night when he was asleep."

"He was put aboard Brandt Airlines Flight 203 to San Francisco today?"

"Yes. It was a through flight."

"Who saw him off?"

"Mrs. Brown, our housekeeper. She took him to the airport in the Embassy car and turned him over to airlines personnel."

" 'Turned him over?' "

"Yes. You know how the airlines do these things. Putting a child alone on an airplane is rather like sending off a package. They get name tags stuck on them and packets full of names and addresses. It's all quite safe."

"Usually," said Colonel Turnbull. "Usually."

"My wife was to meet him at the San Francisco airport at about four o'clock. She was there in plenty of time, but...no Toby."

The Ambassador paused a moment. He knew his voice was about to crack.

Finally, he said, "My wife immediately appealed to airlines' personnel for help in locating Toby. Here's a fact for you, Colonel

Turnbull: the airlines manager in San Francisco told Christina that Toby's reservation had been canceled. In New York, the night before."

"What?" The Ambassador thought he'd let Turnbull put his mind around that hard fact himself. "What did you say?"

"Toby's reservation was canceled. And not by my office."

"Then Toby is still in New York?"

The Ambassador raised his hands. "Toby could be anywhere."

"Who made the travel arrangements for your son?"

"The Embassy. Overseen by my secretary, Sylvia Menninges."

"Did the Embassy Intelligence Section know about your son's travel plans?"

"Of course."

"Who else knew?" asked Colonel Turnbull.

"The travel agency—"

"What travel agency?"

"We always use the Mideast Airlines office here in New York for any family or Embassy traveling. We're obliged to. They make all the arrangements."

"So, doubtlessly, there were Embassy stickers all over the tickets...."

"I suppose so."

"Therefore an unknown number of airlines personnel also knew that the Ambassador's eight-year-old son was skittering off to Fantazyland?"

The Ambassador's eyes ran along the top shelf of books across the room. "Skittering." Colonel Turnbull made it all seem very irresponsible.

He said, "My wife and son were taking a vacation. This was not an official trip."

The fat man flopped his hand impatiently.

"Who's this Mrs. Brown?"

"Our housekeeper."

"How long has she been with you?"

"Almost nine years. Since just before Toby was born, when we were stationed in London. She's sort of doubled as a nurse."

"Is she the woman who opened the door to me?"

"I suppose so."

"Is she a British citizen?"

"I think she's taken the opportunity to become an American citizen."

"I see. What other household staff is there?"

"Two drivers—"

"You mean, chauffeurs."

"Yes."

"Are they both Americans?"

"No. One is a Jamaican. The other is an American. From Brooklyn."

"Anyone else?"

"There's the cook."

"American?"

The Ambassador shook his head. "French. The houseman, who doubles as my valet—Pav—is a loyal subject. I've known him since we were boys."

The Colonel was shaking his head sadly.

"Are there complete intelligence dossiers on each of these people?"

"I trust so. You'd have to ask Major Mustafa."

"I will. Please ask this Mrs. Brown to come in. I want to question her."

As Ambassador Teodoro Rinaldi walked across the library to summon Mrs. Brown, he felt his legs hard with tension and already heavy from exhaustion.

Five

"Mrs. Brown, are you an American citizen?"

"I am, sir. Naturalized."

She sat on the edge of the library chair facing Colonel Turnbull, glancing nervously sideways at Ambassador Rinaldi.

"Toby," Colonel Turnbull said. "You picked him up at the airport yesterday at what time?"

"Oh, my God!" Her hand flew to her mouth. "Toby!" As she looked at the Ambassador, her sky-blue eyes seemed to shatter like glass. "Something's happened to Toby!"

"Mrs. Brown—" the Ambassador began.

"If you please, Ambassador," Colonel Turnbull said sternly.

"I do please," said the Ambassador firmly. "Mrs. Brown has been a member of this family since before Toby was born."

"I'd rather she had no information before I question her!"

Mrs. Brown, frightened eyes brimming with tears, was taking short gasps of air. "Toby?"

The Ambassador turned to the little, gray-haired woman in the big leather chair. "Mrs. Brown, I'm sure all this is just a false alarm… we're just being extra cautious. Toby seems to be missing…."

"Missing?"

The Ambassador could only guess at what she was imagining.

"This is Colonel Turnbull, sent here by His Majesty to help us."

She looked untrustingly at the Colonel. "I've never seen him before in my life."

The Ambassador smiled. "Neither have I, Mrs. Brown. Neither have I."

"Call the police," she blurted. "Call the New York police. Call the F.B.I."

"We can't do that. The Colonel is here to help us. If you'd just tell him everything you know…"

Mrs. Brown found a handkerchief in her pocket and brought it to her face. She would be a good soldier. She would rise to the demand. She always had.

Colonel Turnbull said, "Mrs. Brown, what time did you pick Toby up at the airport yesterday?"

"Does Mrs. Rinaldi know?" she asked the Ambassador with renewed sharpness. "I mean, that Toby is lost?"

"Yes."

To her hands in her lap, to herself, she muttered, "Poor Christina."

"What time did you pick Toby up at the airport yesterday?"

"Five thirty."

"Was he on the Eastern Airlines shuttle flight from Boston?"

"Of course not. American Airlines. First class."

"Arriving in New York at five thirty?"

"The plane was due at five ten. It arrived a little before five thirty. At LaGuardia Airport."

"Where, precisely, in the airport did you meet Toby?"

"At the security gate. I had to wait outside. Only ticketed passengers are allowed through the security gate, the sign said."

Colonel Turnbull's eyes flickered at her. A sensible woman: one who obeyed signs. He said, "Was Toby alone when you found him?"

"I didn't 'find' him. He wasn't lost." Her eyes were wet. "At that point, anyway. He came walkin' down the corridor like the darlin' little man he is, grinnin' at me, his suitcase bangin' against his knee every step."

"Was he alone?"

"No, sir. There was a stewardess with him. From off the plane. They were quite chummy. She even bent and kissed him goodbye."

"The stewardess left you immediately?"

"Yes, sir."

"Then what did you and Toby do?"

"We went straight to the car."

"You didn't have to stop for baggage?"

"Toby had his bag. Didn't I already say that? The poor lad didn't have all that much to carry."

"Where was the car?"

"It was in the taxi area. Double parked. DPL license plates, you know. Max didn't even open the trunk. He took Toby's bag in the front seat and we jumped in the back."

"Max?"

"Our driver," the Ambassador said. "One of our drivers."

"Mrs. Brown, while waiting at the airport, and after picking up Toby, going through the airport with him, were you aware of anyone watching you or following you?"

"Good heavens, no, sir. Then again, I'm not one to see evil lurking behind every bush."

"Then you shouldn't be working for an embassy," muttered the Colonel. "At least, not this Embassy."

"Of course, goin' through the airport with Toby, some people looked at him and smiled. People do that with Toby. He's such a beguilin' child."

Mrs. Brown blew her nose.

"Mrs. Brown," the Ambassador said gently.

Colonel Turnbull rolled on his hams. "What did you and Toby talk about?"

"You mean in the car?"

"At the airport, in the car, at the Residence...."

"Well. First he told me about the stewardess. How he found out so much about her in an hour's flight, I'll never know."

"What was her name?"

"Ms. Gunn."

"One N or two N's?"

"How would I know?"

"What did he say about her?"

"He said she wasn't too shabby."

" 'Wasn't too shabby?' What does that mean?"

"I think it means that he thought her beautiful."

"Oh."

"Her father was a doctor in Mississippi. She had a boyfriend in Atlanta, Georgia. The plane was going there next, and she would have dinner with him. His name was Jim."

"Did you understand from this that Ms. Gunn, the stewardess, was going back to the airplane and continuing her flight to Atlanta, Georgia, last night?"

"Yes, sir."

"Do you have any idea what Toby told her about himself?"

Mrs. Brown's eyebrows creased. "No, sir. Not at all."

"What else did Toby talk about?"

"He congratulated me on bein' pasteurized, the darlin'."

"'Pasteurized'?"

Mrs. Brown smiled. "He called me a 'pasteurized United States citizen.'"

"I still don't get it," Colonel Turnbull said. "Mrs. Brown, will you please speak English?"

Quietly, the Ambassador said, "Pasteurized: naturalized."

"I had been writin' him about my becoming a naturalized United States citizen," Mrs. Brown said. "So he congratulated me on becomin' pasteurized."

Colonel Turnbull shook his head. "What else did you and Toby talk about?"

"The trip to Fantazyland with his mother. He kept askin' me what I really thought it was like."

"What did you tell him?"

"I told him I'd never had the pleasure of bein' there."

"How much time did you spend with Toby last night, Mrs. Brown?"

"Well, we had supper together, in the kitchen, I went in on him while he was tubbin', and then talked with him for a while before he went to sleep."

"Mrs. Brown, was he in your opinion a well child?"

"'Well?'" Her eyes popped wide. "You never saw a handsomer, healthier child. Eight years old and not a speck of baby fat on him. His skin and his eyes and his hair just shine with health."

"Did he seem worried about anything? School? Work? Sports?"

"At supper he told me about his teachers and all his courses, and that he was the fastest runner in his class, beat everybody at the hundred-yard dash and made a record for his age running around the quadrangle in under three minutes. A very happy child, Colonel Turnbull."

"Neither you nor he left the Residence once you came home from the airport and you did come straight here, no stops?"

"We made no stops, and neither of us left the Residence last night, or this morning, for that matter, until it was time for the car to take us to the airport."

"Was it the same driver who took you?" The Colonel looked at his notes. "This man you identified earlier as Max?"

"Yes. It's usually Max on duty during the daytime."

"Do you know this Max person well, Mrs. Brown?"

"As I say, Colonel, he's usually the driver on duty during the days. So he's usually the one who takes me shopping. He comes to the kitchen for coffee if he has to wait for the Ambassador or Mrs. Rinaldi, or soup and sandwich if he's ferrying people in and out for a luncheon party."

"You're a widow, Mrs. Brown?"

"That has nothing to do with Max. Max lives in Brooklyn with his wife of twenty-six years and the three of his five children who still live at home."

"Was there a Mr. Brown?"

"Of course there was."

"What happened to him?"

"He was run over by a bus. Twelve years ago. On the Kingsland Road. A good man, you may be sure, but not one noted for his sobriety."

"All right, now. Mrs. Brown." The Colonel's tone gentled. "I want you to tell me about taking Toby to the airport earlier today. Everything you can think of. Especially whether—at any point— you noticed anyone watching you and Toby. Whether you remember seeing any person—no matter what he or she looked like—more than once."

"It went as smooth as canned applesauce," Mrs. Brown said. "Max was waiting for us downstairs with the car. We went directly to the airport. I can hardly be expected to know if anyone was following us in a car. Wait a minute." Mrs. Brown frowned. "There was a funny vehicle that was in the lane next to us for a long time. Pulled up beside us at two or three red lights. Toby and I got a good look at it and laughed about it. It was a yellow van, with blue and red bugs painted all over it."

"Bugs?"

"The slogan written on the side was, *Get the bugs out.* Call Whatsis Termite Company."

"I see. Do you remember the name of the termite company?"

"No. I'd say it was a French name. Or Italian," she said hesitantly.

"This truck stayed with you a long time?"

"Two or three miles. But not 'with us.' More beside us. In the next lane."

"Did it go all the way to the airport with you?"

"No. I wouldn't say so."

"Did the driver of that truck show any curiosity regarding you and Toby? Did he look at you?"

"Of course. People are always curious about people riding in the back of a limousine. But the funny thing about that truck was that it had wiggly antennas just over the windscreen...."

"You mean, radio antennae?"

"No," Mrs. Brown said decisively. "Bug antennas. Like bugs have. They wiggled as the truck moved along. Most comical, they were. Toby had never seen such a truck, no more'n I had."

"All right, Mrs. Brown. At the airport, what did you do?"

"Went to the Brandt Airlines ticket counter, waited only a few minutes. I did change queues. First queue I got into there was a man at the counter makin' a perfect nuisance of himself, something about his refusing to pay overweight charges on his luggage, a lot of camera equipment, I understood him to be talkin' about, so I went to the next queue and the man there was very friendly, smiled at Toby and with a straight face asked if he wanted to sit in the Smoking or the Non-Smoking section. Toby, being Toby, said he wanted to sit in the Pizza section.

"I told the airline's representative Toby was traveling alone, and I tried to show the man our ticket, I mean, Toby's ticket, and the packet of information the airlines people had given us, but after a minute or two talking to Toby the man said, 'Seeing you have a special person here, we're going to let you both go right through security down to the waiting area for Gate 18.' He said someone would meet us there and check us through so I could meet the stewardess or steward who would be on the plane with Toby, and I said—"

"Wait a minute, Mrs. Brown." Colonel Turnbull held up his hand. "Are you saying that the man at the airline's counter did not look at Toby's ticket?"

"No. He didn't. He understood this was a child traveling cross-country alone and special arrangements had been made for him."

"As far as you know, he did not even check to confirm Toby's reservation on that flight?"

"No. Why should he? We were there in plenty of time, and someone was going to do that 'specially for us at the gate."

"Did you give him Toby's name?"

"Not his whole name. I think the first thing I said was, 'This is Toby. He'll be traveling with you to San Francisco, Flight 203. Here's his travel packet. What do we do?'"

"And, although layin' his charm out for you and the boy, Mrs. Brown, in fact the airline's counter representative told you to wait until you got to the gate before checking in?"

"Yes. So I'd be sure to meet the stewardess." Mrs. Brown's cheeks turned pink. "I'm pretty sure the young man thought I was Toby's grandmother."

Colonel Turnbull said to the Ambassador, "The reservation was not confirmed."

The Ambassador said, "I see that."

Mrs. Brown looked worriedly from one to the other. "Did I do something wrong?"

Colonel Turnbull said, "No, Mrs. Brown. It's just that we need to check Brandt Airlines' routine for children traveling alone."

The Ambassador said, "It would make sense to have children checked in at the boarding gate. It would make sure that they were accompanied by an adult to that point. And it would allow the adult to meet the flight's stewardess, to have personal contact with whoever would be with the child during the flight."

"Steward," said Mrs. Brown. "It was a steward. He was waiting for us. And he told me I couldn't go through security with Toby."

"Wait a minute, Mrs. Brown," Colonel Turnbull said.

"I'm just saying I never did go to Gate 18 with Toby. The airline's steward met us in the corridor. Just as we were comin' to security, this young man came up to us. He said, 'Is this Toby Rinaldi?' I said, 'Yes, he is. I'm Mrs. Brown. Are you the young man from the airline?' and he said he was."

"Did you get his name?"

"Of course I got his' name. Willins."

"Willins?"

"Willins," said Mrs. Brown. "Two I's, two L's. I always make sure of names, especially if I'm handing Toby over to someone. He asked for Toby's ticket and his information packet, looked at them as well as he could, poor boy, said, 'That's okay,' then picked up Toby's bag and headed back toward the airline terminal with it. He told us to wait for him there."

"Mrs. Brown, did this person show you any credentials proving he was an airline's representative?"

"No, sir. I didn't ask."

"Then how do you know he was from the airline?"

"He was waiting for us. He knew Toby's name. He was wearing one of those blazers all the airlines' representatives wear. At least, the men do."

Colonel Turnbull sighed. "Can you describe this man Willins to us?"

"I didn't like him, at first. He wasn't tall, but he had very big shoulders and chest. At first, something about him struck me as untrustworthy, but then I saw one of his eyes was perfectly still. I guess it was glass."

Turnbull's head jerked up.

"He had a glass eye?"

"Yes, sir, I think so. And his face was rough and scratched. He had my sympathy, lookin' at him."

Colonel Turnbull hesitated. "What else did you and this Willins man say to each other?"

"He didn't say much. When he came back, Toby asked to have his name tag pinned on him. The man—Willins—didn't seem to care much about that, so I asked him if I could do it, and he said, 'Sure,' so I pinned it on Toby, makin' a kind of ceremony out of it."

The Colonel cut in. "Is there anything else you can think of that might help us, Mrs. Brown?"

"Why, no, sir. I don't think so." Agony was in her eyes.

"Just one more thing, Mrs. Brown: you didn't actually see Toby get aboard that airplane?"

"How could I have, sir? I was left way down the corridor. Last I saw of Toby was walkin' down that corridor beside the airline's representative."

"I see."

Mrs. Brown was crying quietly.

Colonel Turnbull said to the room at large, "I'd like to interview the rest of the staff."

Mrs. Brown said, "I'll get them, sir."

The two men watched Mrs. Brown walk across the bare floor to the library door.

The Ambassador asked, "You'll be joining my wife, Colonel?"

The Colonel looked at his watch. "I'll fly to the Coast immediately."

"That's good," the Ambassador said. "Someone should be with her."

Six

Closer to Baltimore than Washington, Simon Cord pulled off the highway into a McDonald's parking lot.

He held the door open for a family leaving the restaurant, a mother carrying one child while towing another along by hand, followed by a tired-looking husband putting his billfold back into his pocket. The man nodded his thanks at Cord.

At the side of the restaurant, Cord dialed the Rinaldi family's private number at the Residence in New York. At the instructions of the operator, he stuck a correct assortment of coins into the slot.

The phone answered on the first ring.

"Ambassador Rinaldi," Cord said.

"Speaking."

"You're Ambassador Rinaldi?"

"Yes. What is it?"

Cord was surprised the Ambassador answered his own phone, and on the first ring. That was good: he had already gotten the message.

"Mr. Ambassador, we have your son. Tobias."

Cord listened to the silence for a moment. Then he heard the Ambassador take a breath.

"Let there be no mistake about it, Mr. Ambassador. The people I work for do not want Resolution 1176R submitted to the United Nations."

"What have you to do with the closing of the Persian Gulf to the shipping of oil?" The Ambassador was expostulating, nearly blurting. "What has that to do with my son?"

"I don't know anything about that, Mr. Ambassador."

"What has it to do with you?"

"I don't know anything about it. All I know is what I'm told by the people I work for."

"Who do you work for?" The Ambassador was shouting. "Who's hired you?"

"I'm just hired to do a job—"

"What job?"

"Kidnap your son. We've done that."

"Brave! Some man you must be. Kidnap an eight-year-old child—"

"Man enough to murder him."

"What?"

"If you give that speech. If you submit Resolution 1176R to the United Nations, we'll kill your son. And we won't give him a nice death. Child or no. We'll make sure the body is found so you and your wife will see what your child went through before he died."

Cord listened. The Ambassador was breathing heavily.

The Ambassador said, "Bastard."

"Oh, I'm much worse than a bastard, Mr. Ambassador. Do you doubt it?"

"…No."

"Listen: if you're having any problems with this—if you think we haven't got your kid, or if you think we won't kill him—would you like us to send you his ear, or a finger or something?"

"Where are you?" the Ambassador said.

"How about answering my question? You want to get your son's foot in the mail? We don't want you to have any doubt at all."

"I have no doubt," the Ambassador said.

"No doubt?"

"No."

"Okay. Just be a good boy, Mr. Ambassador, and do what you're supposed to do. No Resolution."

Cord hung up.

The restaurant was about half full. Every table where people sat was littered with paper. There was more paper visible than food.

Cord walked down an aisle between the tables, toward the front door. A handbag was on the floor. He picked it up and handed it to an elderly woman eating a hamburger.

He smiled. "You might lose it," he said.

"How nice of you," she said, taking it with her free hand. "There are still gentlemen in the world…."

Seven

Going to the airport, Christina had been happier than she had been in a long time. She had had ten days of good exercise, tennis morning and afternoon, plenty of sunshine by the pool, healthy diet, early nights, good novels to read. Better than all that, for ten days she had been away from New York, away from the Embassy, away from Teddy, with his tired, drawn face, his long, diplomatic, involved answers to her most simple questions. Better than anything, relaxed, refreshed, she now got to spend a few days with her son, Toby, alone, together with him, exploring Fantazyland. She had felt fit to take on the world.

In recent months, no matter how she had tried to suppress it, her discontent had been growing. *Nothing is ideal*, she had tried to assure herself. *No one is perfectly happy. What is that line? Every happily married woman is putting up with something she can't stand? Something like that....*

Day in and day out, night after night, Christina realized she was putting up with more and more things she really couldn't stand. At breakfast every morning, gently, firmly, conversationally, Teddy, in fact, would give her her orders for the day: what invitations she was to accept, what invitations she was to send, what letters she was to write, what phone calls she was to make, what, in each case, she was to say and how she was to say it. He would tell her with whom she was to have lunch, and where, and what was to be said at lunch. In the afternoon, what members of the legation staff she was to see and how she was to handle them. Where dinner would be and at what time, roughly how she should dress, with whom she should make a point of speaking, and again, what she should say— always what she should say. And late at night, she and Teddy would sit in their robes in their bedroom for another half hour or hour, and again conversationally, as if it weren't desperately important, Christina would report to Teddy in detail everything she had seen, heard or otherwise perceived during that day. Teddy complimented her continually and referred to her as "my eyes, my ears, my heart."

She had become better at her job as she had come to know well most of the people with whom she had to deal. She developed a subtlety at working around evasive answers while answering evasively herself. Sometimes she even saw the whole diplomatic process as an amusing game: *You've got a fact, and I want it; I've got a fact and you're not going to get it unless I want you to have it.*

Odd things bothered her. At first, her facial muscles literally hurt from smiling. Her feet and the small of her back hurt from the constant cocktail parties and receptions. She consulted a doctor, who told her that standing still for prolonged periods was the most difficult and unnatural exercise the human body could perform. She learned to find excuses for walking across a room, up or down a flight of stairs, to the ladies' room, to go sit next to someone for a five- or six-minute chat. Whenever she could escape the legation, she would go for as much of a walk around New York as time permitted. And even though she would restrict herself to a single glass of wine at each function, every morning when she awoke there would be the mild headache, the stale taste in her mouth—complaints from sinuses and lungs that had consumed too much of other people's cigar, pipe, cigarette smoke and whiskey, gin and vodka fumes.

Her job. Her sensible mother had said that marriage was *a job.* What she meant, of course, was the job of being a wife, helpmate, mother, friend, sexual partner.... She did not mean the job of being a professional diplomat.

Christina Finch was born and raised in Flemmington, Pennsylvania, which in those days was shifting from a strictly agricultural area to a mixed suburban, rural community. Most of the farms were being given up. Two, redesigned to look like college campuses, had become headquarters for international corporations. One had been turned into a country club. Most had been turned into housing developments.

Her mother's family, the Reardons, owned most of the best farmland and, except for a few acres of road frontage here and there, had held onto it. Each of her three uncles still ran a sizable farm. Her father had put together his initially small country law practice with a real estate brokerage firm and an insurance agency and done very well. There was some grumbling among the established families of the town that Ol' Finch had made a fortune developing everybody's real estate but his wife's family's, which was left intact at ever-increasing values. But the town elected him mayor four terms running.

Christina's two older brothers had been the football and basketball stars of the town. One had gone on to West Point. The younger had taken his medical degree from the University of Pennsylvania and then surprised the world by becoming a minister.

Christina's own youth had been as ideal as possible. At school, although no mean basketball player herself, she led the cheerleading at her brothers' more noted athletic events, absolutely secure in their protection of her. Summers she spent working around her uncles' farms, again absolutely secure in their protection. Being the mayor's daughter, Christina became an expert buffer, making peace between youngsters born in the town and those moving into it. She was vice-president of her sophomore class and president of her senior class.

She had had no difficulty adjusting to college in North Carolina. Knowing her home would always be waiting, she dreamed vague dreams of New York and London and Paris but had no real expectation of ever being part of that world.

Then some committee asked her to play hostess to this diplomat from the Middle East who was coming to Chapel Hill to give a lecture.

She was at the airport on time, looking for a man in flowing robes and thick dark glasses. No such man appeared.

Finally, a slim, handsome but slightly tired-looking man, dressed in blue corduroy trousers, came up to her and said, "Hey, are you from the college?"

"Yes."

"Here to pick up someone named Rinaldi?"

"Yes," she said. "Are you here to see him, too?"

"I'm Rinaldi," he said.

"My God!" she said. "You're a diplomat?"

Seeing her shock, he said, "I guess I'm not."

The hotel where he was to stay, being state owned and run, did not serve meals on Sunday, so Christina found herself spending more time with him than she expected. She discovered he loved roast beef sandwiches with mayonnaise and strawberry milk shakes. Sunday night he said he didn't particularly want to go back to the hotel and rest, so they saw a movie. They stopped by an off-campus eatery and had beer and pizza. He didn't say much about himself, and she was too mystified by him to ask. He did say he had gone to school in Switzerland and to college in the United States. He said he liked listening to The Who but liked Eric Clapton even better.

The next day at the lecture she saw him for the first time as a diplomat, dressed in a dark blue suit, white shirt and red tie. She thought his lecture brilliant. Members of the audience that she knew were there to boo ended up asking respectful questions.

At the airport, saying goodbye to her, he touched his lips to her cheek so easily, so briefly, she wasn't really aware he had kissed her until after he had left. She knew she had fallen in love with Teddy Rinaldi, but she told herself it was just a schoolgirl infatuation for a sophisticated older man.

Wednesday he called her and asked if she could spend the weekend with him in Washington. She said no, thought for forty-five minutes, called him back and yelled, "Yes!"

Shortly, she knew it was Teddy Rinaldi she loved, his children she wished to be her children. Over long dinners he would try to describe the world of diplomacy. Only vaguely did she realize he was trying to warn her. Dumbly, she kept nodding her head yes.

Diplomacy: hadn't she been the town peacemaker? President of her senior class? Hadn't her father been reelected three times as mayor of Flemmington, Pennsylvania?

When they were first married, stationed in London, there had been frequent trips, vacations, breaks from routine. There had been Teddy's business trips home, long weekends in Scotland or Wales, or an occasional week in Portugal, or on the King's yacht in the Mediterranean, or skiing as part of the entourage in Switzerland. Even after Teddy was assigned to the United Nations in New York, there had been summer weekends on Long Island or Martha's Vineyard, winter weekends in Stowe, and vacations in Saint Croix or the Laurentians. And she and Toby and Mrs. Brown had spent many happy weeks at Christina's home in Pennsylvania.

Since Resolution 1176R had been conceived by Teddy and the King, there had been no such breaks.

In fact, she could not remember a single quiet dinner alone with her husband in over a year. Once, when Teddy had flu, he spent three days in bed. He worked there, too, but at least for three days she felt she had some of his personal attention.

What was most wrong with present circumstances was that it never let up. Christina was never seeing Teddy except formally, professionally. She was never seeing Toby at all. She felt she was losing touch with herself. One night before she had left New York, Teddy, tired and discouraged, had told her that it might be months yet before he would be scheduled to submit Resolution 1176R to the United Nations. Some African emergency had arisen. Christina was no longer sure she believed in Resolution 1176R.

Despite what her life had become, regardless of how hard she tried at her job, she remained Christina Finch, from Flemmington, Pennsylvania. To the diplomatic community (and to Teddy, she knew) she was *only* the Ambassador's young American wife, bright, attractive, very nice, of course, but without the training, the background necessary for such a position.

During crisis circumstances, Christina was not considered. Suddenly, Ria Marti would appear at Teddy's left elbow. Ria would know what was going on. Ria would represent the legation at receptions and dinners. Christina would find herself waiting in the bedroom late at night while Teddy and Ria consulted in the legation's office, or at Ria's apartment. At four o'clock one morning when Teddy came in from Ria's apartment, Christina threw a framed photograph of Toby at him.

He had never mentioned the incident. He had understood. Diplomats always understood.

But the incident had happened.

Christina was a terrific asset during business as usual, but given a crisis, she was supposed to withdraw and leave matters in the hands of the professionals. And they had been living under crisis circumstances for an inhumanly long time.

She still loved Teddy, but flying out to California, alone, divorce had been very much on her mind. She could make a home for Toby in Flemmington, Pennsylvania, where he would be safe and would know he was loved. She could go back to being involved in the lives of the people in her town, people she knew and loved— real people.

After her ten days of tennis and sunlight and swimming at the All Stars' Tennis Camp, Christina felt much stronger. She had not dropped the idea of divorce or, at least, separation from Teddy. She could, though, admit she still loved him.

For the moment she had decided to spend as much time as possible with Toby and try to discover how he felt about the school in New Hampshire, about never seeing his parents, about being yanked about by one adult after another.

She believed her vacation with Toby was going to be the most crucial few days of her life.

In leaving the airport, Christina suffered an agony the likes of which she had never known nor thought possible. Her heart, her mind, her nerves could not accept the idea of Toby *kidnapped*.

She drove stiffly, her legs braced with tension, fingers tight on the wheel, tears rolling down her cheeks below her sunglasses.

Rested, relaxed, she had begun to think she could get on top of her problems.

Someone has taken Toby!…Toby!…My God, my God.…Someone has taken Toby.…

Eight

In his apartment in Washington, Cord came out of the bathroom and answered the bedside princess phone.

"Cord? Something's wrong."

Cord's answer was sharp, annoyed. "How could there be? The kid was snatched. I already spoke with the Ambassador. On that private number you gave me."

"He was snatched, but not by Dubrowski."

"Turnbull, what are you talking about?"

"The chap at the airport who picked up Tobias Rinaldi was not Dubrowski. The housekeeper's description doesn't fit. Dubrowski's a big, muscular, handsome guy. Mrs. Brown describes the airline representative who snatched the kid as short, heavy shouldered—"

"Descriptions people give are never accurate."

"—with a glass eye. She couldn't have been mistaken about that, Cord."

Cord sat on the edge of his bed. "Gus...."

"What happened to Dubrowski, Cord?"

"I don't know."

"Did you give him any money in advance?"

"Yes. Some."

"How much?"

"Five thousand dollars."

"You gave five thousand dollars to a junkie?"

"He's been straight, Gus. Gone into the body-beautiful bit. I used him on that thing in Rome, the bomb—"

"Cord, right now we don't know where the kid is or who has him. Where's Dubrowski? Answer me that! Who is this other boyo who grabbed the kid?"

Simon Cord studied his white feet on the aquamarine rug. "I don't know, Gus."

"You bloody well better find out, Cord."

"I'll go to New York—"

"I'm on my way to the West Coast. The kid's mother is out there, and the kid knows it. You find Dubrowski."

"I will, Gus. Don't agitate your fat."

Simon Cord shaved as carefully as always.

When he had been called to the United Nations and given the assignment to kidnap the Rinaldi boy by the Nine Nation Coalition, by training he immediately had set about two tasks. The first was to get someone else to commit the actual crime, preferably a known criminal, an ex-convict, devoid of political interest, for an amount of money substantial enough so that when the time arrived to maim the boy, later to murder him, the tasks would be carried off without hesitation. Donald Dubrowski had served two sentences for robbery. Twice he had been indicted for but not convicted of murder. He had had a drug habit, but the last time he had left prison he was clean and determined to stay clean. Although a little past his prime for such a sport, he had put in between forty and fifty hours a week body-building. For ten thousand dollars, Cord had assigned him to blow up the car of an Italian banker in Rome. Dubrowski had done so, killing the banker, his driver, and a woman and child who had been waiting on the sidewalk for a bus. The assignment had not fazed him even slightly. For this Rinaldi assignment Cord had agreed to pay Dubrowski fifty thousand dollars. He had given him five thousand in advance.

Cord's second immediate task had been to secure someone in the Rinaldi household to cooperate with him, provide information about the family's travel plans, security arrangements, etc. This had proved remarkably easy. A decade before, he and Augustus Turnbull had known each other in Cairo. It was simple enough, as an old friend, to call up Turnbull and invite him to lunch. The representatives of the Nine Nation Coalition had identified Augustus Turnbull as His Majesty's chief of Secret Intelligence in the United States.

Like any two businessmen discussing a deal of some dimensions, they enjoyed a long lunch against one wall of the Four

Seasons. Cord saw to it that Turnbull had plenty of gin. Gently, he sounded Turnbull out about the Rinaldi family. Turnbull's caginess dissipated with remarkable alacrity.

Turnbull's hatred for the Rinaldi family was personal, profound, obsessive, insane. Speaking of them, his face reddened, his hands shook. Cord was surprised to see Turnbull had gained so much weight in ten years. He did not seem to be in complete control of his emotions. Cord gave him a long, drinking afternoon and early evening. Turnbull fantasized they were back in Cairo and told Cord everything.

A few days later, they met again. Turnbull did not remember having told Cord so much. Cord remembered. He assured Turnbull he would spoil Turnbull's plans for the Rinaldi family if Turnbull did not cooperate with him. He also assured Turnbull that Turnbull's best way of implementing his own plans for the Rinaldi family was to work with Cord. Once they had completed this assignment successfully, Turnbull could destroy the Rinaldi family, individually and as savagely as he liked. Cord would help.

Turnbull, Turnbull, Turnbull. Cord wiped the lather off his face. He wondered if he had made two mistakes: Dubrowski and Turnbull.

Nine

"Have there been any calls for me?" The young woman behind the tennis camp's reception desk radiated untroubled health and happiness. "Christina Rinaldi. Has anyone called for me?"

"No, Mrs. Rinaldi. No calls."

"I mean, someone didn't call and you said I'd checked out, or anything?"

"No. I've been here at the switchboard since two o'clock."

Christina found herself leaning forward, ribs suddenly against the high reception desk.

"No calls for me…?"

Concern flickered in the young woman's face. *She thinks I'm staggering drunk*, Christina realized.

"Listen," Christina said. "I have a problem. Something's come up. I have to have my room back."

"Your room?"

"Yes. I need to—I have to stay the night."

"I'm sorry, Mrs. Rinaldi." The girl looked at her chalk board. "We've given your room to a Mrs. Uhlmann, from Toronto. She's already arrived, I'm afraid."

"Some other room," Christina said. "You must have some other room available. Anything."

"No," the girl said. "This is our busy season. Every room is taken." Again she looked at her chalk board. "If you're having trouble with your travel arrangements, I could phone around and find a room for you in a motel until you get things straightened out—"

"No!" Christina's right hand was a tight fist on the reception desk. "I have to stay here! It's very important!" She knew she was speaking too loudly. People always speak too loudly when there are things they can't say. "Please," Christina said senselessly, "can't you help me?"

The young woman stared into Christina's eyes.

"Mrs. Rinaldi, are you all right?"

"Look," Christina said. *Tell no one Toby is missing*, Teddy had said. "Listen. This is the only telephone number my son has for me. If I'm not here…"

"Your son can't be very old," the girl commented.

"He isn't. He's just a little boy."

The girl looked at her chalk board again, hesitated.

"Please," Christina said.

"I suppose you could take a staff bungalow. Mark, one of our tennis pros, is away, playing in the C.R.A. tournament in Santa Barbara."

"Oh, yes. Please. Anything."

The young woman looked into Christina's eyes again, to confirm that something was seriously wrong, something she didn't understand. "We've never done this before. The bungalow's probably quite a mess. Twenty-five-year-old bachelor—God knows what you'll find. No housekeeping."

"That's marvelous," Christina said. "I really appreciate this."

"Hang on," the young woman said. "I'll get Mark's key. I'm sure he won't mind. I—I think it's upstairs in my jacket."

Ten

On the flight to San Francisco, Colonel Augustus Turnbull was assigned an aisle seat in the Non-Smoking, first-class section.

A man was sitting in the window seat.

When Turnbull opened the overhead locker to stow his own coat, the other man's coat and two packages fell out.

Turnbull dumped them in his lap.

"Why don't you go sit somewhere else?" Turnbull asked.

He slammed the locker hatch closed and fitted his girth to the wide seat. He then aimed a kick at the man's attaché case, under the chair in front of them. The man's case sprung open.

Turnbull turned slightly toward the man, folded his hands over his stomach and stared at him.

The man's eyes were roaming around the first-class section.

The stewardess leaned over them. "Is there a problem?"

"Nothing I can't solve," the man said.

Leaning over, he closed his attaché case and picked it up. Holding it and his coat and packages, he stood up. "I'm changing my seat, stewardess."

The stewardess glanced at Turnbull. "That's fine, sir. There are other seats available."

Turnbull snorted.

"Would you let the gentleman out, please, sir?"

Sighing, as if he were doing everyone a favor, Turnbull stood up and moved into the aisle. At the man's first step into the aisle, Turnbull pushed past him and squeezed into his own seat again.

He listened to the stewardess settling the man into a seat two rows behind him.

The stewardess then leaned over Turnbull again.

"Is there anything else I can do for you, sir?"

"Yes," Turnbull answered. "You can turn off that scratching music."

"The music, sir, is for the enjoyment of the other passengers."

"This passenger isn't enjoying it."

"Once airborne, sir, would you like me to bring you a glass of champagne?"

"Double bourbon for me."

"Yes, sir. Please fasten your safety belt. I'd hate to lose you, sir."

Turnbull leaned out to watch the muscles in the stewardess's calves as she walked up the aisle. He sighed. He pulled up the chair arm to his left and let himself expand wider in the seats.

Turnbull didn't know quite how he became so fat. One day he just noticed a pounding in his temples, a ringing in his ears, a shortness of breath and looked at himself.

He was covered with blubber.

His life had been active—physically very active. He had always been able to eat five square meals a day. It had always burned off in physical activity.

Once he became His Majesty's chief of Intelligence in the United States, his physical activity became negligible. He spent hours a day on the telephone directing his operatives, hours a day in cocktail lounges and restaurants, wining and dining government officials: members of Congress, the military, the various departments.

Again, Turnbull snorted. *That blithering idiot Rinaldi—Ambassador Teodoro Rinaldi—thinks he's done the work on Resolution 1176R.* Turnbull patted his stomach.

Colonel Augustus Turnbull knew the truth.

The music went off. They became airborne. The stewardess immediately brought him a plastic glass with ice cubes in it and two shot-bottles of bourbon.

Colonel Augustus Turnbull had had great difficulty even being in a room with Teodoro Rinaldi. Looking at him. Talking to him. Listening to him. Pretending to question him. Watching the man's servants march before him.

Turnbull realized it was a good thing he had played out the

questioning. He had expected to know the answers. Impatiently, brusquely, he had interrogated the Ambassador, savoring his own superior knowledge and role in this affair. He had Rinaldi where he wanted him.

Mrs. Brown was speaking. Turnbull was not listening closely. What was she saying? What did the man at the airport look like? He asked for the man's description again.

It wasn't Dubrowski.

The Rinaldi child was really missing....

Turnbull swallowed his double bourbon in one gulp. He slammed his chair back into a reclining position. He heard the woman behind him say, "Ouch! Hey...." He put his head back against the cushion.

He'd have to be far more coy with Christina Rinaldi than he had been with the Ambassador. *To find the kitten, follow the cat.*

The bourbon sloshed in his stomach.

The man who rode in the Jeep. The small, white man with the mustache that was too big for his face. The plantation owner. A high government official. Very close to the King.

The boy, Augustus, knew this was only one of the rich man's plantations. Far from the capitol.

The owner visited the plantation only twice a year, once in the fall and once in the spring. He was driven around in his Jeep.

When he would pass by the small, dusty frame house where Augustus lived with his mother, she would watch the Jeep, watch him. Her face would be totally expressionless.

The rich man in the Jeep would never wave or look her way.

When the rich man came to their house after dark, he always drove the Jeep himself. There was never anyone with him.

There had been other children in the Turnbull family, but they were so much older Augustus had only a dim impression of them. One son went to work on a neighboring plantation and was never heard from again. Another joined His Majesty's Army. Turnbull discovered later he had been beaten to death in a barracks fight. Still later he heard a whorehouse in Mosul, Iraq, was run by a woman named Turnbull, and Augustus wondered if she were his half sister. He never went to that whorehouse.

The senior Turnbull had been the overseer of the rich man's plantation.

Augustus had heard the story of his death many times. It had happened two or three years before he was born.

Turnbull had fallen into a threshing machine.

The workers brought him back to the house in a wagon dragged by a mule, but by the time they got him there he had bled to death.

His mother told him many times of her looking into the back of the wagon. Her husband's body was so bloody and mangled she had difficulty understanding what it was.

She always spoke of the flies. Her husband's body was black with flies.

Augustus and his mother lived alone in the house—except for the nights the owner was there.

The man who rode in the Jeep. The small, white man with the mustache that was too big for his face.

The man who rode his mother.

Rinaldi.

"Augustus! Come here! Come here this instant!!"

He was eight years old. Just the age, now, of Teodoro Rinaldi's son.

"Augustus!! Here!"

It was his mother calling.

When the owner came to the house in the Jeep after dark, Augustus always stayed in the back of the house. Sometimes there was yelling, sometimes laughter.

Tonight there had been yelling.

The kerosene light in the front room was hard on his eyes.

His mother's nightdress had been torn. Her left breast hung out. The nipple looked red, inflamed.

Rinaldi stood near the upright piano. There was something wrong with his eyes. They were watery, red. He was swaying.

"Your son, Rinaldi," his mother said.

Rinaldi said, "So what?"

"So don't think I can't get myself to the capitol."

Rinaldi put his hand on top of the piano, lowered his forehead onto his wrist. "You'd be shot before you were ten miles from here. Who cares anyway? Who'd believe you?"

His mother said, "Everyone."

"Who cares?" Rinaldi asked again.

"You have another son now. Your official son. Little Teodoro. Your wife."

"Shut up."

"You promised a lot, Rinaldi, Enough money to live on. Luther died working for you."

"He fell in the threshing machine. He was drunk."

"You're sober?"

"I'm not working a threshing machine."

"You said proper education for the boy—for Augustus—a proper education."

Rinaldi raised his head. He was sweating. It took him a moment to refocus his eyes.

"What do you want?"

"Money to go to England. I can't stand this heat anymore. The food. The flies. I'm old, Rinaldi, now. I'm thirty-nine. I look like I'm in my fifties. The heat, the sun. The flies. Just money. Just to go to England. That's all I want now."

"You'd never adjust."

"I can't live here anymore. I can't stand it. The isolation. I've given you enough. You've got to let me go!"

Rinaldi focused on Augustus.

"Yes," she said. "School. School for the boy."

Rinaldi came across the room. Passing Augustus, he didn't even stop.

The back of his hand smashed into Augustus's face.

The side of Augustus's head hit the wall He found himself sitting on the floor next to the wall.

"Little bastard," Rinaldi said.

Augustus remained on the floor. He heard the Jeep start and immediately gun down the road.

"It's all right," his mother said. "He'll do something now."

They arrived in Liverpool, England, in November, when Augustus was eight years old. His mother never did adjust. She worked in a factory, joined a church and went to a neighborhood pub on Saturday nights.

When Augustus was twelve years old, he came home from school on a January Monday to find his mother hanging by her neck from a pipe in the kitchen. For him, then, it was institutions until he was old enough to be put into the Army.

He served two hitches, then spent eight years in various African nations as a mercenary. Finally he returned to England and rejoined the British Army with the understanding he would be assigned to Army Intelligence. Of course, after full training, he was assigned to the Persian Gulf States.

It was while he was recovering from a three-day drunk in a fleabag hotel in Sirik, Iran, that the idea occurred to Augustus Turnbull. Was it an idea or a realization…a goal toward which he had been moving unconsciously all his life?

Old Rinaldi was dead. His *other son*, Teodoro, *little Teodoro*, was alive. Over the years, Augustus had heard Teodoro was in school in Switzerland, in school in America, assigned to the legation in London. Skiing, yachting, playing polo. He was being groomed for the highest posts in His Majesty's government. *Precious little Teodoro.*

The idea was so grand, so basic, so simple that lying on his flea-infested bed, he felt it between his legs.

Infiltrate and destroy.

He would wipe out the Rinaldi family. Nice and slow. He would give himself the pleasure of doing it

Nineteen months later, Augustus Turnbull changed employers again.

He used everything he had: having been born in that nation, having been trained by British Intelligence, having an intimate knowledge of the politics and the sewers of the Middle East, the Persian Gulf. He was accepted readily into His Majesty's Intelligence Service. Within three years of his decision in Sirik he was chief of His Majesty's secret intelligence wing in the United States.

And Teodoro Rinaldi, married, with a child, a son, was stationed in the United States as Ambassador to the United Nations.

Faithful to the King—oh, Colonel Augustus Turnbull had been faithful to the King, was faithfully doing the legwork, the blackmail and the bribery, to get Resolution 1176R passed in the United Nations, when along came his old friend from mercenary days Simon Cord with a proposition, an idea so grand, so basic, so simple, again Augustus Turnbull felt it between his legs....

Eleven

In the lobby of San Francisco's Fairmont Hotel, Spike put a quarter into a pay phone, carefully dialed 0, the Manhattan exchange and then the number.

The operator said, "May I help you, please?"

"Yeah. Oh. This is a collect call."

"Your name, sir?"

"Ah—Wilkins."

"Thank you, sir. I'm ringing. Will you talk with anyone?"

Spike said, "Just the guy who answers." A few meters away from him sat Tobias Rinaldi. His back was straight, his hands folded in his lap. Near him on the divan sat a girl in a brown velvet suit and leather boots reading *Vogue*. Toby was looking at her.

"Jeez," Spike said into the phone. "That kid's used to bein' pushed around."

"Pardon me, sir?" the operator asked.

"I wasn't speakin' to you."

"There doesn't seem to be an answer, sir."

"There hasta be."

"Well, there isn't, sir. No one seems to be answering."

"What number did I give you—I mean, dial?"

The operator recited the number.

"Yeah, that's right."

"Would you like me to try it again?"

"Yeah. There must be some mistake. The guy said he'd be there. This number."

"Very good, sir."

Again, there was the ringing. The girl who had been sitting next to Toby was gone and Toby was looking down at his fingers as if he'd never seen them.

"Jeez, what a punk kid."

"Sir? There is no answer at that number."

"Oh, yeah? How can that be?"

"I don't know, sir."

"Aw, okay, operator. But don't go home yet. I'll try later."

Twelve

Christina dragged her suitcases from her rented car in the parking lot down the long, dark path between a high hedge and the All Stars' Tennis Camp's staff bungalows. The young woman who showed Christina to the bungalow referred to the path as "Slave Alley." As a guest, Christina had never noticed the area or known of its existence. A party was going on in one of the other bungalows. Music was playing softly over the murmur of voices.

She stayed under a hot shower a long time, hoping it would relax her, make her feel better.

It didn't.

In her robe she sat on the lumpy divan, glancing frequently at her wristwatch, observing time stand still. Next to the divan was the telephone.

The bungalow was tiny. There was a Pullman kitchen, a bathroom with shower, a bedroom barely big enough for the bed and a dresser, and the living room with one long couch, two wicker chairs and a pine coffee table. There was no air conditioning.

On the walls were posters of the two popular model-filmstars of the moment, in poses more athletic than seductive, a T-shirt tacked up by its shoulders saying FOREST HILLS, an autographed tennis schedule and a large number of fly stains.

In every corner of the bungalow, it seemed, was something discarded—one sneaker, one sock, an empty rum bottle, a torn tennis magazine, a cracked Frisbee, a pair of blue jeans torn at the crotch.

Christina thought of getting up and finding something to eat. She felt slightly nauseous.

Again she glanced at her watch.

There was a rapping on the window of the bungalow door. Hearing it, the only immediate thought she had was that the pane of glass was loose in its frame.

Someone rapped again.

Remaining seated, Christina called out, "He's not here. Mark's away—at a tennis tournament."

Outside, a voice said, "Mrs. Rinaldi?"

"Yes." She got up. "Yes."

She opened the door.

A heavy man in a bulky tweed suit stood on the path.

"I'm Mrs. Rinaldi," she said.

"Augustus Turnbull, ma'am. Colonel Augustus Turnbull. Here to do anything I can to help."

"Oh, yes. Come in. Please."

After he entered, she saw that his tweed suit was green.

"I'm alone," she heard herself say.

"Your husband mentioned me?"

"Yes, I think he did. I don't know. He mentioned someone would be here. I'm so—"

"You're in a state of shock, Mrs. Rinaldi. A terrible state of shock. Over this terrible thing that has happened to your family."

"I was hoping someone would appear. I—I'm not thinking too well."

"Of course."

"I'm not sure what I'm supposed to be doing just now. I don't know what I can do."

She had difficulty seeing the man's eyes in his fat face.

"I don't think there's anything to be done just now. Get some sleep. We both need sleep."

"But Toby could be anywhere…anything could be happening to him."

Turnbull put his hand on her arm. "You can't think that way, Mrs. Rinaldi. I'm here now. Everything will be all right."

"That's very kind," she said. "But I don't know what it means."

"There are people in Washington and New York working on this, and there'll be more in the morning. Have you eaten? Would you like a drink? A sedative?"

"No. I don't want anything."

"This is very difficult." Turnbull moved around the living room, apparently seeing everything.

He picked up a broken tennis racket and went to one corner of the room. Stooping, he picked something up with the racket's handle. Christina saw it was a jock strap. Turnbull carried it to the door and threw it outside.

She smiled at him.

"There's one bed, I suppose?" he asked. "One bedroom?"

"Yes."

"I'll sleep there. On the couch." He could not conceal his look of dismay.

"There are no other rooms available," she said, "but there are motels nearby. I'll be all right."

"I'd rather stay with you," he said quietly, "for what comfort I may be to you."

"You really needn't."

"That's all right, Mrs. Rinaldi." He asked, "May I call you Christina?"

"Yes." She looked away. "Of course."

"All right, then. Good night, Christina. Try to sleep."

At the bedroom door, she said, "And what do we do? What do we do in the morning?"

"I'll need to make some phone calls," he answered. "I'll need to go out for a while. Don't you worry yourself. Just follow your own instincts. Leave everything in my hands."

Christina looked at his hands. The backs of his hands faced forward.

"All right…" she said.

"Not to worry, Christina. We'll find your child. Believe me."

Thirteen

"Anyway—" Toby sat on the edge of the bed in Room 102 in the Red Star–Silvermine Motel continuing to tell the story he had begun in the car with Spike. Spike had never seemed much interested in it.

When they had arrived at the motel, Spike had left Toby in the car while he talked to the man in the office.

Spike and Toby had gone to the room alone.

Over the phone, Spike had ordered cheeseburgers, french fries and milk for them both.

Then he made another call. He dialed a lot of numbers, told the operator it was to be a collect call and said his name was Wilkins. He held the phone to his ear a long time before hanging up. There was no answer.

As Toby talked, Spike prowled around the room, looking in the closets, out the window, walking in and out of the bathroom several times.

Toby thought telling Spike a story might make him more peaceful. Stories always made Toby more peaceful.

"This policeman says to this newspaper reporter, Clark Kent, who really is Superman, you see, in different clothes—do you remember my telling you that, Spike?—'If we don't catch this crook soon, we can wave goodbye to all decency in this city!' I told you, Spike, that this terrible crook was stealing buses right off the city streets so everybody had to walk to the store. He would go disguised as a bus driver, you see, and knock out the real bus driver and then drive the bus away. He was selling them to some poor city in China. They could never catch him because all bus drivers look the same in their bus driver's uniforms—"

Spike turned from the window. "Shut up, kid. Go to the bathroom."

"What?"

"Get into the bathroom."

"I went when I came in."

"Get into the bathroom!" Spike put his head too close to Toby's, his glass eye staring. "Or I will twist off two of your fingers and make you eat 'em!"

Toby wrinkled his nose. He put his hands in his pockets.

He went into the bathroom.

"Lissen," Spike said. They were sitting on the edges of their beds, eating the cheeseburgers and french fries. Each had a pint of milk on the floor by his feet. "Sick of your stories. Fac' is, you don't know what you're talkin' about. How old are you? Twelve years old?"

Pleased, Toby said, "No."

"How old?"

"Eight."

"Eight years old. Shit. I don't even remember eight years ago hardly. Eight years is nothin'." He tried to snap his fingers, but they were too greasy. "Eight years means nothin'. What you ever done?"

"I done plenty," Toby said. He looked up from under his eyebrows at Spike. "I mean, I have done plenty."

"Yeah? You don' sound it. You sound like an ignoramus kid."

"I've done plenty. I go to school."

"Everybody goes to school," Spike said. "Mos'ly."

"I've done the quad in under three. I'm age champion in the hundred-yard dash...."

" 'Done the quad in under three.' What kinda language is that?"

"Yes. And I've studied French—"

"Who needs to speak French? Everybody I ever come across speak one of those crazy languages all you have to do is say shut up to, and if they don't, you punch 'em out. Stupid shits."

"I can sail a Beetle Cat—"

"Anybody can do thatl You pick it up by its stupid tail, swing it through the air and let go! 'Sail a cat.' Fancy Dan talk."

"In Gstaad last year, skiing with His Majesty, they allowed me on the medium–advanced slopes. That's pretty good for a kid my age. And it wasn't because of anything His Majesty said, either."

"What's a Gstaad? Ko-zum-tite!"

"It's a place we go skiing. With His Majesty."

"Who's 'His Majesty'? Your old man?"

"Old man?"

"Your father?"

"No. The King."

" 'The King.' Jeez, ignoramus kid."

"Sure. And the King has put me on some of his ponies. He even had a special short mallet made for me."

"What for? What's a mallet?"

"For polo."

"Jeez, kid. Ignoramus kid. Fancy Dan talk. You're outa your tree. Fac' is, you've had too much of that red horse."

"What red horse?"

"That red-horse stuff you were always talkin' about on the plane. In your suitcase."

"That's Red Pony."

"There's a diff'runce?"

"Where is my suitcase?"

"I tol' ya, kid. Fac' is, the airlines lost it. You need a fix, kid? Ahh, you don't know what you're talkin' about. Fac' is, you confuse me."

"I don't have any clothes. Any pajamas. Any clothes for the morning."

"What'sa matter with the clothes you got on?"

Toby looked down at the sleeves of his jacket. "I've been wearing them all day."

" 'Wearing 'em all day'! I wear clothes two, three weeks. Then I throw them away."

"Two, three weeks at a time?"

"Yeah. See, I got money now. I can do that."

"Don't you itch?"

"When I itch, I go to the store."

"So that's why you don't have any luggage, either?"

"That's right, kid. Travel light. On the road. Keep movin'."

"Why wasn't my mother at that big hotel we went to?"

"You already ast me that."

"In the car I said, 'Where's my mother?' and you didn't answer."

"You saw me on the phone?"

"Of course I saw you on the phone."

"Fac' is, they tol' me she couldn't make it. She was gonna be late. Real late. Maybe two, three days late."

"Oh. You were talking with my mother?"

"No. 'Course not. The airlines. I was talkin' to the people at the airlines. 'Cause your mother wasn't at the hotel, see?"

Toby said, "You never asked at the desk."

"Fac' is, she supposed to be waitin' for us in the lobby, see? So I called the airlines."

"Oh."

"They said to come over here. Cheaper, you know? Who needs a big hotel like that?"

"But if my mother's going there—"

"Oh, yeah, kid. When she arrives, she'll call us here. That's why we're supposed to stay here, see? Wait for her to call us. Then we'll go back to that other hotel." Spike ran his index finger around his teeth, wiped his fingers on his pants and smiled at Toby. "See? You don't know everything. Just an ignoramus kid."

Toby said, "I need a toothbrush."

"In the morning, kid. Maybe we'll get things in the morning."

"Pajamas?"

"Shit, no. Pajamas is for sissies."

Toby said, "Why?"

"Why? I dunno. 'Cause you don' know much, that's why. Just an ignoramus kid. Swingin' a cat—"

"Sailing a cat."

"We used to call it swingin' a cat. You don't think I never swung a cat?" His eyes narrowed. "Lissen, you pour kerosene on it, set a match to it, set the cat on fire, then you swing it by its tail over your head a few times. Then you let go."

Toby felt his blood fall down through his body.

"You never did that, did you, kid?"

Toby swallowed hard.

"See? Fac' is, you don' know nothin'. Nothin' at all. This stuff you make up. His Majesty. The King. Jeez, kid."

"There is a King."

"There are no kings."

"My father works for him."

"Yeah? You're full of bullshit."

"There are lots of kings."

"There are no kings. They're called presidents nowadays, stupid. Fac' is, I even been in some places they call 'em *presidentes*. There are no kings, but I can tell you some real stories. You want to hear some real stories?"

They were surrounded by greasy cheeseburger wrappings, french fries containers, milk cartons. Toby was looking from one scrap to another. He was thinking about going to bed without pajamas.

Uncertainly, he said, "Sure."

"Okay." Hands behind his head, Spike lay back on his bed. "Fac' is, there are no crooks, either."

Toby said, "Oh."

"Just guys who have a job to do, makin' a livin' at what they can, like bankrobbin' or knockin' over a liquor store, burglarin', like that. It's a profession, see? Like, I'll bet your daddy is a banker or somethin', isn't he? Rich guy?"

Toby hesitated. "He talks to people."

"See? Okay. He's a salesman. That's his profession. Other people rob. Run numbers. Sharks. That's their business. See? It all works out. Everybody has kids, see."

"You have kids?"

"I dunno. None nobody ever tol' me about." Spike laughed. "And there's no Superman, neither. There are cops, sure, but they don't go flyin' through the air in no big cape." Looking at Toby, Spike's good eye glinted. "Mos'ly, they sit in the middle doin' as well as they can for themselves, if you get what I mean, takin' any-thin' that comes down the pike." He continued to look at Toby. "I see you don' unnerstand me. Lemme say this: people you call cops are always botherin' people tryin' to make their way. Got that?"

Toby ran his eyes over the scraps of paper and cardboard again.

Spike returned to examining the ceiling. "Fac' is, there was this cop in Newark—this big, fat cop, a detective, belly hangin' over his belt, life had been so good to him, big, fat belly. And he shot a frien' of mine. Kilt him. That wasn't fair. All this frien' of mine was doin' was takin' things outa a warehouse after dark. Nothin' to get kilt about. The cop said my frien' had a gun and pulled it. See, that isn't fair, Toby. The cop shoulda least let my frien' get off a shot or two at him before he shot him dead. Right?

"So what they do in a case like this—when a cop shoots somebody they give him a vacation, a kinda reward, only they call it a suspension and they have a big investigation while everybody forgets about it ever happening, and so they can say, sure, it was all right for the cop to shoot ol' Joe or Pete or whatever the stiff's name. You probably know all this from television. You gotta know something. Where you been all your life? Eight years old!"

Sitting on the edge of a bed in a San Francisco motel, Toby's eyes began to close. He was hot. Only two days before he had been in school in New Hampshire.

"But I didn't forget. This particular guy was a frien' o' mine.

"So while this particular big, fat cop was on vacation, I hung aroun' outside his house one morning. He came out. Swimming suit. Beach towels. Six-pack beer. Put the stuff in the trunk of his car. Nice vacation. Shot somebody so he got to go to the beach.

"I follow him down outside Red Bank. Watch him take a swim, swallow couple beers, begin to settle down on the beach.

"Hour or so later, he stands up, all hot and sweaty, jumps in the ocean again, starts back.

"Only, I'm on the beach with my knife. Big knife."

Through his eyelashes Toby watched Spike show with his hands how big a knife it was.

"He looks at me funny like, 'cause I'm the only one on the beach in clothes."

"Anyway, I stick the knife into the top of his big belly, push it sideways and down. Then I do the same with the other side of his stomach. Make a big flap, you know? Then I stuck my fingers in along the top of the flap, grabbed a lota flesh and guts and pulled down.

"With him lookin' down at himself, all his guts spillin' out on the beach."

For an instant, Toby saw Spike clearly, very clearly—more clearly than he had ever seen anything or anyone before. Then he saw Spike lurch, the room heave.

Spike said, "I didn't stay for a swim. It was a hot day, too."

Toby ran for the bathroom.

Kneeling by the toilet, vomiting cheeseburger, french fries, milk, he heard Spike in the bedroom laughing so hard he was coughing for breath.

"Hey, kid. You awake?"

In his bed in the dark motel room, Toby was awake. He was naked. He was hungry.

He didn't answer.

Spike said, "I tol' ya I'd tell ya a story. A *real* story."

Fourteen

"I don't know," Ria Marti said.

In the back of the limousine she was sitting on the right-hand side. The car was oozing up the Avenue of the Americas. It was quarter to eleven at night.

The Ambassador had gotten himself through a long cocktail party at the Italian Embassy. He had even had a forty-five minute private consultation with the Japanese Ambassador in the Embassy's library. They had gone on to the CBS television studio, where the Ambassador had taped an interview for the next day's morning news.

Neither had had anything much to eat. Ria thought Teddy unusually pale.

"You don't know what?" Rinaldi asked absently.

"I'm sitting on some kind of a powder keg," Ria said. "And I don't know what it is."

"What makes you think so?"

"You can't be public relations officer for an embassy without developing a sixth sense. Something's wrong, and I know it."

"First time I've ever heard you plead female intuition."

"It's more than that. I suspect you almost goofed."

"Oh? How?"

"When Roger Mudd asked you if His Majesty has a secret police force to keep track of students and radicals...."

"I get asked that all the time. Funny how some rumors never die."

"And you deny it all the time."

"I denied it tonight."

Ria put her hand on his. "Teddy, you hesitated. You licked your lips. When you answered, your mouth was dry."

He took his hand away and said nothing.

"You can't get away with that on television," she said. "Just wait. Tomorrow every news group in the country will call with the same damned question."

They were being driven by Louis, the Jamaican.

"Something is going on," he said.

She said, "Is it Toby?"

He said, "Wait until we get to the Residence."

The houseman-valet, Pav, as usual, was on late-night duty. He had set out cold sandwiches and brandy in the library.

After the library door was closed, Ria handed Teddy a plate of sandwiches and a brandy and soda. The hand that took the sandwich plate was shaking. He put the plate down, drank half the brandy and soda, went to the side table and refilled the glass.

Ria watched him silently.

"Guess I'm not very good at my job," he said.

"In fact," she said, sitting on the divan and drawing her legs up, "you are."

"Funny," he said. "The boss wasn't too pleased by my marrying an American citizen. Especially an American girl with the Christian name Christina."

Ria was just listening.

"Yet he expressed enough joy when Toby was born. Regarded him almost as one of his own sons."

"Toby," Ria said.

Teddy drew a deep breath. "Toby is missing."

Ria sat up, putting her feet on the floor.

"We're pretty sure kidnapped. Mrs. Brown put him on the plane to San Francisco this afternoon. He did not get off the plane. Christina was waiting to meet him."

"Oh, Teddy! God! How *awful*!"

Teddy shrugged at the inadequacy of the word.

"The Resolution," Ria said.

"I've had a call. Ria, Toby's dead if I submit the Resolution."

"Teddy, Teddy," Ria said.

"So…"

"Is Christina returning?"

Teddy hesitated. "Not at the moment. Makes more sense to leave her out there—where Toby knows she is." He turned his back on Ria. "The point is…" He choked. "…We don't know where Toby is."

"Oh, Teddy."

She started across the room toward him, but he turned abruptly.

"Regarding the press, Ria: no notice of this is to be given out. The Residence staff, of course, knows about it because most of them have been questioned. They've been sworn to silence. For Toby's sake, your staff and the Embassy staff in general is not to know about it. There are to be no leaks."

"I'll take care of it," she said.

"Business as usual. To get the Resolution accepted, it is imperative no one thinks this Embassy is under any particular strain. If the press should make any inquiries on this matter, you are to stonewall them absolutely. Toby is at Fantazyland with his mother."

"Don't worry about that part of it," Ria said. "I'll do my job."

"I know. I'm sure of it."

"What's being done?" she asked. "You haven't gone to the local police, have you? You couldn't have. The F.B.I.?"

"No." He looked into his brandy glass. "No."

"Oh!" she said. Her eyes grew wide. "Oh! It is true!"

Teddy was looking at her blankly.

"That's why you clutched up on television!"

"I deny it." Teddy put down his glass. "His Majesty's government does not have a secret intelligence arm in this country."

"And you never knew it!" She collapsed on the divan. "I never knew it. It's true!"

Teddy said, "Some jobs are more difficult than others."

"Are they any good?" she asked. "I mean, is this the best way…?"

Teddy said, "They haven't made a good impression on me so far, but I don't know. Don't seem to have many choices just now."

He gave himself more brandy, this time adding soda.

"Look, Ria. I'd rather be left alone just now. I suspect we've got long days ahead of us…"

She stood up immediately.

"Can't I help you, Teddy? Are you sure you wouldn't want me to stay with you tonight?"

"Thanks," he said. "No."

"It might be a good idea," she said.

"Yes," he said. "It might be."

"Then let me stay."

"No," he said. "Somehow it would be too…I don't know, Ria… significant?"

Fifteen

The beam from Cord's penlight ran down the chipped directory in the outer lobby of the apartment house on New York's West Eighty-Ninth Street. It stopped at "4C—Du owski."

Cord did not ring the bell. He pressed the palm of his gloved hand against the glass door. It swung open.

In the dimly lit lobby, he found the door to the fire stairs next to the elevator. It being quarter past three in the morning, he used the stairs. He did not know what he would find, or do, in Apartment 4C, but he did not want restless residents of the building remembering they heard someone using the elevator at that hour.

The fourth-floor corridor walls were yellow veneered brick. There was the smell of fish.

The door to 4C was locked. Again, he did not ring the bell. He kicked the door handle hard with his heel. The door sprang open, bounced off the wall.

There were no lights on in the apartment.

Cord entered and closed the door.

"Dubrowski?" he said quietly.

With his penlight he found a light switch and clicked it on.

There was one camp chair next to a floor lamp facing a small, portable television set on its own packing crate. There was a record player, five or six albums propped against it. Against one wall was a large, cheap mirror. Strewn on the floor in front of it on a six-by-six plastic mat was a complete set of weights. The place smelled of stale sweat.

Cord switched on the bedroom light before entering. Against the far wall near the windows were stacks of magazines. There were also two or three cardboard containers of Kaufmann's Hi-Protein tablets. Next to the head of the bed a telephone was on an orange crate. On the floor right next to the cot was a pair of hand weights.

There were also a hypodermic syringe, a tablespoon with a blackened bowl, a paper packet of matches, a half dozen burned-out matches on the floor, and four clear plastic packets. Only one of the packets was empty.

Dubrowski was on the cot. His eyes were open, the pupils angled oddly, downward, toward the floor. His teeth were deep in his tongue. The tip of his tongue was purple. There was dried blood on his teeth.

He was naked. Dubrowski was broad shouldered, thin hipped. There was not an ounce of fat on him. His pectoral, stomach, thigh and calf muscles had been highly developed.

He was in tip-top shape, for a corpse—for someone who had OD'd.

Cord turned off the lights and left the apartment, closing the door behind him.

Sixteen

Christina was awake. She had spent the night awake, staring at the bedroom ceiling, trying not to think of what might be happening to Toby, not to sob out loud. If Colonel Turnbull hadn't been on the living-room couch, she would have turned on her light, gotten up, taken another warm shower, prowled around. Instead she had passed the night listening to him through the thin door, snoring, coughing.

Shortly after dawn she heard him get up, rumble around the living room. The only access to the bathroom was through her bedroom.

The bungalow's front door closed, and then there was silence.

Christina got up and went into the living room. The sofa looked more lumpy than ever. It looked like it had been through a wrestling match with a bear.

It was too early to call Teddy in New York. She was sure he wasn't sleeping, either. But she was also sure he would call her if there had been any news.

"Just follow your own instincts," Colonel Turnbull had said.

Christina returned to the bedroom to get dressed.

Seventeen

At five minutes past seven in the morning, Toby walked into the lobby of the Red Star–Silvermine Motel.

There was a man behind the reception desk, seventy years old or more, sorting slips of paper. His head was bald on top but white hair fluffed out over his ears.

Toby said to him, "Where's the silver mine?"

The man said, "You're lookin'at it. I'm the Silvermine. My name could be Goldmine or Platinummine, I suppose, but the natural humility of my family limited their aspirations. Still, better to be a Silvermine than a Coppermine or a Coalmine, I've always figured. I'm one of the natural wonders of California, son. Right up there with Disneyland, Fantazyland and Hollywood. I'm a walkin' Silvermine."

"I'm going to Fantazyland," Toby said.

"Are you, now? Better watch out those mechanical crocodiles don't get a bite of you." Silvermine put down his sorted papers. "Nothin's worse than bein' bitten by a crocodile with automatic dentures."

"Have you even been bitten by a mechanical crocodile?"

" 'Course! How do you suppose my hair got this way? When I was bit, the ouch was so bad my hair shot out over my ears and it's been stuck out that way ever since. You wouldn't want your hair to look like this, would you?"

"No, sir."

"I thought not. I haven't seen you before. You must be young Jackson. When your Pa came in last night, he just wrote in the register, 'Jackson, son.' I obliged him to write down his first name and he wrote, 'Jack Jackson, son.' I asked him to impart your name. He wrote, 'Jack Jackson, son, Jack Jackson.' Are you Jack Jackson, son, Jack Jackson's son?"

Toby didn't understand. He said, "My mother's coming to get me. She's late. Then we're going to Fantazyland."

"Well, then, Jack Jackson, Jack Jackson's son. What can I do for you? You're up early."

"The waitress said I had to ask you if I can charge breakfast in the coffee shop."

"Old man not up yet, uh? Sure you can. Kids get hungry whether other people are awake or asleep. I remember that. Let's see, you're in Room 102, right?"

Mr. Silvermine came from behind the counter. He was wearing plaid shorts and sandals.

"I'll come down and introduce you properly to the waitress. How come you're dressed that way? Long pants, blazer. Don't see many people 'round here dressed that way. Least not kids. You'll be hot."

Going down the corridor, Mr. Silvermine pointed through a window. "You seen our swimming pool?"

"Yes," Toby said. "It's nice."

"That's a special kind of water we have in the swimming pool, you know. You jump into it and you're guaranteed to get wet. All over. Try it. You might like it."

"Where can we buy things?"

"Like what?"

"Toothbrush. Pajamas. Clothes."

"You guys travel light, uh? Sure you're not a couple of desperadoes? Bank robbers on the lam?"

"My luggage got lost. On the airplane."

"Oh. Well, that's how they keep airplanes flyin', you know. They feed 'em a whole mess of luggage, and the airplane chews it all up and just spits out what it don't want. Luggage is airplane condiments. Gives 'em energy. I guess your particular airplane found your suitcase mighty tasty. Anyway, there's a shopping center across the road." As he walked, Mr. Silvermine waved his hand over his shoulder. "Get anything you want there. Only, you'd better drive across. Motorists don't respect you enough to slow down for you unless you're wrapped in just as much tin as they are."

"If a telephone call comes for us and we're at the pool, would you let us know?"

"Better'n that. I'd transfer the call out to you."

"My mother's going to call," Toby said.

Mr. Silvermine said to the waitress: "This is Jack Jackson, Jack Jackson's son. Feed him up and put it on the bill for Room 102. This young man's goin' to Fantazyland, and we ought to fatten him up for the crocodiles. An airplane's already eaten his luggage."

Toby had to knock several times on the door to Room 102.

Finally, hair tousled, a towel wrapped around him, Spike opened the door.

Both his eyes were wide, staring. His mouth was slightly open.

He looked up and down the corridor quickly, grabbed Toby by the neck and yanked him into the room.

"How did you get out? Where did you go?"

"I went to breakfast."

"Jeez!"

"I was hungry."

"You're supposed to stay with me!"

"You were asleep."

"I know I was asleep. I'm supposed to sit up with you all night, starin' at cha? Fac' is, you're a dumb kid!"

Quietly, Toby said, "I got breakfast."

"Stay there! Don't move a Goddamned inch!"

"I lost my supper last night!"

Before going into the shower, Spike said, "You stay there!"

Toby stayed there.

When Spike came out of the shower, Toby said, "Spike? When you take a shower, do you take the glass eye out of your head first?"

"Jeez!"

"I just want to know."

Spike said, "It's not gonna be hard to twist your head off. Fac' is, it'll be a pleasure."

He began getting dressed.

"There's a swimming pool," Toby said.

Spike said nothing.

"Special kind of water. Guaranteed to get you wet."

Spike looked at him.

"It's a nice day," Toby said. "Sun's out hot."

Spike checked his hair in the mirror.

"There's a place across the street. A shopping center. We can get all kinds of things there. Pajamas. Toothbrushes. Clothes. Swim suits."

"You think you know everythin', doncha?"

"I went on an explore." Toby giggled. "I even found the Silver-mine."

"Well, you don' know nothin'. Fac' is, I'm goin' for breakfast. And you're goin' to stay here. Then we're goin' to stay in this room until we get a telephone call. Until your mother calls." Spike checked his pants pocket for the room key. He switched on the television. "Here, you look at T.V. See if you can learn somethin'."

After Spike left, Toby heard the sound of the key in the lock. On the television a man in a yellow suit was telling the story of Moses in the bulrushes. *"And Pharaoh charged all his people, saying, Every son that is born ye shall cast into the river, and every daughter ye shall save alive...."*

Toby got off the bed and went to the door. He tried the handle. The door opened. No one was in the corridor. He went back into the room, pushed a chair into line with the television and sat down.

"And Pharaoh's daughter said to her, Go. And the maid went and called the child's mother...."

Eighteen

"Mr. Ambassador?"

Sylvia Menninges's voice blurted through the intercom. Again, Teddy had been sitting at his desk, staring at his wastebasket.

"Yes."

"Assistant Secretary of State Skinner. Line 253."

"Yes." He picked up the phone. "Yes?"

"Teddy! How goes the battle?"

Teddy remembered he was to be hearty with Pat Skinner. Characteristically hearty. He and Pat had known each other since Government 101 at Harvard. They were friends. Which was why Patrick Skinner had been named Assistant Secretary of State when Teodoro Rinaldi had been named Ambassador to the United Nations: almost exclusively to deal with Teddy.

The Ambassador tried to lighten his voice. "How be Frannie and the little skinnies?"

It was stupid of him to ask about Pat's wife and children. They had talked just after lunch yesterday.

"Teddy, what's the matter?"

"Guess I didn't sleep too well last night."

"Well, you must be relieved at the good news this morning."

"What good news?"

"Monday night. You get to introduce your Resolution Monday night."

"Oh."

"You didn't know that?"

"No."

"I should think your office would have had that information by seven thirty this morning. Don't they check?"

Teddy's eyes wandered slowly to his desk calendar. *It's Friday noon.*

"I mean, it's sort of imperative you know how much more time you have to negotiate."

Indeed, Teddy thought, *to negotiate the life of my son.*

"How did the meeting with the Iranian bunch go this morning?"

"I'm sorry?"

"The Iranian delegation. You said you were going to meet with them at eight thirty,"

"...I didn't see them."

"Oh. You were meeting with the East German delegation at ten." Teddy said, "I didn't."

The extension buttons on his telephone had been flashing all morning, but Teddy had been only dimly aware of them. *They've been leaving me alone! The staff has been leaving me alone. Damn, dear Ria Marti. Now they all must know something's wrong.*

"Mr. Ambassador," Pat Skinner said. "You have a bit of a hangover this morning, or something?"

"Yes," Teddy said. "It's possible. Something like that."

"Well, you have the weekend," Pat said.

"Yes. I have the weekend," Teddy said. "Pat, I'll call you back."

Pat Skinner walked into the enormous office of the Secretary of State. The Secretary, coat off, shoes off, was sitting back in a recliner lounge near the fireplace, reading. His briefcase was open on the floor beside him.

"Morning," Pat said. "Just talked with Rinaldi."

"And how's Rinaldi?"

"Showing signs of stress."

"Oh?"

"His concert's Monday night. Eight P.M."

"Resolution 1176R...." the Secretary said, "to work longer, harder, more intelligently...diplomatically—if I may use such a stupid word—than Teddy Rinaldi has on Resolution 1176R."

"All that won't do any good, Mr. Secretary, if when the curtain goes up, ol' Teddy can't play his fiddle."

"That bad?"

"Stress level seven...nine..."

"This whole world," the Secretary said, "is run, always, by tired people. People who eat a little too much, drink a little too much, take a few too many pills, sleep too little. History," he said, looking over the rims of his glasses, "is nothing more than the best arrangements that can be achieved by tired minds."

"Just thought I'd alert you," Pat said.

"It would be too bad if we had to back away from this Resolution, from supporting it."

"It would."

"Which of course we'll have to do if you tell me Teddy's chances of carrying it off are slipping."

Pat Skinner took a deep breath. "I know."

The Secretary of State said, "Keep me informed."

Alone in his office, Teddy was staring off into space. Earlier that morning, Mrs. Brown had come into the dining room where he was breakfasting alone.

"Nobody slept," she said. "I spent the night awake. Whatever I did, it wasn't sleepin'. No more the same for you, Mr. Ambassador."

Her presence made him put some egg in his mouth.

"Oh, I had some horrible thoughts. I'm sure we all did." She was pretending to do something at the sideboard—straighten something. "But I had some good thoughts, too, Mr. Ambassador. You know your son is a rare cookie."

The egg yolk wouldn't stay on his fork. "Is he?"

"Indeed he is, sir. He can handle himself, take care of himself, better than anyone would suspect. A genius at handling people. Put him in almost any situation, sir, and he never loses sight of his direction. Remember his wantin' to go to that sailin' camp? And the time he wanted that Egyptian boy to stay with him when our two countries weren't precisely talkin' that week? Well, sir, I tell you. If there's a way out, don't be too surprised if Toby finds it for himself."

The Ambassador knew Mrs. Brown had been awake all night trying to think of something to say to make himself, Christina, the staff feel better.

He also knew his son, Toby, was only eight years old.

Standing by the kitchen door, innocent blue eyes sad, she said, "Now, what should I do about the carpets, sir?"

"Carpets?"

"Yes, sir."

He stood up from the dining-room table.

"I don't care. Give 'em to the Salvation Army."

Nineteen

In Room 102 at the Red Star–Silvermine Motel, Spike and Toby were on their beds.

On the television there was a game show.

The telephone had not rung.

The air conditioner was making a boring noise.

At breakfast, Spike had bought a newspaper he had been reading ever since. The headline read: WOMAN KEEPS HER BABY'S SKULL IN PURSE SEVENTEEN YEARS. The one under that read: STARS PREDICT FALL FROM HORSE FOR EX-PRESIDENT'S WIFE— *Your Horoscope, page 36.* I'LL NEVER LOVE AGAIN, *Says Teenaged Star of TV's "There's Always Tomorrow."* Spike was taking a half hour to read each page.

"Spike?"

No answer.

"I'm hot."

On the TV, people were guessing whether a particular young husband had ever tried on his wife's brassiere.

"What's a brassiere?"

"Dumb kid. Don't know nothin' 'bout nothin'."

It turned out the young man *had* tried on his wife's brassiere, and everyone laughed, including the young man. Someone referred to it just as a bra. Toby knew what a bra was.

He got up and opened the drapes. A wide shaft of sunlight came into the room. It bleached the images on the TV screen. The noon news was coming on. Toby turned the TV off and flopped on his bed, belly down.

"Swim," Toby said. "Pool."

Spike said nothing.

"Place across the street. We can get toothpaste, swimming trunks, pajamas. Only, Mr. Silvermine says we have to drive across, because of the traffic."

"Who's Mr. Silvermine?"

"The owner. He wears shorts."

Spike's look was sharp. "You talked with him?"

"Had to. To get breakfast."

Spike shook his head. "Jeez."

Aloud, Toby read a headline from an inside page of the newspaper: "*War Predicted for Persian Gulf. President Terms Oil Flow Essential for Free World Survival.* What does that mean, Spike?"

"Means you're a dumb kid what don' know nothin' 'bout nothin'," Spike muttered.

"Oh," Toby said. "I see." Smiling, he put his face against his arms. "I get it now," he said. "Anyway, I know what a bra is."

Spike had unbuttoned his shirt.

"Spike? You like stayin' in a room, just one little room like this, all the time?"

"Fac' is, I'm used to it."

Toby said, "So am I."

"Sure, kid. You been in jail, too. Right?"

Toby lifted his head. "You been in jail?"

Spike shrugged. "Like everybody else. Twic't."

"For tearing that man's stomach off?"

"Naw. They never caught me for that. The guy croaked. They never caught me for a lot of things. Just chicken-shit stuff."

"Like what? What'd they catch you for?"

"Oh, when I was fourteen I borried a car. Somethin' was wrong with the steerin', you know? So I went a block or two and smashed into another car. Knocked me silly. So when the cops arrived, there I was, high as a grasshopper, asleep at the wheel. Unconscious. Reformed school for me." Spike had put the newspaper aside. "For two years I had to eat burned rice. A lot a wet, burned rice."

"We get rice at school."

"Not wet, burned rice."

"Wet, burned rice."

"Not a lot of it."

"A lot of it."

"Other time, I was just outa reformed school. I was hungry. You never been hungry."

"I been hungry."

"No money. Unemployed. Who'd hire a kid who'd been in jail? All day I'd been waiting, you know? Money, food come from somewhere. Well, it didn't. Ten thirty at night, I couldn't stand it no more. Waited outside a bar. Decided to mug the next guy who came out. Well, fac' is, I did, and fac' is, he was a cop. Bye, bye, Spike, so long, nice to know ya. That place even had rice soup. You know, water with rice in it?"

"I know."

"Whadda you know?"

"What's jail like?"

"Spend a lot of time locked in a room. Even have the crapper in there so you smell yourself all the time; don't have no place to go. No toilet seat. 'Fraid you'd wear it as a necklace or somethin'. Sit around the machine shop. Sit around the cell. Shavin' and takin' a shower, fresh clothes—things you really get to look forward to. And the guys you have to talk to! Stupid shits. If they weren't stupid, they wouldna got caught."

"You got caught."

Spike looked at him. "I was just a dumb kid. Like you. Didn't know nothin'. I know a lot more now than I did then. You'd better believe it. You don't see me in jail now, do you?"

"It seems like we're in jail."

"Well, we're not. I can walk outa this room anytime I want to."

"Why don't we?"

"You don't know what you're talkin' about. School. Home to Mommy. Cookie-milk anytime you want it. Hugs and kisses, sleep tight, don't let no skeeters bite."

"No."

"Whaddaya mean, 'no'?"

"I don't go to that kind of school. I don't live at home."

"If you don't live at home, where do you live?"

"School. I live at school."

"You live there?"

"Yeah."

"Alla time?"

"Mostly."

"No foolin'. What's it like?"

"Big. Heavy, gray stone."

"You have a room there?"

"A little room."

"But you're never locked in it."

"Sort of. Every afternoon from four thirty to six, I have to be in there doin' homework, and then again at night from seven thirty to nine. The lights go out at nine twenty, ready or not."

"Yeah. But where's the crapper?"

"Down the hall."

"You can go there anytime you want...."

"You're not supposed to. If you're out of your room during those times and they catch you, you have to spend Sunday afternoon in detention hall."

"But you can take a crap?"

"You're supposed to before or after."

"Jeez! Strict! Can't even take a crap in your place or it's solitary for you—no shit! What'd you ever do to get sent to a place like that?"

Toby shrugged. "I don't know. I'm gettin' a fine education, I guess."

"Sounds worse'n my reformed school. They feed you good?"

"Lot a rice," Toby said. "Lot a rice."

"Where is this place of yours?"

"New Hampshire."

"In the sticks?"

"What?"

"I mean, is it in the city or the woods?"

"Woods. Country."

"You mean, even when you look through the window there's nothin' to see? No girls? Just fuckin' trees?"

"I don't think the trees around there fuck." Toby smiled. "At least, I've never seen them."

"You know what fuck means?"

"Yeah," Toby said.

"Jeez. No wonder you're in reformed school, age of ten."

"Eight. I'm eight."

"Worse. And you never get to go anywhere? You never get to go home?"

"Sometimes. Ten days. Last summer I went to a sailing camp."

"Yeah, they were startin' the furlough program second place I was at. Just like your place. Out in the sticks."

"You know this motel has a swimming pool?" Toby said.

"I seen it."

"Mr. Silvermine says it has a special kind of water. I mean, in the swimming pool."

"Yeah?"

"Guaranteed to get you wet all over."

"I don't swim so good."

"I can teach you. A little."

"I don't need you teachin' me nothin'."

"Hot in here, isn't it?"

Spike sighed. "Yeah. What's on the television?"

"Golf," said Toby.

"Anybody who watches golf on television is a birdie," said Spike.

"We can use the pool, you know," Toby said. "Because we're guests here."

"Yeah? I suppose so."

"Spike?"

"What."

"Let's go for a swim."

"Naw. Have to wait for the telephone."

"No, we don't. I asked Mr. Silvermine. He said if a call came for us, I mean, if my mother calls, he'd transfer the call out to the pool."

"You said what?"

"There's a telephone by the pool."

"Jeez, you had quite a chin wag with that old coot, didn't ya?"

"He's a nice man. Though I didn't understand a lot of what he said. He's been to Fantazyland, too."

"You tol' him you're goin' to Fantazyland?"

"Sure."

"What else did ya tell him?"

"Nothin'. Waitin' for my mother to call."

"Tha's good. Jeez, kid, you're dumb."

"Anyway," Toby said, "we could get swimming trunks and tooth-paste and clothes at this place across the freeway."

"Jeez. Why didn't cha call the cops?"

"Cops? Why would I call the cops?"

"I dunno, kid. I dunno."

"Fact is, Spike, I need clothes. I'm hot. Mr. Silvermine says everybody here wears shorts. He wears shorts. He said you don't see many people around here dressed like this."

Spike tossed him a quick look. "He said that?"

"Yeah."

Spike was biting the end of his thumb. "You may be right, kid. At that. Yeah."

Spike sat up on the edge of his bed. "Yeah. Let's go get you some clothes. Fac' is, you don't look right. Not at all. And that's a fac'."

Toby jumped off the bed.

"And swimming trunks, and pajamas?"

"Yeah, yeah. Maybe."

"And then we'll go to the pool?"

"Yeah. Maybe. Dirty bastids. Allus puttin' us in a room and tellin' us to stay there. Fuck 'em's what I say."

"Right!" Toby said. "Fuck 'em!"

Twenty

"Dubrowski's OD'd," Cord said over the phone to Turnbull. "Like fish on ice."

"You gave money to a junkie before he did his job!"

"Okay, Gus. I made a mistake. We gotta work our way out of it."

"What do you mean, 'we'?"

"You want what you want, Gus, and I want what my employers want."

"So who snatched the kid?"

"Maybe a guy named Mullins. Spike Mullins. He and Dubrowski knew each other at Attica. Last night I went to this bar where I used to meet Dubrowski. I bought a lot of drinks, you know? Tuesday, Dubrowski was flying pretty high. Zonked. Wednesday, he was seen looking pretty seedy in a corner of the bar, talking to this jail buddy of his. The bartender said he saw Dubrowski hand Mullins a wad of bills. My guess is Dubrowski hired this buddy to stand in for him on the grab until he got himself together and got out to the Coast to take over."

"Then Dubrowski went home and OD'd."

"Yeah."

"So we don't know how to get in touch with Mullins and Mullins doesn't know how to get in touch with us."

"Yeah."

"You do nice work, Cord. What do you know about this Mullins?"

"Dumb and vicious. I got the people in the bar to tell me stories about him. A real psychotic thug."

"Another druggie?"

"No. Apparently not. Gus, we've got to find that kid."

"I will."

"I mean, what would you do if you were this guy Mullins and someone got you into a situation like this and then didn't follow through? I mean, you've got a kidnapped kid on your hands you don't know what to do with?"

"Kill him and dump him."

"Yeah. The kid is no good to us dead, Gus. At least until Monday night. I said you could do whatever you wanted to the kid—to the family—after Monday night. I mean, to Christina Rinaldi and the Ambassador and all. A dead kid's a dead threat."

"I don't see we have a deal anymore, Cord."

"Maybe I ought to come out to the Coast, Gus."

"Stay out of my way, Cord."

"We'll meet. We'll talk."

"Cord. Stay out of my way."

Twenty-One

"MARCO!"

"POLO!"

"...MARCO!"

"...POLO!"

Spike watched the kids play in the motel pool. They were all about the same size. Three boys and two girls. Wet, skinny, darting kids, faces, shoulders, arms, legs, flashing in the sunlight, their hair changing color and texture every time their heads came up from the water.

Sitting in a swim suit in a long chair, his legs stretched out before him, Spike finished his second beer.

"MARCO!"

"...POLO!"

Across the pool under an umbrella sat a woman in a swim suit, knitting. Her yarn was in a plastic Sachs bag at her feet. At least one of the kids, one of the boys, belonged to her. He'd climb out to her once in a while, use a towel, stand in the shade of the umbrella, catch his breath. Occasionally, she would look up from her knitting at the kids in the pool and smile.

I ought to go give her a pound of the best. One-two-three behind your tree. Spike glowered at her and the rest of the world. *Bastids. Put me in a room, tell me to stay there. Cheap bastids.*

"MARCO!"

Spike figured the game the kids were playing had something to do with people who couldn't see so well. They'd grope around the pool for each other, in turn, as if blind. All the kids who had their eyes open would tease and taunt the person with his eyes closed— call to him loudly from close up, then swim away quickly and quietly.

Little bastids. Think it's funny bein' short of sight. Think it's funny never knowin' what's goin' on outa the left side of your head....

"POLO!"

Spike's head lowered to the cushion. *Nice. Nice bein' out. Nice havin' a job to do, and doin' it. Nice bein' in the sun. Nice havin' a beer just 'cause you want it....*

But where the hell is Dubrowski?

"Come on," the boy said. "Want a Coke? Who wants a Coke?"

Standing in the pool, Toby looked at Spike asleep in the chair.

"No," he said. "I don't think so."

"Haven't you got any money?" The boy looked at Spike. "Oh, your dad's asleep. That's okay." He started walking out of the pool. "Maybe my mom will buy you one."

By the time Toby got to the lady under the umbrella, she had picked up her purse and was counting out change.

"There's a Coke machine by the door to the ladies' room," she said. "I saw it."

She looked into Toby's eyes and smiled.

All the kids ran to the Coke machine, coins in hand, yelling, "Yeaaa!"

On the way, one of the girls dropped her towel. Toby jumped over it. After they got their Cokes and wandered back, the lady said, "Why don't you all sit in the shade now while you're drinking your Cokes? Relax a minute. That was quite a game!"

"And we're going to play again!" her son announced.

Toby sat cross-legged on the pool deck, drinking his Coke.

The rest of the kids were teasing a girl who never had succeeded in catching anyone during the game.

Toby said to the lady, "Thank you. Thank you for the Coke."

"You're welcome. Are you staying at the motel?"

"Yes, ma'am."

"I haven't seen you before. What's your name?"

"I'm Dink," her son said.

"Toby."

Toby saw a shadow fall over his body. It extended to the shade of the lady's feet.

"Toby Rinaldi."

The lady looked up.

Toby looked around and up.

Standing over him, fists clenched, face red, one eye gleaming furiously, was Spike.

"Get outa here," he said. "Get over there!" He pointed across the pool to his long chair. "Get your towel. You hear me? Get goin'!"

Toby lowered the Coke bottle from his mouth and swallowed.

Clearly, he had done something terribly wrong.

He didn't know what to do with the bottle. It wasn't empty. He shouldn't leave it on the pool deck.

The lady put out her hand. "That's all right. I'll take it. You'd better go with your father."

Toby stood up.

Spike hit him in the back of the head, making him fall forward a step or two, then grabbed him, nearly lifting him off the pool deck, and hurried him along.

Twenty-Two

Teddy's voice answering the phone was subdued.

"Teddy! Any news?"

"Not really," he said slowly. "Did you get any sleep?"

"I just keep thinking, Teddy—"

"It's not thinking. It's worrying." His voice fell lower. "It's agony."

"I don't know what—we must—"

"Did Turnbull or any of his henchmen show up there last night?"

"Yes. Colonel Turnbull spent the night sleeping on my couch. He's very nice."

"He didn't strike me as very nice," Teddy said.

"And a couple of men in a yellow Toyota followed me here to the airport. I guess they're his men."

"You're at the airport? In San Francisco?"

"I didn't know what else to do. I came here thinking there just must be some mistake—he got lost, or—"

"There's no mistake, Christina."

"Turnbull belongs to the boss's secret intelligence force, doesn't he?"

Teddy hesitated. "Something like that. Maybe."

"Teddy, you've always known such a thing exists."

"Have I?"

"Well, I have."

"Frankly, Christina, he struck me as sort of vicious."

"Maybe what we need here is 'vicious.'"

"Maybe."

"Oh, Teddy, where is Toby?" Christina held her breath a moment to prevent her crying. "Oh, God, where is Toby? Hasn't there been any word—any ransom demand? Anything?"

There was a long pause before Teddy answered. "No, Christina. There's been no ransom demand."

"Maybe this morning. Most likely this morning," she said. "You'll call the hotel—I mean, the tennis camp—as soon as such a message comes...."

"I'll keep in close touch. Let you know anything we hear. Immediately....What do you think you should do, Christina?"

"I don't know. I guess stay here. At least another twenty-four hours. I keep thinking there must be some terrible mistake. It isn't real. Suddenly Toby will just show up. We don't know what's happening, Teddy. You're there. I should be here....I don't know."

"I don't know, either. I'll call the minute we have any news."

Twenty-Three

"I heard you were on your way." Turnbull was sitting on the couch, his feet on the coffee table. On the end table next to him was a bottle of bourbon and a half-empty glass.

"Those men who have been following me all day, do they work for you?" Christina asked.

"For us, dear lady, for us. They are there solely for your protection."

"They—whoever—have got Toby. Why would anyone hurt me?"

"Would you like a drink?"

"No," Christina said. "I'm afraid it would knock me over. Do you have any news for me?"

"Actually, I have." He put his feet on the floor and sat forward. "Not much, but something. Perhaps we should go have dinner. I expect you haven't been treating yourself very well."

"Maybe later." Christina sat in a wicker chair. "Please tell me."

"As I say," Turnbull said, picking up his glass and drinking from it. "Not much. Your little boy's suitcase was found in the airport in New York. Airport maintenance found it in a men's room and brought it to Lost and Found."

"You mean, he's in New York? You know he's in New York?"

"We don't know anything," Turnbull said. "We know his suitcase was found."

Christina swallowed hard. "Makes it sound—I mean, if they dumped his suitcase—as if they didn't expect him to need a change of clothes, or anything...."

"Now, now, Christina. Mustn't think that way." An odd smile came on Turnbull's face. "It might have been left there as a false clue, you know. To make us think Tobias is still in New York."

"Oh, I see." In her lap her fingers were knotted. "I—of course, I don't understand much about these things."

"Of course you don't, Christina. Just leave everything to me."

"It's been twenty-four hours," Christina said.

"Yes, and a lot has been done. People have been working on this all night, all day. The suitcase was turned in at two thirty this morning. Our people identified it at six thirty."

She exhaled. "I'm sorry. I can't…"

"The other thing I have to tell you is that all flights out of that airport yesterday, all airlines, from noon on, were checked. Children traveling alone, as well as with adults. Mammoth job."

"I'm sure."

"All children flying out of that airport yesterday have been accounted for. Phone calls to the reference numbers established they were who they said they were—except for four. Two couldn't be checked because there was no answer at the phone numbers given. But one of those was a girl and the other a fifteen-year-old boy. One kid was a no-show, but her name was Elizabeth. Another child's phone number must have been given wrong. It didn't exist. But his name was Ling Pao."

Christina was listening intently. "Colonel, why—?"

"I'm trying to show you how thoroughly my people are working, Christina."

"Did they check private airplanes?"

"Yes. Apparently, they can't be as sure who's aboard private aircraft. Just names.…"

"So, Colonel, Toby could be on the East Coast, the West Coast, or anyplace in between. You haven't narrowed it down much."

"Those who kidnapped your child, Christina, have the advantage." The Colonel stared at her solemnly. "They knew they were going to do it. They were able to plan. You and your husband, I must add, did nothing to prevent it."

"Oh…"

"I know you haven't much confidence in your Major Mustafa.…"

"I am blaming myself," Christina said.

"There, there, Christina." The Colonel's smile was kindly. "Why don't you go change? We'll have a nice dinner."

Twenty-Four

"Wandering around the airport all day," Christina said, sitting back in her chair, waiting for her soup, "I felt like one of those shopping bag women, you know? You see them in New York, London. Women with broken shoes, coming from nowhere, going nowhere, going in circles, looking in refuse baskets for God knows what, some evidence of their own existence, some evidence of someone else's existence."

Across from her at the small table in the main dining room of the tennis camp, Colonel Turnbull had his fist firmly around a glass of bourbon and ice.

"What were you looking for?" he asked.

It took her a moment to get her face under control.

"Toby."

Colonel Turnbull had prevailed upon her to order a decent dinner: mock turtle soup, a rare steak with salad.

The soup was placed in front of her.

"It seemed a senseless thing to do," Christina said, lifting her spoon. "Wandering around an airport all day. I just didn't know where else to go, what else to do. I couldn't sit by the phone all day. I would have gone completely crazy."

"You just follow your instincts," Colonel Turnbull said. "I have great faith in maternal instincts."

"I have great faith in rationality," Christina said. "And I don t see anything here that makes any sense yet. I called Teddy from the airport—I mean, the Ambassador—"

The Colonel smiled. "You may refer to the Ambassador as Teddy, Christina. I well know who he is."

"He said there had been no ransom demand. No one had been in touch with him at all about Toby, why he's missing, why they took him."

Across the table, Turnbull allowed his face to become thoughtful, concerned, hesitant.

Christina ate most of her soup before their steaks arrived.

After the waiter left, Colonel Turnbull said, "I'm afraid the Ambassador is being less than frank with you, Christina." As she stared at him, he repeated his point, almost as if enjoying it: "Less than honest."

"There *has* been a ransom demand? Why didn't he tell me?"

"No, not a ransom demand. There's a great deal more at stake here than the mere exchange of money for human life. Doubtlessly, he felt he was sparing you."

Colonel Turnbull shoveled some salad into his mouth.

Chewing, he said, "Your husband received a call last night. From someone who obviously would not identify himself, or for whom he works. We traced the call to a hamburger stand near Baltimore."

"Baltimore? Why Baltimore?"

"Why anyplace? I think the call coming from Baltimore is a pretty good indication of the size of the team we're up against. They're everywhere, nowhere...."

"Are you going to tell me what the man said?"

Colonel Turnbull was now chewing a large piece of steak.

"The man said that if your husband submits Resolution 1176R to the United Nations when he is called upon to do so, your son will be killed."

"Oh." Christina put down her fork. "Oh." She sat back in her chair. "Oh."

"You might as well know everything, Christina. This is the worst kind of political blackmail. You know the flow of oil through the Persian Gulf is slowing down. You know there are people who want the Persian Gulf completely shut. They are willing to go to war over it. His Majesty and your husband drafted this brave little resolution to prevent precisely that happening. It could work." Despite what he was saying, the Colonel appeared to be relishing his dinner. "If your husband gives that speech, your son is dead."

Listening to him, Christina was having a mad rush of thoughts, feelings.

This, too, Toby's kidnapping, has to do with our lives in diplomacy. A little boy who has no more idea of the movement of oil tankers, or concern about it, is kidnapped and facing murder because of the good his father is trying to create....

Why didn't Teddy tell me? I couldn't be worried more or less than I already am....

Oh, yes: when a crisis appears, the nonprofessional, dear-darling-wife Christina, gets shoved aside....

"Poor Teddy," Christina said.

"I'm sure he thought he was being kind—in not telling you."

"He wasn't, you know. Not a bit kind."

"If you're going to help me find Toby," Turnbull said, "I think you should know everything—no matter how difficult for you it is."

"Yes."

"And we must find Toby."

"He could be in New York, in Baltimore—"

"He could be anywhere."

"Colonel, I—I would like to return to the bungalow now. I feel a little woozy. Think I should lie down."

He looked over at her plate. "You didn't eat much, did you?"

"Did the best I could," she said. "Under the circumstances." Christina stood up. "You finish your dinner. I'll be at the bungalow."

Augustus Turnbull did finish his dinner.

Christina got up from her bed and went into the living room when she heard him return.

He had just taken off his coat.

He was wearing a shoulder holster. The black metal of the gun gleamed in the weak light of the room.

"Colonel Turnbull," Christina said. "I want to thank you—for being so honest with me."

"Think nothing of it." Turnbull let himself down heavily on the couch and picked up one of the torn magazines. "Can't solve the problem if we don't have all the facts, can we?"

Twenty-Five

"Operator? Is this the Information operator, New York City? I'm trying to check a phone number."

In a phone booth outside a garage, Spike Mullins had been trying to check a number for more than fifteen minutes. First he dialed the local operator, who gave him the number of local information but did not give him his coin back. He had to get change from the garage. The local Information operator gave him the number to dial for Information New York City. The boulevard traffic outside the phone booth was so noisy he yelled at that operator, who hung up on him.

Now, with the phone booth door closed, Spike was sweating but speaking quietly and hearing fairly clearly.

"The name is Dubrowski," Spike said. "Donny Dubrowski."

"Would you spell that for me, sir?"

"Yeah. Sure. Uh. Du-D-U-ah-browski."

"B-R-O-W-S-K-I?"

"Yeah. That's right. Donald. West Eighty-ninth Street, New York City."

"Would that be a new listing, sir?"

"Naw. Donny's been free as a bird seven, eight months now."

The operator recited a number to him. Spike asked her to repeat. She did so while he held the slip of paper up to the phone booth's light. They were the same number.

"Would you try that number for me, operator? It doesn't answer."

"Sir, you may direct dial."

Again the phone went dead.

Standing in the phone booth, glancing over at his rented car, Spike dialed the number three times. He let it ring a dozen times or more each time. Spike could see Toby's head in the passenger seat of the car, watching the cars go by on the boulevard. Finally,

Spike hung up, kicked the phone booth's door and returned to the car.

Turning the ignition key, Spike said, "That was your mother, kid. Some delay."

In the dark of the passenger seat, silently Toby was looking at Spike.

"Got to go somewhere else. Wait for her."

Racing the engine, Spike sped back onto the boulevard.

Toby was still looking at him.

"Broke her ankle," Spike said. "Hit a grease spot in the kitchen."

After hustling Toby in from the swimming pool, Spike had scolded him about talking to strangers. Quickly, they had checked out of the Red Star–Silvermine Motel.

They had been driving around ever since, stopping at phone booths.

"Well," Spike said. "Don't blame me! Shit! Ain't my fault your old lady broke her ankle."

After driving awhile again in the dark, they passed a sign saying:

FANTAZYLAND 10

Neither of them said anything.

Twenty-Six

Bernard Silvermine stood in the small ballroom of the Ramada Inn. He was wearing a kilt, a brooch and sporran. In his hand was his second scotch and soda.

The piper had not yet come to pipe them to dinner tables across the room. The Highland-dressed people were gathered around the cash bar, catching up on the month's news. For as long as it had existed, twenty-nine years, The Ancient and Honorable Scottish Auxiliary Fusileers—A Charitable Organization had had dinner meetings the second Friday of each month, except June, July, August and September.

Bernard Silvermine had said hello to the hardware man and his wife, asked the price of new faucets; the dentist and his wife, asked about their daughter at U.C.L.A.; the United Parcel delivery man, asked about his wife, forgetting he was recently divorced—and gotten himself a second scotch.

Bernard Silvermine's own wife, sipping her once-a-month gimlet, was standing by the door in a group of everybody's wives except the U.P. delivery man's.

Three men were sitting at the corner of one of the tables. *Good.* One of them was Ed Noakes. Bernard Silvermine wanted to speak to Ed Noakes.

He walked over and sat down.

The three men greeted Bernard Silvermine.

"How's the Red Star–Silvermine Motel working out for you, Bernie?"

"Red Star," said Ed Noakes. "Communist."

"Better than retirement did," Bernard Silvermine said. "Couldn't stand retirement. I recognized I was beginnin' to form opinions about things I knew nothin' about."

"Missus happy?"

"I think so. Hadn't realized it, but she'd sort of been forced into retirement when the kids left home. Least now she doesn't tell me I don't know what I'm talkin' about so much. 'Course I don't have the time to develop great theories about Pakistani politics."

Each of the younger men mentioned his retirement plans. One said he was just going to sit in the sun, and the others—especially Bernard Silvermine—assured him he would do that for three weeks at the most before he found himself wanting to do something else.

"Maybe after thirty years," the man said, "I'll start a garden."

"What're you goin' to do till then?"

"Study up on it."

"Say, Ed," Bernard Silvermine said. "Something I thought I might mention to you."

The other two men didn't hesitate to listen.

"Man and boy checked into the motel yesterday. Rented car. No luggage."

"Jeez, you runnin' that kind of a place now, Bernie?" one of the men asked. "No wonder you can afford a new Buick."

"The boy was no more'n ten years old. He stayed in the car while the man registered. Didn't see the boy until this morning. Registered as Jack Jackson and son, Jack Jackson, Junior."

The expression on Ed Noakes's face didn't change.

"Thing of it is, I don't think they were father and son at all. The man was a real dese-dose-and-dem guy, talked in grunts and groans, you know? And frankly he smelled a little ripe. Looked like an ex-fighter to me, if you know what I mean: face all marked up, glass eye, smashed nose, thick knuckles. Lace burns, the back of his neck. Clothes he was wearing were bought off the rack, and probably outdoors.

"The kid, on the other hand, was wearing a blue blazer, gray slacks, white shirt, black shoes. His jacket alone probably cost two hundred dollars. And he spoke—his accent was almost English."

Ed Noakes finished his drink.

"This morning the kid said they were waiting for a phone call from his mother. Late this afternoon, way after checkout time, they checked out and left in a hurry. I charged them for an extra night, just to see if the man would give me a story, but he didn't say a word. Paid cash. And they never did get a phone call."

Ed Noakes said, "Did they say where they were goin'?"

"This morning the kid said they were going to Fantazyland. Waiting for his mother, to go to Fantazyland. When I threw him a lot of noise about Jack Jackson and son, Jack Jackson, the kid just looked at me as if I was crazy."

Ed Noakes said, "Anyone for another drink? I do believe I hear the pipes wheezin' up."

"I'll get 'em." The real estate man stood up. "Had a big week last week. Sold a five-story building to a guy who wants to knock it down for a parking lot. Scotch all around? Scotch for you, Bernie?"

"Mine with soda."

The truth was Bernard Silvermine didn't like scotch very much; he also didn't like soda. Too, he always felt a little silly driving through San Francisco and walking into the Ramada Inn in a kilt, brooch and sporran. But The Ancient and Honorable Scottish Auxiliary Fusileers did good, charitable work. Last year they raised all the funds for a new therapy wing of the children's hospital.

And the club was good, too, when you wanted to ask a hardware man informally about the wholesale price of faucets for the motel, or mention something to a Federal Bureau of Investigation agent like Ed Noakes.

Twenty-Seven

"I don't know," Teddy said. "My mind keeps closing down. It seems to go to sleep without me. With my eyes open. Suddenly, it's twenty minutes later, a half hour. I forget...."

In Christina's usual place across the breakfast table sat Ria Marti.

Grapefruit halves were before them, but neither was eating.

"...I forget things. Last night, for the life of me, I couldn't remember the name of the head of the Italian legation. I've known him fifteen years. Can't remember whom I'm supposed to see next, or why. Just now I got a necktie out of the closet, went to the mirror and discovered I already had a tie on. Senile....Too young for this stuff.... I just keep seeing Toby's face."

"I think it's called exhaustion," Ria said. "Understandable, justified exhaustion."

"Does one get over it?" he asked innocently.

"You need some time off," she said. "A lot of time off."

"Sounds boring."

"Time doing something else."

"I'd really love to teach for a while now. Put my papers in order, my thoughts....Put my life in order. Some peace and quiet: exciting, stimulating young minds coming to me with urgent questions instead of urgent dispatches. Spend a lot of time with Christina, Toby...."

"Why don't you eat your breakfast?" Ria Marti said.

"I may not be making decisions very well, but it's still my responsibility. I've still got to make 'em."

"Yes, Ambassador."

Twenty-Eight

"Are you in the office, Teddy?"

"Yes. Listen, Christina: maybe some real news."

"What?"

It was Saturday morning and Christina was packed and dressed. Colonel Turnbull had left the bungalow before she woke up. She had made a reservation on the one thirty P.M. flight to New York. She was just about to call Teddy when he called her.

It was less than forty-eight hours since Christina had discovered Toby was missing. It seemed an eternity: nothing before that continued to exist with any real clarity; she did not believe this period would ever end.

Packing, she divided this eternity into two periods. At first, in shock, in horror, she had expected all information to come from Teddy. She had waited for him to give her direction. Then she realized there were things she could do, would do—there was a viciousness she could attain to fight this viciousness directed at her child. But she had no fact, no idea, not a scintilla of evidence of any kind to commence with, to direct and guide herself.

Teddy had been less than candid with her. Toby had not been kidnapped for ransom: *"I'm sure he thought he was being kind,"* Colonel Turnbull had said.

Sure, Christina had thought while in the shower washing her hair vigorously. *Little woman. Don't distress her. Save her. Keep her down. Lie to her, or, at least, don't tell her the whole truth. Believe her capable of nothing, don't distress/trust her, keep her in the background....*

On the coffee table in front of her was the note she had written:

"Dear Colonel—Finally slept. This morning I'm still confused, but at least I'm thinking clearer. If I can't accomplish anything here, at least I can be with Teddy. If I have no way of finding Toby, maybe at least Teddy and I should be together through this terrible thing. You have my appreciation for your honesty."

On the telephone, Teddy's voice had slightly more spirit to it.

"There was a message on the F.B.I. telex last night. Just one of a million advisories—"

"I thought we hadn't involved the F.B.I., Teddy."

"Well, ah…I guess it was intercepted by our chaps. I guess, ah…our chaps had a tap on it.…"

There are things Teddy is not willing to tell himself, either—things he's never been willing to tell himself—like the boss's secret intelligence group in this country. He's still not looking straight at that fact, admitting to himself he's been diplomatically dissembling all these years.…

"May mean nothing, of course," Teddy continued, "but I'm very hopeful it does mean something. A San Francisco agent reported on the wire last night that a man and a boy checked into a motel called—let's see, I wrote it down—Red Star-Silvermine Motel. The motel manager got suspicious of them. I guess he didn't believe they were really father and son. The boy was about Toby's age and the manager reported he was dressed expensively, blue blazer, gray slacks, spoke well. He thought the man seemed like kind of a tough guy—a gangster. They registered under the names Jack Jackson and son, Jack Jackson. Of more importance than all that, the description of the man fits the description Mrs. Brown gave of the man at the airport here—the man who was supposed to take Toby to the airplane, Willins. Name of Willins. About thirty, heavy shoulders, glass eye. All this may mean nothing—"

"Was the boy—was Toby all right?"

Teddy's voice took on a steadying edge. "Christina, we don't know that it was Toby."

Christina's heart was pounding.

"Are they still at the motel?"

"No. They left hurriedly. Listen to this: the boy told the motel manager they were waiting for a call from his mother—who was going to take him to Fantazyland."

"Oh, Teddy." Christina ran her eyes over her suitcases neatly lined up by the bungalow door. "Teddy, listen carefully, why was Toby's suitcase left in the men's room in the airport in New York?"

There was a silence before Teddy said, "I'm listening."

"To convince us Toby is still in the New York area. That, at least, he was taken away from the boarding gates, back through the terminal—"

"You're saying it was left as a false clue? That therefore Toby was taken from the airport by plane? Christina, we've already checked the airlines, accounted for every kid on every plane all Thursday afternoon and night."

"No. There's one plane you didn't check. One last question—"

"Christina, you know how I am about riddles. At the moment, I find them especially nerve-wracking."

"Why was Toby's reservation canceled?"

Teddy thought a moment. "That's a good question. To convince us he wasn't on that plane?"

"Also, Teddy, maybe to make room for someone who was on that plane...."

"Toby."

"Under another name. Your gnomes didn't check the plane Toby was scheduled to be on, did they?"

"No. I don't think so."

"Would you please ask them to do so?"

"Yes. Of course. I—ah—Where did you get such an idea?"

"Quickly, Teddy. Ask them to check quickly."

"I don't know...I don't know that it would help—"

"It would help give some credence that that boy at the Red Silver Mine Motel—"

"Red Star–Silvermine. Silvermine, one word."

"—was Toby."

"Yes," Teddy said. "Colonel Turnbull doesn't believe—"

"Teddy?" Christina pressed the phone closer to her ear. "You knew all along Toby wasn't kidnapped for ransom, didn't you?"

"No," Teddy said. "I didn't know it. But I was pretty sure. The Resolution...Turnbull told me this morning that he's told you the truth about that telephone call...threatening Toby's life if I submit the Resolution. Christina, you know there are people who would rather go to war than have me introduce that Resolution Monday night. It's going to cause a complete shift in political alignments—"

"Thanks, Teddy."

"What do you mean?"

"Sorry."

"Look, Christina—"

"I don't know what I mean."

For a long moment, husband and wife listened to each other breathing over long-distance telephone.

Finally, he said, "I'm sorry. Are you staying out there?"

She looked at her suitcases. "Yes."

"I'll call you as soon as I hear anything more," he said.

"Just tell me the truth, Teddy. Please."

Christina placed the telephone receiver in its cradle.

She looked at her suitcases. She looked at the note she had written. She reached out, took the note from the coffee table, crumpled it in her hand and dropped it in a wastebasket.

Twenty-Nine

Ria Marti came into the Ambassador's office. Immediately he hung up.

"His Majesty's on the phone," she said. "He asked Sylvia not to break in on you when he understood you were talking with your wife."

"Is he on scrambler?"

"Yes."

Teddy reached for the phone.

"Mr. Ambassador," Ria said. "He's making arrangements to fly to New York."

"Oh?"

"Thought I'd warn you. His being here would make things much more difficult for me. I'd have to explain his sudden arrival." She opened the palms of her hands in a futile gesture. "It would make everything even more impossible than they are for you."

"Yes," Teddy said.

"I'm sure he thinks his being here would be a help—"

Teddy spoke into the phone: "Good morning, Your Majesty."

"Teodoro…" The distorted voice was ponderous. "How is Christina?"

"She's handling herself well, sir. Under the circumstances."

"Colonel Turnbull spoke to me a few moments ago from San Francisco, California. His report is not encouraging."

Teddy spoke carefully. "We're slightly encouraged."

"He tells me you received a threatening call which he knows originated in Baltimore, Maryland, that your son's luggage was found in the airport in New York, that there is a highly unreliable report that your son may have been seen in California."

Teddy sighed. His Majesty's ability to cut to the bone often removed hopeful illusions. "That's about it."

Teddy waved Ria Marti out of the room.

"The Colonel tells me he doesn't believe this report of Toby's being at this motel in California—what is it called, the Red Silvermine?—"

"Red Star–Silvermine."

"—is even worth following up. Worth investigating."

"He doesn't? He said that?"

"Yes."

"Then may I ask what the hell is he doing in California?"

"…Teddy?"

"Sorry."

"I know you're distraught. Are you all right?"

"Yes."

"You can carry on?"

"Your Majesty, this Colonel Augustus Turnbull…"

"Yes?"

"He is someone you know personally?"

"I have met with him several times. Of course."

"He is unknown to me."

Teddy had to make that point. Ria had been right: the national news organizations had been on the phone all morning asking for confirmation of the Ambassador's statement that the King did not have a secret intelligence force operating in the United States. Teddy had not spoken with them.

The King simply said, "Yes. He is."

"At this moment, I do not share your confidence in him."

"You are in a position, Teddy, where you have every reason to be critical. Overcritical."

"I'm not sure I'm being overcritical. The other night, questioning me and the staff at the Residence, he struck me as impatient, brusque, abrasive—"

"You can hardly blame him for being impatient, Teddy."

"On occasion, I was convinced that he wasn't even listening. He acted like he knew the answers to questions before he heard them."

"He's a bright man, Teddy. I'm sure the process of questioning people can be tiresome."

"For some reason, I seemed to detect genuine animosity on his part for me."

"He told me." The King paused. "He told me how wrong and… irresponsible…he thought you were to allow your family to be traveling, especially for pleasure, at such a time as this."

"I admit that," Teddy said. "But I have obligations to my family as well."

"I understand."

"Last night, Turnbull told Christina about the phone call I had received saying that if I offer the Resolution, Toby will be killed. She had been believing this was a matter of kidnap-for-ransom."

"I'm sure the Colonel thought it better she know the truth."

"Frankly, Your Majesty, I think it was uncommonly cruel of him."

"Let's not quarrel with the man's methods just now. He has an impossible job to do, and little time in which to do it."

"I do not have your faith in him."

"But you do have faith in me, Teddy?"

The phone was hurting Teddy's ear. He tried to relax his hand. "Of course."

"Teodoro, I am arranging to come to New York."

"May I ask that you do not do so?"

"I thought I should be with you and your wife—"

"Your Majesty, you cannot submit the Resolution yourself."

"No. I realize that. It would make the Resolution appear far more controversial than it already *is*. It would extend the debate."

"Also," Teddy said, "it would greatly lessen the chances for the Resolution's being accepted."

"Yes. I understand that. Clearly. And I cannot ask either the Ambassador to the United States or the Ambassador to the Court of Saint James's to substitute for you in submitting the Resolution—"

"That would make the Resolution look like a ploy—something we're just throwing out while really trying to accomplish something else."

His Majesty said, "I'm afraid I'm entirely dependent upon you, Rinaldi."

"Your sudden arrival here would have two negative effects.

First, it would direct too much press attention to the Resolution—too many spotlights on the negotiations as they now stand. Other ambassadors would begin grandstanding. I suspect several would vote against us just to strike a tough, popular pose in the world's press."

"I could explain I have arrived suddenly in the United States for medical reasons. Americans are always quick to believe other nations have no doctors."

"Second, Your Majesty, your arrival here would give us the usual intense security problems."

"I'm used to that."

"Pardon me, sir, for being blunt."

"Go ahead."

"You'd be using personnel who instead should be out looking for my son."

There was a long pause. Teddy envisioned His Majesty sitting at his massive desk under the white, fluttering canopy on the terrace, looking out at the Arabian Sea through his dark sunglasses.

"I never thought of that, Teddy. You are quite right. I am delighted to witness that you are thinking clearly."

"May we speak of Turnbull again?"

"Colonel Turnbull? I thought we—"

"No, sir, we haven't. You have arranged matters in such a way that I do not know Colonel Turnbull; I do not know the people he has working for him; I do not know the manner in which he and his people work."

"I thought it wise—"

"It may have been wise. But, at this moment, my ignorance of him is not helpful."

"Again, I fear I must apologize to you."

"No, sir."

"What can I say? Colonel Augustus Turnbull is a native, having been—"

"He is?"

"Yes."

"I thought he was brought up English."

"He was born on a farm near Dahrbahr. His father was a plantation overseer. Didn't your father have a plantation near there, Teddy?"

"I see."

"His father was killed in a farm accident. Augustus and his mother went to England, where he was educated. He joined the British Army, was decorated two or three times and eventually trained in Army Intelligence."

"Oh."

"A rather fine record, as I read it. He came home and joined our Intelligence Service only after a distinguished career with British Intelligence. Of course, it's always so hard to know what these intelligence people actually have done. So much of their lives are closed to us."

"Your Majesty, you consider Augustus Turnbull a loyal subject?"

"Yes. Indeed I do. Why not?"

"Then I request that you apply to him the maximum pressure. Toby must be returned safely to us before the Resolution is submitted Monday night."

There was another long pause. "Mr. Ambassador," the King asked, "are you giving me an ultimatum?"

"I'm requesting that maximum pressure be placed on Augustus Turnbull." Teddy noticed that during this conversation his fingers had shredded the near edge of his blotter. "You see…" Teddy swallowed slowly. "We don't have much time.…"

"No," His Majesty said, "we don't. Teddy, maximum pressure is being exerted on Augustus Turnbull and his people there. I have complete confidence in him. Give us the weekend."

"We only have the weekend."

"And, Mr. Ambassador? Monday, in the light of facts then prevailing, I will give you a directive. You will follow that directive."

It was not a question.

"Goodbye, Mr. Ambassador."

Thirty

From the motel room not only could Toby hear the music from the carousel, but through the window from almost a mile away he could see Uncle Whimsy's mountain-sized Stovepipe Hat.

He had gotten up and peeked at it through the edge of the window shade at dawn. Somehow he had known it would be there that morning, right in the middle of his window, regardless of whether the window faced north, south, east or west. It had to be there. It was the symbol of Uncle Whimsy, of Fantazyland, which he had seen on comic-book covers, in magazines, on television a thousand times.

Toby had known he would get to see Uncle Whimsy's great Hat, as tall as the sky, in reality sometime.

Quietly, he had crawled back into bed. Beyond the shades, the sunlight on the window became brighter and brighter. The air conditioner went on and off. With increasing urgency and frequency, Toby's stomach notified him he was hungry. He told it to be patient and kept still.

Finally, Spike rolled onto his back.

"Ho-hum," said Toby loudly. "Ho-hum."

Spike raised his elbows and rubbed his eyes with his fists.

Toby jumped up, opened the window shades, went into the bathroom, brushed his teeth, showered, dressed in the shorts and sneakers, socks and shirt Spike had bought him the day before, combed his hair somewhat.

When he came out, Spike was sitting on the edge of his bed. He was rolling his glass eye around on the palm of his hand. He carried it with him into the bathroom, tossing it into the air and catching it as he walked.

Toby waited.

First he waited while Spike shaved and then while Spike showered. He waited while Spike dressed. He waited while Spike went to the bureau mirror and popped the glass eye back into his socket.

"Goin' to get a newspaper. You wait here."

"Breakfast," Toby said. "Food. Don't you want your coffee?"

"Dunno about breakfast."

Spike swung the door closed behind him.

And Toby, showered, dressed, ravenously hungry, waited while Spike went to the lobby for a newspaper.

He stood at the window, staring at Uncle Whimsy's Stovepipe Hat standing up like a mountain in the landscape. Its black, cylindrical sides glistened in the morning sunlight. The carousel music was light on the morning air. Occasionally, there was the sound of a man's voice announcing something through a public address system. Toby could not make out the words exactly, but the tone of voice was cheerful. And frequently there was an enormous roar, deeper in tone and louder in volume than any jet engine Toby had ever heard. He tried to envision what sort of a machine would make such a roar. What would it do? Maybe the machine existed simply because of the lovely, awful noise it could make.

It was a temptation for him to sneak out of the motel room, as he did at the Red Star–Silvermine Motel, and get breakfast. The Motel Rancho O'Grady was much bigger, much busier. After Spike had registered the night before, he had returned to the car to get Toby. The only way to their room, Spike had said, was through the lobby. Even at that hour there had been many kids in the lobby, most of them wearing shorts and Uncle Whimsy T-shirts. Spike had hurried Toby through the lobby, even though Toby, too, was wearing shorts and at least no adult had looked at him. A few girls had looked at him; a couple of boys. Toby's T-shirt read, VALVOLINE.

The longer he waited for Spike, the more he wished he had snuck out of the room before Spike had awoken and had breakfast.

But, clearly, today he did not wish to make Spike angry.

When the motel room door opened, Toby turned from the window.

Spike did not have a newspaper in his hand.

Spike's head was so straight he appeared to be looking at Toby with both eyes.

There was the roar of that mysterious machine from Fantazyland.

"Telephones don't work," Spike said. "Fuckin' telephones."

"I'm sorry," Toby said.

Spike sat on the edge of his bed. His shoulders were slumped. His head was low. He was staring at the floor.

"Eggs," Toby said. "Cereal. Bacon. Sausage. Orange juice. Toast. Coffee for you."

Spike said absently, "What? What're you talkin' about?"

"Breakfast!" Toby said. "A little thing called breakfast! Breakfast is next!"

"Oh, yeah." Spike reached for the phone between the unmade beds. "Sure, kid. I'll call up. We'll have it here."

Spike sent Toby to the bathroom while breakfast was being laid out in their room.

Toby popped out of the bathroom and sat down at the portable table as soon as he heard the door close.

Spike had repeated into the telephone everything Toby had said. And there everything was, jammed on the table: eggs, cereal, bacon, sausage, orange juice, toast and coffee.

Toby began eating everything at once.

Spike was slow to sit down. He drank a cup of coffee before he touched any food.

Toby thought Spike was looking, sounding, acting like his math teacher the mornings he smelled of whiskey and the other kids said he had a hangover. Spike was moving slowly, not saying much. His face looked like he would be glad to burp. Even his real eye was slightly glassy. He did not smell of whiskey, though.

After Spike began eating, Toby said, "Spike? If you wanted to hide a shoe, where would you hide it?"

"What?"

"Simple question: where would you hide a shoe?"

"Stupid question."

"Sensible question. Where would you hide a shoe?"

"Another one of your stories about damn fools who fly through the air in their pajamas?"

"Where would you hide a shoe?"

Spike blinked around the room. "Under the bed."

"Why under the bed?"

"No one would see it there."

"They would, if they were looking for the shoe."

"Why would anybody be looking for the shoe?"

"Are there many shoes under the bed?"

"I dunno. I haven't looked. Could be corpses, for all I know." Spike stabbed his scrambled eggs. "Why are you talking this way? I didn't take your shoe. Dumb kid."

"Ask me where I'd hide a shoe—if I had to hide a shoe."

"In a closet."

Toby shook his head. "First place anyone would look for a shoe. That's where a shoe's supposed to be."

"It is? I never put no shoes in no closets."

"Ask me."

"Ask you what, for Chrissake?"

"If I had to hide a shoe," Toby said, "I'd hide it in a shoe store."

"Oh, yeah." Spike chewed thoughtfully. "Like hidin' a needle in a haystack."

"No," said Toby. "Like hiding a piece of hay in a haystack. I'd hide a needle in a sewing box."

"But a needle's supposed to be in a sewing box."

"Yeah. But no one would expect you to *hide* a needle in a sewing box."

Toby munched awhile, then said, "Spike, where would you hide a speck of sand?"

"Anywhere."

"A speck of sand you know other people are looking for."

"Why would anyone look for a speck of sand?"

"You'd hide in on the beach."

"I would not."

"Why not?"

"I'd never find it again."

"That's true," Toby said.

They ate in silence for a while.

Toby said, "Are we going to stay in this room all day?"

"Why?"

"I noticed you made me go into the bathroom when the man brought breakfast to us."

"Oh. Fac' is, you needed to go to the bathroom, anyway."

Toby ate another piece of toast

He then said, "I guess when people tell you and me to stay in a room, Spike, we have to do it. Right, Spike?"

Spike looked annoyed. "It's the telephone. Can't get nobody to answer the telephone."

Faintly, they could hear the carousel music from Fantazyland.

"Spike?"

"Why don't you stifle it? Punk kid."

"If you had to hide a kid, where would you hide him?"

Spike glanced at the bathroom door.

Then he stared at Toby.

Toby said, "I think a school yard would be a pretty good place to hide a kid."

Spike continued to stare at him.

"Don't you think a school yard would be a pretty good place to hide a kid?"

"Yeah, kid. Sure. A school yard would be a fine place to hide a kid."

He poured himself some more coffee.

Toby said, "Anywhere there are lots of other kids."

Again, Fantazyland's mysterious machine roared.

Toby continued to look at Spike. The man's fists were clenched tight. He was looking over his shoulder at the window, through the window, maybe seeing the top of Uncle Whimsy's Hat.

Spike picked up his coffee cup and took it to the window. His back was to Toby.

After a moment, very cheerfully, Toby said, "Hey, Spike! We goin' to Fantazyland now? Nice day for it...."

Spike drained his coffee cup before turning around.

"Fac' is," he said, "we are."

He left the coffee cup on the bureau and picked up the car keys.

"Fac' is, I'm sick of your conversation."

Thirty-One

The old man in short pants, standing on a ladder puttying in a window, didn't see her.

"Good afternoon," Christina said.

The man looked down. "Hi."

"You're Mr. Silvermine?"

"Always have been," the man said.

"The person in the motel office said I might find you here."

"Well. You have."

Christina opened her wallet and handed it up to him.

He squinted at it, took it in his hand, held it out of the sunlight. Then he looked at her.

"Oh. You his mother?"

"Yes. Do you recognize him?"

"Sure do." He handed the wallet back to her and, leaving his tools on top of the step ladder, climbed down. "Thought I hadn't heard the end of this."

The man was looking carefully at her. "That man. Traveling with the boy. Your son. Jackson. Not the boy's father, was he? Your husband?"

"No."

"Thought not." He shook his head, blinked. "This is the quietest kidnapping I've ever heard of—now that I know it's a kidnapping. 'Spose there's a reason for it? I mean, you all being so quiet about it."

"Yes."

"But the F.B.I. must be involved," Mr. Silvermine said. "Ed Noakes is the only one I spoke to about it."

"No," said Christina. "They're not."

"Come on. Let's go into the office. Get out of this sun, even though, like me, it's past its prime."

Walking with him across the patch of lawn, Christina said, "I just wonder if there's anything you can tell me. Anything. For example, by any chance do you have the registration of the car?"

"Sure do. Didn't give it to Ed Noakes 'cause I had just the faintest suspicion that I was bein' a busybody. Not my role in life to harass people if they don't need harassin'. Enough people have taken on that role for themselves."

In the office, he copied down the registration of the car on a slip of paper and handed it to her. "Not sure that will do you any good. Pretty sure it's a rented car. People change cars these days faster than they change facial expressions. All the cars look alike, anyway, whether they call 'em Chryslers or Oldsmobiles. All the facial expressions look alike, too, come to think of it. Orthodontisized grills up front, ears you can't see. Teeth everywhere you look. How about some iced tea?"

"Love it."

"Let's go into the dining room and see if anybody workin' for me is workin' for me."

At the table, over tall glasses of iced tea, Mr. Silvermine leaned forward and said, "Arrived Thursday night. Man came in to register, boy stayed in car. That's unusual. Little kids usually like to come in with their fathers, 'specially boys. If they're awake. Saw his head through the window, stickin' up over the dashboard. Wide awake. Didn't really lay eyes on your little boy till next morning, real early. As soon as the dining room opened for breakfast, he presented himself in the lobby, enlisting my authority to permit him to order breakfast. I was taken by the way he was dressed— black shoes, gray slacks, white shirt, blue blazer. Even the president of the United States wouldn't be dressed that way in the lobby of a motel at seven o'clock in the morning, if he had other clothes. Struck me that if the boy had any other clothes, shorts or jeans or somethin', he'd be wearin' 'em. Then I perceived he was a well-spoken child, and the man who registered as his father had given me the distinct impression he believed vocabulary was something meant for other people. I guess I was a little suspicious. I threw a quick routine at him about his name, Jack Jackson, son of Jack

Jackson, and although he didn't answer me, he also didn't particularly seem to know what I was talking about."

"How did he seem to you?"

"Right as rain. Hungry. Mostly anxious about his breakfast."

"He wasn't wounded in any way?"

"No. Not at all. I saw him later playing in the swimming pool. No bruises as far as I could see."

"He was playing in the swimming pool?"

"Later. Later in the afternoon."

"Was this man, Jackson, with him at that time?"

"Yup. He was sittin' to the side, dozin'."

"This is hard for me to understand," Christina said. "I've been envisioning…gagged, tied in a closet, beat up."

"I'm sure you have. None of that was goin' on, as far as I could see." Bernard Silvermine thought a minute. "'Course, it would be pretty hard to move a child around in that condition, bound and gagged. You'd sort of have to keep him in one place, if you know what I mean. Lose your freedom of movement."

"But how are they doing it? What have they told him?"

"Oldest story in the world," Bernard Silvermine said. "Get a child to come along with you by the promise of candy. Con him. Make him think if he comes along nicely, he'll get somethin' he wants. Isn't that always the story?"

Christina had not touched her iced tea. "Tell me about this man. Jackson."

"Not terribly tall, but heavily, I mean, powerfully built. Big shoulders, chest, thick arms and neck. Glass eye. His face was pretty well cut up."

"What do you mean, 'cut up'? Acne? Chicken pox? Knife scars?"

"Very distinctive scars. Follow the fights somewhat, you know. Always fascinates me how one man can make a business out of knockin' other men senseless."

"I don't get you."

"He had the scars of a fighter. A professional fighter. Scars over his eyes, mashed nose, lace cuts the back of his neck."

"A fighter."

"Boxer. Retired boxer."

"Why do you say 'retired'? Because of his age?"

"No. He wasn't that old. Didn't I say he had a glass eye? Can't fight with a blind side. Have to be able to see out of both sides of your head."

"He sounds pretty ugly."

"Well, I doubt he'd ever be taken up as a model for aftershave."

"But what kind of a person did he seem like? I know that's a stupid question...."

Bernard Silvermine looked at her a long moment before answering. "Frankly, he seemed a pretty tough character. But don't take that too much to heart. I'm older than you, by a day or two, and I can tell you I've never met a person yet who is what he looks like. People with wide open, innocent faces seem to have more latitude in bein' rotten. I find that people who are born lookin' rotten already seem to have to toe the line a little closer. All I can say is your boy seemed all right when I saw him."

"Any idea where they went?"

"No, ma'am. People aren't apt to leave forwardin' addresses at a motel. The home address Jackson signed was 200 Park Avenue, Saint Louis, Kentucky. The imponderability of all that didn't strike me until later. Paid cash. No credit card. The boy—your son—told me he was goin' to Fantazyland—which might have been the candy Jackson was usin' to keep him in line. Then again, the boy also told me he was waitin' on a call from his mother—you. You were comin' to take him to Fantazyland."

Christina's eyes roamed around the empty dining room.

Bernard Silvermine waited patiently, to hear if she had any other questions.

Finally, he said, "California's just one big parking lot, you know —strips of it movin'."

"What do you mean?"

"Even highway patrol doesn't seem to be able to find any particular car too quickly."

"No," she said. "I don't suppose so."

"I don't know what to tell you," Bernard Silvermine said. "Anything at all I can do to help?"

"No." Christina took her handbag off the table and stood up. "Really, I'm very grateful to you. This is the first real lead we've had."

Bernard Silvermine said, "Delighted to hear I'm not a busy-body. Not that I was losin' any sleep over the possibility."

He had risen and she had put her hand in his. "Thank you so very much, Mr. Silvermine."

"I have a question. Busybody question. What's your son's name?"

"Toby."

"That's a right nice name," Bernard Silvermine said. "Right nice. You know, I wouldn't mind too much knowin' where there's good news."

"What? Yes. Of course."

"Otherwise, I won't want to know, if you understand me."

"Yes."

"I'd rather think maybe you just forgot to tell me."

"I understand," Christina said. "…I understand."

Thirty-Two

The parking lot at Fantazyland was the largest Toby had ever seen. They had to follow the hand signals of six people before they were parked properly.

And Uncle Whimsy's Stovepipe Hat rose up into the sky from the nearby landscape higher than Toby had ever dared think possible. He could see the little gondolas, bright red, yellow, green, pop out of the hole near the Top of The Hat, the people in them barely distinguishable, zip around a curve, vanish into another hole in The Hat, reappear from a tunnel a little further down, climb slowly, plunge down into another tunnel.

They had to walk a long way through the sun-dazzled parking lot to get to Fantazyland's main gate. And then wait in line for tickets.

UNCLE WHIMSY WELCOMES YOU—ONE AND ALL—TO FANTAZYLAND. Toby read the sign a million times. He had known, really known, that someday he would get to read that sign.

If you need help at Fantazyland, ask your Constable. Emergency medical facilities are available near main gate.

Spike bought two books of tickets, good for two days' admission, a ticket for every ride.

Inside the main gate, constables stood around, men in blue suits, wide belts, truncheons hanging from them, handlebar mustaches and helmets.

A giant Uncle Whimsy, stovepipe hat, bright pink face with white-painted smile and smiling eyes, baggy pants and three-foot-long high-button shoes, greeted them. His gloved hand on Toby's head was so big and floppy it fell over Toby's shoulders.

Spike's hand disappeared in Uncle Whimsy's glove.

"Glad to meetcha, glad to meetcha," Spike said. "You're a big bastid, arncha?"

A nearby constable gave Spike a sharp look.

And Uncle Whimsy moved away.

Immediately inside the main gate, they were in the square of a town that had never existed, except in people's longings.

In the middle of a green, four-squared park was a bandstand on which mustached firemen played trumpets and saxophones and an oboe and drums, *When the saints come marchin' in....* Horse-drawn carriages went around the square and up and down the main street. One horse relieved itself and instantly a man in a white suit was there with shovel and broom and a barrel on wheels to clean it up.

On one side of the square was a Fire Station, its doors open. Inside was a horse-drawn pumper and an antique fire truck, kids swarming over both, ringing the bells. Next to it was a Candy Store (the biggest store in the square).

Also on the square was an Emporium, a Mercantile Establishment, a Newspaper Office *(People with press passes please check in here)*, a Drug Store *(Ice Cream, Notions & Sundries)*, a small Lawyer's Office, a large Doctor's Office with a Red Cross flag outside *(Doctor Is In—for medical emergencies)*, a Chamber of Commerce Office *(Special Guests of Fantazyland, please check in here)*, a movie theater *(See Charlie Chaplin! Harold Lloyd! Abbott & Costello!)* and a Sandwich Shoppe. Poles atop the buildings flew the flags of all nations, although Toby could not find the flag of his nation.

"Jeez," Spike said, standing, staring. "Just like Newark."

First they went to the Candy Store, where Spike bought a bag of peppermints ("Good for your breath") and Toby a bag of licorice ("That stuff shits," Spike said.)

Munching, they listened to the band music for a while. Spike hummed along with such a dreadful voice the space around them cleared. Then they ambled around the square. Going by the Fire Station, Toby looked in and guessed it wouldn't take him all that long to work his way through the crowd of kids, take his turn in the drivers' seats and ring the fire bells.

Spike said, "Kids' stuff. Ya see, that's kids' stuff."

Continuing to look around doors, Toby noticed that although the dresses in the windows of the Emporium had hoops and hobbles and bustles and veils for sale at low, low prices, inside the store were jeans and T-shirts and shorts with no prices visible.

At the end of the street was a signpost with three arrows. The one pointing right said, TO THE FUTURE; to the left, TO THE PAST; straight ahead, THRILLS, CHILLS AND SPILLS.

Toby wanted to go straight ahead. He knew that path led to Uncle Whimsy's Hat.

Spike said they would go to the left.

On the main street of Wild West City stood a man dressed in black cowboy gear, snarling at the people, cracking a bullwhip. He wore a black patch over one eye.

"Look at that turkey," Spike said.

They tried their luck in a shooting gallery. Toby's score was twelve hits out of twenty shots. He was awarded an Uncle Whimsy Comic Book. Spike's score was seven.

"Rigged," Spike said. "Can't trust nobody. Bastids."

Walking along, Spike said, "I ain't tol' you 'bout the time I shot this guy.... He was up on a roof in Newark, eight, nine storys high. I was in the street, block away. Single shot with my pistol, from my hip. That was a real gun, none of this shooting-gallery crap. Fac' is...."

The cracks of the bullwhip became sharper, more frequent, more insistent. A cowboy dressed in white came out of The Marshal's Office. He and the villain glared at each other. The marshal stepped into the street. The villain dropped his whip. They circled around each other. The large semicircle of tourists, dressed in bright shirts and shorts, grew six deep.

The two cowboys drew on each other and fired. For a moment, each stood there. Then a red stain appeared on the villain's shirt, over the heart, and he fell forward, biting the dust.

The tourists smiled and laughed and applauded and took pictures.

Four other cowboys appeared, picked the villain up by his hands and feet and carried him off.

"Make believe," Spike said. "Fac' is, it ain't real, ya know. None of this stuff."

There was a Wild West Clothing Store—more jeans, shorts and Uncle Whimsy T-shirts, ten-gallon hats and big belt buckles—

a Dance Hall Saloon with a list of prices outside for fruit juices, soft drinks. Toby heard a piano tinkling. Two or three heavily made-up women, hair piled on top of their heads, gowns cut low, stood outside, saying to the men, "Hiya, honey…"

Spike reached into the skirt of one and pinched her bottom.

"Hiya, honey," he said. "Whatcha doin' after the show?"

At first the woman looked shocked, then disgusted; then she looked away.

In various places, when they were just standing there looking around, Toby heard the hum of machinery. He didn't ask if Spike heard it too. He noticed little booths here and there (in the village by the main gate they were old-fashioned telephone booths, without windows; in the Wild West village they were outhouses)—all marked *Employees Only*. Especially standing near these booths, he heard the humming noises. He thought the sounds nearest the booths sounded like elevators.

There was a corral with live ponies, one of which Toby rode; another area of mechanical horses, bucking broncos, which they both rode. The mechanical horses were more lively than the live.

They were in Wild West City so long the villain reappeared in the street, with a fresh black shirt, again cracking his whip at people.

"Turkey," Spike said.

Over the tuna sandwiches at an outdoor pavilion, they studied their ticket books and discussed where they'd go next. Toby pressed for THRILLS, CHILLS AND SPILLS, but Spike said he thought THE FUTURE would be more interesting. Near them was a seven-foot-tall white stem of a ship's air vent. At the beginning of lunch, Toby saw a constable step up to the vent, open a door in it with a key, step inside and close the door. Toby kept careful watch all through lunch. The constable never came back out of the vent. However, near the end of lunch, the door in the vent opened again and out stepped a woman in a space suit, carrying her helmet.

Everywhere they had gone in the park, people dressed as constables, clowns, bears, space travelers, rabbits, shook hands with people, patted children's heads, held babies, struck silly poses with tourists while having their pictures taken. While they were finishing up their sandwiches, a fountain in the middle of the pavilion rose up slowly. Music became louder and louder. Under the fountain rose a stage. On it, a band with electric guitars and drums played; four girls, all blondes in slinky red dresses, sang. *Why don't you love me, baby? I can bake a cake...*

Spike turned around. "Where'd they come from?"

"Look, Spike." Toby pointed up in the air. "The fountain's still working! Over their heads!"

"Well, I'll be a goose's rear door!"

That afternoon they visited THE FUTURE: circled a lake in a ship that traveled on an air cushion, its engines making the lovely, awful noise Toby had heard from the motel; visited the bottom of the lake in a submarine, stared through the portholes at simulated ocean growths and fish; whipped around the lake on a Future Bus that also traveled on an air cushion, making a ground noise; talked into telephones that permitted them to hear Japanese ("What's that shit?" Spike said as he listened. "Not me!"); blasted off in a space ship, rushed through the atmosphere, watching the world become smaller behind them, then burst into the galaxy and floated among the stars to tinkling music.

"Whaddaya think of this?" Spike asked himself out loud.

"Inneresting," he answered. "Inneresting."

They also visited the Spooky House. Eyeballs of portraits followed them; ghosts walked by them in the dark, moaning. Chains rattled. The room lurched, suddenly changing dimensions. Headless ladies and gentlemen appeared, dancing a minuet.

And The Pirate's Caravelle. Gold spilled from a chest on the lower deck. Sailors languished in the brig. On the upper deck a sailor, dressed only in torn-off pants and a blindfold, hands tied tightly behind his back, was forced to walk the plank.

The tourists smiled and laughed and applauded and took pictures.

Spike and Toby watched a long time, but the man never rose to the surface of the water.

"Poor dude," Spike said. "He croaked."

They went in a dugout through The Dangerous Swamp. Mechanical alligators and crocodiles came to the edge of the boat and snapped their teeth at them. The dugout veered away. Along the embankment, ten-foot mechanical bears waved them nearer and roared at them. Huge snakes slithered down the trees. On a little island they passed, there was a log cabin burning.

"Fantastic!" Spike said, "fac' is, you know, all this is fake, you know. I mean, that cabin isn't really burnin'. It's takin' too long. It just looks like it's burnin'."

They were walking across an old wooden bridge. It began to tremor. It wobbled. It lurched down to the left. They could see and hear the timber supports breaking. Three sharks appeared across the lagoon and came at them with horrendous speed. One after the other, they came to the edge of the bridge, their mouths open, reaching for them....

"Jeez," said Spike, drawing back. "Getcha to believe it."

Toby knew they were coming to the base of Uncle Whimsy's Stovepipe Hat.

But down a path, Spike saw a great, smooth cement bowl in the landscape. In it, people were driving brightly painted, rubber-wheeled, rubber-bumpered cars, gathering speed, smashing into each other, laughing, bouncing off.

"I gotta try that!" Spike said.

Spike hustled into the driver's seat.

"Hey, Spike! I'm drivin'!"

"Bullshit you are, kid. You're too young."

"Other kids my size are driving!"

Spike looked around. "Oh, yeah. So they are. Next time. Next time you get to drive."

Spike drove. He gave himself the maximum space to gather the maximum momentum to crash into people with the maximum force.

"Hyaaa! Gotcha, ya bastids!"

Some of his victims looked offended.

Spike gave them the raspberry.

When Toby drove, it took him a while to discover how the pedal and steering wheel worked.

"Go get those dudes!" Spike shouted. Toby was nudging other cars gently. "Smash 'em! Smash 'em!"

A plaid car came from nowhere and hit them so hard their car rocked sideways.

"Why, you bastids!" Spike tried to stand up in the car to get out. He shook his fist at them. "Let me outa here! I'll kill the bastids!"

Toby started the car with a jerk and Spike fell back into his seat.

"Ah, dumb kid," Spike said when the ride was over. "Whaddaya you know? Nothin'! Nothin' at all. All you think life is is fun fun fun fun."

Ultimately, they came to the line at the base of Uncle Whimsy's Hat.

Spike put his hands on his hips, leaned back and stared up at the top. Directly over them, on little tracks, the gondolas were zooming in and out of The Hat, down the sides. "Jeez, kid. Look at that."

"Let's get in line, Spike."

Spike waggled his head. "Not safe."

"Whaddaya mean, 'not safe'? Spike, it's been working for years!"

"Not safe," Spike said.

Quietly, Toby said, "Chicken."

Spike took a step toward him. "Whad you say?"

"Cluck-cluck-cluck," Toby said. "Chicken!"

"Don' you never say nothin' like that to me!"

"All right, then. Let's get in line."

"No."

"CLUCK-CLUCK-CLUCK!"

"Dumb kid, whadda you know?"

"I know you're a chicken."

Spike looked at the ground, at the people waiting in line to go on the ride down Uncle Whimsy's Hat. He looked at the ground again.

"Cluck," Toby said.

Spike broke into the head of the line, pushing people aside. Toby stayed right with him.

The shadows were longer.

Spike sat on a cement bench. His face was ashen. His lips were slack. His hands were shaking.

Toby stood on the sidewalk, facing him.

"Have I still got my eye?" Spike felt for it with his fingers.

"Yeah."

On the ride coming down The Hat, through The Hat, down, down, plunging through black tunnels, roaring out into sunlit space, twirling around in midair, down, down, rushing down, Spike sat, back straight, clutching the safety bar with both hands. His mouth was open, his neck muscles strained.

He was bellowing, "Oh—hhhhhhhh!"

Laughing, Toby joined him. "Ah—hhhhhh!"

Going through the pitch-black tunnels, Toby had the impression Spike's head was a white balloon on a string being towed along beside him.

It wasn't until the little gondola slowed down, near the bottom, that Toby realized Spike wasn't having fun.

Spike wanted to get out of the gondola immediately. He saw the platform, but his movements were uncertain. His knees wobbled.

Spike was a shaken man. He went to the nearest bench and sat down.

"That's enough for today, kid," he finally said. "This place gives me the creeps. Hard to remember nothin's real, ya know?"

He stood up, putting his hand on the back of Toby's neck.

"Let's go back to the motel now."

"We can come back tomorrow, though. Right, Spike?"

"Sure, sure," Spike said.

"There's lots we haven't seen yet."

"Yeah," Spike said as they walked along. "The Wax Museum. The Duck Pond. Princess Daphne's Flower Castle…"

Thirty-Three

Bernard Silvermine saw the green four-door sedan pull into the parking lot in front of the Red Star–Silvermine Motel and park immediately in front of the main door, where there was a sign saying, NO PARKING — LOADING AREA.

A heavy man rolled out of the driver's seat, slammed the door and stood a moment looking at the motel. He wore a rumpled green tweed suit. Before he adjusted his jacket there was a noticeable bulge under his left shoulder.

When the man stood at the reception counter, Bernard Silvermine looked up at him inquiringly, but said nothing.

The man put a school photo of Toby on the counter. Bernard noticed that in laying the picture on the counter, the man had his thumb on Toby's face.

"Ever seen that child before?" the man asked.

Bernard Silvermine looked at the sweaty thumbprint. "Who are you?"

The man's tone was official, if not authoritative. "You, or someone else at this motel, reported to the Federal Bureau of Investigation your suspicion that a boy staying at this motel the night before last in the company of an unidentified man was the victim of kidnap."

"Are you with the F.B.I.?" Bernard Silvermine asked mildly.

The man's small eyes were impudent, Bernard Silvermine thought. "How else would I know you reported it?"

"That I don't know," Bernard Silvermine said. "But I know you're not with the F.B.I."

"I'm with a private police agency," the man said. His hand went to his back pocket.

"That's all right," Bernard Silvermine said. "There's no need to show me credentials." He picked up Toby's picture, held it in the light of the plate-glass windows, shook his head and said, "That's not the boy, anyway."

"It's not?"

Bernard Silvermine put the photograph back on the counter.

"No, indeedy," he said. "The boy who was here had red hair and freckles."

The man took the picture off the counter. He hesitated before putting it back in his pocket. He appeared to have more questions for Bernard Silvermine, but didn't seem immediately sure what they were.

"I wonder," Bernard Silvermine said, "if you'd be good enough to remove your car from my loading zone?"

Outside, a chambermaid was trying to get her laundry wagon by the green sedan.

Bernard Silvermine said, "I mean, like move it. Now."

He watched the heavy man cross the lobby, push through the glass door and, with deliberate slowness, get into the car and start it while the chambermaid waited in the hot sun.

I wonder if Toby's mother knows, Bernard Silvermine thought, *that someone else is looking for her son—and that that someone is no particular friend.*

Thirty-Four

"I wonder if you could help me," Christina said to the young woman behind the car rental counter at San Francisco Airport. "I'm Mrs. Cummings. I live in Los Altos Hills...."

Christina had given the same story to the other two car rental agencies at the airport and drawn a blank.

She held the piece of paper Bernard Silvermine had given her with the registration number written on it.

"...Do you ride bicycles?" she suddenly asked the young woman behind the counter.

"Yes, I do," the young woman said. "My husband races."

The two women smiled at each other at the thought of a representative of a car rental agency riding a bicycle.

"My son has a very precious bicycle," Christina said. "He paid for it himself. A Motobecane Gran Record."

There was clear recognition in the young woman's face. "That's a hell of a bike," she said.

"Not inexpensive," Christina agreed.

"Does your son race? I mean, your son must be pretty young."

"I think he means to try," Christina said. *Oh, my. Don't they make Motobecane Gran Records for youngsters?* She had first seen one only the previous week. Her pro at the All Stars' Tennis Camp had one. *This person knows bicycles. Have I made a mistake?* "Actually, he's my husband's son," Christina said. "He's seventeen."

"Oh. I was wondering. That's a professional kind of bike for a kid. I mean, a little kid."

Christina nodded. "It's a very good bike. Anyway, he had it with him at the ball field the other night, and a car hit it. Squished it."

The young woman's face fell.

Christina assured her, "My son wasn't on it. The bicycle was just on the grass, you see...."

The young woman's face didn't seem relieved. *My God. This person is struck dumb by the tragedy of a bike's being run over.*

"Anyway"—Christina held up the piece of paper—"my neighbor-friend, Mrs. Scalise, took down the registration number of the car that ran over the bike and gave it to me. See? 7NP 4484. And she said she thought she saw one of those car-rental stickers near the back bumper. I'm just wondering if the car belongs to your agency, and if possibly you could give me the name and address of who-ever rented the car from you?"

The young woman had read the registration number. She said, "We're not liable for accidents—"

"Oh, no," Christina said quickly, "I'm not thinking that. I'm just thinking that I'd write to the person who squished the bike—"

"He might have insurance," the girl said. "Well, he ought to have insurance."

"Yes," Christina said.

"But I don't want the agency held responsible."

"Of course not," Christina said. "But don't you think someone who squished a bike should be told he had done so? Especially a Motobecane Gran Record?"

The young woman nodded firmly. "Especially a Motobecane Gran Record."

"At least," Christina said, "he ought to be told what it was he squished."

"Indeed, yes." The young woman took the paper. "I'll find out what I can."

While the young woman was going through her agency records, Christina turned her back to the counter and looked at the airport.

Such an odd mix of sights and sounds.There were little people with big suitcases, big people with little cases; people dressed in three-piece suits, people dressed in cut-offs and jerseys; people hurrying madly, people standing looking bored out of full con-sciousness. The general sounds were cavernous; the public address announcements penetrating; the occasional whine and roar of the jets taking off and landing oddly suppressed.

Airports had always been happy places for Christina. She had met Teddy for the first time at an airport. She recalled the days flying back and forth from New York and college to spend weekends with him. Later, after they were married, flying from London to Geneva, New York to St. Croix for vacations...flying in His Majesty's private jet.

She wasn't sure she'd ever like airports again. An airport, this airport, was where Toby hadn't shown up when he was supposed to. *Perhaps I'm obsessed by this airport*, she thought. *I keep coming back to it. In this airport, there has to be a lead, somewhere, somehow.*

"Mrs. Cummings?"

Christina turned around. The young woman had a long, yellow piece of paper in her hand.

"That car was rented by a Charles Mullins, a driver licensed by the state of New Jersey."

She handed Christina back the small piece of paper that had the registration number on it. "Here, I wrote down his name and home address for you."

Christina looked at the paper, feigning great interest in it. She still did not know what she wanted to know.

"Tell me," Christina said easily. "Has the man turned the car back in yet?"

The young woman looked at her curiously.

"What I mean is," Christina said, "there's no hurry in writing him if we know he hasn't gone home yet."

"Oh." The young woman consulted her piece of paper. "No. It's an open-ended return."

"He has not returned the car?"

"No. If he had, the computer would have marked it available."

"I can't thank you enough," Christina said. "It's a small matter, of course, but my son—"

The young woman flipped her index finger at Christina. "Squishing a good bike is no small matter."

Thirty-Five

Christina ran the last few meters down Slave Alley in the dusk. She'd heard the phone ringing in the bungalow.

Once inside the bungalow, she instantly picked up the receiver. "Hello?"

The reading lamp near the telephone was on.

"Christina? Good guess."

"Teddy, listen—"

"You were right about the flight Toby was supposed to be on. In fact, it looks like he was on it. There was a last-minute reservation for a man and a boy. Reservation in the name of Doland. Major Mustafa found one of the stewardesses who had served that flight and spoke to her by phone. Caught her between flights in Toronto. She remembers the man because, well, she saw him do something unusual to the boy, and—"

"What do you mean, 'do something unusual to the boy'? Teddy, what did he do to Toby?"

"Nothing, really. It's all right. A small thing."

"Teddy, you'd better tell me what the stewardess saw the man do to Toby!"

"He twisted Toby's fingers. Bent them back. Apparently to make him shut up. A childish thing, really."

"Was Toby all right? It must have hurt him."

"Well, Christina, this whole—"

"Oh, Teddy."

"Anyway, he fits the description Mrs. Brown gave us of the guy at the airport. The stewardess remembers his glass eye. And her description of the boy pretty well fits Toby—age, coloring, dress."

"Teddy, listen. Toby is here."

"What?"

"No, I'm sorry. Not here. I mean, on the West Coast. The man at the motel, the Red Star–Silvermine Motel, identified Toby from that little picture I keep in my wallet."

"Positively?"

"No doubt at all. Toby was there two nights ago. Again, the same description of the man with Toby. Mr. Silvermine thinks the man may have been a boxer."

"Did he have any idea where they might have gone?"

"None. But I have the registration number of the car they were driving."

Teddy thought before speaking. "Give it to Colonel Turnbull."

"I checked it out as much as I could. The car is rented to a Charles Mullins, of New Jersey."

Teddy's voice was becoming increasingly thoughtful. "I don't think the name means anything, Christina. How many names has he used so far? Willins, Doland, Jackson—"

"Teddy, the important thing is that the car hasn't been returned to the rental agency yet. That means they're still somewhere in this area." Teddy did not say anything. "Here in the San Francisco Bay area."

Finally Teddy said, "I guess that narrows it down somewhat."

"Only somewhat," she said. "But before we had the whole world to search! And now we have the car registration number." Again, Teddy was saying nothing. "What do I do now?" Christina asked.

"Give any information you have to Colonel Turnbull."

"Yes. All right. I will."

"The boss has complete faith in him." Teddy was now using the voice he used in giving directives late at night: low, tired, efficient. "By the way, Christina, His Majesty is being totally supportive."

"Does he still say you have to give that speech?"

Teddy's voice became lower, tireder, more efficient. "There is no doubt in his mind about that, Christina."

Still standing, facing the side wall of the living room, Christina realized she was staring at a film-star poster on the wall. Seen from this short distance, the girl's bathing suit was transparent.

"Teddy? I don't mean to add to your burdens, right now, and that's not why I'm saying this…."

"Saying what?"

"After we get Toby back…What I mean is…we have to find some other way of life.…I mean, if we're going to live together.…Teddy? Are you there?"

"Yes."

"It was bad enough before, never seeing Toby, never being able to spend any time with you, I mean, *real* time, but I never knew, I never even thought Toby's life could be at stake." The poster on the wall blurred watery. The upper part of her index finger was in her mouth. She was biting on it, hard. "I can't stand this!"

Quietly, Teddy said, "We have to stand this."

"I do love you, Teddy."

Teddy said, "Let's keep doing the best we can." He exhaled. "Are you sleeping?"

"I fell asleep near dawn this morning. I slept a few hours."

"Is Colonel Turnbull there?"

"No." She looked at the end table. The bottle of bourbon had not been touched. "I haven't seen him all day."

"I suggest you find him. Tell him about the car and the motel. Leave everything in his hands. Try to get some sleep."

"All right, Teddy." She began to hang up, then raised the phone to her ear again. "Teddy?"

"Yes?"

"Sorry about what I said. But we have to do something else."

Teddy said, "It would be nice."

Christina said "Nothing like this must ever happen to us again."

After she hung up, she turned to get a tissue in the bathroom, not bothering to switch on the bedroom light. She was halfway across the bedroom when a man who had been sitting on the bed stood up.

Thirty-Six

"Let me turn on the light," Colonel Turnbull said.

He turned on the bedside lamp.

Christina had one hand on top of the bureau, the other on her breasts. She was trying to suck in breath.

"I'm so sorry to have given you a fright," Colonel Turnbull said. "I was just coming out of the bathroom when I heard you dash in and answer the phone. I didn't want to disturb you." He waved his arm at the tiny bedroom. "There was no place else I could go."

Christina found enough breath to say, "That's all right." She put her foot out toward the bed. "Just let me sit down a moment."

Taking her by the arm, he helped her to sit on the edge of the bed.

He was smiling.

"I'm so sorry," he repeated. "Was that your husband on the phone?"

"Yes." Her pulse was pounding in her ears. "Did you hear everything?"

Again, he waved his arm around the room. "There was nowhere else I could go, you see. Perhaps I should have let you know I was here…but you sounded so…distraught."

"No," she said. Then she said, "Yes."

"My dear child. Just give yourself a moment to recover. I'm so sorry."

"No, no," she said. "It's all right. I got the registration number of the kidnapper's car. It's right there in my purse."

Colonel Turnbull went into the living room. He picked up the purse from where she had dumped it on the divan. He took out the piece of paper and studied it in the light. Coming back to the bedroom, he put the paper in his pocket.

"Really doesn't help much, I'm afraid," he said. "Not at all, really."

"But Toby was at that motel. Two nights ago. Mr. Silvermine positively identified him!"

"Did he indeed?"

"And he gave me the car registration number. It's a rented car. It hasn't been turned in yet. Can't you find the car?"

"How?"

"The police. Put out an all-points bulletin, or whatever they call it."

"My dear Christina. Don't believe what you hear on television. There are thousands of cars missing in California alone. The police don't find any of them, unless one happens to drop from a helicopter through the police station roof."

"Still—"

"Christina, we are not going to the police on this matter. Do you want this story on the front page of the *San Francisco Examiner*, *New York Times*, *London Times* by tomorrow morning? That wouldn't leave your husband much room to negotiate, would it?"

"I don't care!"

"Others do," Colonel Turnbull said primly. "And, too, I'm talking about negotiating for your son's life."

"Your own men! They've been following me for two days. Tell them to go look for the car."

"Yes, of course," he said. "I'll do just that."

He went back into the living room. "You just rest awhile," he said. "I'll be back shortly."

"Why don't you use the telephone here?" she asked.

"I've disturbed you enough," he said at the door. "Get some rest."

Thirty-Seven

A young couple scampered past Turnbull on their way to the tennis courts. The girl's tennis skirt and panties were so short easily pinchable areas of her cheeks were showing. The boy's legs were slim and sinewy.

"Rotten sods," Turnbull muttered.

The boy glanced over his shoulder angrily. The girl giggled and pulled on the boy's hand.

"It's almost nine," the girl said. "We'll miss the court."

The double rows of clay courts were superbly bathed in white light. Most of the players were dressed in whites: shorts, short dresses, jerseys, except for the odd blue, green or red shirt. All the balls that went back and forth over the nets were colored—yellow, pink, red.

To Turnbull, the lit courts were like a station in space. It was a wholly unreal, synthetic environment, with intent people hurrying about doing things of which he had no comprehension.

The tennis courts were for people's pleasure. As were yacht clubs, ski centers, polo fields, race courses and other places Teodoro Rinaldi had enjoyed all his life and understood completely.

Official son: precious little Teodoro.

At the Orphanage of Saints John and Thomas outside Liverpool, where Augustus Turnbull had spent much of his less than precious youth, only one game had been encouraged by the staff, a particularly vicious form of rugby. As Turnbull remembered it, oversized teams of undersized boys would surround a ball and kick out their aggressions on each other's bare shins. Every boy was obliged to play. Shinbones that were not raw and bleeding by the end of the game drew contemptuous glances from mates and staff alike.

It was not a game for pleasure. It was a painful torture, exercised methodically, to keep boys beaten back and in hand.

He walked along the fence outside the tennis courts.

"Good shot," he heard someone say.

Turnbull knew what a "good shot" is. A "good shot" is a shot which gives the victim just enough time to shit in his pants before dying.

Turnbull had made many "good shots."

The lanky man waiting for Turnbull near Court 7 was watching the people play. Dressed in a gray suit, hands behind his back, Cord seemed absorbed in the game.

Turnbull knew Cord was only pretending not to know Turnbull was behind him.

"Thinking of taking up the game, Simon?" Turnbull said.

Cord turned slightly to him. "I have played," he said. "I spent fifteen months in Hong Kong once when people thought I might be useful there."

"Were you useful there?"

Cord said, "Yes. Had a lot of time off. One of those stop-and-go situations while the diplomacy boys seesawed. Yes," he smiled. "At the end I proved to be very useful."

"Same employers then as now?"

"No," Cord said. "I have no particular credit with my current employers."

"You don't deserve much," Turnbull said.

The overhead lights whitened Cord's short gray hair, long gray face, gray eyes.

"How are things going?" Cord asked.

"Bloody awful!"

"How about giving me some facts, Gus?" Cord asked politely.

"Facts?" Turnbull put his face closer to Cord's and fixed him in the eye. "Fact one: they know we got the boy away from New York by using his own plane reservation. Fact two: they know he's here somewhere in the Bay area. Fact three: they know what motel he stayed at two nights ago. Fact four: they not only have a full and accurate description of this Mullins character, they know his full name and home address." Cord turned his head. "Fact five: they even have the registration number of the car Mullins is using."

Cord's eyes were directed at the tennis players, but they were not focused.

"You're right, Gus. This is bloody awful."

Turnbull hit Cord's shoulder with the heel of his hand.

"One bloody, silly, spoiled bitch has been able to trail you right up to your bloody ass!"

Cord looked at the ground. "The Ambassador's wife? Christina Rinaldi?"

"Rinaldi!" Turnbull shouted.

A tennis player shouted to them, "Quiet, please!" He said to his opponent, "Take two serves."

"Christina Rinaldi," Turnbull finally said.

"Hard to believe." Cord shook his head.

Turnbull took Christina's piece of paper out of his pocket and slammed it against Cord's stomach.

"Hard to believe, eh? This was in Christina's purse. Mullins's name, address, car registration number."

Cord tipped the paper toward the tennis lights to read the handwriting.

"And," Turnbull said, "they know Mullins and the kid are still floating around this area somewhere. Mullins didn't even have the sense to change cars. He's still driving the car he picked up from the airport when he arrived!"

"They said he was thick," Cord said. "Dubrowski's friends said there's nothing between his ears but dead roaches."

Turnbull put his finger against Cord's lapel. "Tell me, Cord, why can't we be perfectly certain right now that Tobias Rinaldi is dead and his body's just waiting for Sunday morning's sunlight to be discovered?"

Cord cleared his throat. "It would be the most natural thing to presume."

"You sound like a ruddy professor!"

"Listen, Turnbull, this is my job—"

"—And a ruddy good job you've made of it, too!"

"Gus, you're out of control. I've got to see this thing through, with or without you. Do you understand?"

Turnbull pushed his finger hard against Cord's chest. "If Mullins has wasted the kid because he doesn't know what else to do, and the kid's body is found tomorrow, you and I have had it. The world isn't big enough for you and me to hide in."

A tennis player was standing inside the fence, peering through the edge of light at them in the shadows. He said quietly, "Are you gentlemen guests here?"

"We own the place," Turnbull said.

"That's not true. Please leave." The tennis player went back to his baseline.

Cord said, "Gus, get control of yourself—or else. Try to keep your sanity—at least until Monday night."

Turnbull hit Cord hard on the side of his head. As Cord staggered off-balance, Turnbull aimed a kick at his groin but instead contacted with his kneecap.

Cord's hands began to rise.

Turnbull hit Cord with all his weight and power just below the short ribs. As Cord fell forward, Turnbull hit him in the face.

A woman screamed.

The tennis player ran back to the inside of the fence.

"Hey!" he yelled.

Cord's head was on the ground. Turnbull kicked it just above the ear.

All the witnesses were on the other side of the tennis fence.

Turnbull turned his back on them and walked out of the lit area. He found a path winding among some rhododendron bushes.

Thirty-Eight

"Ah, Colonel Turnbull."

Christina had spent a long time standing under the shower, letting the hot spray play on her neck and shoulders. Dressed in a robe, she had opened her bedroom door to see if Turnbull had returned. Just as she was closing the door, the front door to the bungalow opened and Turnbull stepped in.

"I was looking for you," Christina said. "Thought I'd turn in, see if I have any luck sleeping."

The expression on Turnbull's face Christina had never seen before. His ruddy skin seemed redder than usual. In his eyes, for the first time, seemed to be some recognition of her as a person—a body.

She gathered her robe more tightly around her.

"Before I try to sleep, I just wonder if…the car's registration…"

Turnbull closed the door behind him. He took a long, narrow black case out of his jacket's inside pocket. He went directly to the tall reading lamp on the divan's end table.

"…if you'd tell me what I should do next, what we should do next. I'd feel so much better if we had a plan, if I had a plan…if I knew what the plan is…what…"

Turnbull turned around. "You're not supposed to be doing anything, Christina. Just being quiet."

There was a hypodermic syringe in his right hand.

"Let me handle everything from this point."

He held the syringe up to the lamp and pushed the plunger. A colorless fluid jetted from the needle.

"What are you doing?" she asked.

"This won't take a moment." He walked toward her. "Please cooperate."

"No!"

Christina tried to get by him, tried to get to the front door. He grabbed her wrist and swung her around. She felt the back of her leg against the coffee table.

"No!"

Turnbull's left hand was grabbing for her arm.

She pulled it away from him, regained her footing. She put the flat of her hand against his chest and pushed.

Suddenly, Turnbull's left fist smashed against her right cheekbone.

There were darting silver slivers of light against a deep, black field. Her knees were on the floor. She saw the surface of the coffee table.

The flesh of her arm was being squeezed. She pulled in breath. Her cheek was on the coffee table.

She was tumbling, going among, through, the moving silver streaks into the blackness.

Thirty-Nine

In Room 39 at the Motel Rancho O'Grady, Spike dropped his newspaper from his bed onto the floor. For a while, he looked at the opposite wall.

Then he said, "Once there was this gang after me—a gang of real badasses—Holy Devils, they called 'emselves. This was in Passaic, see? Fac' is, I had killed one of their gang members, with a knife. Clean, fair, honest fight, all that. This guy had tromped on my foot at a disco place, see? So I invited him outside, to kill him.

"First, he didn't wanna go, see, 'cause he didn't have no gang with him. But I poked fun at him, and all, and the girls laughed at him.

"So I laughed him into comin' out to get killed.

"He came out with me, back o' this place, and he pulled a knife. I had a knife, too. I only had to sashay around with him a little before I stuck my knife in his eye, see? Deep...."

Spike looked at Toby.

On the other bed, Toby lay on top of his blanket, head on the pillow. Facedown on his chest was the Uncle Whimsy Comic Book.

Toby was asleep. On his face was a happy smile.

It was ten fifteen. Spike chuckled and turned out the light.

Forty

Christina could not understand what she was doing on the floor. Looking up, she was seeing partly the underside of the coffee table, partly the ceiling.

The telephone was ringing.

Her neck was twisted so that one ear was almost pressing against her shoulder. A part of her face hurt. Her cheekbone. She explored it with her fingers. Her skin stung to the touch.

Sitting up, she discovered her neck was stiff. There was daylight in the room. The reading lamp was still on. She reached up for the telephone. She wanted to stop its ringing.

"Hello?"

"Hello, Mrs. Rinaldi? Christina, it's me. Mary Brown."

"Hello, Mrs. Brown…Mary."

"You all right, Christina?"

"I don't know. I guess so."

"You don't sound it."

"Guess I just woke up."

"I know I'm not supposed to be using the Residence's phone long-distance without permission," Mrs. Brown said, "especially for any personal craziness of my own—"

"That's okay."

"I waited until nine thirty. I couldn't figure if it's six thirty in the morning where you are or twelve thirty noon, so I thought I'd be safe if I called at nine thirty. I guess it's six thirty where you are."

It seemed the most natural thing in the world to be chatting with her housekeeper, listening to Mrs. Brown's voice in the morning, dressed in her robe. But why was she sitting on the floor?

"It doesn't cost so much callin' on Sundays, anyway, does it?"

"No. That's all right. I'm glad you called. I suppose I should have called you."

"Well, that's why I'm calling. You're going to think I'm crazy, but I had a dream. And I've been thinking about it. I haven't been sleeping—at all. So last night I took one of those pills Mr. Ambassador keeps in his medicine chest, secondaries or something, you know, sleeping pills?"

"Seconal?"

"Yes. Well, maybe it made me dream. Anyway, it made me sleep. Electronic age. Here's an old woman telling you about her dream over three thousand miles of telephone wire."

"What was it?"

"I dreamt Toby's at Fantazyland."

The fingers of Christina's free hand kneaded the back of her neck.

"Mrs. Rinaldi, you know I'm not someone to believe in dreams. Although, I will say, the Old Testament's full of 'em and I understand some head doctors make a business of 'em. But this dream was too real. I saw Toby. You know Uncle Whimsy's Hat? Fantazyland has made some kind of mountain out of it, and there are rides through it or something. I saw Toby staring up at it. Big bears and rabbits all around him. He was wearing white shorts and a blue shirt. His hand was up, I mean, his arm was, you know? As if his hand was in the hand of someone else—an adult. And then there was this rush of air, and darkness, in my dream, and I felt Toby going through some kind of a tunnel. He was laughing. Crazy, isn't it? But it was so real."

"Mrs. Brown, I'm sure it was real. It was what you wanted to dream. It's what you want to think."

"I thought so, too. I'm not as crazy as all that. Have I ever told you a dream before? I've never had one so real. Then I began thinking. Since three fifteen this morning, when I woke up, after the dream. I've been thinking and remembering certain things."

"Mrs. Brown—"

"Half a moment, Christina. That boy's been determined to get to Fantazyland for longer than you know. More than two years ago, I first heard of it. On the plane, that time we were flyin' to Mexico to talk to them about oil or whatever. I went forward in the cabin to get Toby away to bed and His Majesty had just finished readin' him a chapter of *Winnie-the-Pooh*, and Toby was askin' him, the King, 'Will we go to Fantazyland, sir?' and His Majesty looked at the Ambassador, and the Ambassador said, 'Not this trip, Toby. We'll be too far south. Maybe someday we'll get there, if they have us,' and it was I, Mrs. Rinaldi, who took Toby back to the little bunk and strapped him in, and he said he was goin' to Fantazyland. First I'd heard of it. And he's been talkin' about it ever since, to you, to me, to the Ambassador...."

"Yes but—"

"And, by God, Christina, I believe he's there. I know Toby. He's a determined little chap. Knows what he's doing every minute. He looks like he's puttin' up with things, he does, but he's a genius at settin' himself a goal and gettin' there. You don't even see him doin' it. Like his father, he knows how to handle people, and like you, Christina, he knows how to mark time and appear to be patient and then assert himself at just the right moment, in just the right way. Forgive me for complimenting you both. But I know you a great deal better than maybe you think I do, after nine years bein' with you. Great believer in blood, I am, especially where your son, Toby, is concerned. Put Toby on the West Coast of this country, within a few miles of Fantazyland, and, by God, Christina, even bound hand and foot, he'll see himself there."

Christina said nothing: she was envisioning Toby at Fantazyland. Toby had shown her the pictures, too.

Where had the idea of this trip to the West Coast really come from? Christina had thought it was her idea—a family vacation, an attempt to give Teddy a break.

But the timing of it was so bad. Resolution 1176R. Who laid down the timing of this trip?

"Oh, Mrs. Brown...."

"Think I'm crazy if you want. I'll probably think I'm crazy myself after the sun gets a little higher in the sky. Burns away the nighttime fantasies. But I had to tell you about it."

"I'm glad you did."

"A thing like this drives everybody crazy," Mrs. Brown said.

"Makes us all do and think crazy things. I'll never take one of those secondaries again. Never had such a real dream."

"I understand. Anything any one of us thinks—"

"Now, what about the carpets?"

"What carpets?"

"I was supposed to get the carpets cleaned while you were gone. No cleaner will take 'em without a billion dollars of insurance."

"Forget about the carpets, Mrs. Brown."

"They do need cleaning. And we've got them up in a big pile in the foyer. Mr. Ambassador's forever trippin' over 'em—"

"Forget about the carpets. I don't give two hoots about the damned carpets. Let 'em rot."

"All right."

"Mrs. Brown...Mary. If you think anything else, have any other ideas, call me right away and let me know."

"I tell you what I think, Christina," Mrs. Brown said. "Toby's at Fantazyland."

Forty-One

Over the intercom Sylvia Menninges's voice said, "Mr. Ambassador? Assistant Secretary of State Skinner is here to see you. Says he's just dropped by to say hello."

Ambassador Teodoro Rinaldi's finger hesitated on the intercom button. He glanced at his watch and the typed schedule on his desk. It was twelve thirty-nine, Sunday noon hour. He was due at lunch with the Security Council at one o'clock. It was key he be there, and be there on time. Yesterday, and so far today, he had been keeping his schedule well, continuing, hour by hour, meeting by meeting, word by word, to develop delegate support for Resolution 1176R. He had even managed to meet or talk with most of the people he had missed Friday. He sincerely hoped he had carried it all off well, looking tired, he knew, under pressure, of course. He believed no one had discerned from his performance how distraught, sick at heart, he was.

Now, Pat Skinner, who probably knew the Ambassador's schedule better than the Ambassador himself did, suddenly was dropping in, from Washington, to "say hello"; in fact, to look into the eyes of someone he knew twenty-five years and assess for the diplomatic community Teddy's true condition. Would the Ambassador's appeal to the United Nations the following night be strong, stirring, convincing, successful? Or would it be delivered as one more diplomatic essay, an exaggerated position paper meant to cause nothing more real than slight and slighting reference in subsequent cocktail chatter? The Ambassador knew he could not conceal his true condition from Pat Skinner.

Before he responded, Sylvia Menninges said, "Mr. Ambassador? Your tailor on 270."

"Your tailor": code for His Majesty. On scrambler.

Pat Skinner must be standing right next to her desk, listening.

Teddy said, "Ask Mr. Skinner to wait a moment, please. And make sure the car is out front, will you, please?"

"It's waiting now, sir."

He pushed button 270—the green button. "Sir?"

A long pause, then the funny voice of Donald Duck, the boss's voice over the scrambler phone.

"Teddy? I'm not hearing any good news."

"Neither am I. Sir."

"How do you feel?"

"All right."

"Do you feel you can carry on?"

"Yes."

"The terrible thing about this, Teddy, is that I don't see any options. I don't see we have any choice but for you to carry on. In kidnapping your son, they've hit you personally. But if you personally don't get up there in front of the United Nations tomorrow night and submit Resolution 1176R, it has no chance of passing. Diplomacy is a personal business. There's no one I can substitute for you."

"I know that."

"I can't see any plan other than the plan we decided upon first: that we keep this matter as quiet as possible, and, that you proceed as normally as possible."

"Yes, sir."

"I mean, to the end, Teddy. To the end."

"Yes."

"I have a terrible thing to say."

Teddy waited.

"Teddy, if this Resolution doesn't pass, tanks are going to roll. They are going to roll across the sands of this nation, down the streets of our villages, into the cities. It will mean war, Teddy, within the year. The major powers will fight each other on this poor speck of sand. They will destroy this nation over our ability to ship oil through the Persian Gulf. There is no doubt about it. You know this to be true. Don't you, Teddy?"

"Yes. Yes, I do."

"You might be wise to consider that we are at war now. Teddy, your son may be a casualty of that war."

Teddy looked across his office at a complicated tapestry on the far wall.

Teddy said, "He's only eight years old, sir."

"Given a war, Teddy, there will be many eight-year-old casualties."

"I understand."

"I'm asking you to understand and accept something no one can reasonably ask a father of a child to understand and accept. You have to think of your son, no matter how little he is, as a soldier. Right now, they've got him. We cannot permit the utter destruction of this nation and most likely several other nations—if not the world—because of the loss of one soldier."

"I hear you. Sir."

"I think this is the most terrible thing I've ever had to say. No matter what happens, I trust, in time, you'll forgive me. Understand…."

The Donald Duck voice faded off. There was a snap on the line, then a high-pitched whirring noise.

Teddy hung up.

In a moment, the door to his office opened and Pat Skinner stepped around it, his eyes immediately on Teddy's face.

The Ambassador had not signaled Sylvia to permit him to enter. She had seen the yellow light on line 270 go out and knew he was on a tight schedule.

Pat said, "Am I disturbing?"

At first, Pat's look was normally curious. As he came across the office, looking at Teddy, the expression on his face became one of shock and then alarm.

"Ted, are you all right?"

"Haven't been getting all the sleep I should. Burning the candle at both ends."

"That's true, but—" Pat Skinner sat down.

"Figure I'll start a vacation sometime this week. Maybe as early as Tuesday. See how things go Monday night. Maybe I'll even join Christina and Toby out at Fantazyland."

"They're at Fantazyland?"

"Sure. Why not? Toby had a school break. He's been pressing for a trip to Fantazyland for as long as anybody can remember. You know Toby. This seems as good a time as any."

Skinner was now looking as if Teddy had taken leave of his senses.

"Once Toby sets his mind to something…" Teddy said.

"I hear you dropped a few stitches Friday."

"'Dropped a few stitches'?"

"Yeah. Got around the community. Canceled appointments. Not available."

"Oh, that. Had a terrible sore throat. Couldn't speak above a whisper."

"I spoke to you on the phone Friday."

"Right. Then you know what I mean."

"You didn't sound—uh—right."

"Ready to sing Wagner now."

"How do you think things are going? I mean, for the passage of the Resolution? Got your ducks all lined up?"

"It will go down like Kentucky bourbon, Pat. I have no doubt of it. The Resolution is vital not only to our national interests, but essential to the best interests of nearly every nation in the world."

"The Islamic groundswell—"

"—is entirely understandable." Teddy stood up. "I can't be late for lunch, Pat. Not only is it diplomatically essential, but, also, I'm hungry. Can I give you a lift?"

"No. Uh, no. Thanks."

"Let's get together, Pat. I mean, let's get the families together. A weekend somewhere. Chew things over. Maybe after my vacation…."

Forty-Two

...7NP 4484...7NP 4484...7NP 4484...7NP 4484...7NP 4484...7NP 4484...7NP 4484...7NP 4484...7NP 4484...7NP 4484...7NP 4484...
...7NP 4484
7NP 4484!

Dazed as she was, having read thousands of license plates in Fantazyland's enormous parking lot, driving slowly up and down every row, watching out for children and parents cutting across the lot in front of her every minute (they looking to neither the right nor the left, having been guaranteed every safety while enjoying their stay at Fantazyland), having to argue with at least one parking-lot attendant at the end of every row who did not like her driving up and down the rows, insisted she park, ignored her statement that this was an emergency and she was looking for a car and could never walk all those miles, up and down, up and down, driving off on them, driving around them, evading them, ignoring their shouts, mile after mile.

Finally, when she saw it, she stopped. She blinked. Registration number 7NP 4484. A blue two-door car. She read the number again and again. She thought she so much wanted to see it she had created the illusion of seeing it.

No. Right beside her, parked near the front of the Fantazyland parking lot, was a blue car, registration number 7NP 4484.

"Oh, my God. Toby is here!"

Up the row, twenty cars away, was an empty slot. Christina sped her car into it, locked it and ran back to the blue two-door.

The registration plate still read 7NP 4484.

She peered through the windows to see some evidence of Toby. On the front seat there was an Uncle Whimsy Comic Book. Probably ninety-nine percent of the cars in Fantazyland's parking lot had Uncle Whimsy Comic Books in them. There were some gum wrappers on the floor. Nothing else. The car was as neutral as any other rented car.

She looked around the lot. The men Turnbull had had following her were nowhere in sight. She hadn't seen them all morning. After days of uselessly spooking her, they were not around when she could use them.

Neither were there any parking-lot attendants in sight.

In her purse she found a fingernail file. With this, she let the air out of three of the car's tires. Working the release of each tire valve seemed to take forever. She wanted the tires absolutely flat.

It took her as long to work the hood latch. Finally getting it into a position where it had some give to it, she yanked it up, breaking something.

She studied the motor a long moment. She could see nothing obviously devastating to do. There were some black hoses, and she tugged those free. She tugged free every hose and wire she could find, ripping out altogether those that would come.

Finally, she took off her shoe and beat the engine with her heel.

When she was trying to close the hood, she noticed a parking-lot attendant had driven up in an electric cart. He had stopped and was looking at the flat tires, the wires on the ground.

"Need help, lady?"

"Somebody vandalized my car!" she said.

"Gosh...."

He stepped off his cart to examine the damage.

Christina said, "I've got to call my husband," and began running across the lot.

"Hey, wait! Lady! I'll give you a lift."

Running across one row, she was nearly hit by a station wagon full of Girl Scouts.

"Stoooo-pid!" yelled all the girls.

UNCLE WHIMSY WELCOMES YOU—ONE AND ALL—TO FANTAZYLAND.

Right at the main gate, to the left of the box offices, was a row of public telephones.

Christina slowed to a walk. She knew the park was enormous. Uncle Whimsy's mountainous Hat was in the middle, and it looked a long way away.

I found the car, I found the car....

Forty-Three

When Pat Skinner entered the Waldorf Astoria suite of the United States Ambassador to the United Nations, the Secretary of State was sitting on the divan, shoes off, wriggling his toes. For socks, the Secretary was known to wear only lisle, which, of course, gave rise to jokes about "our Secretary with cold feet." (At the Pentagon, the Secretary of Defense had become referred to, therefore, as "ol' Iron Socks.")

The Secretary of State was due downstairs in a few minutes to give an after-luncheon speech to The National Association of Christians and Jews. The Secretary had arranged to miss lunch. Experience had taught him he was better off sitting alone somewhere, resting, sipping a vodka martini, shoes off, wriggling his toes, than keeping up luncheon and dinner conversations.

"Hallo, Pat!" said the Secretary of State.

Skinner said, "Glad I caught you."

The Secretary jiggled his martini glass and laughed. "Caught me at what?"

At the sideboard Skinner mixed himself a very weak scotch and soda.

"How's your friend Rinaldi? That thing going to work?"

Skinner said, "No. Doubt it. He's a mess."

"How do you mean?"

Skinner sat down. "He looks in such bad shape I don't see how he can make it through the day, let alone tomorrow and tomorrow night."

"Physically?"

"Looks like he should be hospitalized. Mentally, he may have cracked. He had no very reasonable excuse for being incommunicado Friday. Pleaded sore throat, but he had forgotten I had spoken to him on the phone myself. Would you believe his wife and kid are at Fantazyland? You'd think His Majesty would have better use for his illegal secret intelligence in this country these days—I mean, in lining up ducks—than having them escort the Ambassador's wife and child around an amusement park. Teddy is sitting there in his office, being late for lunch with the Security Council while chatting on the phone with his tailor. He's almost incoherent. All he talked to me about was his vacation and that he's ready to sing Wagner."

"Wagner?"

"Wagner."

The Secretary of State said, "Nobody's ever ready to sing Wagner." He stared into the dark fireplace. "Some guys just can't take the pressure. I'll inform the President. I'm stopping to pick him up at Camp David at five o'clock. Want a ride in the chopper?"

"I think I'd better stay here. What will the President say?"

The Secretary shrugged. " 'Pull.' He'll say, 'Pull.' " He drained his glass. "The old boy's in no mood to back another dead horse. This administration has already bought so many we can supply a glue factory for a decade."

The Secretary put his glass down and leaned over to tie on his shoes. "Surprising. Thought Teddy had more stuff in him. We all react to pressure in this business, Skinner. Trick is to let no one see it." Red-faced, the Secretary sat up. "Not even," he said, "your alleged best friend."

Forty-Four

"Sylvia? Quick! This is Christina Rinaldi. Get me the Ambassador!"

Phone to one ear, fingers pressed against the other, Christina ran her eyes along the lines of people waiting for tickets at Fantazyland's box offices.

"I'm sorry, Mrs. Rinaldi. The Ambassador is at a special luncheon meeting with the United Nations Security Council."

"Can you transfer me somehow?"

"No. I'm sorry, I can't."

"It's terribly important."

"Mrs. Rinaldi, even the President of the United States isn't allowed to interrupt a special meeting of the Security Council."

"Oh, dear."

"Christina, can't I take a message?"

"Yes. Get to Teddy as soon as you can."

"I will."

"Tell him I found the car. He'll know what I mean. In the parking lot at Fantazyland."

"You found the car."

"The car we were looking for. Willins'–Doland's–Jackson's–Mullins's car."

"Wait, I didn't get all those names."

"Never mind. He'll know which car I mean. Tell him I'm at Fantazyland now, and I need help. I need a lot of help. Tell him to tell Major Mustafa I need people here now."

"You need people at Fantazyland."

"And, Sylvia. Tell him not to trust Colonel Turnbull."

"Not to trust Colonel who?"

"Turnbull. You don't know him. Last night he stuck a needle in my arm. Gave me some kind of drug—a sedative. Do you have that?"

"Yes. I think so."

"Get to Teddy as fast as you can, tell him these two things and ask him to get people here as fast as he can."

"To Fantazyland?"

"Yes. To Fantazyland."

Forty-Five

"Look at them flowers!" Spike said. He and Toby were in the garden of Princess Daphne's Flower Palace. "I never knew there was so many different kinds'a roses."

"What roses?" Toby said.

"Those roses."

"Those are tulips," Toby said.

"Yeah, tha's right, kid. They're tulip roses."

"No," Toby said. "Those are daffodils."

"Did I ast you? Punk kid. Whaddayou know? I said those are daffadil-kind of tulip roses."

Toby pointed. "Those are roses over there. On the trellis."

"Talkin' fancy again, uh? Thought I knocked that outa you."

"What's fancy in what I said?"

"These flowers out here are nicer than them inside Princess Daphne's pad," Spike said. "These are real, you see, real flowers growing in the earth."

Toby said, "I think they're fresh planted."

"Don't be wise, punk. The ones inside were phonies. Dincha know that? They was glass and plastic and stuff like that."

A barefoot girl dressed entirely in flowers drifted by them. Flowers were twisted neatly in her hair. She carried a yellow sunflower.

Watching her, Spike said, "I'd like to pluck her."

"Shh," Toby said. "That's Princess Daphne."

The girl looked at Spike. Her face reddened. Either she was blushing or angry.

"Aw," Spike said, "she's nothin' more than a Uncle Whimsy groupie gettin' the minimum wage."

"Come on over here, Spike," Toby said. "There are some more roses."

"Yeah!" Spike said "I never seen a garden like this!"

❊

Spike wanted to drive a bumper car again, so he did. He smashed into everyone he could with maximum force, calling everybody in sight "Bastid!" shaking his fist in all directions at once, not seeing any cars that came at him from his left.

Toby watched through the fence. He had had his last bumper car ride with Spike.

Toby did get him to go with him through The Hall of Knives.

In the first room they came to, there was a polite, museumlike display of every sort of knife, sword, dagger ever invented by man. In the next room, some people in baggy trousers performed a sword dance. In the third room, furnished as a banquet hall, two cavaliers fought a duel down stone steps, across the room, up onto and along the dining table, scattering roast pigs and fowls and wine glasses.

Then they were walked through a dark, scary, menacing place. Knives flew through the air. A guillotine clanged down just as they passed it. A great, gleaming, sharpened pendulum swung over their heads, dropping lower and lower. A huge barrel, spinning seemingly out of control, rolling on armatures, approached them from the dark. Swords stuck out all sides of it, at all angles.

The tourists smiled and laughed and applauded and took pictures.

Spike backed into the far railing. His face was ashen.

Then they went back to Wild West City to try the shooting gallery again.

Forty-Six

Sylvia Menninges followed the Ambassador into his office.

"The luncheon ran late," he said.

He sat at his desk.

Sylvia said, "Mrs. Rinaldi called."

"Oh?"

"She left a message. She was talking so fast I had trouble getting it all down." Sylvia looked at her steno pad. "First she said she found the car and that you would know what that means."

"She did? She found the car?"

Sylvia nodded. "In the parking lot at Fantazyland."

Teddy sat back. "Well, I'll be damned."

Sylvia read from her pad. "Please ask Major Mustafa to send people, a lot of people, to assist her right away."

"Major Mustafa?" Teddy wrinkled his brow. "Why Major Mustafa?"

"I don't know. She also said you were not to trust a Colonel Turnbull."

"She said that?" Teddy looked extremely curious. "Why did she say that?"

"She said…Colonel Turnbull, I guess she meant…gave her a sedative last night."

"I see." Teddy's face returned to normal. "I see. I'm sure Christina needed a sedative. I'm also sure she resented the hell out of being slipped one. Okay." He sat up and looked at the papers Sylvia had put on his desk since he had left. "Get on to Colonel Turnbull immediately. Tell him Christina has found the car we've been looking for in the parking lot of Fantazyland and he and his men are to join her there immediately."

"Shall I say anything to Major Mustafa?"

"No," Teddy said. "Leave everything in the hands of Colonel Turnbull."

Forty-Seven

Cord had followed Christina from the bungalow.

He had parked where he was directed to park in Fantazyland's huge lot and then stood by his car, looking over the rooftops of other cars sparkling in the sunlight. He watched her drive up and down the rows of parked cars, evading the attendants who yelled and waved at her. He figured she was looking for Mullins' car, but he had no idea what led her to look for the car in Fantazyland's parking lot.

He saw her stop near the front of the lot, in front of a blue two-door car. She parked nearby. Watching her, he began walking at an angle among the cars to where she was. She ran from her car back to the blue two-door.

From a distance, he watched her flatten the car's tires, break open the hood and rip things out of the engine.

When the attendant in the electric cart came along, she ran toward the main entrance to Fantazyland.

By the time Cord got there, she was using one of the telephones.

He waited in one of the box-office lines. After telephoning, she got into his line, about a dozen people behind him. Simon Cord preceded Christina Rinaldi into Fantazyland.

When she came through the main gate, he was standing, hands behind his back, listening to the music from the bandstand.

Cord ambled into the shade of a giant pink mushroom and stopped. A child went by, accidentally brushing his cotton candy against the sleeve of Cord's gray suit. He brushed it off and looked at his watch. It was five minutes past five.

Christina Rinaldi, dressed in a light, beige suit, was standing near the cotton candy stand. Her eyes were roaming high and low in each direction, methodically. She was alone.

Slowly, she began to move in the sunlight in the direction pointed by a sign saying, TO THE PAST.

At a good distance to the side and a little behind her, keeping in the shade as much as possible, at her pace, Cord followed her.

She was passing a carousel, slowly, looking at the children revolving on it, the air filled with the loud, clanging carousel music, *London Bridge is falling down....* After watching it go around once, she looked off to her left.

Suddenly, Christina's body braced as if jolted by an electric shock. She was screaming. She was yelling something.

She began to run.

Cord glanced down the slope to see what she was seeing, but saw only a crowd of tourists going through the fortlike gates of Wild West City.

A man ran past her. In his left hand was a gun. He reached the crowd at the gate wall before her and began to weave through them, pushing and shoving, waving his gun.

The people smiled and stepped aside for him.

Another man ran up behind Christina, a man wearing an Uncle Whimsy T-shirt under his jacket. As he passed her, he pushed Christina's shoulder, making her land too hard on her right shoe heel, snapping it. As she fell to the walkway's hard surface, he spilled his bag of peppermints. By the time he got to the crowded Wild West City gate, he, too, had a gun in his hand.

The people smiled and let him through.

Smiling, they even let long-legged Cord stride through.

In the middle of the main street of Wild West City, a cowboy, wearing a black hat, black shirt, black patch over one eye, was cracking a bullwhip and snarling.

Among the whipcracks was a gunshot. The cowboy's head jerked toward the gate. He saw two men running toward him with drawn guns. The cowboy dropped his whip, vaulted a water trough and dropped to the ground, facedown, hands over his hat.

Down the street, Cord saw a man and a boy. They looked around.

Toby Rinaldi and...Mullins.

There was another pistol shot.

Three constables came out of the crowd at the entrance gate and began running down the street.

The marshal came out of his office. He looked for the whip-cracking villain. There was another gunshot and the marshal ducked back into the office.

Mullins and Toby ran to their right, up onto a raised-board side-walk.

The two men fired at them nearly simultaneously.

At the end of the block, Mullins tripped off the sidewalk. He stumbled in the street. The child ran back for him, grabbed his arm and pulled him along.

None of the tourists screamed or backed away.

The tourists smiled and laughed and applauded and took pictures.

Mullins and the boy were halfway up the next block. The man in the Uncle Whimsy T-shirt fired again into the crowd.

Cord could see neither the boy nor Mullins.

The crowd did not disperse. They laughed at the two men, standing in the middle of the street, their faces agape.

The three constables, mustaches bobbing, billy clubs in hand, were running up the street toward them. The helmet of one fell off. Long, blond hair streamed behind her.

The men stuffed their guns into their pockets and took off at an angle to each other. One ran through the swinging doors of a saloon. The other went up the street before darting through the open door of The Glassware and China Shoppe. The constables ran after them.

The tourists gave a hearty round of applause.

Down the street, Christina was standing by the gate, her shoes in her hand. Even from a block away, Cord could see her eyes moving wildly.

She had a black eye.

Moving at an angle, Cord walked half a block to where he had last seen Mullins and the boy.

It was not obvious from a distance, but there was a narrow space between two frame buildings, covered by a board fence. Cord pushed up against it with his fingers. It swung open. He stepped through it.

There was a narrow alley running between the two buildings. At the far end of the alley were covered garbage buckets.

Cord walked to them and turned the corner of the building. Near the back wall were scuff marks in the dirt. He crouched.

In the dirt was half-dried blood.

Cord stood up and looked around. It was becoming dusk. The light in the alley was diminishing rapidly. He went back and forth, up and down, but could find no more blood. He could not discover which way Mullins and the boy had gone.

He went back down the alley and through the fence. There was almost no one in the main street.

But in the middle of it, shoes in hand, the shoulder of her suit jacket torn, staring at him as he came through the gate, was Christina Rinaldi.

UNCLE WHIMSY IS GLAD YOU HAVE ENJOYED YOUR DAY AT FANTAZYLAND BUT NOW MUST BID YOU GOOD NIGHT SO ALL UNCLE WHIMSY'S FRIENDS CAN GET THEIR REST AND COME OUT TO PLAY TOMORROW.

A woman's voice sang over the loudspeakers: *Good night until tomorrow…Sweet dreams you shall have…*

Cord turned left and walked along with his head down until Christina was no longer watching him.

Forty-Eight

Had there been, or had there not been, a shooting incident at Fantazyland that afternoon?

The question was bursting Drew Keosian's gut.

He stood at the podium, waiting for the last few constables to straggle in after patrolling the grounds one last time before complete dark. They were to make sure all the guests of Fantazyland had returned to their homes, hotels, motels, campers to dream their sweet dreams so they could come out to play tomorrow.

Infrequently, but occasionally, they would discover someone still on the grounds, incredibly drunk (only beer was provided at Fantazyland) or stoned, after closing. Once they found an old senile woman wandering; another time, a veteran lying in a path, immobilized because the metal pin in his hip had suddenly disintegrated. Another time the body of a thirteen-year-old girl had been found, abandoned by her terrified friends when she had died of a coronary infarction in the Doll Museum.

More frequently, they had to search for the missing child while keeping frantic parents calm in Drew's office. Almost invariably, the child was found asleep somewhere, under a bush or near the waterfall. (They had learned from experience to look first for sleeping children near the waterfall.)

There were always the two or three cars left in the parking lot without explanation. Had friends met or been made and gone off in one car? Had engine trouble or personal illness gone unreported but just caused the car to be left there overnight? The next day they would be gone. There were seldom the same cars there for more than one night. About six stolen cars a year were found abandoned in Fantazyland's parking lot.

Through the window Drew could see the headlights of the electric patrol tricycles still pulling up.

At thirty-seven, Drew Keosian was a professional lawman of a rare type. A graduate of Oral Roberts University, he had had his early police training with the Chattanooga, Tennessee, police force. He hated having to deal with the poor, the disenfranchised, the ill, the violent.

Drew believed absolutely in the thick line between the lawful and the lawless, right and wrong, good and evil. He loved his job at Fantazyland. He considered it a great moral experiment, an imitation of God's creating Eden. Fantazyland was a beautiful garden filled with innocence, where people could be children forever. It was his job to make this moral experiment work.

As chief constable he had few, if any, of the problems of chiefs of police forces of similar size. In his eight years at Fantazyland there had been only one serious crime, and that was the rape of an employee, an older lady who worked at a hot dog stand. There was the occasional purse mislaid. Every few months a gang of pickpockets would work Fantazyland for a day, but the constables were trained to spot them quickly and deal with them summarily. There was some petty shoplifting.

Fantazyland was private property. Constables could and would deny obviously drunk, stoned, or seemingly disturbed people entrance. Everyone coming into Fantazyland was scrutinized by at least one constable.

It was Drew's job to keep the snake from Eden, to keep genuine evil from Fantazyland, and he took it as his holy mission to do so.

An hour or two earlier, Constable Hidgson had phoned in breathlessly saying there were two men firing guns in the middle of Wild West City. Tourists. Real guns.

Drew had hurried to Wild West City (he had not run; the tourists might be alarmed) and found nothing in particular going on.

The cowboy villain told him people were shooting at him, and he didn't like it. The cowboy marshal said he wasn't sure. He said he had come out onto the boardwalk, not seen the cowboy villain, saw the whip on the ground, yet heard what he thought were whip-cracks. He wasn't absolutely sure what else he had seen.

Constable Gladstein told him there had been no shooting as far as he knew, but he might have been on his break at that moment.

Before him now in the police station briefing room, all the constables were seated in their chairs, all with their helmets off, some with their mustaches off, the black handlebar mustaches of the rest clashing weirdly with their blond, brown, red or even natural black hair.

From the podium, Drew asked, "Any bodies tonight? Anyone missing, drunk, lost?"

There was no response.

He said, "Box office tells us supposedly there's an eight-count difference between ins and outs. Eight people who entered Fantazyland today but didn't leave it." He looked at the roomful of tired constables. "Anybody seen any strays? No?"

The chief parking-lot attendant (the only person in the room dressed in khaki; the night watchmen wore undecorated blue suits) said, "Drew? There are seven automobiles left in the parking lot tonight."

"Seven? That's unusually high."

"One looks like it's been vandalized. Three flat tires. Motor wires and hoses on the ground."

"No one complained?"

"Yes and no. Jack Dibbs said the lady who owned or rented the car spoke to him and ran off saying she was going to call her husband. He must have come and picked her up."

"I see. Anything else unusual?" Drew Keosian felt his stomach muscles tighten. "Hidgson, what about this shooting incident you reported?"

"Three of us saw it," he said.

Katy chimed in right away. "Two men with handguns ran into Wild West City and fired several shots. Couldn't tell what they were firing at."

Katy, at twenty-three, was the most definite member of the force. Her reports were always the most clear, succinct and certain. Two months before, she had identified and turned in Alf Worsham, known pickpocket. His own pockets were clean, but the state of California was grateful to collect Worsham, anyway, as there were several bad check charges outstanding against him.

"Was it some kind of a gag?" Drew asked.

Katy said, "I don't think so."

"Who was the third constable?"

"I was," Mac Innes said.

"Do you think it was a gag?"

"Guess so. Musta been blanks. Couldn't been shootin' like that, really shootin', without hittin' somebody."

"Did you apprehend these characters?"

"Got away," Hidgson said. "We waited in turns at the main gate, but couldn't recognize them as they went out—if they went out the main gate."

"Description?"

"Two men," Katy said. "One wore an Uncle Whimsy T-shirt."

"No one has complained," Drew said carefully. "That right?"

The constables looked at each other and at him.

Drew exhaled slowly. "Must have been a gag. Remember that time that gang from some fraternity got naked out at the ice cream parlor and sang, *Beat me, daddy, eight to the bar*...? You weren't here then, Katy."

"We caught them," Mac Innes said.

"We could pick them out of the crowd," Hidgson said.

Drew said, "Okay, everybody. See you tomorrow."

Drew went into his office. His hands were shaking. *Katy did not think it was a gag.*

If there had been a shooting incident at Fantazyland this afternoon—even as a gag—the public must never, never know about it.

Forty-Nine

"Shit, Toby. They took down ol' Spike."

"Shh."

"They got me. They shot me. They put a bullet in me."

Spike was lying on the floor of Ms. Lillyperson's Cottage, clutching the calf of his leg. His hand was covered with blood.

Toby was sitting cross-legged near him. He was peering through the cottage's second-story dormer window.

Outside, Ms. Lillyperson's residence looked a graystone cottage on a rise above the walkway up to Princess Daphne's Flower Palace. Inside, it looked like a packing crate.

"Not in you," Toby said. "They put a bullet through you. Through your leg."

Toby already had rolled up Spike's pant leg and examined the wound. He thought it something, seeing Spike's zebra sock all bloody.

"Never thought nobody would get ol' Spike down. Who'd want to shoot me?"

"Somebody…" Toby said.

"Yeah, kid. Somebody shot me. Who?"

"Fac' is…" Toby said, "I dunno."

"Shootin' ol' Spike. I didn't think it was real. Never saw those guys before in my life."

"Shh," Toby said. "Be quiet."

Through the window, Toby watched an electric patrol tricycle go up the path. Its headlight was on. The man driving it was not wearing a constable's uniform, just blue pants and a shirt. It went over the hill.

"When it's really dark, I'll bring you over to that log cabin," Toby said. "The burning log cabin. On the island. Nobody will find us there. Come on. Let me make a tourniquet for your leg."

"Yeah? A tourniquet? You know about things like that?"

"Sure," Toby said. "I got to find the stuff first. A stick and a hunk of rope, or cloth."

"Yeah?"

"I'll be right back."

"Sure," Spike said. "Sure. Only, just don't get lost, kid."

Fifty

Once inside Wild West City, Christina had not understood what was happening. Through the milling crowd on the main street she had seen three constables chasing the two men with guns. About a block and a half up a street, she saw the two men stop, face the buildings to the right, then turn and run in different directions.

Carrying her shoes, the shoulder of her suit torn, Christina then wandered up and down the main street of Wild West City, as she had spent a day wandering in the airport, looking for she knew not what—some sign of Toby, some clue. She was only dimly aware of the fading light, dimly aware of the thinning crowd looking at her: a disheveled, distraught woman, prowling aimlessly, staring intently.

The street was nearly empty. She heard the announcement Fantazyland was closing for the night

A man came through the board fence in the middle of the block. His pale eyes looked at her expressionlessly. He turned to his left, walked up the boardwalk and around the corner.

Leaving Wild West City, Christina went to her right. Small safety lights, inset in the path, came on. She went off the path to her left, down to a small gulley where there were bushes, and took off her torn pantyhose. She rolled them in a ball and, putting her broken pair of shoes with them, stuffed them under a bush. The ground felt cool and soothing on the stinging soles of her bare feet. She remembered the pleasant sensation from being a kid on her Uncle Toby's farm, summertimes in Pennsylvania.

A constable on an electric patrol tricycle trundled by her. Watching him from the bushes, Christina restrained herself from calling out, explaining everything, asking for help. Fantazyland was enormous. It was becoming dark. Toby was here somewhere. And his kidnapper now knew he was being pursued. Making its little noise, the cart disappeared around a curve to the right.

Stumbling on bruised feet, her ankles becoming increasingly scratched, Christina spent hours wandering around Fantazyland in the dark.

Softly: "Toby…?"

"…Toby?"

"Toby…"

Occasionally, at a distance, she would see the headlight of an electric patrol vehicle jiggling along a path.

More than once, in the dark, she would realize she had returned to an area she thought she had left far behind her. The paths went in deceptive circles. A small moon rose. She stayed away from the turn-of-the-century square just inside the main gate. She knew some administration offices were there, including the police station. The hard, white, metallic, glossy surfaces of The City of The Future aggravated her: there seemed to be no nooks or crannies, no places to peer into, no places for people to hide. The area around Uncle Whimsy's mountainous Hat was completely fenced off and locked. She wandered again through Wild West City, trying every door, through every building that was unlocked, found the alleys, prowled them.

"Toby…?"

And Pirate's Cove, and the Pirate's Caravelle, and The Victorian Graveyard (a few hands sticking above the graves, pasty in the moonlight), and Princess Daphne's Flower Garden.

In The Mercantile Establishment (Notions, Novelties & Sundries) she heard something clatter to the floor behind her.

"Toby!"

No answer.

"…Toby?"

Again, standing deep in The Pirates' Cove, she thought—she was certain—she heard someone breathing.

"Toby…"

The sound stopped.

She found herself, exhausted, in topographically the lowest area of Fantazyland, The Swamp. She stood for a moment at its edge, her sore bare feet enjoying the dampness of the earth.

Behind her, to her right, was the white Riverboat at its dock. Beyond that, the bare spars and crow's nest of The Pirate's Caravelle rose against the sky. Ahead of her, what little moonlight there was reflecting on the river's surface made stark the jungle tree trunks and branches.

She walked, the mud becoming deeper, into the trees along the riverbank.

At one point, stopped, listening, she heard a twig snap.

"Toby!"

There was no answer.

The mud was up to her ankles. She went up the bank, looking for drier ground.

She walked into a tangle of foul-smelling fur.

She jumped back.

Above her was the massive head of a bear. Its eyes glittered in the moonlight. The head was moving. Its upright arm descended toward her.

Christina's hand grabbed her mouth. She screamed.

A mechanical voice said, "Grr."

Christina stumbled backward. Her hair snagged in the branches of a tree.

She turned and scrambled up the slope.

Fifty-One

Billy Joe Carfer stopped the patrol vehicle at the top of the rise overlooking, to his right, the river, The Riverboat, The Pirate's Caravelle—beyond that, the lake. To his left were the roofs and fake stone turrets of Princess Daphne's Flower Palace. Well behind him, but still looming like a black hole in the sky, was Uncle Whimsy's goony great Hat.

He performed his midnight ritual.

Other night watchmen had a break for coffee or a sandwich and soft drink. Billy Joe believed coffee made him nervous. He was seldom hungry. He had been told enough times soft drinks were bad for his teeth.

Settling back in his seat, putting one work boot up against his handlebar, he took a cigarette box out of his shirt pocket. He did not smoke cigarettes, either. Cigarettes caused cancer.

Billy Joe unwrapped his joint from its tinfoil, lit up and inhaled deeply. Pot caused pleasant sensations.

Billy Joe had no feelings about his job as a Fantazyland night watchman. Fantazyland was weird. Perverted. Fantazyland's message to the world was: rats are cute, lions are cowardly, ducks make puns; pirates are heroes, astronauts are Boy Scouts, outlaws are comic. From all the signs around Fantazyland one had to think the only threatening things in all this world were paying customers. Don't touch this. Don't touch that. His boss, Drew Keosian, was a turkey. He talked about Fantazyland as if it were the United States Constitution, to be protected from overt and covert aggression from all sources and at any cost.

Fantazyland offered a world view—something in which to believe. It was a religion. A fenced-in religion.

Billy Joe did not consider his job as work. Nothing ever happened. Being a night watchman at Fantazyland was like being a scarecrow in a cactus patch.

The job permitted him to spend his days painting. Or so he had planned.

His goal was thirty great canvasses. Including the few good works he had kept upon graduating from U.C.L.A., he now felt he had twelve good canvasses.

He had never sold any, but he felt—he just knew—that if he put thirty good canvasses together, any broker, agent, gallery owner, critic would be able to perceive the certainty of his style, the consistent high level of his ability.

Trouble was, he hadn't painted anything in over three months. California days were full of distractions: swimming pools, beaches, movies, girls, galleries filled with other people's work…

As he inhaled his midnight joint, the view of Fantazyland laid out before him took on a delightful aspect. He only smoked grass while on the grounds of Fantazyland. The irony pleased his sensibilities. The lights along the paths became softer. The amusement park objects, ships and castle turrets and the enormous Hat, took on an incredible, stark, funny reality. The fantasy became abstract. One could believe anything, believe one was seeing anything. Polonius pot.

Tonight Billy Joe Carfer heard a woman scream. One loud, protracted, frightened scream. He heard it come from the riverbank, down to his right.

Billy Joe chuckled.

He knew, intellectually, he really had not heard a woman scream.

If nothing else, the study of art had taught Billy Joe Carfer that any perception can be distorted. Reality is better perceived slightly distorted.

After his pot break, Billy Joe Carfer started his electric patrol wagon and joggled down the path to scoot around Princess Daphne's Flower Palace, pass The Hall of Knives, Spooky House…

After his midnight joint, Billy Joe Carfer got a real thrill out of cornering his patrol vehicle at speeds up to twelve miles per hour.

Fifty-Two

Goddamn everybody.

Colonel Augustus Turnbull gave his suit coat, bunched under his head, a punch with his fist.

He was lying on the bench along the inside wall of Fantazyland's Victorian Station. The bench was made of horizontal rolls of wood. It dipped considerably before joining its back. Lying on his back or front was impossible. Lying on his side, facing forward, Colonel Turnbull was too fat to fit his hips securely into the dip. His belly hung over the edge of the bench, pulled him toward the floor.

His three men were sprawled around the railroad station. One, on the floor, was snoring loudly.

"Stop that snoring!" Turnbull roared.

The snoring did not stop.

Augustus Turnbull recalled an incident that had happened almost twenty years before, when he had come back from his years as a mercenary in Africa and rejoined the British Army.

He had gone to London for a night on the town. He was a non-commissioned officer, nearly thirty years old. He wore his uniform because that was all he had to wear. For two or three hours he had done whiskey-beer at a pub off Fleet Street. His uniform was sweaty and crumpled. Cigarette ashes had spilled on it.

Finally, there had been a girl to talk to. He bought her drinks and told her stories of the people he had killed. War stories, when there had been no wars she had heard of.

She said, "Be a good laddie and get us a cab. We'll go to my place."

He looked at his drink. "Now?"

"Before it's too late for you, sweets," she said.

So they stumbled out into the street, his arm around her shoulder. Taxi drivers ignored them.

"Come on," she said. "We can get one up at that posh hotel up there."

There were no taxis outside the hotel.

There was a Rolls-Royce saloon car waiting. The uniformed chauffeur standing by the car's back door did not even look at the soldier and the girl swaying on the sidewalk.

He opened the back door.

Three young women in evening gowns and furs and jewels, chatting and laughing, skipped out of the hotel and into the back seat. Two young men in black tie accompanied them. They, too, climbed into the back seat.

"Oooo," the girl with Turnbull said. "Look at them. The pashas."

The chauffeur did not close the car door. He waited. They all waited.

One of the young men finally shouted through the back door at the hotel entrance.

"Rinaldi! Come on!"

Turnbull turned.

A slim, attractive man in his early twenties, beautifully groomed, wearing black tie, ran out of the hotel. The young people in the car cheered as he jumped into the back seat, laughing. He sat among the beautiful women, the jewels, the furs.

The chauffeur closed the door carefully, softly, then ran around to the driver's seat. Even the car's exhaust seemed an expensive perfume.

As it drove off, Turnbull watched through the rear window the heads of gilded youth, chatting, laughing.

It was the first time he had seen Teodoro Rinaldi.

Precious Teodoro.

An hour later, the girl threw Turnbull out of bed.

Now, in The Victorian Railroad Station at Fantazyland, he gave the tweed suit coat bunched under his head another punch.

"Goddamn," he said softly.

Fifty-Three

Exhausted, Christina sat by the waterfall awhile. So many nights as a young girl in Pennsylvania, she had sat out, enjoying the night, dreaming of a husband, children. *Children…Child…Toby…*

Now, even though she leaned against nothing, tried to keep her back straight, her breathing became deeper, more rhythmical. Her chin rested on her collarbone.

She snapped her head awake and watched the headlight of a patrol vehicle as it came along a path, closer to her. It veered off to her left.

It approached a dim square of light in the hillside.

It disappeared.

It took her a long moment to realize the vehicle had gone into the patch of light. Actually gone into it.

It had gone into a tunnel.

She got up and walked toward the patch of light. She was at the rear of Fantazyland, next to the Victorian Graveyard. In the dark, she went through a garden of plastic flowers. They cut the insteps of her feet badly.

There was a chain-linked fence outside the tunnel. The sign was red, with black lettering. DANGER! EMPLOYEES ONLY—SERVICE AREA.

The gate was open. She went through it and a few meters along the path entered the tunnel.

She heard the hum of machinery.

Inset into the base of the tunnel's walls, spaced widely, were lights covered with frosted glass.

The tunnel was cement floored, walled and roofed, of good dimensions, about four meters high. It was wide enough for two patrol vehicles to pass each other. Ahead twenty meters the tunnel curved, dipped smoothly to the left, went back deeper, under the ground level of Fantazyland.

Half awake but fascinated, Christina padded along. After she passed the curve, the tunnel flattened out.

She passed double steel doors to her left. DANGER! HIGH VOLTAGE AREA. GREEN CARD EMPLOYEES ONLY. There were more such doors to her right. She heard voices. A radio playing. Light spilled into the tunnel from her right. On tiptoes she approached the door and peeked through its small, round window.

A bake shop. She could smell the bread and pastry. There were bakers baking. One, whose elbow had been dipped in flour, was saying, "…massage parlors that don't do nothin' for you are a crock a shit. I mean, they know you can't complain to no Chamber of Commerce or…"

She crossed the tunnel to the far wall and continued. Shortly, the tunnel widened. There were sidewalks on both sides. Christina began passing many closed doors. They were the sort you'd see in any office building. Stenciled on them were signs which read, CREDIT UNION, Ms. Jameson; HEALTH; COSTUMES, Mr. Roark.

Elevators were between some of the office doors. They were marked: Area 12, BLUE MUSHROOM; Area 9, OUTHOUSE; Area 9, SALOON KITCHEN. Wide corridors went off to the right and left. Yellow lights blinked at the intersections. There were sidewalks and doors in these corridors as well. In the roof of the tunnel, behind grilles, air conditioners whirred.

More doors: Maintenance SPEED TUNNEL Red Card Employees; Maintenance HALL OF KNIVES Red Card Employees; Maintenance SPOOKY HOUSE LIFTS Red Card Employees…

She went by two lit locker rooms. From one she could hear a shower running and a man singing *Blue Moon*.

From across the corridor, Christina looked into a small, lit lounge area. A man in blue shirt and slacks sat doubled over in a chair, changing his boot laces. He did not look up as she glided by.

A ramp swooped down on her right. REPAIR VEHICLES ONLY.

More doors: POST OFFICE; SECRETARIAL, Mr. Tanney; ACCOUNTING, Ms. Engel.

Christina came to a large, semidark room. Its entrance was wide and doorless.

Peering into it, her eyes adjusted. It was a large lounge, comfortable chairs, divans, big tables with lamps and magazines neatly on them. There was a television against each of the three walls. Crepe paper streamers dangled from the walls. A homemade sign read: SO LONG, MARTY! Another read: MAINTENANCE DEPT WILL MISS YOU, MARTY! There were paper cups on some of the tables, and depleted hors d'oeuvre trays.

In the light from the corridor, Christina found a hunk of cheese on one tray. She sat on a divan in the back of the room and dry-swallowed the cheese.

Her feet were stinging.

Am I just going on instinct? Why can't I figure out where Toby is rationally…?

Sitting on the divan in the back of the semidark lounge, feeling her feet sting, Christina realized that if she had not been having a drug reaction from Turnbull's shot, she probably would not have reacted to Mrs. Brown's dream and looked for the car at Fantazyland. In the condition she was in when Mrs. Brown called, sitting on the floor in her robe, her cheekbone throbbing, her neck aching, her arm sore, her housekeeper's voice over the phone appeared to Christina to have the certainty of God. Toby is at Fantazyland. Christina was off the floor, dressed, and had her foot jammed on the accelerator, headed for Fantazyland, before she knew what she was doing.

Of course, she had had nothing else to do. She had spent all Friday wandering around the airport for no rational reason.

At least she had caught a glimpse of Toby. And he was dressed in white shorts and a blue jersey….

Christina curled up on the divan. But, she told herself, for only a moment, a short moment….

Something awoke her. Some noise. She glanced toward the dim light from the corridor. Again, Christina was certain she heard breathing. Someone sniffed.

Quietly, she got up and padded across the room.

Between the divan and the door was a tall-backed Naugahyde chair. Asleep in it was the man she had seen before. The gray-eyed man who had come through the fence in Wild West City and looked at her.

Quietly, breathing through her mouth, she looked at him closely.

He was gray haired; his face was long and sallow; his suit was gray. Some blood vessels had been broken recently on his nose and upper lip. There was a large bump above one ear. Beneath his short hair, on the bump, there was a hairline, half-moon cut. His hands were folded in his lap, his fingers lightly laced.

Softly Christina tiptoed out of the lounge.

She went to the left along the corridor, having no idea in this underground world what time it was.

Fifty-Four

"Jeez. This is the coldest house afire I ever been in."

Spike was lying on his back on the floor of The Burning House. He was soaking wet and shivering violently. The raging flames were turned off for the night, but everywhere there was the slightly oniony smell of gas.

After full darkness, they had crawled out of Ms. Lillyperson's Cottage and worked their way down to the swamp and along the riverbank until they were just across from The Burning House Island. Looking across, they could even see in the moonlight the silhouettes of the Indian mannequins attacking the house.

"How deep is the river?" Spike asked. "You go first."

"Not deep, I guess."

"I've lost a whole lotta blood."

"The river will wash out your cut."

"'Cut!' Some cut. Some dude shot me!"

"Come on."

Toby took off his clothes, made a bundle of them and stepped into the water, holding them over his head.

Clad, pantleg torn, leg bloody, Spike slipped into the river. He scraped his feet in their shoes along the river bottom. He felt for holes before taking each step.

"Come on, Spike."

Toby was in the middle of the river. The water was up to his shoulders. He waited.

From downriver there was a noise. Something had moved in the water. A wet, black triangle appeared in the moonlight on the surface of the water.

There was a rushing noise, the sound of water rushing, the sound of some huge thing rushing through the water at them.

Spike saw the eyes. They were imbecile, gleaming, wet. He saw the jaws. He saw the massive white teeth separating.

"Oh, Jesus!"

Mouth open, head and body rolling, a shark rushed by him.

It knocked Spike over. His head went underwater.

A few meters beyond where Spike floundered, the shark suddenly stopped. It had come to the end of its track.

"Jesus!"

Spike regained his footing and stared at it. The shark was bubbling. After a moment, it sank. Spike could feel it moving slowly past him again, going backward underwater.

Through the dark, Toby said calmly, "You must have triggered something with your feet."

"Jesus! Real! I thought it was a real shark!"

"Rivers don't have sharks," Toby said simply. "Except, of course, at Fantazyland."

"Thanks, kid. 'Ppreciate that. Really 'ppreciate it."

"Come on, Spike. Pick your feet up."

By the time Spike reached the riverbank, Toby was nearly dressed in his still dry clothes.

Spike caused a commotion scrambling up the riverbank. A crocodile rose, turned its head toward him, appeared to reach for a bite.

Spike kicked it in the head with his soaked shoe. He slipped in the mud and found himself sitting.

"Good way to make your cut bleed again," Toby commented.

Spike's wound bled again. The blood on his leg was warmer than the river water.

In The Burning House, Toby worked the tourniquet again.

"Should work even better now," Toby said, twisting. "Now that it's wet. Leave it tight until I come back."

"Where you goin'?"

"Outside. I saw a blanket."

In the moonlight Toby walked up behind the mannequin Indian Chief and said, "Excuse me, sir. We need your blanket." He gave it a tug. It snapped free from around the mannequin's neck.

Spike was a dark form on the floor of the cabin. Toby could hear him shivering.

"Should have taken your clothes off, Spike."

"You shoulda tol' me."

"Take 'em off now. Otherwise the blanket will get wet too."

Without getting up, Spike struggled out of his clothes. He threw them on the floor and grabbed the blanket over him.

In a minute, Spike said, "Jeez. This is terrible, kid. They got ol' Spike down. You know?"

Fifty-Five

"Spike?"

"Yeah, kid?"

Toby was sitting with his back against the inside wall of The Burning House. His arms were around his knees. To him, Spike was a long, dark bulk on the floor. Only Spike's toes, nose and chin were discernible from Toby's view.

"Am I kidnapped?"

"Yeah, kid…Toby. I guess you are."

"And you're the kidnapper?"

Shivering: "Yeah. Guess I am. Fac' is….That all right? I mean, that all right with you, Toby?"

"Sure. Just wondering. You know?"

"Sure, kid. Toby. I know. Forget your las' name."

"What?"

"I forget your last name."

"Rinaldi."

"Yeah. Tha's right. Don't take it personal. You know what I mean, kid?"

"Sure."

"I mean. You know. Everybody's gotta make his way. In this world. In this real world out there."

"It's okay."

"Well frankly…fac' is…I'm not so sure." He shivered again. "I'm not so sure no more."

"…And my mother?"

"What about her?"

"She didn't really break her ankle, did she?"

"Naw. How would I know? I never seen your old lady."

"You said so. You said she broke her ankle."

"Well. You see. Toby. Fac' is…not everything I say is exactly the truth. You oughta know that."

"How?"

"Well, see, I blow out a lotta air. It's how I get by, if you can dig that. I mean, it's how I do."

"Do what?"

"Get by. If you know what I mean."

"Those other stories, Spike…"

"What stories?"

"About rippin' that guy's stomach off. With a knife. With your hands. On the beach."

"Ah, shit. I made that up. You were makin' up stories. Tellin' me stories about some super-creep flyin' through the air in his drawers and a cape, someone stealin' city buses. Whaddaya expect? I told you a story. I made that up. Tearin' off a guy's stomach. I used that story lotsa times. Makes me puke."

"Made me puke."

"Yeah, well, see? That was funny."

"What about the cat?"

"What cat?"

"You ever set fire to a cat?"

"Jeez, no, kid. I never set fire to no cat. Spin her through the air like that by her tail. I'm no mean guy. Swingin' a cat. When I was a kid in Newark—your age—there was this mean guy on the block, though. I seen him do it. Real mean guy. I hated him. Really hated him. He usta make me toss my cookies. Mean…His name was Spike, see?"

"'Spike'? Then what's your name?"

"It's Spike, now."

"What was your name? What's your real name?"

"…Charles."

"Oh. I know someone named Charles."

"Sure you do. See, I hated this guy so much I took the name Spike when I went inta fightin'. Figured if anybody was gonna get his head beat in, better him 'n me. Make sense?"

"Not really."

"See when I was in reformed school, they made me fight. Taught me a skill: getting' beat up." Shivering: "I was never any good. They paroled me right to this guy, name of Brian, big promoter he was, full of the manly sport of bleedin'. I spent months fightin' down south. They flew me right outa Newark Airport. Long ways south. Colombia, Venezuela, Bolivia—those places I tol' you about, where they don't speak English too good. Fightin' two, three times a week. Fuckin' face never got time to heal. Every time I fought they gave me twenty-five dollars. Then they'd change it for me into the local money, so I could have a beer, you know? Didn't seem to make any difference whether I won or lost: twenty-five dollars. Always the same twenty-five dollars. I came to recognize the bills. I didn't care. I knew they were poppin' eyes down there. I heard enough about it round the gyms. Brian was always warnin' me. Don't let 'em pop your eye, Spike. I was scared shitless of that. Win or lose: I didn't care. As long as no one popped one of my peepers."

"What do you mean, Spike?"

"You know, during a fight, get a thumb in behind an eyeball. Pop it out."

"Oh."

"Takes a special kind of glove. Less than regulation, Brian called 'em."

"Oh."

"Sure. Fac' is…it happened. The night came. Brian was very upset. Sent me home. Newark."

"Oh."

"Didn't hurt so much. Quick, you know? Some reason, less blood comes from the eye like that than usually comes from the nose alla time. Always bein' afraid of its happenin' was much worse. Losin' an eye 'cause some mean guy really popped it out with his thumb on purpose to win a twenty-five dollar fight really rots. You know what I mean? I mean, it's only a fight. Twenty-five dollars. How many beers is that? Jeez. You know what I mean?"

"Yeah. I guess so."

"That's some kinda mean."

"But, Spike, you have been in jail?"

"Yeah. Sure. Twice't. Tol' you about that." Shivering: "When I was fourteen, borried a car, didn't know how to drive, smacked it into another car, knocked myself silly. Tweet-tweet. Cops come— there I was, sleeping prince of a jerk. Second time was after I came back from Bolivia. I was starvin', you know. I mean, havin' trouble standin' up I was so hungry. Waited outside a bar one night. Said to myself, next drunk out loses his wallet. Hamburger heaven, here I come! Next drunk out was a plainclothes cop. Bye-bye, Spike. Least the state of New Jersey plugged the hole in my head with a glass marble. For free, too. 'Ppreciated that. I've kept good care of it, too. Before that I had to wear a dollar patch. Like a old pair of pants."

"You mean your glass eye?"

"Yeah. See, kid, in reformed school, you learn to say terrible things about yourself, what you done. Make up big stories, people back off. Stay outa your pants. Fac' is, I'm mostly good at takin' stories from the newspapers, then makin' 'em up about myself. I make 'em real, know what I mean? What I do, see, see, is I stand around the bars in Newark, some of 'em, tellin' stories. I guess I look like I should be believed. This face…People believe me, see? I scare 'em shitless. Then, every once't in a while someone comes up to me, says, 'Spike, there's this guy needs his legs broken, his head beat in, his house torched, car kaboomed.' And I say, 'Sure, how much?' real easy, just like that, as if I'm beatin' up on so many people I have difficulty fittin' one more into my busy schedule. I allus take half up front. Cash money. I'm no dope."

"Then do you do it?"

"Do what?"

"Beat up on somebody?"

"Shit, no. I move on to another bar. There's lotsa bars in Newark."

"Don't they come after you? They gave you money. Why don't they beat you up?"

"If they weren't so chickenshit about beatin' people up themselves, they wouldna hired me. Right? What money? Most I ever took, twenty dollars, fifty, once't a C-note. Anyhow, they're all too scared o' me! Scared shitless. This face o' mine…. If I ever saw 'em again, I'd say, 'Oh, yeah. I forgot. Been busy. I'll get to it next week.' See? Like that. A little business."

For a while they both sat in the dark, listening to Spike's teeth chattering.

Then Toby asked, "So how come you kidnapped me?"

"Aw, that was nothing," Spike said. "Just doin' a friend a favor."

"Nice friend," Toby said. "Nice favor."

"Aw, don't go all snotty on me, kid. Don't take it personal. Ain't you never done a friend a favor?"

"Yes," Toby said.

"Well, tha's what I was doin'. I was doin' a friend a favor. Name o' Donny Dubrowski. Swell guy. You'd like him, kid. Knew him in prison, up in Attica. He was in for this and that. Only, he was smart, see? None of this fightin' shit for him. He lifted weights. Worked out real hard. You know, developed his body? He got as strong as a horse. Two horses maybe. Body building is a smart sport. Nobody hits ya. Nobody pulls your eye out. Only, there you are lookin' like you could beat up the whole world with one twitch of a deltoid."

"What's a deltoid?"

"Anyway, Donny got sprung seven, eight months ago. We saw each other sometimes. I didn't exactly know what he was doin', exactly, but fact is, he always had money in his jeans. He knew the stories I was tellin' in the bars were full of shit. Jus' my way of doin' business. I'd tol' the same kinda stories up in Attica. To keep guys off'n me.

"Then just the other day, like, last week, Donny come to me and ast me to do him a favor. One look at him…'Aw, Donny,' I said. 'You got a snootful.'"

"What's a snootful?"

"He'd climbed the ladder, kid."

"What ladder?"

"He was flyin' without wings. Seems someone gave him a job to do—kidnappin' you—and Donny had temporarily messed up his head. He knew he could come down, though. Just take time."

"I don't understand you, Spike. What was wrong with your friend?"

Shivering: "He was sick, kid. Had the flu."

"Oh."

"So he ast me if I'd stand in for him while he got better. He said, 'How'd you like a ride to California on an airplane?' I said, 'Sure.' He said, 'Pick up this kid at the airport'—that's you, Toby—and he tol' me how, and what to say, and give me this special jacket to wear, and he gived me two thousand bucks. Think of it! Two thousand of 'em, all in my pocket at the same time, me owin' nobody.

"But I owed Donny I do this job for him. So I did it. And that's a fac'. You saw me do it, dincha, Toby?"

"Yeah."

"I did a good job kidnappin' you, too, dinnin' I?"

"Guess so."

"Sure I did."

"So what happened to your friend, Spike?"

"Tha's the fac' I dunno. See, I suppost to fly out here with you, lyin' to you all the way, grab a car, drive you to that fancy Dan hotel, the Fairmont, then call Donny for further instructions, he said."

"So what happened? What happened when you called him?"

"He wasn't home."

Toby ran his finger along the scratch on his forehead. He had discovered the cut after the men had shot at him and Spike. He figured his forehead had been grazed by a wood chip, or a bullet.

Spike shivered. "He never answered the phone. Fac' is, he never answered the phone."

"He must be real sick," Toby said.

"Must be," Spike agreed.

"Could your friend be dead of the flu, Spike?"

"I dunno, kid. Could be."

Toby said, "Good night, Spike."

He stretched out along the wall of The Burning House.

"Toby?"

"Yeah?"

"You want the blanket?"

"No, thanks. My clothes are dry."

"Sorry that you ain't got no pajamas. I know how you like 'em."

"That's okay," Toby said. "I'm not in bed."

Shivering: "Jeez, I thought that shark was real. Jus' for a minute, there…"

Fifty-Six

"Wake up, Spike! Come on! Wake up! I found a whole world, with nobody in it!"

Kneeling over him, Toby was shaking Spike's shoulder.

Spike opened his eyes. His right eye focused on the door of The Burning House. It was just after dawn. There was a wind.

"Look!" Toby moved to the back corner of the cabin. There was a thin railing in a half circle. "Stairs. We didn't see them last night. I've already been down, on an explore. There's a big tunnel down there. I smelled food. Bread cooking. Come on!"

He returned and pulled the blanket off Spike.

"Sorry," Toby said. "Forgot you're naked."

Spike sat up and looked at the floor near his leg. There was wet blood. "I been leakin'," Spike said.

"Not much."

"I feel bushed."

"We'll eat," Toby said brightly.

"I need blood. God. I seen more of my own blood than any other dude alive."

Toby picked up Spike's trousers. "They're still damp. Should have hung them up."

"You didn't tell me."

"Let's go."

"No, I can't move, kid. They've really got Spike down this time."

Toby handed Spike his shirt. "Put it on."

Spike said, "Not going anywhere." He put on his clammy shirt.

Toby forced Spike's sticky socks on his feet.

From the front of the cabin there was a single quiet pop. Suddenly, the front of the cabin, near the window and door, was a mass of shooting, licking, whooshing flames.

"Jesus Christ!"

"Asbestos," Toby said. "Can't burn, remember?"

"Like hell!" Spike was up, hopping around trying to pull on his trousers.

Toby's head was visible at the top of the stairwell. "Must be an automatic pilot light," he commented.

"Hot as hell!"

"Come on, then."

Spike hobbled after Toby down the long, circular iron staircase. By the time he reached the bottom, Toby had opened the door to the tunnel.

Spike looked to his right and his left along the corridor lit dimly by the inset-base lights.

"I'll be a goose's rear end. So that's how they run this place! What a basement!"

Toby let the door close. The sign on it said: Maintenance BURNING HOUSE Red Card Employees Only.

"Smell food?" Toby asked.

"Fac' is, I do. Yes, I do."

They went along the corridor slowly. Spike stayed near the right wall, putting his hand out to it frequently.

They followed their noses to the large, still darkened employees' cafeteria. In the dim light from the corridor, they found the serving counters and went behind them. Most were bare. On one near the cash registers there were some sandwiches wrapped in cellophane and some half-pint cartons of milk.

They stood in the dark and munched.

"What did you get?" Toby asked.

"Roas' beef."

"I got tuna....What did you get this time?"

"Roas' beef."

"I did, too."

The great fluorescent ceiling lights began to flicker on in waves.

A man in a white apron stood in the kitchen door holding a large spoon.

"Hey!" he said.

Toby dropped his sandwich. "Let's go!"

"Nice to know ya," Spike said.

They dodged around the counter and ran through the dining area.

"Hey, you! Come back here!"

They turned left down the corridor and kept running.

Toby looked back.

The cook was standing in the middle of the corridor. "HEY!"

Toby pushed limping Spike around a corner into another corridor that ran to the left.

Fifty-Seven

Christina felt her feet were buried in hot sand.

She woke up, sat up and looked at them. She was on a couch in the Health Office.

She couldn't see her feet very well in the semidark, but her fingers told her how swollen and lacerated they were.

Standing on them was agony.

There was a lamp on the desk. She snapped it on.

On the wall beside the desk was a medicine cabinet with a glass front. It was locked. She broke the glass with a desk stapler. Inside were liquid antiseptics, salves, ointments. Sitting in the desk chair, she poured almost everything she could find onto her feet, one after the other, rubbing them as hard as she could stand. The pain and the pleasure went up the back of her legs to the back of her head.

Under the typewriter was a pair of nurse's white shoes. Gingerly, she tried one on. It was blissfully loose.

Removing the shoe, she wrapped both feet in Ace bandages she found in the medicine cabinet. Then she put the shoes on and laced them tight. She stood up. It would be possible to walk. She would walk. She snapped out the desk light and opened the door.

Fifty-Eight

Colonel Turnbull was under the bench in The Victorian Railroad Station, hands folded across his chest, suit coat bunched under his head, finally asleep.

"Colonel?"

"Shut up."

Monks was over him, on one knee.

"Shut your face."

"People around here," Monks said softly. "Employees arriving. Better move."

"I said, *Shut up!*"

Reaching around, Turnbull used the edge of the bench to pull himself into a sitting position. He worked his way up to his feet.

"Rinaldi," Turnbull said. Coughing, he corkscrewed phlegm out of his chest and spat it on the railroad station's floor.

"Shh," Monks said. He retrieved the Colonel's coat from under the bench.

"There's an elevator in there." Monks held the Colonel's coat. "It goes down somewhere."

The other two men were standing in the stationmaster's office. The elevator door was open.

His eyes red, his hands shaking, Turnbull stepped into the elevator.

Fifty-Nine

MEMO

INTERNAL ONLY

FANTAZYLAND CONSTABULARY DEPARTMENT

MONDAY A.M.

FIRST REPORT

COPY NUMBER: *One*

Drew Keosian

Item 1: Dodge Aspen Stationwagon left in main parking lot last Saturday P.M. identified by Nevada Police as stolen. Owner notified. Will pick up Wednesday. Name of Gotlieb.

Item 2: Pink Card Employee (cook) José Jones reported seven twenty A.M. two persons in or near employees' cafeteria: man, about thirty, torn trousers, limping; boy, about ten, white shorts, blue shirt; together.

Item 3: Pink Card Employee (aquamaid) Kathy Runson reported eight-three A.M. bikini top missing from locker third time in week.

Item 4: Black Card Employee (watchman) Grieves reported eight-thirty A.M. meeting Black Card Employee (watchman) Billy Joe Carfer on path near Future Transport Rocket at one-fifteen A.M. driving patrol vehicle erratically. Not responsive when spoken to. Carfer, age twenty-two, is known to have an interest in art.

Item 5: White Card Employee (nurse) Lydia Kozol reported eight-thirty A.M. office medicine chest broken into, salves, bandages missing. Also missing were her shoes.

Item 6: Disturbance reported in aquamaids' locker room eight-forty-seven A.M. Pink Card Employee Kathy Runson sent to Personnel.

❖

Chief Constable Drew Keosian had his hand on his desk telephone before he finished reading the morning report.

Joe Grady, his second-in-command (Mobile Unit), picked up.

"Read the morning report yet, Joe?"

"Yeah. That Kathy Runson sounds like a hot ticket. What's she got the other aquamaids haven't got? That's what I'd like to know."

Keosian had never been keen on indecent reference. In his job, he had to accept a certain amount of it.

"A man and a boy in Fantazyland Under. At dawn. The man possibly wounded."

Drew Keosian had not slept well. He had tried to conceptualize how there could have been a real shooting incident in the Wild West City—how two men could possibly have shot into that crowd without hitting anybody. He told himself it couldn't have happened.

"Yeah."

"And I doubt either the man or the boy stole Nurse Kozol's shoes."

"Or Kathy Runson's bikini top…"

"Put half the available constables into the Underground. Tell them what they're looking for. I'll be going right down myself."

"Yes, sir."

"And, Joe, this character, Item Four, Billy Joe Carfer, watchman?"

"Yes, sir?"

"Fire him."

"Yes, sir."

Drew put the telephone receiver back on its yoke. From his desk drawer he took a .38 caliber handgun. He checked it quickly. Standing up, he dropped it into his pants pocket.

Leaving his office, crossing to the elevator, he reminded himself, *Even in Eden, the snakes….*

Sixty

In the dim light of the main corridor of the tunnel there were four people.

Christina was aware that far up the corridor a man was limping away from her. She had no idea who he was. More to her interest, behind her down the corridor was the tall man in the gray suit she had last seen asleep in the chair. *I'm seeing rather too much of him*, she thought. Behind him, a constable had stepped into the corridor. He was standing still, looking in her direction.

Christina looked back and forth.

Around a corner came a monkey wearing a red hat. It was riding a green unicycle. Over its shoulder it carried a yellow umbrella.

The monkey chattered at Christina insistently. In warning? In anger?

The walls echoed the monkey's chatter.

Suddenly, there was light. Everywhere. Blinding light. It poured from the tops of both walls. Triangled behind glass between walls and ceilings were fluorescent lights.

The tall man in the gray suit shouted, "Mullins!"

On top of his echo the constable shouted, "Hey! Freeze!"

Chattering nervously, the monkey made a perfect U-turn on its unicycle. Furiously it pedaled up the corridor and around a corner.

Christina shouted, "What's happening?"

Pale eyes staring, the tall man in the gray suit strode quickly past her.

The constable flung off his helmet and ran after him. His nightstick bounced against his leg.

The man with the limp had disappeared.

Christina yelled after the constable, "What's happening?"

In the corner remained only the echo of her own voice.

Sixty-One

Toby, walking ahead of Spike in the tunnel, had just turned a corner. Behind him, instead of Spike, came a monkey on a unicycle, shaking its fist. It rode in a circle around Toby and tried to hit him over the head with an umbrella.

"Hey, lay off!" Toby said.

As the lights in this corridor came on, the monkey rode away, looking back at him angrily.

From around the corner came the sound of shouting. A woman's voice was shouting a question. A man's voice was shouting a statement, or a name. The edges of the voices were blurred by the hard tunnel walls.

Spike came around the corner, favoring his wounded leg. He was moving fast.

"Let's go," Spike said. "Go, go!"

They went.

Spike dragged his leg after him. He kept his hand behind his thigh to continue pushing his leg forward. He was still losing blood. His face was drained, white.

Leading, Toby decided their direction.

"Come on, Spike. In here!"

"Aw, shut up, ya little punk."

"Through here, Spike! Hurry up!"

"Punk kid. I'm hurryin'!"

They went up an elevator marked, RED CARD EMPLOYEES ONLY.

Just after the elevator door closed behind them, they discovered they were in the target area of a shooting gallery.

"Aw, shit!" Spike dropped to all fours. Rifle pellets shot over their heads and thwacked against a thick mat. "Now everybody's shootin' at ol' Spike!"

They crawled through a cabin tunnel and dropped into a room full of loud, huge, hot machinery.

"Wait a minute, Toby! Gotta sit down. Gotta rest. All my blood leaked out, ya know…"

"Too noisy here," Toby shouted.

"Gimme a chance, willya, kid?"

Spike followed him.

Underground, they went along iron scaffolding. Deep pits of machinery—humming, hissing, thumping, pumping machinery— yawned below them. Toby ran from pit to pit. Waiting for Spike, he looked down at the machinery, studying it. The machines were enormous, but intricate.

Spike worked his way along the scaffold, averting his eyes from everything below him. He kept both hands on the thin railing.

"Wow!" Toby said. "Look at that!"

"Yeah, yeah, kid. You look at it."

They went through various twists and turns of a tunnel not big enough for a horse. An organ was screeching shrill, spine-tingling music. It reverberated from the walls, ceiling, floor.

"Hey, Spike! Look at this!"

Toby had found a small, narrow, green-tinted window in the wall. It took Spike's eye a moment to adjust.

He was looking into the living room of Spooky House. An open coffin was at one side of the room.

The corpse was a young lady. Her hands were around the stem of a rose upon her breast. At the coffin's foot was a lit candle. A flour-faced hag, a ghost, long white hair down the back of her long nightgown, passed through the room. The arm of a standing suit of armor clanked a chain.

And the organ screeched.

The tourists smiled and laughed and applauded and took pictures.

In the middle of the crowd were the two gunmen who had shot at Spike and Toby the day before. With them was a third man—a heavy man in a bulky, rough suit. Each was looking around and up and down the walls in a far more methodical manner than were the tourists.

"Hey, Spike!" Toby punched him in the arm. "Spooky House. Remember? We're in the walls of Spooky House. Cool, huh?"

Spike looked away. Something in his stomach was bothering him.

"Yeah," he said. "Cool. I think we better keep movin', kid."

"Don't you want to rest? I want to watch the people be scared."

Spike limped on. "You can watch me."

Toby was the first up a metal ladder. At the top, he pushed open a trap door and pulled himself through. In this tunnel there was a railroad track. He stood in the middle of it.

A railroad train was heading straight for him. Its headlight was piercing. The whistle was urgent, shrill.

"Boo!" Toby said to it. "You'll never hit me!"

He helped Spike through the trap door.

"Look at this, Spike. Remember that ride we were on? You go through the tunnel and you think a train is going to hit you and you get right up to it and it's only an illusion and suddenly it isn't there anymore? We're there! I mean, here. There's the train."

Spike stood on the track.

"You forgot somethin', Toby."

"What?"

The structure beneath their feet was trembling.

"A train goes through here. Punk kid! The one we were on."

"Oh, yeah," Toby said. "I forgot."

He had dropped the trap door.

A train of wagonettes came around the curve. Aboard were tourists—so many white arms and faces—screaming and laughing.

Spike said, "Shit!"

He grabbed Toby's shoulder and pulled him against the wall.

The tourists swayed by them, eyes gleaming, mouths open, hair flying, row after row, screaming at the illusion that they were about to be hit by an oncoming train.

The eyes of one girl fell on Toby. Her head snapped around. She looked at him again.

With a final, deafening hoot, the oncoming train disappeared.

The train of wagonettes clattered on.

The tourists shrieked away.

Sixty-Two

We're in The Hat. We're in The Hat, Toby sang to himself. *We're in The Hat. And Spike doesn't know it.*

They had returned to the main tunnels of Fantazyland Underground. Immediately, Toby smelled food. They walked a short way along the sidewalk.

Spike stopped. He leaned his hand against the wall. He lifted his damaged leg as if kicking it slowly and looked at his foot.

"It's all swole," he said.

Keeping his weight off his foot, Spike leaned his back against the wall. In that light, Toby thought Spike looked as white as the girl in the coffin in Spooky House. Even whiter. As white as the ghost.

"People will come along here," Toby warned.

"Like who?" Spike asked. "Ghosts. Sharks. Railroad trains. What else? Jeez, I dunno." He took a deep breath. "I dunno kid."

Toby shrugged. "People," he said.

Spike snorted, coughed. "'People,'" he said.

He rubbed his good eye.

"That's a laugh. 'People.' Tell me another."

Facing Spike, Toby was balancing himself on the sidewalk's curb.

Toby said, "Like the two guys who shot at us yesterday. In Wild West City."

"Them two. They shoulda been taken out with the garbage."

Quietly, Toby said, "They weren't. I'm looking at them."

Spike's head snapped up. "You're lookin' at 'em?"

"Yeah."

"Where?"

Without moving his head, Toby said, "They're coming down the corridor. To my left."

"Yeah? No foolin'."

"No foolin'."

"They see you?"

"Sure, they see me."

"They got guns?"

"Suppose so."

"Why aren't they shootin' at ya?"

"I'm just a kid. Grown-ups can't tell kids apart."

"It's me they'll shoot at. Right?"

Toby said, "I expect so."

"Yeah? So whadda we do? My back's against the wall. See?"

"There's an elevator right next to you."

"Yeah? So there is."

"Press the button."

The sign on the elevator said, DOUBLE RED CARD EMPLOYEES ONLY, NO OTHER ADMITTANCE.

"Guess what, Spike? They see you."

The elevator door opened.

Spike looked around.

"It is them same guys!"

They got into the elevator. Toby pushed the button.

The two men were loping down the corridor toward them.

The elevator door closed and the car shot upward in a surprising, ear-cracking rush. It rose for a fairly long time.

We're in The Hat. We're in The Hat.

"No stops," Spike said.

The elevator door slid open.

Spike looked out. His working eye widened.

"Oh, Lord," he said. "Look where we are."

"Yeah," Toby said. "Top of The Hat."

"Oh, no."

"Can't go back down in the elevator, Spike."

Spike limped off the elevator. "Must be some other way down."

There was a heavy mesh fence between them and the platform where the tourists stood in line. The front of the line fed people into the small, brightly painted gondolas.

When a gondola had a party of two or four in it, it would slip down the track and fall onto the rail outside The Hat. Instantly, the people would begin screaming. They would appear against the sky for only a moment before they would drop down to the left, out of sight.

Music was playing.

Roundsy, roundsy…

Downsy, downsy…

Toby and Spike were on the maintenance men's side of the mesh fence.

A man appeared against the other side. Though it was softened by the fence, Toby thought the man's face dreadful. It was fat and broken with lines and bumps. The red eyes were staring at him.

"Are you Tobias Rinaldi?"

"Yes, sir."

"Well, Tobias Rinaldi, I'm your uncle." The man reached inside his suit coat. "Augustus Turnbull. And I'm going to kill you. And then your mother. And then your precious father!"

Toby sidled along the fence to his left, toward daylight. He felt wind.

There was a ledge. It was black, smooth plastic. Like a lip, it curved outward and downward.

Behind him, Turnbull shouted, "Mullins!"

Toby stepped onto the ledge. From what he could see, it went around the outside of The Hat.

Roundsy, roundsy…

A gondola dropped onto the track. The ledge began to vibrate. The tourists were screaming in their own fright.

Toby tried to jump back, off the ledge. The vibration was too much. He had already been shaken half a meter down the ledge.

The gondola was pirouetting in front of Toby. The people's faces looked truly frightened.

To his right, another gondola dropped onto the track.

Somewhere a voice shouted, "There's a kid out there!"

Toby sat down. Whatever traction the soles of his sneakers had given him he lost. The seat of his shorts gave him none. The vibration of the ledge was banging up his spinal column. His teeth were chattering.

The second gondola was pirouetting in the air in front of him. The tourists were laughing. One, who was not laughing, was trying to point to him. Roundsy, roundsy…

Toby's feet went over the edge. He tried to hold himself back with the flat of his hands. He fell forward. Below him, all Fantazyland moved, tilted. Wind shouted in his ears.

His fingers grabbed the outside gondola track. He was hanging from the rail by his fingers. He held on, dangled in space.

The track began to shake. Toby looked up. A yellow gondola had dropped onto the track. It would run over his fingers.

Toby let go.

Downsy, downsy…

Below him, Fantazyland zoomed closer.

"Ow!"

His mouth banged shut. His knees, the small of his back, his neck jolted. His feet had landed on something. He tried to steady himself. The wind helped. He bent his knees and put out his hands and let himself down.

Toby was well outside The Hat, outside the gondola track. He was on a black guard rail.

Lying on it, he hugged it with his arms and legs. Fantazyland was still far below him. The roofs were many colors and many shapes. The paths seemed aimless. People looked like little bugs. The wind filled his ears, bringing snatches of carousel music. He could hear the lovely, awful noise of the air-cushion boat on the lake.

Then he heard the gondola track rattling.

Toby looked up.

A red gondola was coming. One man was in it. Under his flapping jacket he wore an Uncle Whimsy T-shirt. The man's arm was reaching out of the gondola at him.

Toby put out his left hand for the man to grab.

But instead, he felt the man's hand against his ribs…pushing!

Toby held onto the rail tight, with both arms.

The gondola was gone.

Toby was panting. The wind made his lips flap.

A sudden melody blew in from the carousel. He recognized *Waltzing Matilda.* He had heard that song years ago when he had gone with his parents and His Majesty to some big, sunny country where all the people were big and sunburned and laughed loud and grabbed him and hugged him.

At the sound of the track rattling, he looked up again. A green gondola was coming.

Augustus. He said his name was Augustus. Colonel Augustus Something. Why did he say he was my knuckle?

Colonel Augustus Turnbull was in the gondola. He was aiming a pistol at Toby. He was coming very close. The hole in the pistol's barrel was a perfect circle.

The gondola spun the man around.

The gun went off.

Toby turned his head. He was looking outward at the sky. He looked down. Fantazyland swayed, like a rug moving under his feet.

He shot The Hat! Colonel Augustus Something-or-other shot Uncle Whimsy's Hat!

"TOBY?"

The next gondola was pink. Spike was standing up in it, waving both his arms.

"Wake up, punk! Le's go! Reach out here. Come on! Le go that thing!"

Sitting up a little, keeping both legs wrapped around the guard rail, Toby sent his arms toward Spike.

Spike yelled, "Grab me! Lean in. Come on, le's go!"

The inside of Toby's legs got scraped. His head was moving. He closed his eyes. There was a massive hand on each side of his rib cage. The back of his head bounced on something metallic.

He looked up. He was on the floor of the gondola. The sky above him was spinning. Spike's head was going in a circle. Spike's hand was on Toby's bare stomach.

The sky stopped spinning. Spike's head straightened. The muscles in his neck were bulging. Both his hands grabbed the safety bar.

They were moving straight ahead.

The gondola was gathering speed.

"You know, kid…" The world went dark. "…this ain't percisely my favorite ride…."

Sixty-Three

Christina was looking down from a scaffold into what appeared to be a sixteenth-century banquet hall. Two men dressed as cavaliers, lace collars and cuffs, plumed hats, were dueling with swords. They jumped onto the banquet table, leaped over a soup tureen, kicked aside a roast pig…

The tourists smiled and laughed and applauded and took pictures.

She examined the crowd carefully.

No Toby.

In the crowd there were three boys of about his age. One was blond and overweight and hot. He looked like an apple being baked. One was so skinny his knees looked like doorknobs. The third glowed. She thought he looked rather like Toby.

How many small boys had she seen the last few days that looked something like Toby…? It was a phenomenon with which she was familiar. Missing Toby so much, frequently in a street in New York, in a department store, passing Central Park in the car, Christina would catch her breath at the sight of a boy for a fraction of a second she would think was Toby. For a long moment then, she would be sad at the thought of Toby in school in New Hampshire, at a sailing camp on Cape Cod—being somewhere, anywhere away from her. The last days, in the airport, in the streets, at Fantazyland, the phenomenon of seeing someone who was like Toby, who she wanted to believe was Toby, had been frequent. The psychological phenomenon was cruel.

In the white shoes, Christina had plodded along the main Underground tunnel corridor. The constable, the man in the long overcoat, the limping man—even the chattering monkey—had disappeared.

Wanting to get out, back to the surface of the earth, Christina took elevators.

The first brought her to the inside of a mammoth music box. The din it made was horrible. *The flowers that bloom in spring, tra la…* She knew she was in Princess Daphne's Flower Palace.

She did not know where she was when the door of the second elevator opened. She was facing a green wall. Immediately, a five-foot duck waddled onto the elevator. It stood beside her, looking sideways at her curiously. Silently, Christina rode the elevator down again with the duck.

The third elevator brought her into the stomach of a whale. She looked through a window in the whale's side. Pilot fish dangled on barely visible wires. A submarine glided through the murky water.

She finally went through an ordinary door, up a steep iron ladder and along a scaffold. At least from there she had seen some children, even if Toby wasn't among them.

The metal scaffold began to quiver. At about the pace of a heart-beat. Footsteps. She looked ahead through the gloom. The tall, skinny man in the gray suit appeared in the distance, walking toward her.

Quietly, she moved in the opposite direction.

Below her another room, oddly lit, opened up. She looked over the railing and down into it.

A long rope swung ponderously back and forth. At the end of it gleamed a razor-sharp pendulum. Around the room were guillotines of various sizes and styles. One after another, the blades would rise slowly, then fall with a horrendous clash.

Moving back and forth in the room in a frightening, lurching manner was a huge wooden barrel. It turned slowly as it moved back and forth, up and down. Long, flashing knives stuck out of it at every angle, from every direction. Looking at it, Christina became nauseous.

This must be The Hall of Knives. Behind a rope, tourists stood. For once, they looked solemn, surrounded as they were by machines of death.

Someone grabbed the hair at the back of Christina's head, pulled her back, roughly twisted her head around.

Turnbull's face was an inch from hers. The veins in his eyes bulged.

"Christina…Finch…Rinaldi!" The last word struck her in the

face with spittle. He yanked her hair harder. "Where is the boy?"

"Stop!"

"You don't have the boy, do you?"

"No! Stop!"

"You don't know where the boy is, do you?"

"No. No, I don't!"

"But I have you, haven't I?...Christina Rinaldi."

Holding on to her hair, he pulled her head back, twisting her neck.

"I have you...and I shall have the little bastard...won't I?"

Long, bony white fingers appeared on Turnbull's shoulders.

Turnbull looked around.

The face of the tall man in the gray suit was paper white. In the dim light, the pupils of his eyes were almost colorless.

Turnbull let go of Christina's hair. He turned around to face the man. They all stood close together on the narrow scaffold. Christina's back was against the thin metal railing.

"Yes, Simon?" Turnbull said softly. "What do you want?"

"I need the woman, Gus." Cord's tone was as reasonable as a teacher explaining geometry. "I need the boy. Only another few hours."

"Another few hours for you to mess up again, Cord? For me to lose them both?"

"Gus—"

"No!" Turnbull roared. "I've shit in this bed! If they don't die, and die now..." Holding his hands before his chest, he tightened his fingers as if squeezing tennis balls "...I've yet to get *precious Teodoro*...."

"Another few hours, Gus." Cord's pale eyes flickered at Christina. "Then you can waste the whole family, all we care."

Turnbull swung his fist. He hit Cord on the jaw.

Then his fingers dug into Christina's neck. The balls of his thumbs pressed into her throat

She tried to raise her knee, but Turnbull was too close.

There was a flash of white over Turnbull's shoulder as Cord chopped him in the neck.

Turnbull let go of Christina.

"Gus, you're insane," Cord said conversationally.

Cord slammed the side of his hand against Turnbull's throat.

Turnbull staggered forward. He drew his other hand back to his shoulder to swing at Cord.

Cord laced his fingers together and put them against Turnbull's face. He stepped beside Turnbull and threw his hips against Turnbull's and pushed.

Turnbull's feet rose from the scaffold. Blood was dribbling from his nose and mouth.

Cord, sideways to the railing, had all his weight on one foot.

Immediately, impulsively, instinctively, Christina jumped and hit Cord's near shoulder with both hands. She put her full weight into the blow. Cord's waist was well above the railing, his head already on the other side.

Cord turned his face to Christina. He knew he was falling. The expression on his face was totally indifferent.

Christina's left hand clutched the railing. From below there was a loud, delighted screaming.

She looked over the railing. Both men had landed on the twirling barrel of knives.

Turnbull was spreadeagled on his back. The knives that protruded from his stomach glistened with blood.

Cord had landed on his stomach. Knives pierced his shoulder, his chest, his back, one leg.

The barrel lurched round and round, back and forth, up and down, rotating the bodies. Blood dripped onto the floor in crazy patterns.

The tourists smiled and laughed and applauded and took pictures.

Sixty-Four

"Ma'am, what are you doing here?"

For the moment, Christina could not answer She was in the main corridor of Fantazyland's Underground again. All the lights were on. She could not remember how she got there. Had she ever left?

She pressed the heel of her hand against her temple. She remembered kneeling on some iron rungs…the scaffold…vomiting…dry retching. Then wanting to go somewhere, anywhere, walking…

She looked around the walls and ceiling of the brightly lit tunnel.

There was a constable standing before her. His face was surprisingly tanned, for that handlebar mustache, that bobby's helmet. There was a patrol vehicle standing in the middle of the corridor. There was another man, dressed in a light sports jacket. He had his hand on her arm.

"My name is Drew Keosian," he said. "I work here at Fantazyland. I want to help you."

Far up the corridor, a man limped around the corner. One of his pant legs looked wet, adhered to his leg.

Behind him loped a small boy. White shorts, blue jersey…

"Oh, my God," Christina said.

Keosian looked around.

"Toby!"

He looked straight at his mother.

What is he doing? What is Toby doing?

The boy put his hands on the man's back, turned him around and pushed him. He hurried the man back around the corner, out of sight.

"Toby!" Christina screamed again.

Keosian and the constable jumped onto the patrol vehicle. The cart accelerated instantly, quietly.

Its brake lights flashed as it went around the corner.

Again, Christina was alone in the corridor.

Toby….What is wrong with Toby…?

As well as she could on her damaged feet, Christina ran along the corridor.

He saw me…I know he saw me…He heard me…I know he did. Toby! As she hurried along, Christina tried to clear her eyes of tears. She turned the corner. She looked both ways.

There was no one at all in sight.

A little more slowly, trying to even out her breathing, trying to dry her face, Christina walked. The bandages in her shoes were wet with blood. Her feet slipped in the shoes.

At the next intersection, instead of turning left, Christina crossed the corridor and took the tunnel to the right.

A five-foot beaver, dragging its tail on the floor, hurried past her.

Then she heard Toby's voice. He sounded so casual, as if he were trying to wake her up.

"Hey, Mom?"

Christina spun around, slipping in the big white shoes.

Toby stood against the wall, grinning. Next to him was a door marked, COSTUMES.

All the breath went out of her.

"Where you been, Mom?"

She grabbed him. She folded him into her arms.

"What's the matter with your feet? Did you really break your ankles?"

"Toby, Toby, Toby…"

"Ma'am? Hey, you! Ma'am! Miss!"

A constable down the corridor was waving his arm at them as he jogged toward them. "Wait a minute, miss!"

From under her breasts, Toby looked up at his mother, smiled and said, "Come on!"

He took Christina by the arm and pulled her a few steps. He pushed a button on the wall.

A door slid open.

"In here." He pulled her in. Grinning, he said, "Up?"

He pushed another button. The elevator door closed.

Christina held Toby close to her. She pressed his body against hers.

Then, like a mother cat, she took his hair in her mouth. She put her wet cheeks against the top of his head and kissed it again and again.

"Toby, Toby, Toby, Toby, Toby," she said. "Oh, Toby, Toby, Toby, Toby…"

Sixty-Five

"Mr. Ambassador? I know you asked not to be disturbed at all, but Mrs. Rinaldi is on line 253. She says it is urgent."

At his desk, Ambassador Teodoro Rinaldi looked around his office at his staff. They sat with papers in their laps, pens in their hands. The eyes of each of them had fallen at the sound of Sylvia Menninges's voice over the intercom.

He looked at his watch. In two hours he was scheduled to stand before the assembled delegates to the United Nations and submit Resolution 1176R.

The button on line 253 was flashing. Teddy put his hand on the receiver.

He was not sure that he wanted to, or could, talk to Christina just then. It was her right; it was her need to ask him what he had decided.

That afternoon Teddy had received a coldly worded directive from the King ordering him to submit Resolution 1176R.

Two hours before he was to deliver the speech, Ambassador Teodoro Rinaldi had decided nothing. He had simply continued operating as well as he could, upon the basic principle of diplomacy: *keep all options open as long as possible*. Many, many times he had learned the greatest mistake was in making a decision before it had to be made. Several times in his professional career he had believed he had all the facts necessary, all the facts available, to make a decision, hesitated just a moment longer and been surprised by a new fact, totally unexpected, that changed his decision totally.

Pretending they were not there—not hearing, seeing—his staff, in the final meeting two hours before the culmination of all their work, hopes, just before he was expected to offer a masterwork of diplomacy to create a new economic sanity, a new, essential peace guarantee, for their nation, their people, their homes, for the world, sat there, eyes on their laps, doodling on pads. They were aware of his hesitation in answering the phone.

Urgent? If this was bad news about Toby, the Ambassador was certain he couldn't assimilate it, accept it; he couldn't take it.

He had better hear it.

Teddy put the receiver to his ear, "Christina?"

"Hi, Dad."

The Ambassador looked around at his staff, around the room at the tops of their heads.

"Toby?"

Suddenly he was seeing faces in his office. Faces. Not tops of heads.

"Toby! Are you all right?"

"Sure."

"Your mother with you?"

"Sure."

The faces were beaming.

"Is she all right?"

"Her feet hurt."

"What's wrong with her feet?"

"She walks like one of those ducks out here. She waddles."

"Where are you?"

"Fantazyland. It's a great place, Dad."

"Look." Teddy swallowed. "Don't see everything without me. I'm coming out. In a couple of days. Join you. We'll want to see some of it together."

"I've seen about all of it, Dad. I can show you. I even know how most things work."

Teddy felt he had to hang up. Soon. He had not many moments of control left. "Toby? Ask your mother to call me. Tonight. She knows when and where."

"Okay."

"I'll see you soon, Toby. Wednesday. Thursday at the latest."

"Okay."

Teddy replaced the receiver. He looked around his office—at the faces of the people in his office.

"Well," he said. "Toby seems to have made it to Fantazyland."

Ria's eyes were bathed in tears. She was grinning.

"Excuse me." Teddy stood up. "A moment."

He went into his bathroom and closed the door.

In his office, his staff sat silently.

Ria blew her nose.

Through the bathroom door they could hear the tap water splashing hard into the basin.

Then they heard another sound—frightening, until they recognized it.

They did not look at each other. Of course, they were embarrassed.

Finally, the final-draft speech writer said, "It seems His Excellency, the Ambassador, is blubbering in the bathroom."

Ria Marti closed her notebook.

She said, "I think this meeting is over."

Sixty-Six

There was only one constable at the main gate of Fantazyland. Because of Christina's feet, she and Toby were moving slowly. The constable paid them no particular attention. They had washed their hands and faces, tried to clean their clothes. Fantazyland constables were not very concerned with people who were leaving. Just those who were entering.

Holding his mother's hand, Toby had plenty of time to look around. Of course he looked back at Uncle Whimsy's Hat. From here, the side of the mountainous, black Stovepipe Hat seemed absolutely smooth. The bright-colored gondolas popping out of its top seemed not big enough to carry ants. To its left were the stone turrets of Princess Daphne's Flower Castle.

In the turn-of-the-century square itself, the Flags of All Nations atop the buildings were straight out in the wind. The Firemen's Band was playing, *Glory, glory hallelujah…*

A voice said, "Toby…."

Toby saw no one he recognized. Tourists wandered around. There was the constable; the girl dressed as Princess Daphne, handing flowers to little girls; a sad-faced clown, his white-painted lips curving down; an upright turtle, five and a half feet tall…

"Hey, Toby…."

Toby looked closely at the clown. His makeup didn't seem very well applied. And his eyes seemed odd. Only his right eye was moving, back and forth, back and forth, in some kind of a signal.

Toby looked down the clown's costume. On the ground near his huge feet were a few drops of blood.

Toby looked back up, into the clown's face.

The clown darted his eye back and forth again.

"See ya, kid."

Toby grinned.

He gave a little wave with his free hand, only waist high.

His mother did not see him.

Sixty-Seven

Wednesday, Ambassador Teodoro Rinaldi walked into the V.I.P. lounge at San Francisco Airport, where his wife and son were waiting for him. He dropped his briefcase and put one arm around Toby and the other around Christina.

The family embraced wordlessly.

"Your luggage will be right up, sir," the stewardess said.

"I know." The Ambassador smiled at her. "Someone's downstairs waiting for it."

Finally, Teddy said, "We might as well sit down while we're waiting. What's wrong with your feet?"

Christina dropped back down into her chair. "Plumb wore out. They'll be all better tomorrow."

Toby jumped onto the divan next to his father. "Fac' is," he said. "I'm hungry. Pizza!"

Again, Teddy put his arm around him.

Returning to the airport was not as difficult for Christina as she thought it would be. She had spent such awful hours there. But this time Toby was with her and they hadn't had to wait long for Teddy.

Christina and Teddy had talked at length on the telephone both Monday and Tuesday nights. Monday night Teddy told her Resolution 1176R had passed in the United Nations, with only nine no votes and one abstention—the United States. Tuesday Teddy told her Pat Skinner had been fired from the State Department.

"I guess Pat misread my face at some point," Teddy said.

To them both the grand news was that "the boss" had endowed a chair of international diplomacy at Kennedy, provided Teddy be granted the chair for the first three years. Christina detected the kind hand of Ria Marti behind the endowment and the provision. Surely, "the boss" had not thought of it himself. Three years in Cambridge, living quietly with Teddy and Toby…

Late Monday afternoon, from Fantazyland's parking lot, Christina had called Bernard Silvermine at the Red Star–Silvermine Motel.

"Mr. Silvermine? May I make a reservation for two, for tonight? In the name of Rinaldi—Christina Rinaldi and son, Toby...."

Bernard Silvermine had a kilted bagpiper piping in the motel driveway when they arrived at dusk.

Tuesday and Wednesday, waiting for Teddy, playing around the motel pool, eating in the coffee shop, Toby told Christina some things about what he knew had happened.

His stories, of course, were childish. He was precise about some things: nearly being hit by a train, attacked by a shark in the river, falling down the side of Uncle Whimsy's Hat.

He was most vague about the kidnapper.

When she asked specific questions, Toby seemed to find it difficult to remember. How old was the kidnapper? Well, he was older than Dad—about fifty. Yes, he did limp. He had a wooden leg, you see, like a pirate. Glass eye? No, the man didn't have a glass eye. He said the man had said his name was O'Brien, and he lived on a ranch in Texas.

Christina had not told Teddy about The Hall of Knives—how, without thinking, without even knowing she was doing it, she had killed a man. She would tell him when he was rested. Or maybe never.

Now Toby was sitting on his legs on the airport divan, facing his father, jabbering about Fantazyland and about many people and things that are not what they seem.

Smiling broadly, Teddy looked at Christina.

Christina asked, "Did Mrs. Brown send the carpets to the cleaning department at the museum, as I suggested?"

Teddy looked surprised. "Mrs. Brown?"

"Yes."

Teddy said, "Mrs. Brown isn't at the legation anymore."

"She isn't? Teddy!" Christina sat up in her chair. "Where's Mrs. Brown?"

Teddy's grin was the broadest she'd ever seen on his face. "Downstairs. She insisted on taking charge of our luggage herself. Don't know why she thinks any of it might get lost...."

Toby said, "Yeaaaaaaa! Will she come to Fantazyland with us?"

Teddy said, "I don't think you could keep her away with a bazooka."

Toby said, "I can show you some marvelous things."

"I'm sure you can," his father said.

"I know Fantazyland pretty well now. Almost better than anybody, I bet."

Teddy look at Christina. "Maybe your mother doesn't feel like going back to Fantazyland."

Christina's stomach churned at the thought.

Teddy and Toby were looking at her, hoping she'd say yes.

She put out a hand to each of them.

"Anything to be together," she said.

SAFEKEEPING

(THE SECOND SNATCH)

In memory of M.A.M.,
who told me to close my eyes,
then asked me what I saw.

I
In Which Noses and Other Outstanding Matters Are Discussed

"Burnes?" Mrs. Jencks enquired generally of the small room filled with six beds, six eight-year-old boys scurrying to get dressed, and odd pieces of clothing on the beds, on the boys, in the air, on the floor, underfoot and in hand as weapons.

"Yes, sir?"

"Headmaster wants to see you straight off."

"I can't find my stocking, sir."

In the doorway, Mrs. Jencks still couldn't be sure which boy had answered her and thus identified himself as Burnes. All the youngest gentlemen at Wolsley School called everyone over five feet in height *sir*. At their age everyone, including the gardener and the imbecile from the village who collected the wash, was in a position of authority over them, by size if not by rank, and if there was a word to placate authority, *sir* was the word.

Wisely, Mrs. Jencks maintained her expression of benign maternity while waiting at the door. It was this expression of bemused patience, and her ample, maternal dimensions, which had won and kept for her the job of matron of Wolsley School. Parents and faculty both perceived Mrs. Jencks as a bosom into which anyone would be happy to sob. Three decades of students, however, had penetrated Mrs. Jencks' placid expression and knew it to connote nothing more than painless indifference to the world at large. They also knew that nothing had nestled against her bosom in all those years except crumbs from her tea cakes.

"Hurry along," Mrs. Jencks said, as a general admonition.

Eight-year-old boys haven't that many years' dressing practice behind them. When given a square foot of cold floor on which simultaneously to hop and execute one of life's First Things, including shoe strings and ties, the result is similar to that of any great, unexpected human undertaking: confusion, consternation, and disputation. Out of that room, in twelve minutes, six eight-year-old boys were expected to march, toiletted, washed, brushed, dressed identically in kneepants, kneesocks, shoes, shirt, tie, the Wolsley School blazer and cap, six made beds behind them. Occasionally, it almost happened; expectations were almost fulfilled, but never, of course, with more than two of the six dressed entirely in their own clothes.

Doubtlessly, parents are smarter now, but in the early 1940s they sincerely wished to believe, or wished their friends to believe, or wished their children to believe, that they sent their children off to school or camp with some continuing sense of identity. Name tags were sewn into every article of clothing with thread staunch enough to do its umbilical duty. Traditionally, parents need to believe something of the sort when, in truth, they are throwing their children to the public, their clothes after them.

Jaime Pomfrey, two beds west of Burnes', had name tags in his stockings stiffer than the rest, and placed uncomfortably below the fold. This was one lad at school who seldom forgot his mother. He wrote her each Sunday and cursed her each morning. Very shortly he became adept, via diversionary tactics, argument, offers to dispense bloody noses, at getting anyone's stockings but his own on his legs. His own stockings remained balled neatly in his drawer.

"Burnes," said Mrs. Jencks. "Headmaster wants you before Chapel."

"Yes, sir, but I can't find a stocking."

"Hurry along."

At the shrill sound of a bell, the future of Britain agitated each other to the door, narrowly circumnavigated Mrs. Jencks, and threw themselves suicidally down the stairwell. Left amid the confusion of the room, one bare foot elevated from the cold floor, was—as marked in the school register—Robert James Saint James Burnes Walter Farhall-Pladroman, S.Nob. To this son of a nobleman, Mrs.

Jencks' girth appeared to be holding the door jambs at a distance from each other wider than normal. On the high plateau of her bosom sparkled a necklace of early morning toast crumbs.

"You are Burnes, aren't you?"

"Yes, sir, ma'am."

"You little ones confuse me the first year or two. Until your noses grow."

"Noses, ma'am?"

"Find a stocking somewhere, Burnes. Headmaster's waiting."

As "Headmaster's Waiting" was a disaster on an all-school scale comparable only to the Union Jack's touching the ground, an element of such magnitude that it was capable of causing faculty as well as students to rush from playing field and classroom, even of causing parents to rush from London, Robby was forced to accept the inevitable: that Pomfrey had won again. He went to Pomfrey's drawer and pulled on one of Pomfrey's stockings.

Hopping in a fruitless effort to adjust Pomfrey's identity against his shin, Robby Burnes (as he was generally known by people who had something other to do with their lives than remember all his names) followed Mrs. Jencks down the stairwell, across the courtyard, through the smells of hot chocolate, past the cough-filled, sneeze-filled chapel, and into Admin. Wing, wherein Headmaster had his study. Seeing Mrs. Jencks hurrying from behind over a long course distracted Robby from speculating what difficulty he had caused, precipitating his impending interview with Headmaster. Mrs. Jencks achieved forward motion by the action of each cheek upon the other: The right would rest against the left, which would contract and propel the right outward and onward again—which was intensely interesting to Robby. He wondered if such an athletic device would survive a long scrimmage.

"Aha, there you are, Burnes! That is Burnes, isn't it, Mrs. Jencks?"

"Yes, Headmaster. I have trouble with them, too, sir, until they get noses. A bit slow dressing this morning. Missed breakfast altogether, he has."

"Tadpoles will be tadpoles, Mrs. Jencks."

On Headmaster's desk was a finished breakfast tray.

Headmaster, Robby knew, divided the world between *tadpoles* and *honored parents*. Parents considered him England's greatest boy handler. Boys considered him England's greatest parent handler. He achieved these reputes mainly by keeping a threadbare nine-by-twelve Persian carpet on his study floor. The rug served the double purpose of giving the tadpoles a touch of home (as all, typically, thus far in their lives had been brought up in the back rooms of their parents' homes, those rooms relegated to servants, worn-out rugs and boys) and thus suggested to the boys they could speak freely, confidentially, to Headmaster, as they had been in the habit of speaking at home only to Nanny and Cook. To honored parents, the worn carpet bespoke Headmaster's selfless, soulful dedication to the education of boys. Over the decades, the worn carpet in Headmaster's study had attracted contributions to the school's endowment many, many times its own original worth. Headmaster himself, as he paced restlessly in his black, academic robe, seemed oblivious of the magic carpet beneath his feet. Headmaster's eye, Robby noticed, repeatedly checked the decanter of sherry on the sideboard, as if the rate of evaporation was a cause of concern to him.

"I went to the funeral yesterday," Headmaster said. "Very nice. Although, I must say, two coffins in the one aisle were a bit much, even in this day and age."

"Sit down, Burnes," Mrs. Jencks suggested.

"Yes, yes, sit down, Burnes."

"Funeral, sir?"

"Good heavens. I always start at the back of things. Comes from being a Latin scholar, my wife used to say. She's dead, too, of course."

"Sorry, sir."

"Years ago. Do enough Latin and see what happens to you. Begin starting everything at the wrong end."

"Sir?"

"Latin's the curse of the English school system. Never understand why your honored parents keep expecting us to ladle it out. They conquered Britain, you know."

"Our parents, sir? Did they need to?"

"The Romans. Why should we spend centuries learning the language of a bunch of beasts we spent centuries throwing off the yoke of? Tell me that."

"I'll look it up, sir."

"I daresay if the Germans conquer us, two thousand years from now English schoolboys will be translating *Mein Kampf* as reverently as they're made to swallow Caesar's *Gallic Wars* today. It's all the same bully rubbish, you see."

"I see, sir."

Mrs. Jencks cleared her throat. "Very instructive, sir. I'm sure."

"People wonder why I accepted the position of Headmaster of Wolsley School, ur..."

"Indeed I did, sir."

"...ur. What's your name?"

"Robby Nose, sir."

"Burnes, Headmaster."

"Burnes, yes, of course. The funeral. I accepted the position of Headmaster simply to get away from the teaching of Latin. Can you understand that?"

"Oh, yes, sir."

"How many times can a British subject read the reports of legions of Roman jackanapes marching up and down our green hills, laying waste our villages, slaughtering our young males and despoiling our virgins?"

"I haven't read that book yet, sir."

"No. And it's a jolly good thing you're not going to. You're off to America this afternoon, and the best thing about America is they've never been conquered and therefore have no regard for anyone's language, including the one they pick-pocketed from us. You'll never have to know Latin in America, lad. Or English."

"Sir?"

"Is he sniffling, Mrs. Jencks?"

"I think he's confused, sir, what with the Romans and all."

"Your parents, Burnes. Their London house was in Mayfair?"

"Yes, sir. Mayfair."

"A direct hit. Damned foolish of them, too, I might say. If they ever conquer Britain, they'll want those Mayfair houses, mark my words."

"Who, sir? The Romans?"

"Am I not being clear, Mrs. Jencks?"

"It's the shock, Headmaster. It takes a moment."

"Ah, well, yes. Cheer up, Burnes. Things could be worse, you know. You could have been at home with your honored parents getting bombed instead of enjoying the safety, the staunch peace, the security we provide here at Wolsley School."

"Thank you, sir."

"Any questions?"

"Give him half a moment, Headmaster. He'll understand."

"Chapel," Headmaster said. "Must go do my Christian duty…"

Robby's eyes followed Headmaster's to the sherry decanter, then through the window to the chapel spire. Robby looked at the school emblem on the wall behind Headmaster's desk and at the desk itself. He then studied the threadbare carpet on the floor.

"Are my parents dead, sir?"

"Yes."

"I see, sir. Thank you, sir."

"A bomb. I passed the ruins of your home yesterday, in the taxi on the way to the funeral."

"There was a camera in my room, sir. I got it last birthday. Mums made me leave it home."

"What's he saying, Mrs. Jencks?"

"Something about a camera, Headmaster. But he's not sniffling."

"That's good."

"Did you happen to see my camera?"

"Rubble, my boy, all rubble. Pladroman House is rubble. End of an era and all that. Funeral yesterday."

"Why didn't I go to the funeral?"

"Lord, no place for a tadpole. All that sniffling going on. Press photographers buzzing about, trying to catch someone with her hanky down."

"Sir?"

"Yes, Burnes?"

"Deepest jungle or frozen tundra?"

"I don't get you, my lad."

"You said I'm going to America."

"Yes. You're being evacuated. Cheer up. Plenty of chocolate in America. No Latin."

"But am I going to the deepest jungle or the frozen tundra?"

"I don't know. Never been either place. Never been to America at all. You're going to an uncle in New York."

"But, sir?"

"Yes?"

"I haven't an uncle in New York."

"Of course you have."

"I have a grandaunt, in Scotland."

"Several of us decided yesterday in a meeting after the funeral that you have an uncle in New York. Name of...let me see...Lowry. Thadeus Lowry. Must be an uncle somewhere on your mother's side. A newspaper publisher, someone said. Probably publisher of *The New York Times*. Anyway, that's where you're going."

"Yes, sir."

"Safekeeping."

"Yes, sir."

"There's my brave lad," said Mrs. Jencks.

Headmaster said: "The Evacuation Lady is coming for you at noon. Mrs. Jencks will help you pack while the other tadpoles are in class. We try our best, you know, to keep the war away from the tadpoles at Wolsley School. One only gets to enjoy childhood just so long. Tuition refund will be made to your family's solicitors."

"Thank you, sir."

"Now I really must go and give Chapel."

Thus it was Robert James Saint James Burnes Walter Farhall-Pladroman, S.Nob., found himself seated on his cardboard suitcase the other side of the groundskeeper's lodge at ten o'clock in the morning, as shunted from his mates' view as World War Two itself.

Robby thought of the camera he had never gotten to use. The two coffins in the church aisle. Would his mother have liked the flower arrangements? Mr. Colmap, the butler, would not appreciate the silverware he had polished all those years ending up in rubble. Cook probably wanted to grab her favorite saucepan when she heard the noise of the bomb. Boots was as lucky as Robby to be away from the house when it received a direct hit. Boots was in France with the army. Nanny would not have liked falling down through the whole height of the house in her nightgown. It would have scared her.

Safely out of view of Wolsley School and of everyone left in the world who knew him, Robert James Saint James Burnes Walter Farhall-Pladroman, S.Nob., discovered himself sniffling. All these people who had been good to him were dead. No longer alive. No longer to be seen, heard, smelled, touched. Never.

At first, Robby tried rubbing from his face that offending sniffling instrument, his nose. Then his hands seemed better employed as fists stuck in his eyes to dam the water which wanted out through them. All the rhetoric that had resounded in his head these eight years past—and which he had always supposed had been instilled in his head for just such a moment as this—bounced from one side of his head to the other, trampolined in his throat to hit the roof of his skull. The clearest maxims collided, wrestled with each other, broke each other into a jumble of disjointed syllables. They needed clarifying now. The water which is tears cannot be contained, even by fists. For a long while, the heel of one hand dammed an eye, the other hand rubbed his sniffler; for another long while, the heel of the other hand dammed his other eye, and the hand that had failed so miserably at eye-damming was set to the task of sniffler obliterating. Robby wondered if it might be just such sad exercise that made noses grow, and thus distinguish us.

Robby had missed breakfast. Mightily he came to miss luncheon. Fiercely he came to miss tea.

The Evacuation Lady arrived alone at dusk in a Morris Minor with the news that they were late and had to drive straight through to Southampton, if Robby were to make his ship for America on time.

Voraciously, he missed his supper.

However, by the time the Evacuation Lady arrived, Robby was no longer sniffling. His two eyes and his nose had ceased their mad competition for the attention of his fists. The center of his attention, the center of his being, had slipped millimeters toward his mouth. A single piece of Resounding Rhetoric had won the jumble in his brain. His upper lip was stiff.

2
Water Is Crossed and Thadeus Lowry Is Met

A lifetime later (or so it seemed to him), Robby found himself sitting on his suitcase on a misty, blowing dock in New York Harbor. He had been sitting there since before dawn. Of course he had missed breakfast, and of course he had missed lunch. The past ten days his relationship with food had become strained. He had seen food seldom, and what food he had seen had parted from him quickly. He no longer *missed* his meals; he was simply hungry.

H.M.S. *Scaramouche* had waddled into the harbor at three in the morning. She leaned, wheezing and sagging, against the dock as if hoping never to be asked to confront the sea again. The evacuated children were roused *en masse* for the last time, put together with their belongings, shouted into a double line and marched, slipping, stumbling, staggering down the gangplank, half asleep in the dark. Women with clipboards, in charge of sorting them out, awaited them on the dock. Robby was identified as someone to be picked up by a Mr. Thadeus Lowry. Mr. Thadeus Lowry was paged. Mr. Thadeus Lowry was not present. Robby was told to "Go over there, dear, and sit on your suitcase, out of harm's way," which he did. Other names were paged and women came forward from the group waiting on the dock: women in fur coats, women in cloth coats, women in nuns' habits. Each greeted a child, or two, or three, and took her, or him, or them, off with her, doubtlessly to warm rooms and steaming breakfasts. Men, too, took some children: a man in a homburg, a man in a fedora, two men in yarmulkes. None identified himself as Thadeus Lowry. Each found it possible to leave the dock without Robby Burnes.

After the sorting-out apparently had been fully accomplished, a lady with a clipboard walked over to Robby, said, "You're Burnes, right? Waiting for Mr. Lowry?" The clipboard had told her so. "He must be delayed. Send him to me when he arrives. I'll be in that little office over there."

Robby's eyes followed her to a small, lit office on the side of the dock. Through the wide window he watched her sip a cup of coffee. He had never had coffee, having been assured by Nanny it would stunt his growth, and therefore did not want it now. He thought his recent diet had been sufficiently stunting.

So he sat on his suitcase, scratching at Pomfrey's name tag on a kneesock, then on Robby's left leg. The wind from under the dock whipped up his short pants. His overcoat was precisely the length of his trousers. His blazer was a few inches shorter. Both his overcoat and trousers stopped three inches above his knees, and six inches above the tops of his kneesocks. Schoolboy fashion at that time required that he have a cap, undervest and drawers, a shirt, necktie, blazer, overcoat, shoes, kneesocks and blue knees.

Buses and ambulances pulled onto the dock at dawn. Still keeping out of harm's way, Robby watched as the war wounded, some on stretchers, some on crutches, some hanging on others' shoulders, were unloaded from the ship. It was a silent operation. Except for the wind, and the engine of a bus or ambulance starting off, hundreds of people were moving, being moved on the dock, wordlessly, noiselessly. It took until well past noon to unload the wounded from the ship.

The first Evacuation Lady had taken Robby by car from Wolsley School to the train and then by train to H.M.S. *Scaramouche* in Southampton. "Poor tyke," she announced to the other passengers in the compartment as soon as the train began moving. "Orphaned by one of those nasty bombs. This is the Farhall-Pladroman boy, if you'd believe it. Burnes, they call him. You saw it in the newspapers. Pladroman House in London blown to smithereens. Just shows you: No matter how lucky you are…"

Round, regretful eyes in a row of six contemplated Robby and considered his luck. A lady in a gray tweed suit and heavy brown shoes gave him six ginger cookies she had wrapped in a handkerchief, then used the freed handkerchief to wipe her eyes and blow her nose. Being in public, as he was, Robby ate the ginger cookies more slowly than he wished.

At midnight, three new Evacuation Ladies were aboard ship, sorting things out. They busied themselves by continually referring to their clipboards and calling off names. Responding over and over, "Here, miss!" appearing to do absolutely no good, Robby finally crawled into a corner and slept. Later he was told that by doing so, he had missed several roll calls, sandwiches and warm milk.

In the morning, roll was called again, and again, and Robby admitted to his name again and again. A different and separate roll was called before oatmeal was ladled out.

"Why does everything on this ship smell of wet, rotten pine roots, miss?" asked an older boy.

"That's a disinfectant smell," the Evacuation Lady answered, "so we'll all stay healthy."

"Smells like a bloomin' groundhog's bloomin' parlor," commented the pithy lad. "I can hardly eat my mush, with the stink."

The Evacuation Ladies settled the children in two compartments, divided according to sex, except for someone named Palmerston who was clearly a boy but down on the clipboard as a girl and therefore kept getting shunted back and forth from compartment to compartment, and very shortly got himself put down on the clipboard as a discipline problem.

Sleeping arrangements aboard the *Scaramouche* had been designed with twenty-year-old infantrymen in mind. It took most of the children less time to fall out of the bunks than to climb into them. After the first night they all slept on the steel deck. Childish discussion had resolved that it was much less uncomfortable sleeping on the deck than landing on it time and time again.

It was the strategy of those who arranged the war to build ships as fast as possible to sink other ships even faster. The *Scaramouche*, built as a troop ship, probably between a Monday and a Thursday, undoubtedly had more downward speed than forward.

The survival of these Liberty ships depended greatly upon the strategies of their individual captains. Some captains developed complicated, zig-zag routes to get their ships safely across the water, and some of these ships survived. Other captains simply went in a straight line as fast as their ships could go, and some of these ships survived.

The captain of the *Scaramouche* had his own idea. He wallowed across the Atlantic. Thinking perhaps there was less chance of the ship being seen by the enemy if she were always in the troughs, he kept her broadside to every wave. Or perhaps he thought if he wallowed convincingly enough, with not much power coming from the engines, with no forward motion perceptible whatsoever, the enemies would think the *Scaramouche* already a struck, doomed ship and not spend a shell on her.

The *Scaramouche* survived too, but, if put to a vote, her passengers—the wounded, the evacuated, the Evacuation Ladies—most likely would have opted for a torpedo in the engine room and certain death in the North Atlantic.

The Evacuation Ladies ladled mush into the children, with milk, never spilling a spoonful from bucket to bowl. Yet within twenty minutes, every ounce would be on the deck, looking and smelling much the worse. Whatever the human body does to food, even in hastily rejecting it, does not improve it.

"Children, you must try not to get dehydrated. Now, everyone have a nice cup of warm water and we'll call the roll."

Even warm water is not improved by plunging into the intestines and coming to air again.

"My God!" one of the Evacuation Ladies was heard to mutter. "I didn't know what they really meant when they said these children were to be evacuated."

Some of the children, who, with great perspicacity, decided that part of the problem was caused by the continuous effort to take in food and water, abandoned the effort altogether. Still they stayed on their knees with the rest, vomiting boggy, pine-scented air.

The pithy older lad summed up for everyone by commenting finally, "His Majesty's vomit pit, that's what this is, miss."

Finally sitting on his suitcase on the wintry dock a meter above roiling New York Harbor, Robby Burnes reflected that before leaving Wolsley School, he really had seen his suitcase only once before—the day he left home for Wolsley School.

Nanny, sniffling, carrying the small, black, empty suitcase, appeared in the doorway of Robby's bedroom shortly after breakfast. She put it on the bed, and opened it.

Nanny was hugging Robby when Robby's mother appeared, carrying six school uniforms, including shirts, socks and ties in her arms. Five were to go into the suitcase; one was to be worn. Her disapproval of Nanny's expressions of sorrow made Robby's mother firmly cheerful.

"Here, here, now. Robby will love Wolsley School, won't he?"

Robby was studying the school emblem on the cap and on the blazer: a stag butting its head against an oak tree.

"Robby's been looking forward to going to Wolsley School ever so long now, hasn't he?"

Mothers, universally, when afraid of receiving an unsatisfactory answer, have a way of putting a question into the air. The air never answers, and thus equilibrium is maintained.

"How do you do the tie, Mums? I'll need to do it myself."

"Here, silly."

Robby's mother brought Robby to the mirror and taught Robby the Windsor knot. Thus, with loving hands, was one more colt bridled.

Robby's father stood in the library of Pladroman House, which is what he normally did while at home, awaiting the moment to go off and sit in the House of Lords.

"You're off, are you?" he said, brusque and clubby with his only son newly emblazoned with stags butting their heads against oak trees. "Building blocks behind, balls in front?"

"Yes, sir."

"Any patter at Pater before handing over the sovereign?"

"Yes, sir. I'd like to take my new camera to school. The one I got for my birthday."

"Ah!"

"Mums says I mustn't. Nanny says it will be on the mantel in my room when I get home for Christmas hols."

"I expect Mother's right. I'm sure your teachers won't want you running around snapping at them. Shy lot, teachers—especially in a strong draft."

He rubbed his hands together and then drew a gold sovereign from the pocket of his waistcoat.

"There we are, then." He handed it to Robby. "Traditions must be kept."

"Thank you, sir."

"A sovereign and a few words of wisdom from Pater. Deuced world we live in, Robby, especially at this moment. Your greatest joys, and your greatest hurts, will come from other people. Try to be interested in your fellow creatures, son, and try to be kind."

"Yes, sir."

"Off you go, now. I'll go upstairs and try to cheer up old Nanny."

On the dock Robby's hands were in his pockets for what warmth they provided. The fingers of his right hand were closed tightly around the sovereign.

During the morning the sole remaining Evacuation Lady had looked at him through the window of the dock shed several times. Robby had looked back. No further words had passed between them.

In what Robby knew must be the early afternoon, even for America, a portly man carrying a walking stick in a jaunty manner ambled onto the dock from the street. He stopped, looked this way and that along the cavernous, roofed dock. He apparently did not see the lit window of the little office. He approached Robby as the only animate thing in sight.

Half a meter from Robby, he crouched on his walking stick and peered into his face. "What are you?"

"Cold, sir."

The portly man had a puffy, red face, spotted with razor nicks and most veins showing.

"Did anyone ever suggest within your hearing you're a Robby Burnes?" the man asked.

"Yes, sir. That's what I am. A Robby Burnes."

"God love a goose." The man stood up for a fuller view. "Certainly your legs aren't long fellows."

"Are you my uncle, sir?"

"Did anybody say I am?"

"I think that's the expectation, sir."

"You're not at all what I was expecting, are you?"

"What were you expecting, sir?"

"Approximately nine paragraphs for the morning edition, easily written, gracing my byline, I," the man said rather archly, "go under no name but my own, and that name is Thadeus Lowry. Of *The New York Star*, I might add."

"You're to pick me up," Robby said.

"Pick you up?" said Thadeus Lowry. "Why would I do that?"

Thadeus Lowry's protruding eyes stared down at Robby and watched the boy shrug not once, but twice. Robby finally turned his head away and looked at the hull of the *Scaramouche* leaning against the end of the dock.

The Evacuation Lady, having spotted Thadeus Lowry through the window, approached.

"Are you Mr. Lowry?"

"I am," Thadeus Lowry said, turning himself and his walking stick in a half circle. "Thadeus Lowry of *The New York Star*."

"We tried to phone you at the newspaper. No one there seemed to know where you were." The Evacuation Lady straightened her hat. "In fact, some we talked to there didn't know who you are."

"You must have been talking to the advertising department," said Thadeus Lowry. "Those who sell space for the dollar feel my writing intrudes upon their displays offering hair restoratives."

"Well, if you'd come this way and sign forms…"

"Forms? For what?"

"For Burnes, here. He's an orphan, Mr. Lowry. Don't you understand? He's been evacuated from England."

Thadeus Lowry looked at Robby as if Robby suddenly had grown larger. "An orphan. Oh, yes."

"There's a war on, Mr. Lowry. We all have to do our bit."

"Oh. And what are you saying is my bit?"

The Evacuation Lady jerked her elbow toward Robby Burnes. "That's your bit. Take him along with you."

"Oh, yes," said Thadeus Lowry. "Take him along…"

"He's been here, you know, waiting for you since before dawn. The others were picked up before seven this morning."

"Ah. Well. You see, this way the boy and I will be able to appreciate a timely and leisurely lunch."

"Come into the shed."

Robby picked up his suitcase and followed them into the shed. The office was not much warmer than the dock.

The Evacuation Lady put a sheet of paper on a grimy counter and said, "Have you a pen?"

"Is a carpenter ever without his saw, or a plumber without his wrench? The answer to both questions, of course, as these poltroons of the lower classes are now paid by the hour, is yes. The pen, however, is the tool of my trade, and I know no hours."

"Apparently not. You're a reporter?"

"A man of letters, ma'am, a writer, a journalist…"

"Would you sign the forms, please?"

"Let me see, now: Robert Burnes, male, age eight, English, good God," said Thadeus Lowry, looking down at Robby, "is that all they have to say for you? They ask me to acquit myself little better. Married, yes, American citizen, yes; yes, I promise to run him 'round to the post office to get him stamped English, send him to school, keep him out of the pool room, provide him with clean hankies…" Thadeus Lowry's voice dwindled as he signed the paper with a large hand.

Putting his pen back into his pocket, he said more loudly to the Evacuation Lady, and more precisely: "And now, where is his leash?"

3
Penetrating the Frozen Tundra by Foot

"What a journalist needs most, Burnes, is a good set of legs."

Thadeus Lowry, his walking stick preceding him, and Robby Burnes, running behind, dragging his black suitcase, set off briskly from the customs shed into America. As they stabbed and dragged their way along the sidewalk several taxicabs passed, honking their horns, their drivers shouting through their windows offers of quick, warm, comfortable transportation. The mist had turned to light, blowing snow.

"Am I to be a journalist then, sir?"

"I should certainly hope so," said Thadeus Lowry into the wind, "if you take proper advantage of being under my influence. There's no higher estate to which one may aspire. We're all reporters, one way or another, in life. We'll turn up this street. But only those of us who make a fine art of observation and have good legs are privileged to be employed as the minds and the hearts of The People, as journalists."

"Observation, sir?"

"Observation and legs: the foundation and erection of a noble career in journalism. Look at The People, young Burnes. A story in every one of them. Up this way."

"Look at all the taxicabs, sir."

"Things aren't so easy in England just now, are they? Around this corner."

Robby's legs were still wobbly from his sea voyage. His school shoes were not much good on the frozen slime of the sidewalks. His suitcase was as heavy and as disobedient hanging from his left arm as from his right. And the only area of his body which was partly warm was the section of his left leg being abraded by Pomfrey's kneesock's name tag.

"I daresay you'd like some lunch."

"I'd like anything, sir."

"Something warming."

"Yes, sir."

"Melted cheddar cheese over crackers. A mug of chowder. A warm egg sandwich in the fist. Just the morning for it."

"It's afternoon, sir."

"I know a place just up this street."

After another block or two, Thadeus Lowry opened a recessed brown door. Flashing red neon lights on each side of the door warned MEN ONLY.

Thadeus Lowry was holding the door open. Inside was darkness. The same smell of wet pine-tree disinfectant and vomit emanated from the darkness as had from the ship.

"Is this place called Men Only, sir?"

Thadeus Lowry pointed with his walking stick to three golden orbs stuck together, hanging over the door. "It's called The Three Balls," he said. "It's named after the entire Nazi High Command."

"But, sir, the signs say nothing about small boys."

"That," said Thadeus Lowry, "is because there is nothing to be said about small boys. Will you come in?"

The floor was a pentagonal tile. Green sawdust collected in piles and swirls on it.

Along the right-hand wall ran a tall, brown, wooden bar. A brass rail ran along its base. Half the men at the bar had one foot on the rail.

"Lowry!" shouted one of them. "Great story this morning. Great human interest."

"My byline wasn't in the morning newspaper," Thadeus Lowry said with dignity.

"That's what was so great about it," the man said. "In behalf of human interest, the editors threw your story in the wastebasket!"

Along the wall across from the bar were brown wooden booths with tables in them.

"Who've you got carrying your suitcase now, Thadeus?" asked a man breathing on Robby.

"This is Burnes. My bit for the war effort."

"He's rather short, Thadeus."

"I expect so. It's all right. I'll pay."

Thadeus Lowry raised his stick and called at someone over the bar.

"Solomon! A drink!"

A voice said, "What will you have, Mr. Lowry?"

"A double whiskey for me, please, and a proper Guinness for my friend here."

"What friend, Mr. Lowry?" said the voice. "Are you seeing the small, crawly things again?"

"My friend," said Thadeus Lowry, pointing his stick at Robby. "My friend. Down here."

"Can you spell your name backwards for me, Mr. Lowry?"

"Solomon, if you'd just look over the bar, you'd see my friend. Indulge me this much."

The top of a head, eyeglasses, and a nose appeared over the edge of the bar and peered down at Robby.

"You see, Solomon? A person."

"He drinks Guinness?" asked the head.

"Never touches a thing stronger before lunch."

"He hasn't had lunch?"

"We're coming to that."

"It's quarter to three in the afternoon, Mr. Lowry."

"As long as you're bringing the drinks over to a booth," said Thadeus Lowry, "you might save yourself a truss by bringing me two double whiskeys."

"And two Guinnesses?"

"And two Guinnesses."

"And how many straws?"

After Thadeus Lowry had hung his overcoat and his hat on a peg and propped his walking stick against a wall, he conducted Robby to a booth.

Robby continued wearing his overcoat, as he had since leaving Wolsley School.

"Is this a gentlemen's club, sir?"

"Yes," said Thadeus Lowry, looking at Robby carefully. "It is. In a way."

"And are all these gentlemen members?"

"They are. But in this country we call them regulars."

"Is it terribly difficult to get into a club like this?"

"Allow me to explain," said Thadeus Lowry. "In England, the expression is, you have to stand for a club. In America, being more of a democracy, all you have to do to be admitted to a place like this is to stand."

"You mean: stand up?"

"Yes. That's what I mean. Things are more democratic here."

"Is your newspaper office near here?"

"Not far, not far. We'll go there after lunch. Ah, here's lunch."

On Solomon's tray were two glasses of whiskey, the two glasses of beer, and a bowl of chowder crackers.

Solomon waited at the edge of the table until Thadeus Lowry paid him.

"This is the American bookkeeping system," said Thadeus Lowry. "Nothing on the cuff. Simplifies things."

"It's the only way of getting paid regular," said Solomon, thus allowing Robby to understand why the club members were called *regulars*. "I brought you some *hors de saison*," Solomon said, pushing the bowl of chowder crackers nearer to Robby.

Thadeus Lowry saluted Solomon's back and drained one of the glasses of whiskey. "Now I'll show you how to drink the Guinness." He took one of the glasses of stout, drained it, wiped his mouth with the back of his hand, looked at Robby and said, "Ah, the first drink of the day. Makes sleeping late worthwhile."

Robby was eating the chowder crackers by the fistfuls. "Is that why you missed the boat, Mr. Lowry? You slept late?"

" 'Missed the boat!' I never missed the boat in my life. A true journalist, Robby, strong in the thigh and quick of eye, never misses a story within his purview."

"Am I a story, sir?"

Thadeus Lowry sipped from his second glass of whiskey. "There was a moment, there, when I thought you might be. Why else would I have shown up at the dock this morning?"

"You didn't, sir. You showed up at the dock this afternoon. Everyone else showed up this morning."

"A story, Robby, doesn't happen until a journalist arrives."

"Yes, sir."

"You must learn these things, if you're to take advantage of my influence upon you."

"Yes, sir."

"I received a cable, from London, saying, 'Meet Robby Burnes, H.M.S. *Scaramouche*, New York,' etc., etc. The spelling of your name puzzled me, somewhat, your extra *E* in Burnes, but then again the cable company had managed to spell New York with three *A*'s. Now, I ask you, what journalist in his sane mind wouldn't put in an appearance having received such a cable? As a journalist, Robby, one must consider the best uses of one's valuable time. At best, I reasoned, a dead poet would appear; at worse, a smokeable cigar. A story. You must always think in terms of the story, Robby."

"You're not my uncle, sir."

"Hardly likely," said Thadeus Lowry. "I had only one sibling I knew of, a sister. An impatient child, she was crushed by an ice-cream wagon at the age of six. Story was she was in a mortal rush for a chocolate ripple cone."

"Honorary uncle, sir? Lots of lads have 'em."

"My name must have entered your life, somewhere, been mentioned somehow in your family's progress. Of course, it's entirely possible your parents were admirers of my journalism, perceived my wit, wisdom, sagacity, and agreed between themselves that, should anything befall them, the best thing that could happen to their son would be to be brought up under my tutelage."

"I don't think my parents read *The New York Times*, sir."

"Actually, I don't write for *The New York Times*. I write for *The New York Star*. *The Star* is somewhat smaller than *The Times*, but a livelier newspaper. It has a reputation for attracting the more imaginative writers."

"Is *The New York Star* read in London, sir?"

"Who knows how far the written word flies? Sagacity cannot be confined within borders."

"Could there be some other explanation, sir?"

The redness of Thadeus Lowry's face had increased greatly since coming into the warmth of The Three Balls after his brisk walk in the snow from the dock. His eyes, coursing over the various glasses on the table, had softened. He reached into a pocket. "One thing you can say for your family's attorneys is that they do not fritter away your shillings by being garrulous in a transatlantic cable."

Thadeus Lowry unfolded a yellow rectangle of paper and read from it. " 'Meet Robby Burnes, H.M.S. *Scaramouche*, New York.' It's addressed to me at *The Star*, and it's signed 'Pollack, Carp and Fish, Solicitors.' " Thadeus Lowry dropped the sheet of yellow paper onto the wet table. "Someone at Pollack, Carp and Fish has missed a wonderful career as a headline writer. Or maybe they have T. S. Eliot on retainer to do their cables for them. I could have used a column or two of information. At least a sidebar. And note if you will, young Robby, the cable does not conclude with the usual, forward-looking phrase, *Letter following*. In truth, it doesn't even indicate—at least to the guileless and unwary—*Boy following*."

Robby did not pick up the cable. He said, "Our house was bombed."

"While you were away at school?"

"Yes."

"Good for you. Is that your school uniform?"

"Yes, sir."

"I like the school emblem," Thadeus Lowry said, looking at Robby's cap. "How many years has that moose been sharpening his horns against that tree?"

"Is that what it means, sir? No one ever said. The school is three hundred years old. We're celebrating this year with a special Games Day."

"Sounds drafty."

Robby picked up the cable from where it had been lying wet in a beer ring and handed it back to Thadeus Lowry.

"I've been left in your charge, sir."

Thadeus Lowry studied the cable further. "H.M.S. *Scaramouche* is clearly a ship. Normally, it would have been a simple matter to look up ship arrivals in *The New York Star*, and thus find when, and particularly where, the self-same *Scaramouche* was to dock, but something Pollack, Carp and Fish failed to realize, in their red-hot desire for terseness, is that that sort of information, concerning the comings and goings of ships, is not published information in these dark days of World War Two. It took my best reportorial instincts until late last night to discover against which dock, out of seven thousand miles of New York docks, the *Scaramouche* would nestle this morning. Throughout this entire intellectual exercise, the thought never entered my head—not once—that a small boy was being sent to me for safekeeping."

"I feel rather dizzy, sir."

"I am similarly overwhelmed."

"My stomach, sir. And my head."

"Drink up your stout," said Thadeus Lowry, quaffing the last of his whiskey. "Lots of vitamin P. The thing is," he said, "lots of you children are being shipped over to dodge the bombs."

"You don't have bombs here?"

"Only those we set ourselves. They're all right, if you're careful where you step."

"I'll be careful, sir."

"I spent a few days with an Englishman, once," Thadeus Lowry ruminated. "And got decorated for it. Maybe the occasion meant more to him than it did to me." Thadeus Lowry signalled Solomon for more service. "Allow me to explain."

4
Thadeus Lowry Offers an Explanation

"Twenty-five years ago," Thadeus Lowry explained, his fingers warming a fresh, iced double whiskey, "when I was not that much older than you, it now seems, although three times your size and doubtlessly possessing ten times your wisdom, there was another world war raging—a war now referred to as the First World War, as if we plan a steady succession of them, which probably we do. At that time it was called the Great War; some benighted politician referred to it as 'the war to end all wars.' It wasn't great, in the preferred definition of the word—it was nasty and mean and stupid, and nothing nasty, mean and stupid can be great. It wasn't the war to end all wars, either, as present evidence indicates. In fact, it (and its settlement) went a long way toward causing the present altercation. It will be a lark, I expect, to see what the present war causes."

In the big brown booth of The Three Balls Tavern, Robby Burnes began to feel warm and drowsy. Thadeus Lowry's voice was a sonorous, gravelly growl. Listening to himself, he smiled at certain points he made, and at certain pleasing, well-lathed phrases.

"You see, no civilized adult really likes the young. Whenever you have a universal consensus on such topics as *the loveliness of youth* you know profound feelings run dialectically opposite. The young human being is like a kitten: Everyone thinks kittens are cute and one should have one, but, as the kitten grows and gets older and reveals more and more of its own cold, churlish, independent, insolent, destructive, demanding, and otherwise quite human nature, the more one devises ingenious means to get rid of it. Notice what happens to the human child: Immediately it begins to assert itself, yowling and thrashing, it is put behind bars in something called a crib, or a playpen; as soon as it is able to escape the playpen successfully, it is imprisoned in a building, usually made of stone, brick or concrete, called a school; and once the child grows to the point where school can no longer physically or intellectually confine it, and its own human nature becomes frighteningly assertive, adults arrange a war for it, and off it is sent to destroy itself and other youth. Nothing threatens older people more than the existence of youth. If you ever meet an adult, my boy, who genuinely loves the young and does not fear and resent youth at all, if not murderously, send him or her to me, and I'll see to it a statue is raised in his or her image.

"It was this revelation which allowed me, in all good conscience, to desert."

Thadeus Lowry, smiling, swallowed a fair portion of his drink.

Robby asked, "Aren't deserters shot, sir?"

"Under circumstances then prevailing"—Thadeus Lowry smacked his lips with his tongue like an old cat—"everyone was being shot. Every day, sometimes twice a day, with our officers' handguns at our backs, we were forced to rush forward into the rifles of our enemies. The enemies would push us back with their bayonets. We would go five trenches forward and five trenches back. In the stink and the dust and the smoke of the battle I came to recognize in which trench I was by the bodies in it. I was only sure time was passing in this nightmare by the decomposition of these same bodies—each time I jumped back into a trench, the flesh of these bodies separated more easily from the bone.

"Now, at twenty, one is willing to put up with anything for a while—which is why wars are possible.

"However, after days of this back and forth I aged to the point where I realized there were no grown-ups in these trenches, no one very old at all, no politicians, statesmen, church leaders, captains of industry or officers over the age of twenty-five. There were none of that generation who staunchly had erected the issues, drawn the lines of contention, given the speeches of denouncement and uttered the challenges. In those trenches were youth whose faces had been shot off before being permitted to say anything.

"So, one morning, in a lovely acrid fog, in a comparative silence, with no one pushing me forward or back at the moment, the *we* became *I*. I climbed out of my trench and, hands in pocket, head down to avoid stumbling on felled youth, I walked north.

"After only two or three hours of walking there was a puff of wind, enough to raise the fog like a lady's dress, and I saw a small, stone village. I entered it. The windows of the houses and stores were shuttered. The village appeared abandoned. But I smelled food cooking. I followed my nose to a red plank door, and knocked on it.

"A voice from inside said, '*Entrez! Willkommen! Ich dien!* Come in!' Deciding that anyone who could issue such an invitation, in those languages, under those circumstances, was a man who had made similar peace with himself, I entered without hesitation.

"Inside this cottage, there was a tall, skinny Englishman in an apron standing between a stove and a kitchen table. He gave my muddy uniform a perfunctory eyeing, and said, 'I've just basted the lamb. About to attack the potatoes and onions. Do you know what to do with turnips? Here, a glass of this will make you a more amiable dinner companion.'

"He poured me out a cognac, and brought it to me. I said, '*Mort a guerre*,' and drank it down.

"'*Mort a guerre*,' he said.

"We had lamb basted in *rosé*, potatoes and onions basted in *blanc*, turnips basted in cognac. A meal to remember. You can have no idea how great that meal tasted."

"Are there more biscuits, sir?"

"We kept a fire going on the grate. We ate until we could eat no more, slept, ate some more, rested. We didn't talk much—left the fighting to the soldiers and the talking to the politicians. Ah, you can't imagine what a time that was."

"There's Mr. Solomon now, sir. He might have some more biscuits."

"We spent three or four days there, eating, sleeping, being warm. *Death to the war*."

"It sounds a very good supper, sir."

Rousing himself slightly from his nostalgia for past comforts,

Thadeus Lowry said, "Within three or four days our own British and American armies caught up with us and were most pleased at our having pacified this village ahead of their advance. We were each sent back to our general headquarters, highly decorated, and sent home to heroes' welcomes." Thadeus Lowry laughed. "To answer your earlier question, young Robby Burnes: Armies have a far greater need to acknowledge heroes than deserters."

"My father was decorated during World War One," Robby said. "For capturing a forward village almost single-handedly."

"That was the only Englishman I ever really knew," Thadeus Lowry continued. "If you can say spending a few days with someone eating, drinking, resting, makes for true acquaintance. For obvious reasons, we did not correspond. We both accepted our decorations, I expect, with the silence of due modesty."

His glass of whiskey finished, Thadeus Lowry sat back in the booth, and said, "A tale as good as any other, sufficiently ironic and spotted with proper moral instruction for the young—but I don't see the connection between that Englishman in France, and you. He had sort of an Italian name, as I remember, Romani, or Something-Roman…"

"Pladroman?"

"Yes," Thadeus Lowry said, his voice still somewhat absent. "That was it. Pladroman."

"My father's the Duke of Pladroman," Robby Burnes said.

On the table, Thadeus Lowry's hand jerked and knocked over an empty beer glass.

"That's all right," Robby rushed to say. "We're not royal. Just noble."

He set the glass upright.

"What the hell's the son of a duke?" Thadeus Lowry shouted. "A count? A baron? A marquis? What's the son of a dead duke?"

Robby lowered his eyes. Regulars at the bar had turned to stare at them. "An S.Nob., sir."

"God love a goose!" Thadeus Lowry's eyes were suddenly as tall and wide as if he were seeing heaven open before him. "You're a story!"

5
Advent

"We have plenty of time to catch the first edition," Thadeus Lowry announced after glancing at his pocket watch, which he did after he had put on his hat and his overcoat and picked up his walking stick.

Outside The Three Balls, the wind had increased its bluster. There were two inches of snow on the sidewalks and streets.

"A brisk walk 'round to the office," Thadeus Lowry said, "will help settle lunch."

However, even with the aid of his walking stick, Thadeus Lowry fell against the wall of the recessed doorway when the wind blew the door against him. He grabbed his hat and almost lost his footing.

"You must be tired," he said to Robby, once he had collected himself.

Robby hung onto his suitcase so he wouldn't blow away in the wind.

"There's a cab, now." Thadeus Lowry raised his walking stick to an approaching taxi as if anointing it.

Robby walked into the backseat, dragging his suitcase with him, and sat in the far corner. Through the open door, he watched Thadeus Lowry apparently proceeding to sit down in the street. He was holding his hat on his head against the wind with one hand, his walking stick into the wind with the other. At a certain point in his crouching, when his hat was below roof level, he backed up suddenly and landed cater-cornered on his back on the seat of the taxi.

"The offices of *The New York Star*," Thadeus Lowry spoke up to the driver. "I have a story to write."

"Close the door, willya, Mac?"

"My feet are still out."

"You're in charge of 'em, arncha?" the driver asked.

Thadeus Lowry finally got himself upright on the seat, his hat deeply in place, scrunching his ears, his walking stick between his knees.

Thinking that somewhere in the world there might actually be melted cheddar cheese over crackers, a mug of chowder, and a warm egg sandwich—that such images had not risen entirely from Thadeus Lowry's imagination—Robby tried to complete the image by confirming, "You have a wife, Mr. Lowry?"

"I have," said Thadeus Lowry. "But you won't like her."

"I see, sir."

"She drinks too much," opined Thadeus Lowry, "and cooks too little."

The taxi began to pass department stores with large, brightly lit windows. Robby looked at the Christmas displays. In one window was a manger with Mary and Joseph and the infant, Jesus, and the three adoring Magi. In the next was a lady in a red bathing suit trimmed with white fur.

"Sir?"

"Yes, Robby?"

"Will I grow up in America?"

"No."

"I won't, sir?"

"No one grows up in America."

"What, sir?"

"In America people don't grow up. They just get bigger."

"Yes, sir."

The air of Thadeus Lowry's belch made the atmosphere of the taxi similar to that of The Three Balls Tavern.

"Well," Thadeus Lowry said with contentment. "That was the best interview I've had since this blasted war started. We'll get a good story out of it, never fear. Need a photographer. Put your hat on straight."

"Yes, sir."

The taxi slid sideways to a stop at a red light.

"How does the driver know which red lights to stop at?" Robby enquired. "He drives past most of them."

"Like everyone else in America," intoned Thadeus Lowry, "our driver is an executive. He makes executive decisions instead of doing his job."

On the sidewalk, a Salvation Army band was playing "O, Little Town of Bethlehem."

"Now that," said Thadeus Lowry, nodding through the window toward the band, "is a perfect example of an exception that proves a rule. No matter how much a Salvation Army band plays, it never, never gets better. Practice, in their case, does not make perfect. In fact, it appears to do no good whatsoever. Perhaps if they would take their minds off the serenity of God, and demonstrate mercy for the ears of the general populace, we would all smile more benignly upon them."

The taxi slid forward again.

The sidewalks, and most of the street, were clogged with people carrying gaily wrapped Christmas packages.

"Goddamned people," said the driver. "Why don't they all fall down the sewer?"

"Some of us," sniffed Thadeus Lowry, "apparently already have."

"You bein' wise, mister?" Driving forward, the taxi at an angle to more sedate traffic, the driver fixed Thadeus Lowry, through the rear-view mirror, with a hard stare. "You don't like my cab? You can walk."

"I don't like your cab," said Thadeus Lowry. "And I shall not walk."

"Any more your lip," screamed the driver, "I'll give you a shot in the mouth."

" 'Don't Tread On Me,' " said Thadeus Lowry, fluttering one gloved hand in the air.

A line of nine Christmas shoppers jumped in sequence back onto the sidewalk as the taxi ran through a red light and sprayed their knees with slush.

"Stupid sonsabitches," said the driver.

"Driver?" Thadeus Lowry began enquiringly. "Why aren't you at The Front?"

"I am in the front. What are you, stupid?"

"I said *at* The Front. Where the war is."

"Why aren't you at The Front, you lousy sonofabitch," the driver yelled at his rear-view mirror, "instead of running around in the snow with a little boy in short pants?"

"I'll have you know," announced Thadeus Lowry, with firmness and dignity, "I am a highly decorated veteran of World War One."

"Yeah?" The driver took a more comprehensive look at Thadeus Lowry through the rear-view mirror.

"Yeah."

"Whacha do?"

"I, together with the father of this lad here beside me, went behind enemy lines and held an entire town—just the two of us, mind you—for three days and three nights."

The driver whistled appreciatively through his teeth. "Wow."

"Therefore, I have every right, as a citizen, a taxpayer, and as a highly decorated war veteran, to ask you, an aggressive youth, why you are not at The Front."

"Aw," said the driver. "I have a bad knee."

He rubbed it.

"A bad knee, is it?"

"Terrible right knee. Hurt it when some clown ran his Ford into me just before the war."

"Then," said Thadeus Lowry conclusively, "be apprised that if it is, was, or becomes your intention to assault me once I get out of this cab, it is my intention to kick you in the right knee."

While the driver was staring at Thadeus Lowry through the rear-view mirror, his mouth slightly open, the taxi slid against the curb and bumped to a stop.

Through the windshield Robby saw a Santa Claus, who had been ringing a brass hand-bell on the sidewalk, look at the approaching taxi with alarm. He jumped back out of the way. The taxi's bumper nudged one leg of the tripod holding Santa's charity bucket. Dropping his bell on the sidewalk, Santa tried to catch his bucket. All the coins spilled out of the bucket and scattered in the slush of the gutter.

Santa Claus waved his fist at the taxi driver. "You sonofabitch!" yelled Santa Claus.

"What's that sonofabitch shouting at me for?" asked the taxi driver indignantly, his left hand going for the doorknob.

"That son of a bitch," said Thadeus Lowry, "is the Spirit of Christmas."

"Yeah? Well, I don't give a shit who he is. Nobody's gonna call me a sonofabitch!"

Through the snow-streaked windshield, Robby watched the taxi driver approach Santa Claus and hit him in the mouth.

"Thadeus Lowry!" Robby Burnes shouted. "The sonofabitch hit Santa Claus!"

Santa Claus was sitting on the sidewalk, feeling his mouth with a gloved hand.

"He did," agreed Thadeus Lowry.

The driver had turned back to get into the taxi when Santa Claus rose up from the sidewalk with murder in his eye. Blood dripped from his mouth onto his white beard. He took a long step and belted the taxi driver on the back of his head.

"Never," clucked Thadeus Lowry, shaking his head, "turn your back on the Spirit of Christmas."

The driver bounced off the hood of the taxi. He went after Santa Claus with both fists. Never, in Robby's peaceful weeks at Wolsley School, had he seen fists fly so fast.

"Thadeus Lowry, our driver is beating up Santa Claus! Do something!"

"You must be drunk," said Thadeus Lowry. "Otherwise you wouldn't want to get into it."

Fists and fur flying, the combatants sank out of sight below the hood of the taxicab.

"I suppose we ought to do something," said Thadeus Lowry. He began to get out of the cab. "Leave the meter running."

Robby ran around to the front of the taxi.

The taxi driver was sitting astride Santa Claus, snapping his head up and down on the street. Each time Santa Claus' head hit the street there was a splash of blood and slush. People were standing on the sidewalk, clutching their Christmas packages, watching.

In the middle of the street, Thadeus Lowry flagged another taxi with his walking stick.

"Somebody, please!" Robby cried. "Somebody please stop him! He's killing Santa Claus!"

"Robby! Robby Burnes!" In the middle of the street Thadeus Lowry held open the back door of another taxi. "Come on! I'm on deadline!"

Near blind with tears, Robby walked into the backseat of the taxi.

Thadeus Lowry entered as before, that is, after making his lap in the street.

"*The New York Star*," he announced loudly. "I have a story to write."

"Close the door," the driver said.

"My feet are still out."

Immediately the door was closed and Thadeus Lowry had regained his balance in general, he rolled down the window and shouted through it, "Kick him in the right knee!"

He rolled up the window and settled back in his seat, his walking stick once again between his knees. The taxi started off, at first sliding sideways through the snow.

"Ah, this is a cruel world," Thadeus Lowry observed. "A violent, heartless, indifferent orb." He handed Robby his handkerchief. "Hard it is, to keep childish illusions for long, in this indifferent world."

6
Thadeus Lowry Does a Day's Work

"I'll be ready to take you home in a minute," said Thadeus Lowry, "as soon as I write my story."

Being in the city room of *The New York Star* was rather like still being outside in the street. It was cold. It was dark. And it was noisy. It was a huge room with wet stone walls and a linoleum floor. The windows in the walls were as filthy gray as the snowing sky outside. The floor was strewn with crumpled balls of paper, through which paths had been trampled.

Men in green eyeshades were sitting at desks placed in no discernible order, banging on typewriters hard enough, one would think, to quell them for good. On each desk was a telephone. At any given moment, half the telephones were ringing. About half the ringing phones were being answered. Much noise came from teletypes and police radios along one wall, clattering and squawking like an unpaid chorus line.

In the front of the room, standing in the middle of a U-shaped desk, stood a white-haired, red-faced man shouting huskily at the room at large.

"O'Brien," he shouted. "Fire! Thirty-fourth and Seventh."

"Sanders! B and E, A and B at Sixth and Eighth!"

"Carson! Murder one male Caucasian at Central Park Zoo!"

The news did not disturb the men beating on their typewriters. Buffeted by fire and murder, the journalists' equanimity remained intact.

Thadeus Lowry sat at one of the light metal desks in the middle of the room.

"Are you going to write about the taxi driver beating up Santa Claus?" Robby asked.

"Fist fights aren't news," answered Thadeus Lowry, "unless people pay to see them. That's news."

Rapidly, he typed a line halfway down a sheet of paper.

"What is news, sir?"

"News is what sells newspapers. You're news."

"I, sir?"

"Aye, sir. I'll show you. Go find the men's room, wash your face and brush your hair. By the time you get back, I'll have a photographer here."

By the time Robby returned from the men's room, Thadeus Lowry had typed five pages.

"Sit down," he said. "A photographer will be right up."

So Robby again sat on his suitcase.

Thadeus Lowry was banging on his typewriter awfully hard, and awfully fast. Watching him, Robby realized shortly that Thadeus Lowry's desk was creeping forward. The bouncing of the typewriter, when struck, was making his desk move. Apparently unaware he was doing so, Thadeus Lowry kept hitching his chair forward in pursuit of his story and his desk. Robby looked around at where a man was working at a desk behind him. The space around his suitcase was getting narrower. Robby saw he was about to be squeezed between the two desks.

He picked up his suitcase, moved outside the impending accident area, sat down again, and watched. The desks closed on each other faster than Robby thought possible. They bumped against each other. The typing on each desk surface doubled the vibration on the other. The two desks were bouncing up and down together at a great rate.

Thadeus Lowry stopped typing. He studied the quivering surface of his desk.

The other man stopped typing and looked up angrily at Thadeus Lowry.

Thadeus Lowry screamed, "I told you not to put your desk against mine!"

"I have not moved this desk," screamed the other.

"Who did? Someone moved your desk!"

"Thadeus, you moved your desk!"

"I did not move this desk," said Thadeus Lowry with great certainty. "The desk has not moved."

He stood up and proceeded to push his desk away.

"I'm fed up with what you think is your scintillating sense of humor," said Thadeus Lowry. "If you keep distracting me with your childishness, I'll feed your toupee to a goat."

"Goddamn it," the other man said, giving his desk a violent shove to the left. "I don't know what your game is, Lowry, but if you've made me miss deadline, you'll go home without any teeth."

The two gentlemen of the fourth estate resumed reporting the world to the world.

A man with a camera wandered across the city room to Thadeus Lowry's desk.

"Who's this?" he asked, jerking his thumb at Robby. "The new managing editor?"

"He's an Army Air Corps colonel," said Thadeus Lowry. "He's flown sixty-four missions over Europe."

"I've been hearing our pilots are getting younger."

"Photos to the desk for first edition," said Thadeus Lowry. "Airbrush out the background."

"Anything you say, Tad." Crouching, the photographer was focusing his camera on Robby Burnes sitting on his suitcase. "I'll slug it AIR CORPS STILL FINDS WILLING YOUNG MEN."

"Slug it LOWRY-BURNES."

"I wish it were so."

"I'm not really in the Air Corps," Robby said to the photographer.

"I know, kid. You're really a foreign correspondent."

The photographer left and Thadeus Lowry finished writing before his desk caused another incident.

"Now," he said, putting his typewritten sheets in their proper order, "do you have photographs of your parents?"

"Yes, sir. In my wallet."

"Let me see them."

Robby had been wondering if Thadeus Lowry would like to see a picture of his old First World War friend.

Thadeus Lowry gave the photographs only a glance. "Mother… father…" he said. He clipped them to his folded typewritten sheets and dropped the whole bundle in a wooden box on a corner of the U-shaped desk.

"Let's go home," said Thadeus Lowry, putting on his overcoat.

"The pictures of my parents, sir. Will I get them back, sir?"

"Really, Robby," said Thadeus Lowry. "Journalism does demand its sacrifices, you know."

Passing the colleague whose desk had given Thadeus Lowry trouble, Thadeus Lowry said, "Bastard."

Outside the main door of *The New York Star*, the wind and snow assaulted them again.

"We'll have tea before continuing home," Thadeus Lowry said immediately. "You'd like that, wouldn't you?"

Robby remembered that Thadeus Lowry had said his wife drank much and cooked little. "Yes, sir."

The clock in the city room had read six twenty-five.

The snow was above the ankles of his kneesocks.

They crossed the street and entered an establishment remarkably similar to The Three Balls Tavern. The sign outside this establishment read MONKEY'S MEN ONLY.

A man put his glass on the bar and watched enquiringly while Thadeus Lowry ordered a double martini for himself and a Guinness for Robby.

"A short person is following you, Thadeus," the man said.

"Our bundle from Britain," said Thadeus Lowry. "My bit for the war. Fresh from the briny seas. Ours for safekeeping."

The man examined Robby with crossed eyes. "Can you squeeze a story out of him?"

"Already have. With illustrations. Read *The New York Star*."

"I write for it. Do I have to read it?"

"This is Robby Burnes," said Thadeus Lowry. "Mr. Ronald Jasper, our most esteemed police reporter."

"Robby Burnes?" asked Ronald Jasper. "Who could be verse?"

"Well, son." Gin drink firmly in one hand, Thadeus Lowry handed

Robby the glass of stout with his other. "Do you like journalism?"

"You keep nice hours, sir. My father sits at Lords later."

Ronald Jasper addressed the bartender loudly: "I'll have a drink on Thadeus Lowry! He finally got a story to write."

Thadeus Lowry put his elbows on the bar. His shoulders became round. "Ronald," he said, "I badly need a big story."

"You sure as hell do, Thadeus. You haven't had a big story since the Bishop stole the altar plate in 1938."

"A developing story," said Thadeus Lowry. "A big story that would keep the Thadeus Lowry byline on the front page every day."

"You're on such thin ice at the newspaper," Ronald Jasper said, "you must have water on the knee by now."

"I'd be perfectly happy to go out and wait on an iceberg, if only the *Titanic* could be counted on to sink again."

"That's a hard story to update, Thadeus."

"There must be someone left to interview—an obscure cabin boy, whose imagination is yet to go rampant."

"Nice thing about being a police reporter," Ronald Jasper said, testing his drink, "is that it's steady. Evil lurks constantly in the hearts of Man. You poor feature writers have to go find your own news."

"Maybe I could find a nice Nazi spy somewhere in New York who'd give me his story."

"I don't think they list themselves in the yellow pages, Thadeus."

"The war, the war, the goddamned war. *Mort à guerre.* Nothing makes the front page except the war."

"People are tired of the war, Thadeus. They're tired of reading about it, hearing about it, talking about it, thinking about it. They're even tired of escaping from it."

"What we need," said Thadeus Lowry, "is a good, juicy, sensational murder. Something to take the people's mind off the war for a few days."

"Who would read about a single murder, however sensational, with hundreds a day dying in Flanders Fields?"

"You're right," said Thadeus Lowry. "Individual murder pales next to universal carnage."

Standing on the brass rail, holding on to the raised edge of the bar with his elbows, Robby was eating from a bowl of peanuts.

"What we need is a heartwarming story," said Thadeus Lowry. "One that takes days to unravel. That involves the people, the reader. Tugs at his heartstrings. Allows him to do something. Allows him to be heroic at home by the fireside."

"A kidnapping," said Ronald Jasper. "What New York needs now is a good kidnapping."

"New York!" exclaimed Thadeus Lowry, brightening instantly. "The whole country needs a good kidnapping, Ronald! The whole world!"

Thadeus Lowry expanded physically to such a degree he knocked Robby off his precarious grip on the bar.

"A sensational kidnapping." Thadeus Lowry stepped so close to Ronald Jasper he stood on Robby Burnes' foot. "That kid actress," said Thadeus Lowry, "Shirley Temple. You don't happen to have the name of Shirley Temple's press agent, do you?"

"I don't think they'd go for it, Thadeus. They don't like that kid taking too much time away from the cameras."

"Maybe not, maybe not," said Thadeus Lowry.

He looked down at Robby Burnes. His protuberant eyes protruded even more. He blinked.

"Please, sir. You're stepping on my foot."

"The little bastard looks green, Thadeus."

"Do you think he might be sick?"

"He must be," said Ronald Jasper. "He looks like Eleanor Roosevelt appearing in public with Franklin."

"God love a goose, Ronald. What do I do?"

"I suggest we have a quick one, Thadeus, then you get him out in the air."

7
Held Up on the Way Home

"Homeward the weary workmen wend their way!"

Despite the six inches of snow soundproofing the abandoned streets and sidewalks of New York, Thadeus Lowry's voice echoed from the stone and brick walls on all sides. Stars were visible above the streetlights. Robby sucked in cold, clear air like long drafts of spring water. Thadeus marched on, snow whitening his cuffs, using his walking stick with a brisk beat.

After as many gulps of air as he could manage, to clear his head, to enable his feet to plow through the snow, Robby ran, the suitcase banging against either the front or the back of his right knee at every step, trying to keep up with the man in whose safekeeping he was.

"A brisk walk," Thadeus Lowry encouraged, "home to a nice, warm supper."

It was past eight o'clock.

"You do have a home, sir?" Robby asked with great uncertainty.

"In this city," Thadeus Lowry amended himself, "people do not have homes. Allow me to explain. They have apartments. A few rooms for which they pay endlessly, but never come to possess— pay for the sheer pleasure of running them into filthy, untenable condition before moving out and on."

Robby moved his legs as fast as he could so he wouldn't lose this new instruction, or this new instructor.

"This country is not yet settled," Thadeus Lowry continued, his voice barreling off solid walls on all sides of them. "It's a vast land dotted with impossible, temporary shelters, inhabited by wanderers —travelers from nowhere going nowhere, marking the calendar of their lives by moving days, leaving nothing in their paths but crumpled leases."

"An hotel, sir? Do you live in an hotel? Is that it, then?"

"Not a hotel. Apartment houses have none of the civilities of hotels: no man to greet you at the door; no boys to help you in with your bundles; no warm little bar tucked into a corner of the lobby to make your homecoming convivial—no staff at all, except for a congenital idiot who comes along once a week to dent your waste-baskets against the walls in the pretence that he is emptying them. Hotels, once considered cold shelter for the temporarily home-less, in transient America are the epitome of good living."

"A flat then, sir. Do you live in a flat?"

"Flat is the correct word. We live flat. Oppressed by steam heat. Rooms with walls nearer than we want them. Windows looking out on more walls. We live flat on the level of unembellished boredom. Insipidity as a way of life. Flat, indeed."

"And can you cook at all, sir?"

"By *cook* do you mean opening cans, ladling the contents—which are indiscernible from the contents of all other cans—into a saucepan and then drying out the synthetic garbage over the un-cleansing fire of a two-ring electric stove?"

"I mean preparing any food any how, sir."

"By *cook* do you mean to take what the butcher sells you at a vast price as meat but is less meat than you are gold dust—the frankfurter, ground bread packed in a pigskin casing; the ham-burger, the eyes and entrails of animals spotted with floor-sweepings; the great American steak, leather tightly stitched with dental floss —by *cook* do you mean to plop these flaps of the American life-style into a frying pan greased with oleomargarine, place over a burner until they shrivel to a size right for filling a tooth cavity?"

"Yes, sir. Anything at all like that, sir."

"No," Thadeus Lowry determined, stabbing his walking stick into the snow. "I would not *cook*."

"But your wife, sir. She *can* cook, can't she? I mean, if there were good reason to?"

"Does my wife share in the illusion common to American women that she provides meals? Yes. Occasionally she makes a contribu-tion to the Great American Dream and provides the appearance of a meal by ripping open packaged, prepared food."

"But will she, sir? Will she cook?"

"No."

At that moment they were crossing the end of an alley. They had crossed several before. Snow-capped rubbish barrels lined each side of the alley entrance.

From this alley stepped a man. He blocked their way. He wore a bulky jacket. His hat almost entirely obscured his eyes and ears.

His hands were in his coat pocket.

Gruffly, he said, "Into the alley, mister, and shuddup. Face the wall and lean your hands against it over your head."

"What is this?" shouted Thadeus Lowry as if sincerely in doubt.

Even Robby had read of Robin Hood and knew the goals of such people who interrupt others on the road.

"It's highway robbery, sir!" Robby dropped his suitcase in the snow and threw his hands into the air. "Stand and deliver!"

"Charlie McCarthy's right, Edgar Bergen," said the short thug. "It's a stick-up."

Thadeus Lowry, his stick at parade rest, remained unmoving. He was looking at the thug with pure incredulity.

"I have no intention of standing for this," he stated, "or of delivering anything whatsoever."

Robby, reaching for the moon, felt his fingers get even colder.

"Into the alley, you big-nosed balloon," said the thug. "I have a gun."

"He has a gun, sir. He says he has a gun."

"This," announced Thadeus Lowry, "is Tootsie's corner!"

The thug jerked his head up and looked into Thadeus Lowry's face.

"Tootsie? You know Tootsie?"

"I am Thadeus Lowry of *The New York Star*," intoned Thadeus Lowry of *The New York Star*. "I know everybody."

"How do you know Tootsie?"

"We met on jury duty," announced Thadeus Lowry, "in 1934. After Tootsie used up his *per diem* and was really down on his luck, couldn't talk to a bookie anywhere, I told him I had observed this corner was available. I believe he has done well, over the years, mugging people on this corner. What, young man, are you doing on it?"

"So you're Thadeus Lowry."

"Of *The New York Star*."

"Nice to meetcha, Thadeus, nice to meetcha." The thug began withdrawing his hand from his jacket pocket, possibly to shake hands with Thadeus Lowry.

Thadeus Lowry swung his cane with remarkable force and accuracy through the air and against the thug's head. A swish and a *thwunk*. The thug's cap went into the snow. He raised his empty hands to his head, but did not touch it.

His knees buckled.

He knelt in the snow.

"I asked you," shouted Thadeus Lowry, leaning over him, "how you have the gall, the audacity to work Tootsie's corner?"

The thug sat on his heels, and then leaned forward. His bare hands groped for hard ground beneath the snow to support himself.

Thadeus Lowry struck him on his back with the walking stick.

"Where's Tootsie? What have you done with him?"

"Stop it, willya, mister?"

Thadeus Lowry caned the man's back again.

"I said I have a gun! You'd better watch out," protested the man doubled over in the snow. "I might use it!"

"Do you really have a gun?"

"Yeah. You think I'm a liar?"

"Where is it?"

"In my pocket."

Sitting on his heels, it took the thug a moment to rummage the gun out of his pocket. With it came a packet of chewing gum, a pencil stub and a house key. He held the gun in the flat of his hand. He looked distastefully at it. He blew the lint off it.

Blood was dripping from his ear.

"Where's Tootsie?" Thadeus Lowry demanded.

"In Florida. At the horse races. He goes every year, this time."

Robby's hands were still up. His eyes were wide at the sight of the handgun.

"I had forgotten that." There was a touch of apology in Thadeus Lowry's voice. "Tootsie's winter vacation at Hialeah."

"You're some Edgar Bergen," said the thug.

"Even if Tootsie's away," questioned Thadeus Lowry, "who says you can take over his corner?"

"He did."

"Who did?"

"Tootsie! Tootsie did."

"Why should I believe that?"

"You afraid I might muscle Tootsie out of his corner?"

"The thought had occurred to me."

"I wouldn't do that."

"How do I know that?"

"Tootsie's my uncle, for Pete's sake. He said I could work his corner while he's south for Christmas playing the horses."

"Are you Minnie's boy?"

"Yeah, yeah."

"How is she?"

"She's fine. I'll tell her you asked."

"Still and all," said Thadeus Lowry, possibly trying to justify his having thrashed Minnie's boy, the thug, "how do I know you'll give Tootsie back his corner when he returns?"

"I'm only home for Christmas. I'm in the Navy, stationed somewhere in the South Pacific, like they say. I'm home on furlough. Uncle Tootsie said I could work his corner while he's away so I can make some Christmas money."

"I see. Tootsie always was very kind. Which of Minnie's boys are you?"

"I'm Richard."

"It's nice to meet you, Richard." Thadeus Lowry tucked his walking stick under his arm and helped Richard up. "Well, well. Minnie's boy. Richard."

"It's nice to meetcha, like I said," said Richard, rubbing the blood off his ear. "I heard my uncle speak of you often."

"Well, well. In the Navy. Serving your country. In the South Pacific. Seen any action?"

"Naw. There are no girls out there. I do better at home in Flatbush."

"I mean, fighting."

"Oh, yeah. That. Every once in a while the Japs fly over and drop bombs on things we just got finished buildin'. Maybe they think they're fightin' us. I dunno. Seems like they're just keepin' us employed, you know?"

Robby said, "Sir? May I put my hands down now?"

"Of course, Robby."

"This is still a robbery, you know," said Richard.

"Richard," said Thadeus Lowry, "I don't like your carrying a gun."

Richard looked at his gun, still flat on his hand.

"Your uncle never carried a gun."

"No?"

"If the police pick you up and you have a gun on you, I wouldn't be able to get you out of trouble."

"I have to carry a gun."

"Why?"

Richard looked around warily. "There are some real weirdos around here."

"I think you had better give me the gun."

"I can't, Mr. Lowry."

"Why not?"

"It's my service revolver. I snuck it home in my duffel bag, so I could work Uncle Tootsie's corner for Christmas, you see. I have to bring it back after Christmas, or I'll be in trouble."

"You can give it to me and pick it up at my apartment before you go back to the South Pacific. After Christmas."

"Yeah. Okay."

Richard gave Thadeus Lowry the gun and Thadeus Lowry gave Richard an address on Park Avenue.

"You should have that ear looked after, Richard."

"You gave me quite a crack on the head."

"I didn't realize you were Minnie's boy, Richard, home on furlough."

"That's all right. Any friend of the family. I appreciate your looking out for my uncle's corner."

"Come for a drink," said Thadeus Lowry.

"I can't. I'm workin'. Only eight more shopping days till Christmas."

"Some other time, then. When you come for the gun. After Christmas. We'll sit and talk. Trade war stories."

"Okay," said Richard. "That sounds nice. But now I'm robbing you."

"What?"

"I still mean this to be a stick-up."

"You do?"

"I do. Shouldn't I?"

"Tootsie never robs me."

"Listen, Mr. Lowry, I got a crack on the head. You have my gun. We've been talking here fifteen, maybe twenty minutes. I shouldn't rob you?"

"I guess you're right," said Thadeus Lowry. "After all, one should encourage the young in their work. Let me look in my wallet."

"No," said Richard. "Let me look in your wallet."

Thadeus Lowry had his wallet in his hand, but drew it back. "That," he said, "would be an indignity."

"An in-what?"

"An invasion of privacy. I will look in the wallet."

He did so, in the light of the street lamp.

"There are four ones here," he reported. "Will you settle for three?"

"I want all four. This is a robbery. You can keep the wallet."

"But taxi fare," said Thadeus Lowry. "To get this poor, shivering child home."

"Hungry, too," Robby said.

"This poor, shivering, hungry boy home."

Robby picked Richard's cap up off the snow and handed it to him.

Richard said, "The kid needs pants."

"Here's your three dollars," said Thadeus Lowry, holding the bills in his gloved hand. "Don't get me anything too expensive for Christmas."

"I want all four dollars, dammit."

"You do?"

"I do. Shouldn't I?"

Thadeus Lowry beamed at him, and handed him the other dollar.

"Of course, my boy. Here. Tootsie would be proud of you. Never give the sucker an even break. Here's all four dollars."

"Okay." Richard counted the four dollars twice, perhaps to make the sum eight. "Robbin' you's taken a long time, you know."

"Sorry. Now go back to the alley and lurk some more. I'm sure another customer will be along in just a minute."

"Good night," Richard said.

"Good night," said Thadeus Lowry. "Merry Christmas."

"Mr. Lowry?" Robby called. Two blocks away from where they had been held up, Robby, tripping and slipping, had fallen considerably behind Thadeus Lowry and wanted him to slow down. "Is four dollars a lot to pay for a gun?"

Thadeus Lowry continued his brisk pace, but he did say, "I would have gone higher—if there'd been a need to."

The distance between them grew. Robby heard Thadeus Lowry's voice boom, instructively: "There are lessons to be learned in every business, my boy. Even highway robbery."

8
Care, Feeding and Education Are Discussed

Halfway down the block on a side street they pushed through a glass door into the lobby of Thadeus Lowry's apartment house. There was no man to greet them at the door; no boys to carry the suitcase and, Robby thanked God, no warm little bar tucked into a corner of the lobby to make their homecoming convivial.

While waiting for Robby to catch up, Thadeus Lowry had stood on the front steps of his apartment house and sung sixteen bars of "The Donkey Serenade," loudly.

They went down a long cement corridor with puce cement walls to the elevator, which creaked and swayed as if it were as afraid of torpedoes as H.M.S. *Scaramouche*, but lifted them, over time, to the seventh floor.

"Someone in this place cooks," muttered Robby. "Boiled cabbage."

On the seventh floor they walked down another long corridor to a door marked 7Q. Thadeus Lowry inserted a key and pushed the door open.

"*Chérie*," he called, rather like a lark attaining a treetop. "*Chérie, Chérie.*"

Through the short, narrow, crimson foyer, in another, more brightly lit room, Robby saw a woman's feet suspended thirty centimeters from the floor. The shoes on the feet were polished red leather, with long heels. At the sound of Thadeus Lowry's voice, the feet landed on the floor, and disappeared from view.

"Lover! Is that you?"

"No, *chérie*, sorry. It's your husband."

In small steps the feet came around the corner and into the foyer. Mrs. Thadeus Lowry was not much taller than Robby, but she was a good deal more red. Her hair was ginger, her sweater rose, her skirt brick, her shoes crimson, and her fingernails and lips currant. Her eyes were bloodshot. The walls of the foyer (the walls throughout the apartment, Robby was to discover) were poppy red. Robby blinked slowly and swayed.

"Ah, *chérie…*" she said. She held her martini glass to the side, so it would not spill.

Mr. and Mrs. Thadeus Lowry put their heads together and exchanged fumes.

"Did you have a damaging day?" she asked.

"Brutal. Absolutely brutal." He slipped his walking stick into an umbrella stand like a knight sheathing his sword once inside his own castle walls. "But I filed a wonderful story. Just wonderful."

"You must be exhausted." She nodded. Putting her martini glass down on a hall table, she took his coat and hung it in the hall closet. She gave no appearance of seeing a blue-and-white boy amidst all the red.

"I am, *ma chérie*," he said, handing her his hat. "Simply exhausted."

He stood drooping in the hall while she put his hat on the closet shelf and regained her martini from the Chinese lacquer hall table.

"This is Robby Burnes," noted Thadeus Lowry. "Our bundle from Britain."

Her attention swiveled to Robby. Her eyes grew larger; her face grew larger, her head grew larger; her whole body grew larger. Both hands clutched her martini glass.

Thadeus Lowry said, "Allow me to explain."

"Is he ours?" she asked.

"For the duration."

"The duration of the war?"

"He's the son of a dead duke, it seems. In fact, he must be a duke."

"Are dukes ever that young?"

"Oh, they must be. At some point in their lives."

"Isn't he cute? Look at those knees, Thadeus. Where will he sleep?"

"Too big for a bureau drawer."

"Too small for the bathtub, even with blankets."

"Can't sleep at the foot of our bed. We both have feet."

"And we can't move to a bigger apartment. You remember, Thadeus, I strained my back Christmas shopping."

"Of course, *ma chérie.*"

She spoke slowly, loudly and distinctly to Robby. She even had currant lipstick on her teeth. "What do you want, dear?" Her hands concealed the olive Robby had been eyeing in the martini glass. "What can we give you?"

"Marvelous with children, *chérie*," Thadeus Lowry said. "You're marvelous with children."

"Something to eat, ma'am, and a warm tub, and, please, I'm very tired."

"'A warm tub.' I suppose he means a bath, Thadeus."

"I suppose he does."

Sweat was in Robby's eyes, prickling his scalp, and running down his spinal column. He had never been anywhere as warm as the Lowrys' apartment.

"Please, ma'am, may I have something to eat?"

"Yes, dear, of course. You darling. Go into a nice warm bathtub, and when you come out, I'll have din-din ready for you." She added, "He smells of disinfectant, Thadeus."

"Does he?" Thadeus Lowry sniffed the air. "I've been wondering why I've been nostalgic for the Maine woods all day. Especially seeing I've never been in the Maine woods."

"Right into the tub, darling." Mrs. Lowry pointed ambiguously. "Take your sweet little suitcase. Around to the left."

Robby weaved across the foyer, along the near wall of a red, shimmering, stifling living room, and into the bathroom.

He heard Thadeus Lowry's voice say, "As long as you're having one, I'll join you."

"What did you say his name is?"

"Who?"

"The boy."

"Robby Burnes, with an *E*. Son of the Duke of Pladroman, if I've got it right. Not a very important duke, as dukes go, I suspect."

"He must go to school."

Robby had never lived in the front of a house before, within earshot of grown-ups other than servants. He was uncertain of the decorum of overhearing grown-up conversation. But Thadeus Lowry's domicile had no front or back, no upstairs or downstairs. It had a middle. A very middle. The living room was a divan and two chairs on a rug separated by a coffee table. Steam hissed and snapped from radiators along every wall.

He closed the door to the bathroom and turned the faucets on in the tub and removed the clothes he had been wearing since he had been a very young boy in England. He piled them on the radiator wondering if they would burst into flame.

The only surprise he had in being naked this first time in many, many days, was that his stomach had vanished. It had been a pleasant round object just below his rib cage in which he used to put food. Now he felt for it with his fingertips. Definitely it was gone. Where his stomach had been, Robby's fingers felt a hardness as if touching bone. He had felt that hardness increasing each time he had vomited aboard H.M.S. *Scaramouche*. Water splashing in the tub behind him, Robby jumped up and down, to see himself in the mirror above the wash-basin. Where his stomach had been were horizontal lines of muscle. Robby regretted that: It looked a poor repository for pastry.

Robby lay in the full tub in the company of a bar of soap which floated. It wiggled and wobbled in the waves and went nowhere and reminded him of H.M.S. *Scaramouche*. He thought of the other children aboard ship, and wondered if any of them had been fed yet. And he wondered about the boys at Wolsley School and which meals they were between.

In the living room, Thadeus Lowry was recounting his day. Robby wondered what he could do not to overhear.

"Thus I discovered, *chérie*, it is easier to take over a human life, in these trying times, than to get a small loan from a bank."

"What an amusing thought, Thadeus."

"Then around the corner for a leisurely lunch..."

Robby sank beneath the water and counted his toes.

"...assured him in every way possible," Thadeus Lowry was

continuing. "Told him what great friends his father and I were, what a great hero his father was, how he and I had captured a town behind the lines without firing a single shot…"

Robby went below the surface of the water and extended his fingers, stretched them as far as they would stretch.

"…taxi to the office where I spent the rest of the day trying to hammer out a story."

"You're very generous, Thadeus, giving him so much time and attention."

"Must be a big shock to him—coming from war-torn England to the land of milk and honey."

"We mustn't spoil him, Thadeus."

"I think it was a great thrill for him to see the newspaper office. The hustle and bustle. The crackle of the police radio. The clattering of the teletypes."

"Is he especially bright, do you think?"

"Oh, I wouldn't say so. Ordinary sort of kid. Stares blankly at you while you're speaking to him as if he can't quite grasp what it is he's hearing…"

Underwater, Robby washed his penis. He was glad that it hadn't gone the way of his stomach.

"…On the way home we stopped for tea. I was sure he was missing that sort of thing."

"Then he won't want much supper."

"He ate bowls full of crackers."

Robby went below the water facedown and held his breath. He rose to air only when his lungs hurt.

Mrs. Lowry was saying, "How did you ever find time to file a story for the newspaper today?"

"It wasn't easy, *chérie*, it wasn't easy. But, you know, a real professional can work anywhere, any time, under any circumstances."

Robby was dressing in clean clothes, identical to those he had just taken off, from the suitcase. His used clothes, on the radiator, were scorching nicely.

"What's the story about, lover?"

"I think I'll let you be surprised in the morning. Read *The New*

York Star. Robby should be very surprised indeed. I've arranged a warm welcome for him, to this land where he's come for safe-keeping."

With that much of a clue to reestablish decorum, Robby entered the living room.

"You don't look a bit different," said Mrs. Thadeus Lowry. "Come here and let me smell."

As apparently she was serious about the invitation (her hand was extended limply toward him), Robby drew near.

On the coffee table was a glass of water, with ice in it. On a plate catsup oozed from between two pieces of bread.

"Much better," said Mrs. Lowry; contracting the veins that ran over her nose. "Now sit down and have your supper. Thadeus says you've been eating all day."

"Is that supper, ma'am?"

"I'll get you milk tomorrow, Robby. If my back is better."

In his mind, Robby drank the water and ate the sandwich seventeen times. Sitting on the divan, he drank the water and ate the sandwich once.

"What are we going to do about schooling, Thadeus?"

"He must go to school," said Thadeus.

"But where?"

"The local piss, I suppose."

"The local piss?"

"There must be a P.S. something or other within walking distance. It's the law, isn't it?"

"Quite right. There must be a public school nearby. Well, that's settled. Is tomorrow a school day?"

"Tomorrow is Thursday."

"People go to school on Thursdays, Robby," stated Mrs. Lowry.

"Yes, ma'am."

"It's most important you go to school."

"The trick is," advised Thadeus Lowry, "to leave the apartment in the morning and walk around the blocks in ever widening squares until you find a school."

"Sir?"

Robby's experience on the streets of New York already had caused him to pray that he would never have to enter them alone. If even Santa Claus got it on the streets of New York, who was to protect Robby Burnes? He had seen a highway robber thrashed, then brushed up to rob again.

"But can he find the school by himself, Thadeus?"

"He found America by himself," Thadeus Lowry pointed out. "Children find schools the way women find hat shops. It's a God-given instinct."

"But what about registering?" Mrs. Lowry rubbed her sore back. "Won't he have to register?"

"What's there to register? He's a schoolchild. Any schoolteacher can see that."

"Yes, of course. You'll like going to school in America, won't you, Robby?"

Robby's been looking forward to going to Wolsley School ever so long now, hasn't he? his mother had asked.

"Oh, yes, ma'am."

The catsup in his stomach yearned to be on the maroon divan.

"We'll set you off with a nice warm breakfast in the morning," proffered Mrs. Lowry. "I'm sure you'll have a lovely adventure— going to school first day."

"S-sir?"

"Yes, Robby. What now?"

"Can I take your gun to school with me?"

"A *gun!*" gasped Mrs. Lowry.

"Good heavens, no," chuckled Thadeus Lowry. "What could happen to you on the streets of New York?"

9
The Streets of New York

After dining at the Lowrys', receiving no other instructions or invitations, Robert James Saint James Burnes Walter Farhall-Pladroman, S.Nob., continued to sit quietly on the divan. He closed his eyes against the maroon, crimson, cardinal, auburn, ginger, currant, rose, brick, poppy and puce and concentrated on keeping his catsup in the narrow tubes which once had led to his stomach.

Thadeus Lowry continued to talk to his wife like a Johnson to his Boswell, only in that minor events were given stature in their telling (it was reported that an envious fellow threw his desk at Thadeus Lowry in the city room of *The New York Star* while Thadeus Lowry was composing a piece of literature for first edition), but not in that their telling enhanced the listener's perception of the significant truths of the day.

Robby's attention to Thadeus Lowry's lying discourse was disturbed by concern for what the radiators were doing to Robby, and what more they might do. Again Robby's body was running with sweat. The air was so heavy to breathe Robby's respiratory system was threatening to go on strike. They were circumvallated by radiators. The steam was so charging in the innards of the radiators, so clangorous in its importuning to be released into the room that fear of imminent death by vaporization was not unreasonable. Yet Thadeus Lowry was not condensed.

One ear went to Thadeus Lowry, the other to the radiators. As the evening went on, Thadeus Lowry came to make less sense, the radiators more: There was a more certain rhythm and accurate responsiveness to what was going on in the pipes than in the human colloquy.

Tintinnabulation vanquished confabulation.

Sleep mastered Robby.

Robby had slept at Wolsley School in a room with five other boys, undisturbed by sniffling, snoring, sudden cries in the night for nannies who could not answer, the traffic of uncertain, sleep-sodden prowls to the water closet and back. He had slept aboard H.M.S. *Sacramouche*, lying on a steel-plate deck, vomit and disinfectant in his nose, undisturbed by sudden shifts in elevation and direction, strategic wallowing, undisturbed by Evacuation Ladies stepping on him in the dark to see if he was all right.

Robby's first night's sleep in New York City was disturbed. Thadeus Lowry was giving witness to his day in a waning voice. The radiators hissed at him. Robby slept. A few meters from his head, just the other side of the living room wall, an argument broke out. A man's voice shouted "*I love you!*" and there was the sound of smashing glass. "*I love you!*" and the sound of crashing furniture. "*I love you!*" and a body thudded against the living room wall. "*My head! You broke my head!*" Seven stories below a woman passed by, singing *Carmen*. A fire department went through the narrow street, its sirens amplifying up the walls. (Somnus said, *Right Robby—they're just moving hell*.) An anguished human scream came up from the alleys as the first light of day glazed the windows. (*Someone's just discovered he's alive*.) Snorting, trundling snowplows scraped the streets and shovels sang on the sidewalks. Rubbish barrels were tympanized. Buses roared in the morning like lions looking for people to devour. Robby awoke feeling the concerns of the whole world had prowled his sleep.

Yellow pools of weak light surrounded the table lamps. Robby was still on the divan. Thadeus Lowry was still in his chair, chin on his chest. His *chérie* was curled in her chair, ginger hair on garnet chair arm. The radiators had stopped, and the room was cold. Time had stopped. Getting up quietly and moving around the room, Robby felt himself an imposition—animation in an otherwise still picture.

He looked at his supper plate from the night before and at his empty glass of water and at Thadeus Lowry and his *chérie* and gauged the distance between himself and breakfast as equal to the distance between himself and the nearest school. Even if he'd missed Chapel, he might still be in time for breakfast.

In the bathroom, his suitcase remained gaping on the floor. He took his overcoat and cap from the bathroom doorknob where he had left them the night before, and put them on.

And then Robert James Saint James Burnes Walter Farhall-Pladroman, S.Nob., English-speaking, dressed in a blue blazer and red striped tie, cap and coat emblazoned by stags butting oak trees, short pants and kneesocks, yellow hair over his ears, after finding the elevator and descending in it, stepped out onto a New York City street on a winter morn.

The snow was black. Robby would have sworn the snow had come down white. He shook his head.

Robby walked the four blocks around Thadeus Lowry's apartment house and found himself back at his front door. Although some people had looked at him curiously, and others hadn't seen him at all, Robby was relieved: He had gotten around the block without being accosted once. Neither had he found a school.

Continuing to take Thadeus Lowry's navigational advice, Robby went up a street, went left, and navigated an eight block square. It did not bring him back to Thadeus Lowry's door. He went up another street, went right, and navigated a sixteen block square. In nearly three miles of walking, Robby found nothing which looked like a school to him. Nowhere were there iron gates, a gatekeeper's lodge, a long driveway with playing fields on either side leading to a compound of gray-stone, slate-roofed buildings. There were apartment buildings and office buildings, big stores and little stores. There were people hurrying everywhere, heads down to ignore anyone who might accost them. Robby began up another street, remembering Thadeus Lowry's comment that it was the law there be a school in the neighborhood (and that schoolchildren are drawn to school as are ladies to hat shops), when the simple arithmetic of his search overwhelmed him.

His next square, in the search plan, was to have thirty-two blocks each side. Was New York City big enough? Was he? If he failed to find a school in that square, his next would have sixty-four blocks to a side! Two-hundred-and-fifty-six blocks to a side! Five-hundred-and-twelve blocks to a side!

Robby would miss lunch again.

Therefore, at the corner, he stopped. He looked left, and he looked right. He went in no direction. There were blocks in front of him, blocks behind him, blocks to his left, blocks to his right. Blocks and blocks and blocks and blocks.

Across the street there was a woman who had also stopped. She stood on the curb, squinting at Robby. She wore a brown cloth coat, overshoes, and carried a purse. She was plump.

Robby crossed the street to her. "Please, ma'am, where's the piss?"

"The what?"

"The piss, ma'am. I was told to look for the school which is called a piss. I can't find one."

"The P.S., you darlin' boy." Her hands clutched her purse strap firmly. Through narrowed lids she looked up and down the street. "Yes," she said. "You're lost, aren't you?"

"No, ma'am. I just don't know where I'm going."

Her right hand grabbed Robby's. "I know just where you're goin', you darlin' boy. I'll bring you there."

Greatly relieved, his hand in hers, Robby went down the sidewalk with her. The speed with which the woman moved surprised him. Perhaps she knew that if they didn't hustle he would be late for school. Or perhaps by helping him she was falling behind her own schedule. Attached to her as he was he found that running ten steps, walking five, running ten again was the only way to keep up with her and not have his arm freed from his shoulder.

They came to what appeared to Robby to be wide stairs leading to the basement of New York City.

"Down here, darlin'."

"Is my school underground? No wonder I couldn't find it anywhere I looked."

"That's right, you darlin'. You just come with me."

They went down the steps together. The woman paid money for them both and they went through a turnstile. Robby was astonished to find himself in a train station.

"Oh, ma'am. Do I get to take a train to school?"

"Just this once, darlin'."

With one hand clutching his, the other, with purse dangling from her wrist, pushing his back, the woman shoved Robby aboard a crowded subway train. The door behind them closed, compressing them further. Robby found his face embedded in the rabbit fur of another passenger's coat.

"Glumph!" he said.

The train accelerated quickly to a speed beyond the passengers' ability to adjust. Vertically they squirmed together like eels in a jar. Waist high to most, sometimes Robby's head was twisted upwards. All the tall passengers were pressed so close together they had their faces turned up to the roof for air. Sometimes Robby's head was twisted downwards. The air in neither quarter was desirable. Overshoes, mostly not buckled, took up all but a few inches of floor space. There were two ladies' boots, which did not match, between a pair of man's boots, which did match. One man's boot was way over here; its mate way over there. There was one lady's boot for which Robby could find a match nowhere.

Robby's head was twisted up again. People's arms were raised as if in surrender, clutching at poles and straps. Some ladies' arms appeared to extend from men's armpits. Some men's arms led to ladies' heads.

As they rattled and swayed from stop to stop, the people writhed. More burrowed themselves into the crowd. They turned slow, full circles as people snuggled against them and wriggled around them. All the while their cool, adult, upturned faces studied advertisements above the windows for Alka Seltzer and United States War Bonds. Some tunneled through the crowd to leave the train; others rowed through the crowd with their elbows.

Across the aisle, there was a puddle on the train floor. As the car proceeded and righted itself, the puddle moved to the middle of the floor. The train banked, and the puddle returned to its original bed. The train righted itself again, tipped a little more, and the puddle passed the center of the car. It retreated. At the next inclination of the train, the puddle rushed across the floor and surrounded Robby's shoes. Instantly his feet felt wet.

"Ma'am?" He tugged on her hand. "I'm being stood under by a puddle!"

"This stop's ours." She gave the crushed bones of his hand a further grinding.

"Is my school near here?"

The woman had positioned them so that when the door slid open they virtually were catapulted onto the platform. They ascended stairs carpeted with chewing gum.

Robby rose into a world entirely different from any he had ever seen.

Everywhere there were pushcarts. In each pushcart was an oversized sign saying 23¢ or 12¢ or 9¢ or 32¢. Behind most pushcarts stood men with long white aprons over their overcoats, hats pushed back on their heads. Women at the pushcarts wore bulky sweaters and thick shoes and kerchiefs. They were all singing about potatoes a nickel, oranges a dime. More properly dressed people, men and women, snaked among the pushcarts, testing a tomato here, a melon there. They skirted cast-off cardboard boxes and walked on wood shavings and sawdust and excelsior and slush. Robby's guide pulled him by the hand on a circuitous route through the pushcarts. And on the pushcarts were oranges and apples and bananas and melons and potatoes and tomatoes and heads of lettuce and cabbages and sausages and hams and pudent chickens and many foods Robby had never seen before and whose names he did not know.

Behind the pushcarts the woman rushed Robby down an alley piled high on both sides with empty boxes. They entered a building, went through a cold room of hanging beef carcasses and out again onto a side street. They crossed that street and went along the slush on the sidewalk until they came to the building at the top of a T-intersection.

She pulled him up the steps, through a door, along a dark corridor to an interior door. There she used a key from her purse.

"Is this my school, ma'am?"

She pushed open the door and gently pushed Robby inside.

He was in what appeared to be a kitchen. There was a sink and a stove and a refrigerator. There were also three cots against the walls.

A man in a plaid shirt sat in a wheelchair at the kitchen table. He looked up from the picture puzzle he was doing. He looked directly at Robby, at the woman behind Robby, then even more directly at Robby.

"Who's this?" he asked, as if provoked.

The woman let go of Robby's hand. She closed the door behind them.

Still in her cloth coat, looking at the man in the wheelchair, her body sagged. Her purse dangling from her wrist, she covered her eyes with her hand.

"Oh, Frankie," she said. "*I* don't know. Someone important, I think. I recognize him from the morning newspaper."

The man wheeled back from the table, and turned. Full-faced he stared at Robby.

She said: "I think I've kidnapped him!"

10
Kidnapped

"Whaddaya mean, *kidnapped*?" shouted the man in the wheelchair. "What kidnapped?"

"Shush, Frankie. Someone might hear you."

"Someone might hear me! Call the cops! Whaddaya mean, kidnapped?"

"Please, Frankie." The woman who had escorted Robby through the labyrinths of the world now stood quaking by the door. "I don't know what it is I've done."

Frankie banged the heel of his hand against his own forehead as if trying to escape the immediate situation by knocking himself unconscious. He recovered from the blow. "You kidnapped this? This kid?"

"I think I did, darlin'."

He stared at Robby. There was sleep in the corners of the man's huge brown eyes.

"You're *kidnapped*?"

"I was on my way to school, sir, and this nice woman offered to guide me."

"This nice woman kidnapped you? This nice woman, my wife, Marie Savallo, she kidnapped you?"

"Please, sir, she took me on an underground train and through a market where there was a great lot of food, and it was all jolly interesting."

Frankie's big eyes darted to Marie's face. "Did anyone see you come in?"

"We took the back ways, Frankie."

His arms flung out with astonishing speed. He swept the picture puzzle off the kitchen table. Pieces of it flew to the corners of the room.

"You've kidnapped a child? You, Marie? Marie of the never-ending novena? You musta gone nuts!"

"Saints, I don't know what it is I've done, Frankie. It just came over me in a rush, it did. I saw him in the street. He was so cold and hungry lookin'. So beautiful...lost." Still in her overcoat, Marie Savallo was fighting tears. "So I took him home with me."

"You want a child—so you kidnap one! Right! Call the men in the white coats to come get Marie Savallo! Booby hatch for her!"

She looked to him truly for an explanation. "What's this I've done, Frankie?"

"You've kidnapped a child, that's what you done! You went out to get a job and you come back with a child you kidnapped! That's what you done!"

"I never did get the job, Frankie."

"Of course you didn't get the job! That's what you went out for! Instead you brought home another mouth to feed!" The flat of his hand made an awful bang on the kitchen table. "And you brought him here! My brother Tony's here, the damned draft-dodger, and you walk in—not with a job—not with a loaf of bread—but with a kidnapped kid!"

Marie Savallo agreed. "Things aren't so good, Frankie."

" 'Things aren't so good,' she says. Kidnappin' a kid will make things good?"

"Shush, darlin', please. People shouldn't hear you shoutin' *kidnap* so loud when there's about to be a child found missin'."

"Have you gone nuts, Marie? Who knows about kidnappin'?"

"They'll never suspect us, darlin'. If only you'll lower your voice."

Frankie lowered his voice. "You want to get me sent to prison, is what you want. You want to get rid of me for life?"

"No, darlin'. Never say such a thing. How could I get on without you?"

"God!" said Frankie Savallo. "A wife who kidnaps children!"

"I couldn't resist him, Frankie."

"I marry a sweet Irish girl and she sets me up to go to prison just like a member of my own family!"

"He's such a darlin' boy, Frankie. Just look at him." She took off Robby's hat. "Lost and cold and half starved he was."

"My uncle says it's always the Irish who get the Italians in trouble. My uncle says the prisons are full of good Italians put there by the holy Irish!"

"Frankie, darlin', this opportunity might be the answer to a prayer, you understand."

"Opportunity! What opportunity! Since when is being sent up for life an opportunity?"

"I tell you, Frankie—he's in the newspaper. This lad's a very important package."

"What paper? Lemme see the paper."

"It's here, darlin'. I wrapped the garbage in it."

While another mouth to feed, which hadn't been fed, watched, Marie Savallo went to the sink's sideboard and dumped garbage out of a newspaper. She spread it out on the kitchen table in front of Frankie. "*The New York Star*," she said. "See? His picture, through the eggshells. The very same boy, it is."

Frankie Savallo looked back and forth from Robby in the flesh to Robby through the eggshells.

His left hand plowed percolated coffee beans off the newspaper. He read.

Frankie Savallo exclaimed: "He's an orphan, Marie! You kidnapped an orphan!" His fist banged the kitchen table. In truth, Frankie Savallo had the biggest shoulders and chest Robby had ever seen. The man's body was like a triangle with the broad shoulders on top and the shriveled legs in the wheelchair. Robby knew the legs of the kitchen table couldn't absorb too many more blows from the man's fist. "Who's gonna pay ransom for an orphan?"

"Read the paper, Frankie. He's an English duke, or somethin'."

"What's a duke?"

"It's royalty, darlin'. Up there with the King."

"A king?" Frankie looked around at Robby again, his eyes even wider. "You've stolen a king?"

"Like a king, darlin', only not so royal as all that."

"What the hell are you, kid?"

Robby shrugged. "Burnes, sir."

"See, Marie? He says his name's Burnes. There was a kid in school named Burnes. His father did five to ten for aggravated assault."

"I think he's tryin' to say his name, darlin'. If you'd just look, you'd see in the newspaper that one of the names in this magnificent long string of 'em he has is the name Burnes. See that? You know the English, darlin': When one word will do they squander 'em."

"Oh, yeah. Says here, 'The decision was made in England's highest corridors of power.' Where's that at?"

"Must be the Tower of London, Frankie. Oh, some terrible things have gone on in that place!"

"It says 'special ship,' Marie. Look, it says he was sent to America on a 'special ship.' A special ship for this kid!"

"It quotes the Prime Minister, Frankie, Mr. Winston Churchill himself. You've heard him on the radio. Talking about our wee friend over there."

"Look, Marie. Down here by the jelly. It says the King. The King of England!"

Frankie Savallo, his eyes big, turned the wheelchair and came closer to Robby. "You the kid in the newspaper?"

"I don't know, sir. I haven't read the newspaper. But I do know Mr. Thadeus—"

"Of course he is, Frankie. Look at his clothes."

Frankie squinted at the Wolsley School emblem.

"Why is that moose trying to knock over that tree?"

"Moose, sir?"

"Elk, whatever it is. That big goat on your coat."

Marie Savallo was standing beside Robby. "Tailor-made clothes, Frankie. For a child who'll outgrow them before spring."

"What's tailor-made?"

"Everything, Frankie. Take off your overcoat, sonny. You must be warm."

She ignored Robby's overcoat when he tried to hand it to her. Her fingers unbuttoned his blazer.

"Look at that, Frankie. A tailor-made jacket for a little boy."

Her fingers went between the collar of Robby's shirt and his neck.

"His shirt is hand-sewn, Frankie. And him about to grow like a Jerusalem artichoke."

"I want to know about the moose tryin' to knock over that tree. What does it mean?"

"It means he's very high up, Frankie."

"He's an orphan! Who's gonna pay ransom for an orphan?"

"Well, darlin', someone paid for these clothes. Hand-me-downs they're not."

"Listen, kid." Frankie stuck his finger in Robby's chest. "Are you the kid in the newspaper, or not?"

"I wouldn't know, sir. May I read the newspaper?"

"You can read?"

"Slowly, sir."

"Sure, kid." Frankie wheeled backwards and aside. "Read."

Marie brought a chair upon which Robby knelt as he read, elbows among the coffee grounds. *I think I'll let you be surprised in the morning*, Thadeus Lowry had said. *Read* The New York Star. *Robby should be very surprised indeed.* Robby was very surprised indeed.

At the top of the page was a huge picture of Robby, cap, necktie, blazer, short pants, kneesocks, sitting on his suitcase. There was no background in the picture. Robby appeared to be sitting in space, or on a cloud, or in the land of nowhere. His chin was on his hand, and his elbow on his knee. The expression on his face (which was actually one of curiosity as to how the photographer's big camera worked) looked questioning, pleading, yearning. He looked tired, which he was, and hungry, which he was.

On either side of Robby's picture, in cameo, were the photographs of Robby's parents he had given Thadeus Lowry from his wallet. Their evening wear, and the formal compositions of the portraits made the parents look far removed from the pathetic reality of their son. Too, as their eyes were wide open for their formal sittings, the effect of the arrangements of photographs on the page was that they were considerably concerned, if not startled, at seeing their offspring displayed so prominently within millimeters of their noses.

The photographic layout was held together with the headline:

THE LORD IS AN ORPHAN

Under the photographic display the caption read: *Robert Duke of Pladroman, aged 10, as he arrived in New York from war-torn England yesterday.*

And the story read:

> *The poor little duke!*
>
> *The War ravaging the world is toppling thrones, unsettling the high and the mighty, and making many another distinguished seat uneasy.*
>
> *Not just the people of every nation are distressed.*
>
> *The 10-year-old holder of one of England's most awesome titles arrived in New York yesterday, a homeless orphan, a waif, his eyes hollow from his personal brush with current world history.*
>
> *While other reporters spent the day in pursuit of presidents, dictators and military leaders, your correspondent for* The New York Star *struggled through blistering snow to a cold and wind-swept East Side dock to discover Robert James St. James Burnes Walter Farhall-Pladroman (Duke of Pladroman), aged 10, lost and lonely, trembling with trepidation at these cold shores of a new land, grievous with grief at the recent loss of his beloved parents, victims of war, a small and discouraged figure sitting astride his only remaining possession in the world, a small, black cardboard suitcase (see picture above).*
>
> *"Call me Robby," he said, extending the democracy of childhood while extending a cold and uncertain hand to your* New York Star *correspondent.*
>
> ### LARK
>
> *Weeks ago, happy as a lark, the 10-year-old boy gamboled on England's green glades, the playing fields of his family's public (private boarding) school, Wolsley School, in England.*

Like any other, healthy, high-spirited, 10-year-old boy, he loved to play rugby (football) and cricket (baseball).

The airplanes flying over the school on their flights over the English Channel to deal death blows to the Axis Powers meant no more to him than to any other healthy, happy, 10-year-old boy.

Then came the terrible news that shattered Robby's safe and noble world.

A bomb in the night—a Nazi bomb—emblazoned with the dreaded swastika, directly hit London's famous and fashionable Pladroman House, Mayfair—Robby's home—killing both parents instantly.

Robby's dad, the Duke of Pladroman, a well-decorated hero of World War One, was a distinguished member of the House of Lords (Senate). His mum, the Duchess, was one of London's most noted and loved hostesses, admired for her fragile beauty.

All lost in a single stroke—a school, a home, a family, a way of life.

HAEC

"Forsan et haec olim meminisse juvabit," said the poor little Duke, with a shrug of his thin shoulders, which roughly translates from the vulgate as "I can take anything."

His schoolmates and schoolmasters were open in their sympathy for the noble waif. They tried to assure him their love and friendship were steady in the face of his terrible loss.

But the decision was made in England's highest corridors of power that the young Duke must be evacuated to the shores of England's staunchest ally, the United States of America, for safekeeping.

"We are fighting this terrible evil not for ourselves alone," intoned the English Prime Minister (President) Winston Churchill, "but for the next generation, and the next, and the next. We are fighting for the preservation of our good English way of life."

By dark, heavily curtained trains and devious routes, Robby was brought to his ship in the middle of the night.

SPECIAL

Dodging bombs, his car, without benefit of any headlights at all, sought out the docks and the special ship, His Majesty's Ship Scaramouche.

Fearful days at sea followed his nightmare ashore.

Submarines, with their fearful torpedoes, lurked beneath every wave.

Mid-winter North Atlantic storms were no friends to His Majesty's Ship Scaramouche, her captain, crew, and their special human cargo.

Dodging torpedoes, the storm-tossed little vessel limped into New York Harbor yesterday, her stern in the water.

Asked for his first impression of America, the 10-year-old Duke said, "We are all very grateful for what the people of the United States are doing for the besieged people of Britain. His Majesty, the King, has asked me to transmit his thanks."

CORRESPONDENT

Having no other course to follow, your correspondent for The New York Star *had the poor little Duke accompany him to his own home last evening. There he was warmly greeted by the family and friends of your correspondent.*

The poor little Duke has come to safe harbor, at last, in the warm bosom of your correspondent's family.

When Robby finished reading, slowly, he looked up, slowly, into the blue eyes of Marie Savallo. Slowly he turned his head and looked into the brown eyes of Frankie Savallo.

11
Worthiness

Picking slowly through Thadeus Lowry's account of Robby's narrow escape from peace, he had not been listening closely to the continuing debate between Frankie and Marie Savallo concerning whether Robby had been worth kidnapping, having already been kidnapped. Frankie Savallo continued to exercise the characteristic of an operatic *basso profundo*: Each new fragment of information which came his way he not only assimilated slowly, he took personally. Every aspect in the affair drew from him thirty-two bars in the lower registers. Counterpoint to the depth of his emotions, Marie Savallo's conversational flights fled from her mouth and flittered around the room like so many glib canaries.

Finally the garbage on the newspaper turned Robby away by the nose. He sat facing the room on the kitchen chair. He did think it splendid of Thadeus Lowry to give him such a resounding phrase to say on behalf of the King. Too, Headmaster would be so pleased at Robby's introducing Latin to America. It might enspirit him.

Marie Savallo had removed her coat and hat and now was sitting, sagging, on the other side of the kitchen table, awaiting the teapot to sound. Frankie sat in profile to them, arms folded across his great chest, as if to defend his heart from any further incursions that day.

Their conversation repeated Marie's contention that she hadn't meant to kidnap Robby, Frankie's insistence she shouldn't have kidnapped Robby, and their joint indecisiveness about what to do with the kidnapped Robby.

Frankie twisted his neck further than Robby thought humanly possible, to face him, and said, "Well?"

"Well, sir?"

"Is what the newspaper says about you the truth?"

"No, sir."

"No?"

"No, sir."

"Then what's true?" Frankie shouted.

"I'm eight, sir."

"What?"

"I'm eight, sir. Not ten. Eight."

"Columbus!"

"He's eight years old," said Marie Savallo. "The little darlin'. Hardly old enough to wash between his own toes, he is."

"Dammit, shuddup, Marie! Are you the poor little Duke or not?"

"My name's Burnes, sir. Robby Burnes, S.Nob."

"You know, Frankie," confided Marie, "even his name's familiar to me. I swear I've heard it somewhere."

"Is it true you know the Prime Minister and the King of England?"

Robby asked, "Sir?"

"What?" Frankie said mildly. Then Frankie said not so mildly: "What?"

"Is the Prime Minister the man who rolls instead of walks and talks as if he were upstairs and he wants you to hear him downstairs?"

"How do I know?" expostulated Frankie. "All I know is the King wears a funny hat with diamonds in it."

"Oh, I know the King all right. He comes to tea. We're both rather keen on the strawberry marmalade and I'm always told not to pig it if His Majesty's there. Mums says he has children at home and has to go out for his marmalade. It's the other one I'm not sure of, the Prime Minister one."

"Christopher Columbus, Marie! He knows the King of England!"

"What did you expect, Frankie? He's a duke. Sure, even the King of England has to have somewhere to go when he goes out."

"Kid—"

"He's a duke, Frankie. You're supposed to call him Duke So-And-So. Duke Robby, I guess, is it?"

"We kidnapped him, didn't we? I'll call him any damned thing I please. What did you call your daddy, kid—your papa?"

"Sir."

"What?"

"I called my father *sir*, sir."

"And what did you call the King?"

"Sir."

"You call everybody sir?" Marie asked.

"Yes, sir."

Frankie looked shrewd. "If the King of England likes strawberry whatever-it-is, what does the Prime Minister of England like?"

"If he's the one I think he is, sir, he likes cigars—great, long ones—and he likes other people to light them for him, sir, as long as they don't interrupt him when he's talking, which means he really doesn't smoke all that much, sir. And brandy at tea time. Nanny says it's a sin, anyone having brandy at tea time, and that's why we'll lose the war for sure."

"We'll lose the war because the Prime Minister of England drinks brandy?" Frankie shook his head.

"At tea time, sir. Nanny says a little brandy at breakfast is all right because I've seen her take it then. Knocks on the door of the heart, she says, and tells it to move along."

"Isn't he a darlin' boy?" The teakettle was whistling. "There's our tea now. Would you like a cup of tea yourself, Frankie?"

"I'll have a brandy. I need an excuse for losin' a war."

"Sure, you know we haven't had anything like that…"

She was putting three cups and saucers and spoons on the table. "You'd like tea?" she asked Robby.

"Oh, yes, sir, ma'am."

"I thought you might."

Frankie said, "You just can't ship a kid across the ocean, especially on a special ship! And then just leave him there on the dock! Somebody must be expecting you."

"I was told I have an uncle here, sir, in New York, but I don't."

"The poor darlin'. All on his lonesome."

"Marie." Frankie sighed. He was enjoying dejection. "Let me try to get this through your melon one final time. If the kid don't belong to anyone, who's gonna pay ransom? I ask you!"

"Sure, somebody has to care about the tyke. You should have seen him in the road, Frankie, a wee tired child lookin' as confused as a gentle baker at a butchers' bloody convene."

"Lissen, kid: You got any family? Any family at all?"

"I have a grandaunt in Scotland, sir."

"Fat lot of good that's gonna do us," Frankie said. "From what I hear about the Scottish your grandaunt will send us a rent bill for keeping you. Columbus!" Frankie sighed again and shook his head. "Is your grandaunt rich?"

"Oh, I don't think so, sir. I heard when the war came she had to help her gardeners herself."

"She has gardeners?"

"Sure, Frankie. And we can get the ransom in turnips and squash air-mail from Scotland. Have your tea now, Your Duke-ship." She poured steaming tea into the three chipped cups on the table. "And look what I happen to have." Marie Savallo put an opened jar of grape jelly on the table. And a stack of bread. And a knife. "Dip your knife in that now, lad. And you won't have to wrassle the King for it at all."

"Oh, thank you, ma'am."

"Saints, the child is starved."

"I missed breakfast, ma'am"—which, Robby thought, was as graceful an appraisal of his circumstances as he could muster.

"Look at him eat, Frankie. So delicate he does it there won't be a drop spilled!"

Apologetically, Frankie whispered to Robby, "She can't cook Italian."

"I'm sorry to hear that, sir."

Man-to-man, Frankie continued. "Wait until she gives you what she calls lasagna."

"I'm sure I'll enjoy it, sir."

"You won't recognize it."

"No, sir," Robby admitted. "I wouldn't."

"The way she makes it, it looks like Mulligan stew."

"I'm sure that would be very nice, sir."

"Everything she makes looks like Mulligan stew." Frankie looked at Marie's back to be sure she wasn't listening. "And it tastes—how does it taste?—it tastes like laundry."

Robby was halfway through the jar of grape jelly.

"Her *agnello dorato*? Mulligan stew with lamb. *Scaloppine di vitello*? Mulligan stew with veal. *Anguilla in gratella*?" Frankie and Robby were giggling behind Marie's back. "Mulligan stew with worms. Everything Mulligan stew."

Marie turned from the stove. "Here we've been jawin' away, Frankie, and no one ever had the decency to ask the child if he had a mouth on him."

Frankie cleared his throat. He became businesslike again. "I want him to answer some sharp questions."

Sympathetically, Marie said, "He missed breakfast, Frankie."

Frankie Savallo pushed his teacup away with his thumb. He lowered his two brown eyes like setting suns and they beamed into Robby's eyes. "Who's going to pay your ransom?"

Knife in the jelly jar, Robby hesitated. "Is that like a restaurant bill, sir?"

Marie sat down at the kitchen table. "Sure, the darlin' boy doesn't know what ransom is, Frankie. I don't think previously he's had much conversation with criminal types."

"I remember something about ransom," Robby said. "From *Robin Hood*."

"Now you've got it, lad," Marie cheered.

"He may be a duke," Frankie said, "but he knows less than a newt."

"And how much should a duke know, Frankie? Tell me that. When you're as important as a duke everybody knows things *for* you."

"Lissen, kid: Who would pay a lot of money to have you back?"

"Back where, sir?"

"Back home."

"But I haven't a home, sir. It went under a bomb."

"There must be somebody who cares about you!"

"I don't think so, sir."

"Think a little, willya? Columbus!"

Fortified by bread and jelly, Robby sat back in his chair, folded his fingers in his lap, and to convince them he was cogitating with great sincerity, squeezed his eyes shut.

And sincerely he did try to think who cared enough about him to pay money to have him back. There were his parents, of course, but they last had been reported seen in two coffins in the same aisle. Nanny had had hundreds of pounds under her bed, *for her old age in Bath*, and Robby doubted not at all Nanny would pay every shilling to have him back, but Nanny in her nightdress, and all her pounds, had been blown up by the bomb and fluttered down into rubble. There was Mrs. Jencks, matron at Wolsley School, but surely she wouldn't pay much to have a boy back when she couldn't tell one boy from another until their noses grew. Robby couldn't think Headmaster would take much out of his own pocket to get a tadpole back when he was surrounded by tadpoles. The family solicitors, Pollack, Carp and Fish, which Thadeus Lowry had mentioned, obviously didn't have any money to spare for a boy, or they would have sent a longer, more explanatory cable. And just the evening before Robby had seen Thadeus Lowry robbed in the street, so Robby knew Thadeus Lowry didn't have any money.

Robby opened his eyes. Frankie was still staring at him, awaiting the answer. "Sorry, sir. I can't think of one person who cares for me. Now may I have some more jam?"

"Of course, you can, darlin'. It's a wonder your pants didn't fall down, with your stomach so empty."

Frankie concluded, "We have to throw him back, Marie."

"Throw him back?"

"He's too little a fish to fry."

"Why, he's not a fish at all. He's a wee homeless boy."

"Homeless! That's what you should have thought of before you kidnapped him! There's no one in the world who'd give up a burp for this boy."

"You mean, throw the little fish back into the sewers of New York? There are sharks out there, Frankie. Bad people." Marie rolled her blue eyes to indicate to Frankie how bad those bad people were. "I couldn't sleep if we did that, Frankie. I have a conscience."

"You have a better idea?"

"Ask your Uncle Guido, Frankie. Now there's a man who knows how to turn a dishonest dollar."

"Uncle Guido won't give me the time of day since I married you. He thinks you're a pipe straight to the police. Only Tony he talks to."

"We'll ask Tony then."

"Tony? Give him some of the profits? It's not bad enough we're feedin' him now?"

"He's your brother, Frankie, and may have a better criminal mind than you. He's never seen the inside of a jail, and yet I know he does not tip-toe through the world in an entirely righteous manner."

"That draft-dodger."

"He's a quiet man, Frankie. A man of peace." Marie leaned forward assertively in her chair. "Frankie, darlin', your Uncle Guido doesn't like you because you're bubble-brained. Next to you, a subway train has more originality in the directions it takes."

"He thinks I'm bubble-brained because I married you! He doesn't *think* it! He *knows* it! You have to be one bubble-brained Italian to eat Mulligan stew all your life!"

"Have you noticed all the grape jelly is gone? And the bread? I've never seen anyone eat a whole jar of grape jelly before."

"The King is a hog," decided Frankie.

"It was very good, Mrs. Savallo. Thank you."

"Shush! Is that Tony now?"

Frankie listened. "If that was Tony, you couldn't hear him."

Marie said, "I didn't hear him." She began to gather the teacups from the table. She said, "I felt him."

Robby turned to the door, just as it began to open.

12
A Man of Peace

Tony Savallo's eyes, steady, direct, were in Robby's as the door opened. His eyes clasped onto the new, unexpected element in the room as if he had seen Robby through the door and had only opened the door to get a better look. Robby had the impression that if there had been a mouse in the corner behind the stove Tony would have seen it, too, instantly, and without moving his eyes.

"Hey, Tony," Frankie said loudly from his wheelchair. "Come meet His Lordship!"

"You'll like some tea, Tony?" Marie was bustling faster than ever. "I'll warm the pot."

Without his appearing to move, the door behind Tony closed. It latched with a barely audible click.

"Come sit down, Tony. Quick, Marie, some tea for Tony."

As Tony came across the room to Robby he took his right hand from the pocket of his windbreaker and kept it at the level of Robby's face. Even when Tony moved he seemed absolutely still. Standing directly before Robby, Tony settled the weight of his body on his right hip. His right pant leg brushed Robby's knee. Tony cupped Robby's left jawbone in his right hand and turned Robby's face up fully toward his own. Robby smelled from him the smell of lead pencils. The skin of Tony's face was clear and tight. His eyes were wide-set and black. The immobility of Tony's face appeared to come from its skin having been stretched too tightly over his skull. The long, smooth muscles in his neck were repeated on both sides of his wrist and the back of his hand.

"This is Tony, kid. My brother." Frankie shrugged. "A draft-dodger."

"He's against fighting," amplified Marie. "A man of peace."

"I fall off a roof," Frankie said, "spend the rest of my life in a wheelchair. Tony's got legs, but won't go to war."

Gently, Tony's hand moved up Robby's cheek, opened into fingers and combed through his hair. "War is inefficient," said Tony to Robby. "Don't you agree?"

"It can make a bloody mess, sir."

Tony put his hand back into his pocket and watched Marie putting more tea leaves into the pot.

"Lissen, Tony, sit down."

With his huge arm Frankie swung Marie's chair around, putting it into a more inviting position for Tony.

Even sitting in Marie's chair, Tony still did not seem to be at the table. It was more as if he were on a park bench, looking at everyone across a path.

"See, Tony, it's like this." Frankie was pulled right up to the table, both elbows on the surface. "Marie kidnapped this kid."

Such information, to Tony, was not cause for an aria. It was not even cause for a raised eyebrow.

"Right off the street. He was goin' to school and was lost or somethin'. And he turns out to be this English duke or somethin'. She recognized him from the newspaper. He's in this mornin's paper. Marie, get Tony the paper." Marie hustled from the sinkboard with the crumpled newspaper. "Hey, Marie!" protested Frankie. "The newspaper's still all covered with garbage! Whatsa matter with you?"

She shook the newspaper over the sink. "I didn't know I was going to kidnap a child, especially this child, when I was doin' up the breakfast dishes, darlin'." Quickly she laid the smelly newspaper flat on the kitchen table again in front of Tony. She placed her index finger on Robby's picture. "He ate a whole jar of grape jelly in one sitting, Tony. Would you believe it?"

"See? He's a duke or somethin'. He knows the King. The King of England, Tony."

Tony's eyes flickered acknowledgment of the newspaper laid before him.

"Only, Tony, see? Marie, the dumb broad, when she kidnaps the kid doesn't realize he's an orphan. She has to come home to me to find that out. His parents got killed in the war. Where does it say that? Down here, see? All he's got is an aunt who is a farmer somewhere. It's like that, see? So we've been sittin' here discussin' who's gonna pay his ransom, you got me?"

"Look at his clothes, Tony." Again Marie Savallo tucked her fingers down under Robby's shirt collar as if selling the item through fair examination of detail. "Everything special made for him and hand-sewn like a cardinal at his altar and he's only a wee boy whistlin' in the street."

"But, you see, Tony, we got this big problem: Nobody cares about the kid, see? I mean, that's a big problem for us. An uncle he's supposed to have uptown doesn't exist. The bastard's an orphan, Tony!"

Tony remained like a young lion in sunlight, not blinking.

"And, Tony, you know I can't go to Uncle Guido. You know how it is between us, with Marie and all. He thinks she's an informer or somethin'. And, you know, since I fell off the roof, you know, well, Uncle Guido thinks I got less brains than a mailbox."

Marie put a cup of tea in front of Tony.

He said: "Thank you."

Frankie said, "So what do you think, Tony?"

Marie sat down in the fourth place at table, her hands to her cheeks.

Tony drained his teacup, silently.

"The best idea we got, Tony, is to try hittin' up the King of England." Frankie's laugh at their best idea was a little nervous. "Only you can't just call up the King in England. It's long distance, Tony."

"A fearful long distance," agreed Marie.

"So what do we do, Tony?"

"There must be an embassy," said Marie Savallo. "Of course there is. In Washington, I bet it is. We should call up the Ambassador from England, Frankie." Excited by her own idea, Marie's index fingers made roads through the garbage on the newspaper. "Tell the Ambassador to tell the King we've kidnapped a little friend of his, a nice little lad in short pants named all those names he'll remember from the competition over the strawberry jam pot, and we want one hundred thousand dollars for his return, and none of his English funny money, by the way."

The Savallo brothers were looking at Marie. Frankie's mouth was open. "A hundred thousand dollars! Have you gone nuts?" Frankie jerked his thumb at Robby. "Who'd pay a hundred thousand dollars for this kid? He's not worth his weight in wood the termites have been at!"

Robby didn't know the value of a hundred thousand dollars, but he did consider one hundred thousand anything rather a lot. On the other hand, at Pladroman House in Mayfair he had seen wood the termites had been at and thought himself more substantial than that. If left to his own appraisal, Robby would assess his worth in neither terms whatsoever.

"I tell you, Marie," Frankie reiterated, "no one would pay one hundred thousand dollars for this kid, duke or no."

"Sure," Marie said quietly, but with great determination, "I wouldn't give the darlin' up for a penny less."

"Tony," Frankie shouted. "Make this woman shut up and tell me what to do, willya?"

Tony got up from the table. He put his hands over his head as far as they would go and clutched them together. He stood on tip-toes and stretched his whole body. He rotated his torso and yawned. He said, "Keep him."

"What?"

It was Frankie who spoke, but husband and wife looked equally shocked and perplexed by the comment.

"It's what you want to do." Tony relaxed from his aspirations and put his hands back in his pockets. "You can't have a kid of your own. Marie wants this kid. She kidnapped him, sure, but not for money. For love." Tony's unmoving eyes included Robby in their scope. "Keep him and love him."

"Tony!" Marie seemed embarrassed and appalled that her criminality should be so impugned before her husband. "It's not true at all." Tony's eyes locked in hers.

"We're too poor, Tony, anyway," she said. "This is an expensive lad. You didn't see what the boy had for lunch. A whole jar of grape jelly and a plateful of bread. That's all right as an investment, Tony, the fatted calf and all. But, every day, Tony, feedin' him while he's growin'? And would you have me hand-sewin' things for him till I'm old and blind?"

Frankie's eyes, as he stared at Marie, were incredulous. Marie's eyes shifted lowly as if her mind had been violated.

Tony stood nearer one of the cots.

"Tony, before you nap…" Marie got up from the table. "…I need five dollars for the groceries."

"Sure, Marie." Tony took a bill from his pocket and handed it to her. The number ten was in the corner of the bill Robby saw.

"I'll just get my coat," Marie said. As she moved quickly around the room collecting her coat and hat and purse she kept looking back at Frankie whose incredulous eyes were following her. She seemed to think Frankie was working up to an *aria d'agilita* which would prove too great a strain for her ears. "I'll be back," she said, as she scurried through the door.

"This time bring back the groceries!" Frankie shouted after her. "You bring back a herd of elephants, I'll kill you! Don't bring back a single elephant! Not even one!"

From the cot on which Tony lay came the sound of a chuckle.

Frankie looked at Robby and then at the pieces of his picture puzzle all over the floor. "Columbus," he said to himself. Then he shouted at the closed door again: "You see Mussolini in the street, leave him there! He wouldn't like your Mulligan stew *parmigiana* anyway! Neither would the Roosevelts or the King of France!" In a much lower voice, Frankie said, "Neither do I."

From the cot came no sound at all—not even the sound of breathing.

Frankie muttered, "I wonder what she really went out to do."

13
In Durance

"Columbus!" Frankie Savallo sighed.

Robby was going around the room on one knee picking up the pieces of the picture puzzle. His eyes kept going to one of the unoccupied cots. On one cot Tony Savallo was stretched out, flat on his back, hands folded over his waist. He had not removed his sneakers. Apparently he was asleep—his eyes were closed, his breathing was regular—but there was nothing in his posture which suggested he was relaxed. He looked like a motor which was running in neutral. Working his wheelchair around the room, Frankie scooped the newspaper off the kitchen table, brought it to the sinkboard, and rewrapped the garbage in it. "Columbus!" He sighed again. Robby brought the picture puzzle pieces to the kitchen table in fistfuls. Some of the pieces had been stepped on by Marie.

Finally, Frankie wheeled himself to the table and began studying the puzzle again. Robby stood on one foot, watching him from behind heavy lids. Frankie looked at him. "You must be as tired as a streetwalker in Venice," he said. "Marie pulling you all over the city. Why don't you crawl into that cot there by the stove, and grab some shut-eye?"

Robby was happy to. It had been weeks since he had been in anything resembling a bed. He took off his blazer and shoes, loosened his necktie and got under the blankets.

His pillow was against the white side of the stove. Across the room a torn green shade puffed back and forth in the window draft.

"Got to do something." At the table, Frankie muttered to himself. He had not moved many of the pieces of the puzzle. "What in heck do you say to an ambassador?"

After a few more moments, a few more heavy exhalations on the word *Columbus*, Frankie, with great determination, wheeled himself over to the telephone on a little table by the door. He hesitated, hand on the receiver, then picked it up and dialed *O*.

"Hello, operator? I want to speak to the King's Ambassador in Washington, D.C.…matter of life and death…

"Which king?…The King of England. What's his name, George the Third. No, George the Third was king when I was in fourth grade. By now it must be George the Fourth or Fifth…

"Great Britain? I want the Kingdom of England…U.K.? O.K., that must be it. They musta changed their name, modernized it, you know, keep up with the U.S.…

"Yeah, I'll wait…"

Hand over the mouthpiece Frankie stared solemnly at the floor. "What in hell I say? Hello, Ambassador, this is Frankie Savallo, nice Italian boy, New York. Big kidnapper. My wife she never misses a church but likes a big criminal for a husband…" He put his free hand over his eyes. "Ohhhh," he groaned. "They'll put me in jail for a million years. I'll be a little old man in a wheelchair, goin' around askin' everyone if they remember the taste of mozzarella. 'That's Frankie Savallo,' they'll all say. 'Big kidnapper! Kidnapped the Duke of Tootie-Fruitie. His wife got him sent up for life and married his Uncle Guido…'"

Suddenly Frankie jerked up in his chair as if called to attention. "Hello? Who's this? I'm calling the Ambassador from England. Are you the Ambassador from England?…What am I calling about? I'm calling about a kidnapping, is all. You better let me talk to the Ambassador…All right, I'll wait. But make it snappy, this is long distance…

"Oh, God, what am I doing? They'd never electrocute a man in a wheelchair. It wouldn't be nice…

"Hello? Ambassador?…You're not the Ambassador? Where's the Ambassador?…

"In *Warm Springs*! Doesn't he know there's a war on? Who are you?…Smith-Wilson, head of embassy security. Are you Mr. Smith or Mr. Wilson? What, am I talking to two of you?…Oh, one of you with two names. This is…never mind who this is. Lissen, we've got a little English boy here, calls himself Robert Burnes, but the newspaper says he's a duke, or somethin', an English duke, sent over here to get out of the way of the bombs, or somethin'… Evacuated and sent over here, yes…You are English, aren't you? I mean, you don't sound like Mayor La Guardia. So you should care…We want some money for this kid, if you take my meaning…

"What *for*? So we can give him back! This is an expensive kid. My wife she says he dresses like a cardinal…No, I can't afford to keep him. We live in one room, three of us, myself, my wife, my brother the draft-dodger. Whoops, shouldna said that long distance…Lissen, you don't understand me. We want money for this kid. He's a friend of the King—your King. They arm-wrestle over the strawberry jam or somethin'…Yes, I mean your King. This is an important kid. He doesn't look like much but the newspaper says he's important…Burnes, Robert Burnes. He's got lots of other names, too, just like you, but they're in the newspaper across the room with the garbage wrapped in 'em…" Frankie sat sideways in the chair and studied Robby in the cot. "Yes, he's got a roof over his head. You think I'm calling from Central Park?…Sure we fed him. Who wouldn't feed a starvin' kid?…What do you mean, he's all right! He's not all right! We want money for him! Don't you see what I mean?…Lissen, buddy, don't tell me there's a war on. Isn't my brother a draft-dodger?…Of course you've got funds for such a thing as this. Your King could sell one of his hats, plenty of money…I'm not just a good American, I'm better than that—I'm a good Italian-American!…We have to do our bit for the war effort! You have to do your bit, too, buddy!…Hello? Hello? Mr. Smith? Mr. Wilson?…Hello, English embassy?…It's my dime! I'm talking to you…Guess I'm not talking to you…" Frankie hung up the phone.

He sat where he was, by the phone, a moment. "Columbus," he said. "Phew. What a tight guy. Why should we help out them guys? Won't even pay a little ransom." He wiped the sweat off his face with both hands, sat still another moment, as if exhausted, then turned his wheelchair around. "Least they can't send me to prison for that!"

He wheeled over to the kitchen table and began moving around the pieces of his picture puzzle. "Least I didn't give up a life of mozzarella cheese!"

In his cot, Robby was beginning to think thoughts, hear voices and make choices. *Kidnapped!* He was beginning to understand that he had been taken prisoner, just like an English pilot in Germany or an English soldier in France. The Savallos' one-room apartment did not seem to Robby much like a prison, or a concentration camp. Nevertheless it was durance vile, or it would be durance vile had it not been for the fresh bread, the tea, the jar of grape jelly and the warm cot in which he now snuggled. It was durance.

Robby did not think he was heroic. He did not equate himself with people who could fly airplanes and shoot guns. Nor did he think he was in the hands of enemies, as they spoke nicely of His Majesty, the King. He *was* in a foreign land. Marie and Frankie Savallo had insisted to him he was kidnapped—even going so far as to consult him on how they were to get ransom for him. And they had approached the British government asking for money for Robby at a time when everyone knew the British government was especially hard pressed, financially, keeping all those ships at sea and planes in the air. To that extent they were enemies of His Majesty's Government. Were God and Country awaiting Robby's liberation as breathlessly as They would await the liberation of someone who knew how to fly a plane or shoot a gun? Robby didn't think so.

Having been brought up thus far like every other English boy, on jam and rhetoric, Robby's mind echoed with resounding phrases. *Excelsior! I am not to succumb! I am not to be denied! I am not to suffer the slings and arrows of outrageous fortune! I am to press on relentlessly!* Especially were boys of that era familiar with the wartime code of ethics. Admonitions had been poured into their jugheads through their ears. *It is the duty of every Englishman taken prisoner to escape!*

Robby would escape. He decided that. It was his duty. That much was clear to him. But first he needed sleep, and the cot by the stove was warm and snuggly. Too, he had a curiosity as to whether Marie Savallo's Italian cooking really tasted like laundry. It would be interesting to find that out.

He would escape, all right, but in a proper, gentlemanly, sedate and dignified manner—after he had napped, and after he had dined.

14
With the Aid of the Law

You'd think, in Robby's circumstances (plotting an escape from kidnappers) one would be greatly relieved, upon awakening from a nap, to find a large policeman standing over one's cot, looking down at one. Through shiny round glasses the policeman's eyes smiled; the corners of his lips tucked up into his cheeks in a pleased grin.

Robby had never seen a New York policeman before. The only other day he had spent in New York it was snowing and only the muggers had been out. But he had seen many London policemen and was able to recognize the significance of midnight blue in bulky material, brass buttons and gold insignia. This policeman's coat was generous in front, allowing for a bulging stomach, and furled up on one side, allowing everyone to see the handle of his handgun. Robby had been in New York City not much more than a day and already had seen two handguns; in war-torn England, as he had heard Thadeus Lowry describe his homeland, Robby had never seen a gun. This policeman's hat was different, too, not peaked to impale falling objects as is a London policeman's hat, nor strapped under the chin to prevent its being pinched over a fence by students who believed pinching policemen's hats the literary thing to do. This hat lay upon this policeman's head in a much flatter way, as if nailed on to his head some years earlier with the stern injunction never to pry it up.

Seeing a policeman standing over his cot gleaming down at him should have meant to Robby: Here is an arm of society into which a small boy might fling himself with full surety that Right would be done.

However, simultaneously to awakening and finding the policeman over his bed, Robby awoke to other sensations. The first was hunger. Not just your usual what's-for-dinner sort of hunger but a hunger sent up by a stomach which, having been well fed most of its existence, had been deprived of proper food for days adding to weeks, unable to accept what food had been sent to it, because of strategic wallowing, deprived further of proper food during long treks through snow and cold, and then fed bread, jam and tea, which only reminded the stomach that there was proper food in this world, food which could be properly taken and retained. That sort of hunger. The sort of hunger in which the stomach, having been reminded a few hours previously that food did exist, was wild with hope that it would soon be offered more. The stove atop Robby's head was hot. The room was steamy. He smelled a smell, which, although a new smell to him, he recognized instantly as a delicious smell: the smell of things to put in his mouth, savor, chew, swallow, send to his stomach with warmest regards.

He knew, as certainly as God was Episcopal, supper was in the offing.

Therefore Robby was not that sure he was glad to see a police-man standing over his cot. His nasal perception argued with his visual perception. Had Marie and Frankie Savallo been taken up for questioning? *Not now! Not in this crucial hour!* Since having his future indicated to him by the Headmaster of Wolsley School, Robby's education had increased only regarding the elusiveness of food. Clearly, now, he did not want to be rescued from supper!

"Well, Marie," said the policeman, removing his bulk from the airspace over the cot, "when you take to kidnapping, you don't think very big. Sure, even by the pound I don't think you'd get much for him."

Marie Savallo was setting places for four on the table. In his wheelchair, Frankie Savallo was turned away from the room, playing with the dial of a radio.

The policeman investigated the pots and pans on the stove. "What's this, Marie? More of Frankie's Eye-talian food?"

"More of Marie's Irish stew," said Frankie.

"You'll have supper with us?" Marie asked.

"I'll have a wee taste with you, just a smidgen, understand, before goin' off to headquarters to confirm how hard I've been workin' my shift."

"It's all right, Will'um," Frankie said. "Any brother of Marie's is just like a member of the family."

"Thank you, Frankie," Will'um said as he lowered himself into a seat at table. "I know what that concession means to you."

With hope of being fed before being rescued Robby sat on the edge of the cot and put on his shoes, regretting their lack of polish. He replaced his necktie. Robby was impressed by the civil manner in which this intrusion by the law into criminal matters was taking place. In a Christly manner the policeman was sitting down to break bread with the kidnappers. Difficult social matters hadn't been so smoothly arranged even at Pladroman House. Robby put on his jacket.

Then Robby realized Tony Savallo was gone from the other cot.

Marie's large, blue, wet, soulful eyes looked over at Robby. "Stirrin', are you? You little darlin'. Come up to the table with Frankie and my brother, Will'um, and bring your appetite."

Frankie had turned off the radio and wheeled to the table.

Robby considered it even more socially stressful that a genuine member of the family, Marie's brother, had been sent over to make the arrest. But—Robby was used to people behaving decently under stressful circumstances.

He sat at table himself.

"Lissen, Will'um," Frankie asked eagerly. "Did you read the article in the newspaper?"

"I did, Frankie, I read it chapter and worse. It says 'The Lord Is an Orphan,' which is not news, if I remember my early religious training."

"Yeah. That's the trouble, Will'um. Maybe you can think of somethin'." Frankie sighed into his empty plate. "Has ransom ever been paid for an orphan, Will'um?"

"Not that I remember, Frankie. Adopted orphans, of course, normally attract a better price than natural children, as adoptive parents usually go to greater, less pleasurable extents to have such children…" Will'um placed a baleful gaze on Robby. "But this wee slip of a boy might be the sparrow, Frankie, who falls to earth and causes nothing but universal, human indifference."

"Poor wee bird," muttered Marie at the stove. "Booted from the nest without his own wings."

"So you called the English Ambassador, Frankie," led Will'um, rolling on his hams as if to test for places his supper might settle.

"And I'm sure," said Marie, coming from the stove with pans, "the minute he picked up the phone he got all over nervous and burst out in an Italian accent so thick no one had half a chance to understand him."

"Marie, why you say such a crazy thing?" protested Frankie loudly, with a heavy Italian accent.

"Sure, and don't you always, Frankie? The minute you get nervous you sound like the Pope in a cold shower."

Will'um laughed. "And how would my sister know how the Pope sounds in a cold shower?"

Marie said, "I know he takes cold showers."

"You want to hear what I said to the Ambassador or not?"

"Ah, there he goes, Marie: soundin' like a Napoli thrush."

"You guys don't have an accent?" asked Frankie.

"Sure we do, Frankie. We speak English the way it's meant to be spoken—with the authority of the Irish."

"Irish-American is okay, but Italian-American is no good, is that right?"

"Calm down, Frankie, and tell us your story," said Marie, ladling lamb and vegetables covered with melted cheese and tomato sauce on Robby's plate, "in such a way we can understand it."

Robby leaned his head into the steam of the plate and closed his eyes. He wanted to be wrapped entirely in the atmosphere of food.

"Look at the little darlin', sayin' his grace," chortled Marie. "Isn't he a beautiful child, Will'um?"

The contempt in the policeman's eyes cut through the steam of the plates. "He's English," he said, as if contemplating something for which you could pay one dollar and get two dollars in change.

"Well, she can't cook Italian," Frankie muttered. He lifted part of his supper on a fork. "What is this?"

"It's lamb *Parmesan*, Frankie. Like your mother used to make."

"If my mother ever served my father such a thing," announced Frankie loudly, "I would never have been born!"

"Is it really that good?" Will'um said. "I must try some."

"Italian cooking," protested Frankie. "Marie boils meat and potatoes, pours tomato and cheese over it, calls it Italian cooking!"

Now that his host, Frankie, had picked up a fork, to attack his food but not eat it, Robby picked up his own fork. And Robby ate.

Marie sat in her place. "Now, Frankie, you were saying…?"

"I called the Ambassador. Down in Washington, D.C. Long distance on the phone. They call England the United Kingdom now. Bet you didn't know that, Will'um."

"Sure," said Will'um. "They've been callin' the auld place the United Kingdom ever since it began splittin' up. It's like us chasin' all the Indians out of the middle of the country and then callin' the place Indiana. There's no truth in names, Frank. Take your own, as a case in point."

"You stay calm, too, Will'um," directed Marie. "Don't we want to hear about the one hundred thousand dollars?"

"I'd like to hear about that," Will'um said dubiously.

Robby was not too amazed that Will'um ate with his hat on. Indeed it did look as if it had been nailed to his head. Besides, Robby's parents had had a frequent guest at Pladroman House, Rabbi Michael, who always ate with his hat on. Rabbi Michael had a melodic voice and always said he only came to Pladroman House for the eclairs. Robby was amazed, however, that Will'um ate while still wearing his handgun. Through dinner, while savoring, chewing, swallowing, Robby sneaked looks at Will'um's handgun.

Frankie said, "I goes: Ambassador, this is the biggest gangster in New York!"

Will'um asked, "You gave him your name, Frankie?"

Frankie blushed. "You think I'm stupid?"

Will'um glanced at the wheelchair and the telephone by the front door. "But you did call from here?"

"We keep that telephone in case anything happens to Frankie when I'm not here," Marie said. "Dreadful expense it is, too."

"It's a wonder the police aren't at the door this minute," said the man in the policeman's uniform, under a policeman's hat, wearing a policeman's badge and gun, eating his dinner at the Savallos' table. "If you hear a noise, Frankie, quick slip into me handcuffs— or we'll both be in trouble!"

"I goes: Ambassador, you tell George the King we got a little friend of his who likes strawberry jam—Duke…I still forget his name…and if he doesn't cough up a lot of money he'll never see his friend again."

"How much money, Frankie?" Marie asked. "How much money did you demand?"

Frankie blushed. "A hundred thousand dollars."

Sitting back on his chair, beefy hand on Robby's shoulder, Will'um asked, "Did you actually threaten to kill the child, Frankie?"

Red-faced, Frankie looked apologetically at Robby, who continued to eat his dinner. "Of course I did."

"That's the important thing, Frankie." Will'um shook Robby's shoulder affectionately. "You've really got to threaten to slaughter the tyke. Make it graphic, in the tellin'. You've got to say if they don't pay up, first you'll slice off his ears, then chop off his fingers, his toes, one by one, then chop off his hands, his feet, pluck out his eyes. And if they don't pay up at all you'll sever his head from his body and send it to them in a parcel." Will'um patted the back of Robby's neck. "That's the way to do it, Frankie."

Robby ate quicker.

"Very instructive, Will'um," said Marie Savallo. "That's why I went out and found Will'um in the street, Frankie, and had him home to supper. He has so much more experience in the law than we have."

"Is that about what you said to the Ambassador, Frankie?" Will'um asked.

Frankie swallowed. "Sure. I didn't play around none. He knew I meant business. I told him we want money for the kid."

"And what was the Ambassador's name, Frankie?" asked Will'um.

"I don't know," Frankie said. "How many ambassadors from England are there?"

"Only the one."

"He was the Ambassador, all right," insisted Frankie. "He talked like he had a mouthful of marbles."

"Proof enough," said Will'um.

"And what did the Ambassador say?" asked Marie. "What arrangement did you make to get the one hundred thousand dollars?"

Frankie looked at the center of the table, swallowed, looked at the floor each side of him, swallowed again. Lamely, he said, "I told him I'd call him back in a day or two."

Marie stared at her husband, at her brother, and at her husband again.

Will'um said, "I don't believe a word of it."

"Believe it!" Frankie shouted. "End of the month I'll give you my telephone bill! Long distance to Washington!"

"Well..." said Will'um.

"You're a cop! Believe in the evidence! Even my brother, Tony, knows that! Even in his sleep, Tony says, 'No evidence. There's no evidence'!"

"Shush, Frankie!" Marie gasped. "You're not supposed to mention *your* brother to *my* brother! Tony's a draft-dodger, mind you, and Will'um here is in the law!"

Suddenly, Frankie's face went white. He sat forward and put his elbows on the table. His eyes sought out, searched Will'um's.

"Honest to God, Will'um, we haven't seen Tony in months." Frankie was speaking rapidly. "Last we heard from him he was in Colorado, Texas—"

"Sure, Frankie." Will'um waved Frankie's mouth closed with his hand. "And he works for your Uncle Guido and hasn't been seen since this mornin' on Second Avenue."

"Tony?" Frankie looked pleased. "You say Tony's in town? Hey, Tony! Maybe he'll stop by, see us, Marie!"

"Honest, Will'um," added Marie. "We never see Tony."

"Speaking of evidence..." Will'um cleared his throat. "I observe that there are three beds in this room. Who's the third one for? The maid?"

Frankie and Marie looked at each other.

"That's for the kid," Frankie said, nodding toward Robby.

"But the bed was here last week," Will'um said. "And the kid wasn't."

"Well," laughed Frankie. "We were hopin' you'd stay overnight, Will'um."

"The bed's been there a long time," said Will'um.

"For a long time we been hopin' you'd stay overnight," insisted Frankie.

"And that's all I'll hear about evidence from you, Frank Savallo." Will'um pushed his plate away with his thumb.

Fluttering, Marie stood up. She grabbed Robby's plate. "You'd like some more, wouldn't you, darlin'?"

"I would, ma'am. I missed tea."

"Sure, and doesn't he eat like an Eye-talian, though?" mused Will'um. "Now you see it; now you don't. Food on his plate comes and goes just like that will-o-the-wisp brother of yours, Frankie."

"And without spillin' a drop, Will'um," Marie said from the stove. "Did you notice?"

"He eats like a cop," said Frankie, softly. "The kind who clean out a grocery store without stoppin' at the cash register."

Marie put a filled plate in front of Robby. And Robby ate.

Sitting down at her place at table, Marie asked, "Do you have any ideas, Will'um?"

"What does he know?" scoffed Frankie. "He's a flatfoot! A cop! Your brother!"

"Indeed I do have an idea," said Will'um. "One I think that would work and get you your one hundred thousand dollars. For your old age, Marie."

"Do you, now?"

"I do. Mind you, it's only my sister's old age I'm thinkin' of, seein' Frankie here doesn't work much since fallin' off that roof while doin' a job for his Uncle Guido. A moonlit night it was, too. Tell me, Frankie, did the moonlight get in your eyes?"

"Will'um, be kind," admonished his sister. "A terrible thing. Spendin' your life in a wheelchair just because a shingle gave way." Will'um pinned her with a caustic look. "Of course," she admitted, "the shingle was five stories up on a dark night."

Sitting back in his chair, legs crossed, arms folded across his chest, Will'um waited for the silence indicating complete attention. "It occurs to me," said Will'um, rolling the only R he had to roll, " 'The Lord Is an Orphan' and all that.. . well, it occurs to me that that article in the newspaper we all enjoyed readin' so much... well, you might say it was tinged with the brush of sentimentality. Wouldn't you say it was a wee bit sentimental, Marie?"

"I wept when I read it, Will'um."

"I'm sure," rolled Will'um, "many another woman at her kitchen sink readin' this morning's *Star* felt the same as you did, and wanted to rush out into the streets of New York and clasp the wee, homeless boy to her bosom."

"You think so, Will'um?"

"You're not an unusual gel, Marie, except you married a man who thought he had the wings of an angel right up to the moment he found himself in midflight."

"Go on, Will'um, and stop teasin' my husband."

"Now, who was this man at the *Star* who wrote this piece?"

Marie dashed to the sink counter.

"Thadeus Lowry, the name is."

She brought the smelly newspaper back to the table.

Will'um bent his head to confirm the byline. "Ah, yes. Thadeus Lowry. I think somethin' can be worked out, Marie, considerin' the power of the press, and this man's excitin' literary ability."

Will'um stood up and adjusted the flap of his coat over his holster.

"I don't know what you're thinkin', Will'um," said Marie.

"If I told you," said Will'um, "Frankie here might insist on helpin' me, and we'd never come to know if the plan might have worked on its own merits."

"He's not thinkin' anythin'," scoffed Frankie. "He's eaten, and now he's leavin' so he won't have to help wash the dishes."

"You're good to help us, Will'um," Marie said. "What with your career and all."

"Blood is thicker than water," said Will'um. "Thicker than whiskey, too, although I don't know how I'd ever find that out, havin' supper at your table."

15
The Power of the Press

"My God, Frankie! Look what I've got!" Next morning Marie Savallo stood in the door of the apartment, hat and coat on, eyes big with alarm. Her purse dangled from one forearm. Together, her arms clutched a newspaper to her bosom.

"You go out for a job and kidnap a kid!" shouted Frankie from his wheelchair by the window. "Today you go out to get a job and come back right away with a newspaper!"

Such was the conversation which awakened Robby Burnes next morning. The night before, having eaten more than he ever had in his life, his head lolled, his eyelids had lowered while he was still at the table thinking about getting up and making good his intention to escape. He had felt strong arms putting him into the cot; warm fingers undressing him.

"Look at this, will you?"

Marie put the newspaper on the kitchen table. Frankie wheeled over to it. Instantly his lips began to move as he read.

Robby jumped naked out of bed and looked for his clothes. Between the other side of the stove and the apartment's back wall, cater-corner from wall to wall, ran a short clothes line. Hanging from the line, looking as dejected as only wet laundry hung inside to dry can, were his shirt, his underwear, his stockings. Now, Robby saw, he was a prisoner of wet. His shorts and his blazer were over the back of a kitchen chair. He put those on.

On one leg Robby stood behind Frankie's wheelchair and looked at the newspaper.

EXTRA

ORPHANED DUKE KIDNAPPED

BY THADEUS LOWRY

The same photograph of Robby sitting on his suitcase was on the front page. The caption read: *Save the life of this child!*

A sub-headline read: STAR COLLECTS THE RANSOM. YOU, TOO, CAN GIVE.

In the silence of Frankie's and Marie's reading, Robby also read:

Little Robby Burnes, the 10-year-old Duke of Pladroman, who arrived on these shores a scant two days ago, has been kidnapped.

The New York Star has set up a special fund — The Robby Burnes Ransom Fund — in hopes of fulfilling the ransom demands of those holding the child in captivity.

The Lord is an orphan.

After the special bylined report by this correspondent appearing in yesterday's New York Star, regaling the harrowing and horrendous adventures which have befallen the 10-year-old scion of one of England's most noble families in escaping war-torn England, more misfortune has befallen the blond, blue-eyed, 10-year-old-boy who yesterday captured the hearts of all New York.

And all New York — every New Yorker, every reader of The New York Star, every American — you, dear reader — are asked to contribute to the poor little Duke's return to safekeeping.

RANSOM

The kidnappers telephoned your New York Star correspondent last night and demanded ransom of $100,000 to be raised by public subscription and paid at once — or else.

The voice on the other end of the telephone wire was cold and menacing — surely that of a man who has lived a degenerate, degraded life far outside the law. There was no doubt on the part of your New York Star correspondent that the caller would stop at nothing to attain his ends, however foul these ends are.

Immediately, The New York Star presses were stopped. The front page was ordered remade.

What matters the tides of battles, the oratory of heads of states, when the specter hovers over the city of a little lost boy, cowering in some cold corner, starved and beaten, a knife at his throat?

FATE

Is this American?

Can not even one small boy find peace and security, warmth and love, for one day on these shores that have hosted millions of the poor and needy of other lands, without being confronted by fear and violence, his life imperiled anew?

What are those abroad who send their children to us for safe-keeping during these dire days to think?

"I can take anything," the 10-year-old boy had said the day before, in speaking of his recent past, both parents having been murdered by a Nazi bomb, his school friends lost, a harrowing escape across the cold, storm-tossed North Atlantic dodging torpedoes.

The 10-year-old boy did not know what fate, what new horrors awaited him on these shores he had approached so trustingly.

SPIRIT

Yesterday morning, Robby Burnes (as the 10-year-old Duke of Pladroman democratically calls himself), up from a bed soft but new to him, comforted by the family of your New York Star *correspondent, who had guaranteed his safekeeping in the United States to the government of Great Britain, full of specially ordered kippered herring, muffins and weak tea—his favorite breakfast—set off for his first day of school in the new land.*

As he started bravely down the street, he turned back and waved gaily, full of confidence, at the loving, proud couple in the door seeing him off.

The night before, over a special family celebration dinner of roast duck and sausage and plum pudding with his loving guardians, he insisted that next day he would seek out the school himself, settle himself in, and make his own way, in the true American spirit.

But little Robby Burnes never reached the local public school.

MUM

No word was heard of him until the cold, menacing voice of the kidnapper telephoned your correspondent at The New York Star *last night.*

One hundred thousand dollars in exchange for the freedom—almost certainly, the very life—of a 10-year-old orphan.

The publisher and editorial staff of The New York Star *reached the decision without hesitation to set up a special fund for the return of Robby Burnes. Our prestige abroad, as a responsible people full of heart, is at stake.*

Would you have the free world think of America as a place where a child, sent for safekeeping, disappears within 24 hours?

Robby's mum, the late Duchess of Pladroman, was known as one of England's most charitable ladies. She would rush to benefit any worthy cause, especially any cause concerning the welfare and safety of children.

Consider what your own freedom is worth. Of more importance to you, we are sure, consider what the safety and freedom of your own child is worth.

Send whatever you can afford—a dollar, five dollars or more—to The Robby Burnes Ransom Fund, care of this correspondent, The New York Star, *to help regain the freedom, save the life of this child!*

" 'A little lost boy, cowering in some cold corner, starved and beaten, a knife at his throat'!" expostulated Marie Savallo. "My God, Frankie, this is terrible. I'll go find Will'um at once."

No matter how many times Robby tested his clothes during the day, they remained wet. He did not fancy making his escape into a New York winter without stockings, shirt or underwear. Although aware of his duty as an Englishman, Robby was also aware that he ought not to turn out improperly attired.

At the kitchen table he helped Frankie Savallo with the picture puzzle, which was not at all easy. As the picture developed, Robby discovered it was of the Sahara Desert, which has no landmarks. Fitting pictures of sand which were as big as the top of his finger to other pictures of sand, with neither color nor shape to distinguish piece from piece, soon became one of the more arduous tasks of his life.

Midafternoon, Marie appeared in the door again. This time her arms were stuffed with newspapers.

"Oh, Frankie!" she wailed. "I couldn't find Will'um at all!"

Robby helped her spread the newspapers on the kitchen table. Under the newspapers pieces of the puzzle separated.

HAVE YOU SEEN ROBBY BURNES? shrieked *The New York Star.* There, on the front page, was the same picture of Robby, disembodied. Only his head remained, staring at the reader with such pathos that even Robby himself felt a tinge of sympathy.

EXCLUSIVE

$10,000 TOWARDS $100,000 RAISED
STAR PUBLISHER DONATES $5,000

BY THADEUS LOWRY

Someone has seen Robby Burnes—of that New York Police are certain.

A 10-year-old boy cannot disappear off the streets of New York in broad daylight without someone seeing him.

Have you seen Robby Burnes?

Already, after the report by this correspondent in this morning's Star, *$10,000 has been pledged to The Robby Burnes Ransom Fund.*

The first $5,000 was donated by the publisher of The New York Star.

By decision of the publisher of the New York Star, *after consultation with New York City Police and the Federal Bureau of Investigation, this amount—$10,000—will be given to anyone coming forward with information leading to the rescue of Robby Burnes and the arrest and conviction of his kidnappers.*

UNIFORM

A ransom of $100,000, to be raised from the public, the readers of The New York Star, *has been demanded by the kidnappers for the safe return of Robby Burnes.*

Certainly those involved in his kidnapping—those who know where Robby Burnes is—have seen him.

Distinctive in appearance, the 10-year-old Robert Duke of Pladroman, who arrived, an orphan, after harrowing adventures from war-torn Europe Wednesday, when last seen was still wearing his English school uniform—a blue cap, blue overcoat, blue kneesocks, blue shorts and jacket, white shirt and striped tie.

Emblazoned on both his cap and jacket pocket is the Wolsley School emblem—a stag sharpening his antlers against an oak tree...

The report then went on to recap Thadeus Lowry's Thursday morning story of Robby's arrival and Friday morning's story of his kidnapping, plus instructions to the reader how to subscribe to the Robby Burnes Ransom Fund.

All the other Friday afternoon newspapers which Marie Savallo had brought home clutched to her breast in a jumble reported the juiciest elements of the story which had appeared that morning in "another New York newspaper." At least two of the newspapers announced they were cooperating with "another New York newspaper" to help raise the ransom. Contributions could be sent directly to them.

Robby was reported as ten years old in all the newspapers, which pleased him but made him doubt the accuracy of journalism.

"They've got ten thousand dollars already, Frankie," Marie said, "between breakfast and lunch!"

"And look what they're doin' with it!" shouted Frankie. "The first money they've got they're out lookin' for us with it! They've put bloodhounds on us!"

"A fearful lot of money," said Marie with awe. "Ten thousand dollars. Perhaps we should accept it as a reward, Frankie?"

"Read what it says, Marie! You need a conviction to get a reward! That means somebody has to become a convict. Who are you gonna convict? Frankie Savallo?"

"No, no, darlin'. I wouldn't think of it."

Frankie had wheeled to the windows overlooking the alley at the back of the apartment. He pulled down the green shades. "Lissen, Marie. You sure nobody saw you with the kid?"

"I can't be sure, darlin', but I was circumspect in me comin'. But wasn't it yourself who shouted 'Kidnap!' for all the world to hear the first hour we were at home?"

"I never said a word out loud, Marie. I swear to God!"

" 'Swear to God!' You swore so the whole street could hear you, let alone saints Mary and Margaret takin' their well-earned rest."

"You've done a terrible thing, Marie!" Frankie shook his head violently. "Terrible!"

"I may have done, at that," admitted Marie. "But, Frankie, how are we goin' to get the ransom, if it all keeps goin' to reward money?"

The Savallos remained quietly at home that evening. Frankie played with the radio dial. Each time a news broadcast began he changed the dial to a station offering a comedy or music program. Wordlessly Marie cleaned the one-room apartment as might a woman expecting a great many guests, a wedding or a funeral—or as might a woman expecting to leave the apartment for a prolonged period of time.

During the evening there came a knock on the door. "*Hoosh, Frankie!*" hushed Marie. Frankie snapped the radio off. Marie stood still, listening. The knock was repeated. Marie put her index finger to her lips. Shortly they heard steps retreat down the corridor. Only after a restless fifteen minutes did Frankie click on the radio again.

Trying not to be noticed, Robby tested his clothes hanging on the line time and again. He decided that whatever Marie had done in washing them had made them permanently wet. After a supper of potatoes and bread in warm milk—"Eat up," Frankie said grimly to Robby. "At least she can't say it's Italian"—Robby crawled into the cot to keep warm and, while his clothes tried their best to dry, fell asleep.

E X C L U S I V E

Robby's picture stared out from all of the Saturday newspapers, except *The New York Times*, and they all repeated, with imaginative variations of their own, except *The New York Times*, the legend of Robby Burnes as first written by Thadeus Lowry.

Marie's slinking in and out of the one-room apartment, her coat collar up, her eyes sliding left and right, buying all the editions of all the New York newspapers, clutching to her breast all these pictures of Robby looking pathetic might have indicated her uncommon interest in the crime to a casual observer. Such a casual observer, if pragmatic, might then have called the cops. But, as Robby had already discovered, people in this large city were not apt to be casual observers. For the most part, he had reasoned, they were too wary of being observed themselves.

Again *The New York Star* led the press and ran the EXCLUSIVE banner line.

NEW THREAT TO ROBBY'S LIFE
$27,242 RAISED SO FAR
YOUR HELP NEEDED
POLICE PERPLEXED

BY THADEUS LOWRY

Again last night your correspondent for the New York Star *was confronted by the icy, menacing voice of the kidnapper of 10-year-old Robby Burnes.*

He called, he said, regarding a report by this correspondent in last night's Star. *Your correspondent reported in last night's* Star *that the first $10,000 raised for the release of Robby Burnes would be used as a reward for anyone coming forward with information leading to the discovery and return of Robby Burnes and the arrest and conviction of his kidnappers.*

The first $5,000 was donated to The Robby Burnes Ransom Fund by the publisher of The New York Star.

The cold, metallic voice said that if any of the ransom money were used as a reward, or even as an offer of a reward for information leading to the capture and conviction of the kidnappers, "the kid won't live to say his prayers on Sunday."

Efforts to trace the telephone call were frustrated by electronic failure. Telephone executives said the trace only led back to a police station monitoring the call.

The publisher of The New York Star, *in conjunction with the New York Police, instantly withdrew the offer of a reward.*

GOOD JOB

New York City Police are perplexed by the disappearance of the 10-year-old Duke of Pladroman.

"This is a real professional job," said Police Captain Walter Reagan, in charge of the case. "These kidnappers knew what they were doing."

Repeating "it was a real clean job," Captain Reagan speculated yesterday that an extensive, well-trained gang of professional criminals had this kidnapping planned long before previously thought possible.

Conjecture is that while Robby Burnes was waving goodbye to his loving guardians Thursday morning on his way to school, a net had already been prepared by this unknown professional gang of kidnappers.

"It was neat work," said Captain Reagan. "I take my hat off to them."

RIVETER

So far, $27,242 has been raised toward the $100,000 ransom demanded for little Robby Burnes.

Not enough, if the life of Robby Burnes is to be saved!

Kind people have been giving their hard-earned money unstintingly to The Robby Burnes Ransom Fund.

The children at Manhattan Public School 169 (the school to which Robby Burnes was going Thursday when he was kidnapped) Friday donated $47.

"It's really our War Bond money," said Clarissa Allbright, a student caught in the schoolyard after school. "Principal said for once we can give without interest."

St. Theresa's Parish, in the Bronx, is having a special Holy Name Bingo Evening tonight. Profits will go to The Robby Burnes Ransom Fund.

Bingo organizer Guido Saxallo said, "It's the least we can do. Kidnapping a kid's a terrible thing. I mean, stealin's one thing, but stealin' a kid…you know? I mean, you can tell whoever'd do a thing like that don't have no family of his own, you know what I mean?"

*"I want to donate $1 to The Fund to get the little Duke back,"
said Mrs. Morris Blumgarten, 82, of Brooklyn. "How would I
feel if my husband didn't come home from work one night?"*

*Thomas (Tootsie) Auchinchlos, just back from a vacation in
Florida, donated $116. "That's okay," said the Manhattan street-
worker. "I won it on the ponies anyway."*

One donation, of $20, was signed, simply, "Rosey the Riveter."

*A bowling club in Huntington, workers in a Newark paint
factory, an infantry troop at Fort Dix about to go overseas, perhaps never to return — all have given to The Robby Burnes
Ransom Fund.*

What about you?

"Uncle Guido!" Frankie Savallo screamed as if he could commu-
nicate with his uncle directly through the newspaper. "Whaddaya
mean? Whaddaya mean 'Kidnappin' a kid's a terrible thing'? Always
criticizin' me! Read this, Marie! It's Uncle Guido, runnin' the bingo
up in the Bronx. Right here he says, 'You can tell whoever'd do a
thing like that don't have no family...' My own Uncle Guido said
that! Right here in the newspaper! About me!"

"Hoosh, Frankie. It's all right."

"Here, I fall off a roof for him in the middle of the night, spend
the rest of my life in a wheelchair, and here in the newspaper he
says I ain't got no family! My own Uncle Guido!"

"Frankie, you know he's just sayin' that for the Holy Name,"
Marie soothed. "None of that bingo money will see anythin' but
the darkness of his own pocket. Now you know that, don't you,
darlin'?"

"Yeah, but Marie—insultin' me here in the newspaper. My own
Uncle Guido! What does he mean I don't have no family of my
own? I got my Uncle Guido, don't I? Whatsa matter with him?"

"Console yourself, Frankie. Here's this policeman sayin' it's a
nice professional job and he takes his hat off to us."

" 'Nice professional job'! Even the cops say it's a 'nice professional job.' And my own Uncle Guido says it's notta nice!"

"Calm yourself, Frankie. Your Uncle Guido would be jealous, if
he knew."

The New York Times, on page thirty-six, also reported the kidnapping of Robby. Or reported its having been reported.

BOY REPORTED KIDNAPPED

It has been reported by The New York Star *that Robert James Saint James Burnes Walter Farhall-Pladroman, S.Nob., son of the late William Duke of Pladroman, was kidnapped in New York City Thursday.*

A ransom of $100,000 is demanded by the kidnappers to be raised by public subscription. The boy arrived in New York Wednesday aboard an evacuation ship from England. He is eight years old.

"Hunh!" said Frankie at this last report of a report. "Fat lot of good *The New York Times* does us!"

"But it's right!" chirped Robby. "It says I'm eight years old!"

And the Saturday evening edition of *The New York Star* reported that the Robby Burnes Ransom Fund was up to forty-two thousand dollars.

"Look at that!" exclaimed Frankie. "Forty-two thousand dollars!"

And he looked at Robby with a new appreciation.

"That's all well and good," questioned Marie in a soft voice, "but how do we get the money?"

Frankie thought about that quietly.

"Do you think you might swallow your pride, Frankie darlin'," Marie asked gently, "and ask your Uncle Guido how we collect all this perfectly marvelous ransom people have put up for us?"

"My Uncle Guido!" scoffed Frankie. "He's not my uncle anymore! He says I don't have a family!"

"Anyway, Frankie…" Marie studied her fingers fanned out on the kitchen table. "Precious little of the ransom we'd see if your Uncle Guido collected it for us."

"My Uncle Guido—" Frankie began his expostulatory aria. And he sang and he sang and he sang. He sang high on the scale, and low on the scale. He recited, he declaimed, he reflected. Uncle Guido had never given him much encouragement, he remembered. Uncle Guido had stolen a bicycle for Tony—not Frankie. Uncle

Guido bought off the police the time Tony stole the mail truck; he never did such a thing for Frankie. Uncle Guido gave Tony a job smashing the windows of stores which were late paying protection to Uncle Guido; Frankie had to work putting eggs in boxes in a huge, cold warehouse. Uncle Guido gave Tony a new mohair suit; he sent Frankie up onto an icy roof five stories high. Now Tony came and went as he wanted, and Frankie was in a wheelchair. All because of Uncle Guido! Frankie was inconsolable. Frankie was heartbroken that Uncle Guido should criticize him that way in the public press. "Uncle Guido! Columbus!"

Supper was potatoes and french toast. Frankie wailed all through it. Robby took supper as an excuse to dress in his now dry stockings, underwear, shirt and tie.

After supper, while Frankie continued to expostulate in his chair, Marie undressed him, and bathed him with a sponge. Robby watched from the cot. Like most domestic routines, this scene was enacted without either participant speaking directly of it. Frankie could not undress himself without great difficulty, could not fetch water from the kitchen sink, could not wash himself thoroughly. Therefore Marie did it. And when Marie lifted Frankie bodily from the chair, a look in Frankie's eyes communicated with Robby more completely than could any five-act opera. Frankie's powerful arms were around Marie's neck. Although they were helping him to pull himself up, they were pulling himself up against her strength. Robby saw Frankie's eyes over Marie's bent shoulder. *You shouldn't be here, kid*, Frankie's eyes said to Robby. *No way you should be here.*

So, later, after the radio was off and Marie had helped Frankie lift himself from the wheelchair into his cot and Frankie's eyes had signalled the same message to Robby, *You shouldn't be here*, and the lights were off and Marie was snuzzling in her separate cot and the problem of how they could collect the ransom had not been solved, Robby solved the problem by removing it: Quietly he turned back the blankets of his cot, stepped into his shoes, knotted the strings, tiptoed to his overcoat and cap on a chair, picked them up, tiptoed to the door, and opened it.

"Robby?" Frankie whispered from his cot.

Robby stood still in the open door.

"Good luck, kid. Thanks for helpin' me with the picture puzzle."

Robby closed the door behind him quietly, and tiptoed down the corridor.

16
Philology

Robby escaped.

However, the question presented itself almost immediately upon his arrival on the dark stoop outside the Savallos' tenement that, although escaping is All Well and Good, clearly the Right Thing to Do, to where does one escape in America when one is escaping? From what Robby could see, America was all over the United States. And thus far in America Robby had been left shivering on a dock for eight hours, force-marched through a snowstorm, plied with liquor, starved, robbed of his parents' pictures, marched some more, mugged, starved some more, insulted, sent off on a fool's mission (to find a school in a land where there obviously aren't any), kidnapped, nearly suffocated in an underground train, and finally fed while the adults at table casually talked of his eventual dismemberment. He had escaped...but from what? Jam, lamb and eventual dismemberment. He was to press on relentlessly...but to where?

Subsequently, Robby was to decide that rhetoric is not unlike marmalade: It's exciting enough to take into one's system, but after a slightly sticky sensation turning vapid in one's innards, one is left with little substance other than having had a sweet illusion.

Before him America lay dark and still. He was on the top of a stoop at the top of a T-intersection. The road before him seemed to go nowhere but along itself; it was lightless and changeless. The street that ran from his left to his right was identical in its rightness and leftness; neither side had any characteristic which made him decide in its favor. Robby had already learned that walking blocks and blocks and blocks in New York was no guarantee of getting anywhere, even when one had an idea of where one wanted to get. Both streets before him were broken with potholes and curbs which had not withstood the weight of time. What little light there was reflected icily from the streets' black surfaces. Black snow formed ranges between sidewalks and streets. The hundred or more windows he saw in the brick buildings around him were blind with drawn shades. Smashed vegetable crates and excelsior from Saturday's market hours littered the sidewalks and streets.

To that point in his life Robby had not had great experience in making choices. He had never had to decide before where he was going, because he had always been told. He was going to breakfast, to chapel, to class, to luncheon, to nap, to sports, to tea, to commons, to bed. He was going 'round with Tom the driver to the garage to get petrol for the Rolls; he was going to the zoo; he was going to the Thesigers' for tea. There had always been some place to go; the future was downstream and to get there all one had to do was flow along nicely. Standing on the stoop, Robby even wondered if he might not sneak back into the Savallos' kitchen apartment and whisper-ask Frankie, now that Robby had escaped, where was he supposed to go—but, no, Robby remembered that Frankie seldom went out these days. The last place Frankie had gone had been five stories up to an icy roof on a dark night, from which he had descended involuntarily and speedily.

When escaping from a kidnap situation, Robby expected a logical place to go would be to the police. But the police, in the figure of Will'um, had known of Robby's plight and done nothing to encourage his freedom except advise the kidnappers, share their dinner with them, and recommend dismemberment. Robby had heard his father say that police control crime, but it was an education to Robby to discover how precisely, directly and deliberately police control crime. Subsequently, Robby would phrase the reality of crime as a perfect syllogism. Crime exists; police exist: *ergo* crime and police coexist.

Frankie had already appealed to His Majesty's Ambassador to the United States and even if Frankie hadn't expressed himself clearly regarding the captivity of Robby Burnes, whoever answered the embassy's phones clearly expressed complete indifference. Perhaps there would be more concern if the embassy knew that

Robby was no longer sheltered nor fed, but Robby had understood one fact regarding the British embassy above all others: It was *a long distance*. Supposedly the school to which he had been assigned was within the neighborhood of the Lowrys' flat, and he had never gotten there. *A long distance* in America, Robby already understood, was prohibitive.

Robby wondered where the Evacuation Ladies might be found on a late Saturday evening. At least they knew his name. They had called it enough. They knew Burnes, Robert as coming between Adowitz, Abraham and Collins, Peter. Robby envisioned the Evacuation Ladies' Saturday evening as sitting around a warm parlor in cardigans practicing their roll-calling. Besides having no idea how to contact the Evacuation Ladies, Robby's pride came to the fore. On Wednesday Robby had been a problem which the Evacuation Ladies had solved to their own satisfaction. Problems solved on Wednesdays should not reappear on Saturday evenings. It would disappoint them. Possibly make them think they'd shirked their work.

And Thadeus Lowry. Shivering on the stoop Robby thought long and hard about Thadeus Lowry. Contacting Thadeus Lowry would be easy. All he need do was ask anybody—if there happened to be anybody around. Everyone knew Thadeus Lowry of *The New York Star*, had said Thadeus Lowry of *The New York Star*. Thadeus Lowry might be glad to see him. Thadeus Lowry had done several days' work now, Wednesday, Thursday, Friday, and, Robby presumed, Saturday, and might be glad to return to one of the clubs where he was a regular and discuss again the time in 1938 when the Bishop stole the altar plate. Doubtlessly all this work would have been damaging to Thadeus Lowry, in his *chérie's* terms, brutal, in his own, absolutely exhausting. However, Robby was shrewd enough to realize Thadeus Lowry might not be glad to see him. He and Ronald Jasper had discussed that Thadeus Lowry had not had a good story since the Bishop stole the altar plate in 1938 and that Thadeus Lowry stood on such thin ice regarding his continued employment at the newspaper that he was getting water on the knee. It was clear to Robby that Thadeus Lowry had a good

story now. The Thadeus Lowry byline had been on the front page of
The New York Star three days running. Even *The New York Times*
had reported the news that Thadeus Lowry had a story. The goal of
one hundred thousand dollars raised from the public via Thadeus
Lowry's prose had been set. Robby tried to envision the expression
on the face of Thadeus Lowry if Robby—when less than half the
money had been raised—skipped gaily into the city room of *The
New York Star* chirruping some playful ditty as "Never fear, Uncle
dear, I'm here" between editions. The expression on Thadeus
Lowry's face might be similar to that on the face of Frankie Savallo
on that dark night just after leaving a roof five stories above the
ground and discovering he couldn't fly.

Besides, reasoned Robby, Thadeus Lowry and his wife had a
disdain for food which Robby did not share. In the short time
Robby had spent with Thadeus Lowry, Robby had discovered that
being well-fed was an illusion to which Thadeus Lowry clung most
fervidly and uselessly. He dreamed meals, luncheons, teas, dinners
and breakfasts before they happened and after they had never
happened. He even reported savory meals in the newspaper, dinner
of roast duck, sausage and plum pudding, breakfast of kippered
herring, muffins and weak tea which no one had ever savored.
Robby knew he had had chowder biscuits, bread, water and catsup.

Robby thus came to make his first mature decision in the most
mature way. His criterion was that element upon which all worthy
decisions are made, the fulcrum upon which everyone decides
where he will *go* next, what he will *do* next, upon which all life
plans and employment projections are settled, upon which nations
are constructed and collapsed, governments are elected and ejected,
revolutions are raised and subsided, wars started and stopped.
Robby decided on behalf of his stomach. He was going to *go* where
there was food; he was going to *do* whatever was necessary to eat.
So decide we all.

Robby considered where he had seen food since arriving in this
land of milk and honey. Why, to make the legend good: *right in
front of him!* In bringing him to her home, Marie Savallo had
marched Robby through an open-air market full of oranges and

apples and bananas and melons and potatoes and tomatoes and heads of lettuce and cabbages and sausages and hams and pudent chickens and food Robby had never even seen before. And the market was right in front of him! At most, down half a block and through that building full of animal carcasses now closed. In the dark it did not look it, it did not seem possible that this landscape was the fringe of an area peopled with aproned men and women all trying to empty their pushcarts full of food. Having a memory of the past, Robby knew a hope for the future.

He decided to stay right where he was. He decided to *go* no-where.

Yet it would be a long night, and a cold one. Standing on the Savallos' stoop he already knew it to be a long night and a cold one. He needed shelter. An enclosed place, off the snow and out of the wind. A place where he had some hope of snuggling into warmth.

The landscape didn't offer much. At first he didn't think it offered anything at all. The stoops were solid, the cellar-ways fenced, the sidewalks and streets snowbound and slick. There was a small pan-eled truck parked at the curb in front of him.

He went down to the van, tried the handle of the back door, and, to his surprise, it opened. With his hands he rummaged around inside. On the floor of the van were burlap sacks of potatoes. He had shelter, food, and a place to snuggle himself into warmth.

He had reasoned, sought, and found.

Robby climbed into the back of the paneled truck, pulled the door closed behind him, snuggled among the sacks of potatoes and, having recapitulated ontogeny, fell asleep.

Robby felt and heard a door slam.

Then he heard and felt an engine start.

The motor was making the paneled truck vibrate.

Robby's shelter began to move down the street, away, he feared, from his source of food.

Tossing off the potato sacks, Robby crawled forward and pressed his nose against the glass separating him from the cab. There were no streetlights. Cars and trucks in the wartime streets had hooded headlights. He had only a three-quarter view of the head of the man driving the van.

Yet Robby knew it was Tony Savallo.

He sank back against the potato sacks under the little window. *Good old Tony Savallo. Loving Tony Savallo. He placed the clear, tight skin of his hand against my cheek and tousled my hair. Masculine Tony Savallo. Smelled of lead pencils, as a man should smell of something. Kind and gentle Tony Savallo, a man of peace. Wouldn't go to war; rather help his uncle run bingo for the church. Calm and still Tony Savallo. Said little but "thank you." Slept with the dignity of a kingly sarcophagus at Westminster. Wise, understanding Tony Savallo. Understood more than greed in Marie's kidnapping me, perceived her loneliness and compassion and love. Good old Tony Savallo!*

The van slowed, stopped.

Robby got up again, knelt on the potato sacks, pressed his nose and cheeks against the small, thick window. Behind the driver's wheel, Tony was looking through his open window. He was watching a man walking along the sidewalk. Robby could see the man as a walking silhouette against an empty lot covered with fairly white snow. Tony was pointing something through the window, at the man.

There was a colossal bang.

On the sidewalk the man's back curved. His arms rose above his head. His hat fell off.

There was another colossal bang.

The man staggered sideways on a colt's legs, then crumpled. He sank beneath the knee-high wall of snow.

Robby inhaled, deeply, quickly. His scream rose in volume and pitch. It scraped his throat and vibrated his nose. *Tony shot a man!* Robby screamed even louder and higher on the exhale. *Tony murdered somebody!*

Tony Savallo's eyes, showing vast white areas around the steady brown pupils, appeared in the window. His face had an expression. It was first the expression of horror, then of rage. His face disappeared.

Robby screamed again. The van jerked into gear. Robby fell back onto the potato sacks. The van moved quickly, took corner after corner at high speed, its rear wheels slipping. Robby was rolled left, then right, then left again.

Finally rolling over, Robby spread his knees and his hands wide, got his balance, and worked his way up to the window again. Tony's right hand worked the shift lever and swung the wheel. His left hand steadied the wheel despite its still having a gun in it.

Robby saw the van beginning to pull up at a curb of a narrow street. He darted for the back door.

As soon as the truck stopped, Robby opened the door and jumped out. He slipped on the ice and sprawled on the ground. He saw Tony Savallo's feet land on the ground.

Quickly, Robby scurried under the van.

He watched Tony's feet step up into the back of the van. He heard Tony kicking and tossing potato sacks around.

Tony's sneakers appeared on the street, behind the van. For a moment they did not move. Then lightly, silently, quickly they moved onto the curb, over a low mound of snow. As Tony moved into the alley, Robby could see, from under the truck, that Tony carried the gun in his right hand.

"Whup, whup," said Robby. Lying under the truck at first his legs made a running motion but got him nowhere. "Whup!" Robby ordered. His body organized itself and Robby dragged himself out from under the truck. He became upright. He ran across the street and began to run down the alley opposite from the one taken by Tony.

Robby ran down the middle of the block, across a·street and into the next alley. Even though he assured himself no one, not even Tony Savallo, would spot a small, dark figure pumping down a narrow dark alley, Robby ran as fast as he could. Then he remembered the backs of his knees were white and probably as easy to spot as a bunny's tail in short grass. Then he reasoned that Tony Savallo, being more than twice his size, doubtlessly could run more than twice as fast. Then he recalled from Frankie's comments, Marie's comments, his own observations, that one didn't *hear*

Tony Savallo, one *felt his presence.* Robby felt the presence of Tony Savallo. Then Robby turned his head.

Tony Savallo, gun in hand, appearing to lope easily like a young cheetah out for a preprandial turn in the bush—his face expressionless, the brown of his eyes steady in skies of white—was right behind him.

Robby ran faster than any classmate or games master would ever think possible. However, while running, Robby realized this effort to outrun Tony Savallo down dark, slippery alleys held little future for him.

He took the closest turning, into a yard where a car was up on blocks. Without slowing even slightly, he headed toward a fence which was at least three times his own height. He had no conviction that he could jump the fence. If he had had opportunity to study the matter more at that point in his life, Robby would have known a human being cannot jump a fence three times his own height, without aid. Being ignorant of such conclusions, Robby jumped. However carefully scientists figure all contingent elements into their measurements and equations, sometimes they are ignorant, too, of the human element, which, in this instance, was sheer terror.

"Whup, whup!"

Robby saw the top of the fence pass beneath him and then the ground rush up to greet him. He landed on his feet, knees slightly bent, on cobbled stone.

Crouching, Robby panted and looked around some householder's backyard. In the moonlight he could see that the house along one entire side of the square backyard was brick. There were no lights on. The basement door, down a step or two, had an iron grille over it. In the yard were a few odd boxes, small, round objects which may have been discarded flower pots, and rubbish barrels with lids on them.

In a moment Tony Savallo would clamber over the fence Robby had so astonishingly vaulted.

As noiselessly as possible, with the aid of packed snow, Robby climbed into a rubbish barrel. He squirmed down, and reset the lid on top. Like a mole, trying not to rock the barrel much, he burrowed down into the rubbish. He tossed some old newspapers, cartons, and bottles over his back, shoulders and head. Scrunched thusly, Robby tried to recall some Resounding Rhetoric, from Church or State, encouraging someone Hiding Under Garbage, but nothing came to mind.

He heard nothing.

Until he heard, in almost the exact tone Frankie had used in whispering good-bye to him, "Robby? Hey, Duke?"

Tony Savallo's voice, just outside Robby's rubbish barrel, was calm and gentle.

Robby tried not to breathe. Considering the stink of the air he had to breathe it was comparatively easy for him to breathe little.

"Hey, Duke!"

Something in the rubbish barrel (other than Robby) moved. To keep it quiet, Robby clamped his hand over it. From its contours (although he had never held one before) he guessed (rightly) his coinhabitant of the rubbish barrel was a mouse. Its heartbeat was frantic in Robby's hand.

The air improved. Tony had removed the lid of the rubbish barrel.

"Hey, Duke? You're here somewhere. I know that. I'll hurt you less if you give up now, kid."

Robby, deciding he didn't want to be hurt at all, remained silent.

The lid to the rubbish barrel was replaced. It was not on tight. Robby could feel a draft of air.

"Duke?" Tony's voice, intermittently questioning the air, faded. "Robby?"

Not being able to hear Tony, Robby never was sure when Tony left the yard. After a while, Robby felt less of Tony's presence and made himself more comfortable in the rubbish barrel. Still keeping some rubbish over him, Robby sat on the bottom layer of newspapers and leaned his back against the barrel's curved side.

He brought the mouse to his lap and played with it. He walked it from hand to hand. He tried to hand-feed it some of the commissary from the barrel: eggshells, coffee grounds, cigarette ashes. He could not tell in the dark if the mouse was actually eating the menu, or just investigating each piece offered.

In time, the mouse's heartbeat slowed, as did Robby's.

In the first light of day Robby knelt in the rubbish barrel. He lifted the lid in its center, and, using the rim of the barrel as a turret, had a good look around.

Tony Savallo was nowhere in the yard. Closely Robby scrutinized the top rails of the three sides of fencing. On one board stood a drooped, bedraggled blue jay, looking as if it had spent the evening with Thadeus Lowry. The bird assured Robby no one else was around. There was no door in any of the three fences.

Robby leaned the lid of the rubbish barrel against the barrel's side and stood up. He put the mouse in his overcoat pocket. He arranged the pocket's flap so the mouse would have air to breathe. Then he climbed out of the barrel and replaced the lid.

Intellectually, Robby knew that only hours before he had leaped over that fence in a single bound. Now looking at it in the light of day he swallowed hard. If he had done such a thing once, he must be able to do it twice, but he didn't think so. Backing up across the yard, he contemplated what a running start might do for him and decided not much. Perhaps nighttime terror had taken him over the fence once, but daytime reason would smash him against the fence as certain as the King was English. There were too few boxes to pile up against the fence so he could climb over. He considered a combination of boxes and rubbish barrels might build him a stairway over the fence. The narrow brick house was silent. Dragging a rubbish barrel over the cobblestones would be noisy.

He went down the two steps, put his hand through the grille, turned the handle of the basement door and pushed. It swung open. The basement was pitch black. He pushed the grille and it, too, swung open. Robby stepped into the basement, closed the grille, and closed the door behind him. Then he couldn't find the handle of the door again, to open it, to let in light.

Across the basement from him was a live, red and yellow,

glowing thing. Robby stared back at it. It grew neither more nor less threatening. Then, suddenly, it did flare, grew bigger, redder. There was a wheeze and a dreadful clanking. The noise crossed the basement to him until it was directly overhead. Heat descended upon him. The increased light from the furnace permitted Robby to see its staunch squatness, its ungainly, octopus arms extending, twisting and turning throughout the basement and into the ceiling.

It also permitted him to find the cellar stairs.

On tiptoe he crept up the cellar stairs to the door at the top. Very slowly he turned the doorknob and pushed the door open a few centimeters. He put his face close to the door and peered through the slit between door and door frame.

A woman, entirely naked, stood in the kitchen with a coffeepot in her hand. Startled, she did not turn her head. Only her eyes darted to Robby, then swelled. She threw the coffeepot and hit the cellar door.

Then she screamed.

Robby pushed open the door and ran into the kitchen. He was looking for a door which would let him out of the kitchen. However he was stopped in his tracks, distracted, fascinated by the dance the woman proceeded to do. She began jumping up and down, one leg at a time, as if pedaling a bicycle. Her hands darted from her breasts to her crotch and back again in a great flurry as if she were sending a very urgent message by semaphore.

Her eyes remained round and staring.

"Morning, sir, ma'am."

She released one arm from its futile duty long enough to reach to the sinkboard, pick up a bottle of milk and hurl it at him. It smashed against the wall just over his shoulder, providing plain evidence that her aim was improving. Still doing her silly dance, she moved forward to the stove and grabbed a frying pan by its handle.

Robby pushed backwards through a swing door, turned around and found himself in the main corridor of the house.

A man in a bathrobe, his hand on the bannister, was rushing down the stairs. "Where are my glasses?" he shouted. "What's happening?"

The front door was directly in front of Robby. He ran for it, yanked it open, and scurried through it.

The man, his arms outstretched to grab Robby, dashed into the edge of the open door. "Damn!" he yelled, putting his hand to his face.

The naked lady, still wielding the frying pan, stood on the other side of the man in the front hall.

Robby reached in and pulled the door closed with a slam.

"Damn, damn!" Robby heard through the door.

"A boy!" the woman hollered. "He came up out of our basement! A thief!"

Standing on the front stoop of their house, Robby looked left. And he looked right. And he looked directly across the street.

And directly across the street, leaning against a lamp post, in his green windbreaker, arms folded across his chest, stood Tony Savallo.

The door behind Robby began to open.

17
Taking Stock

"Thief! You little thief!"

Robby jumped off the steps and began running along the sidewalk to his right. Behind him, standing on the steps of his house in his bathrobe stood the householder slandering Robby in a loud voice. Across the street, not far behind him, trotting easily, was Tony Savallo.

"Whup, whup," Robby encouraged himself.

Sunday-dressed people were gathered around a newspaper kiosk on the corner. Some were examining their front pages; others were chatting with each other. There were tall stacks of newspapers awaiting quarters. Leaning against the stacks, hanging from a telephone pole, propped against a No Parking sign, were large posters touched up in color—too much color, red! white! and blue!—of Robby looking cold, lost, hungry, forlorn, sitting on his suitcase. The poster line read:

HAVE YOU SEEN ROBBY?

Robby's blodgy face was on the front of every newspaper he saw. Dashing through the crowd he would have liked to have stopped and given the casual strollers on a nice Sunday morning greater opportunity to *see Robby* but as Tony Savallo was only a few steps behind him Robby decided it was preferable to keep himself a blurred streak. Breathless, the most he managed to utter on his quick passage through the group was "Whup! Whup!" which he knew to be an expression inadequate to his situation. Out of the corner of his eye he did catch the headline of *The New York Star*.

$63,000 RAISED FOR ROBBY

"Whup, whup!" Robby cried out plaintively to no effect, as he darted through the forest of knees. "Whup!"

Halfway down the block, across the street, there was a church. Its bells were tolling. Its doors were open. People were climbing the steps to it. In the street in front of the church were many, many black limousines.

Recollecting from his narrow reading, mostly of *Robin Hood*, that churches universally were regarded as places of sanctuary, Robby quickly decided to attend services. Nearly being hit by a large LaSalle, Robby ran across the street and up the church steps. He received a few sour looks from the parishioners for his shoving them around the knee joints in his hurry, but a few benign looks as well from grown-ups always glad to see the young hasten to suffer unto God.

An ornate, carved sign in the vestibule identified this as the CHURCH OF JESUS CHRIST MATERIALIST. A brass plaque below it notified people that the current pastor was the Reverend John Maple.

Looking back through silk stockings and striped trousers Robby saw a pair of sneakered feet making its way through the mob at the top of the stairs. Apparently Tony Savallo was not going to hold as sacred the sanctity of the church. Clearly he had not read *Robin Hood.*

Robby entered the auditorium of the church, avoided the clogged main aisle, turned to his right, then left, and went down the right aisle. The church was nearly full. He took a seat in a pew just forward of a thick pillar. Two old ladies, one who had a great many chins and the other none at all, made more work of making room for him than was necessary. Their smiles were grimly righteous.

Catching his breath, Robby looked around him. It was a huge church. In place of an altar was a long table with twelve chairs around it. The pulpit was high. In front of the podium at its top was an iron grille, but not of the sort he had seen in English churches. This grille was more like the grilles he had seen tellers sit behind when he had visited English banks.

The bars were thin and vertical; under them was a rectangular open space as if for passing things through. The woodwork of the pulpit had a symbol repeated on it a dizzying number of times. The symbol was a vertical "S" with two vertical lines through it.

Robby recalled that it was Sunday and that a cold, metallic voice had notified Thadeus Lowry that Robby might not live to say his prayers on Sunday. Robby found a shred of cabbage in his hair and dropped it on the floor. The women beside him were beginning to point their noses at him. Robby decided to pray.

He went forward onto the kneeler, folded his hands, and closed his eyes.

Oh, Lord! Giver of life, please don't take away mine while I'm still using it, he began.

The woman beside him, out loud and with some apparent distress, said, "Oh, Lord!"

Why bring me through this vale of sorrow and tears to this crazy place where ill-wishers lurk around every corner? For the paths of righteousness in this new land, unless tread upon carefully, surely lead straight to hell.

Someone else, possibly the man in front of Robby, was heard to say, "Oh, Lord!" Robby also heard a distinct sniffing from the ladies beside him.

Why not bring a scourge of locusts upon the houses and down the necks of all those ill-wishers who are trying to dismember me, in particular one Tony Saxallo, who I'm beginning to suspect is behind me again?

Not meaning to question Your infinite wisdom, Sir, but how come I'm a hundred-thousand-dollar Duke made to lie down with mice in a rubbish barrel?

…Of course, in Your infinite wisdom and mercy I did discover I can run like hell…

The sound of sniffing was growing in a widening pool around Robby. Peeking through his clasped fingers, Robby saw a great many faces were turned toward him, and there was distress upon each face.

Oh, Lord, forgive me, your most unworthy servant, for coming into Your house of worship smelling like a garbage pail. Peeking again through his fingers, Robby saw the ladies beside him had moved as far away from him as possible—which wasn't far. *Perhaps*

it is Your Divine way of making these ladies beside me exercise the
tolerance inherent in Your Divine Teachings.

The sniffing was loud.

Oh, Lord, not a sparrow falls from a tree without Your gracious
Eye upon it.

I was never sure what Your Grace, in His infinite wisdom and
mercy, ever actually did about the sparrow once it clunked to the
ground, but I promise to read that passage again, if I live.

Oh, Lord! Don't forget your tadpole!

Robby felt a sharp pain in his ribs. It was caused by the index
finger of the lady of many chins sitting beside him. For a bad
moment, Robby thought the ladies beside him, flunking Christian
tolerance, were expelling him from the pew, having determined he
enjoyed nothing akin to the odor of sanctity, and thus were sending
him to his certain death. No, the organ was exhaling at a high
volume and it was the need of the ladies that Robby stand with the
rest of the congregation and raise his voice in song. Perhaps they
thought they could be saved by having the air in their immediate
vicinity vigorously stirred. They jammed an opened hymn book
into his hands. "Silence Is Golden" was on the left page; "The
Silver Tongue" on the right.

Robby did not know which song they were singing, so, with
Divine Gusto, he sang one verse of one song and one verse of the
other, alternating lines for the third chorus. This technique had
always worked so well at Wolsley School that he had been permanently excused from choir practice.

The mouse in his coat pocket, doubtlessly invigorated by the
joyful noise, scurried chirruping among the lint. Robby stroked
the wee beastie with his thumb.

As the hymn was wearing down—especially around Robby, where
people were looking at him again, as apparently his noise was not
making them joyful—Pastor Maple climbed into the pulpit so
slowly one would think his every step weighted by centuries of
consideration. His robe was a peculiar shade of green. Stitched
into the robe were faces and pictures Robby couldn't recognize,
and the Arabic numbers 5, 10, 20, 50, 100, 1,000.

"Amen!" Robby always gave his best to every amen to make up for earlier transgressions with both words and music.

The congregation rustled onto their seats, coughing and blowing their noses preemptively.

Pastor Maple blessed the congregation by describing the letter *S* in the air with his hand, then slashing two vertical lines through it.

"*E Pluribus Unum,*" he announced.

The congregation hushed for the lesson.

"Take stock!

" 'Hearken: Behold there went out a sower to sow.

" 'And it came to pass, as he sowed, some fell by the wayside, and fowls of the air came and devoured it up.

" 'And some fell on stony ground, where it had not much earth, and immediately it sprang up, because it had no depth of earth; but when the sun was up, it was scorched; and because it had no root, it withered away.

" 'And some fell among thorns, and the thorns grew up, and choked it, and it yielded no fruit.

" 'And other fell on good ground, and did yield fruit that sprang up and increased; and brought forth, some thirty, and some sixty, and some a hundred.

" 'And he said unto them, He that hath ears to hear, let him hear...'

"...My fellow sowers—are we all reapers?

"Or do we cast our seed upon less than fertile ground and thus cause the gnashing of Divine teeth?

"Are we careful in our sowing?

"Take stock! I say unto you: Take stock!

" 'Is a candle brought to be put under a bushel, or under a bed? And not to be set on a candlestick?'

"Is your seed capital to be hidden away in the dark vaults of banks or in long-term bonds, yielding little interest?

" 'For there is nothing hid,' saith the Lord, 'which shall not be manifested; neither was anything kept secret, but that it should come abroad.'

" 'If any man have ears to hear, let him hear.'

"How many times have you cast your seed upon rocks and thorns?

"How many times have you taken your precious capital and tossed it carelessly into some investment without first thoroughly examining the prospectus?

"One sower carelessly cast his seed into a business whose growth potential had already peaked, and thus lost his capital gains!

"He sowed other seed among over-the-counter stock, and lost his dividends!

"He cast other of his seed among blue-chips preferred and profited neither by capital gains nor high dividends!

" 'If any man have ears to hear, let him hear.'

"But he also cast his seed upon fertile ground: he investigated some companies in depth—he researched their profit margins, knew their price/earnings ratio; he inspected their real estate, visited their factories; he met with their executive staffs, enquired of their home lives, and he judged them. Thus he accurately gauged their potential growth. And on this ground he cast his seed.

"And from these seeds, he brought forth some thirty, and some sixty, and some one hundred percent returns!

"Take stock!

"And the Lord saith, 'It is like a grain of mustard seed, which, when it is sown in the earth, is less than all the seeds that be in the earth.

" 'But when it is sown it groweth up, and becometh greater than all herbs, and shooteth out great branches; so that the fowls of the air may lodge under the shadow of it.'

"Take stock!

" 'Take heed what ye hear. With what measure ye mete, it shall be measured to you.

" 'And unto you that hear shall more be given!'

"The Lord saith, 'For he that hath, to him shall be given; and he that hath not, from him shall be taken even that which he hath!' "

Even though Robby had been intensely interested in this lesson, finding in it Good News indeed, and liked the way Pastor Maple spoke (he kept the cadence of his speech by jiggling coins in his pocket) Robby became aware of an increasing sensation of prickly heat at the back of his neck. Able to stand it no longer, Robby took a quick look behind him. There, only two pews away, sat Tony Savallo in his green windbreaker, expressionlessly listening to the sermon. The pillar of the church had not protected Robby at all! He was within clear view of Tony. Witnessing the mysterious ways of Tony Savallo made Robby very warm.

" 'For the earth bringeth forth fruit of herself; first the blade, then the ear, after that the full corn of the ear!' "

The lady with many chins beside Robby sat listening in rapture to the instructive Pastor Maple. Even with her face raised toward the pulpit she had more than her share of chins.

Robby took the mouse out of his pocket, reached over, and put it in the lady's lap.

" 'Know ye not this parable? And how then will ye know all parables?' "

Robby had not long to wait for a reaction. The lady, however enraptured by the words of Pastor Maple, ultimately became curious regarding what had been put in her lap and was moving about there. She looked down, then drew herself up to such an extent that for a moment she had but a single chin. "Aaaaaark!" she said loudly, and predictably, "a mouse!"

She brushed it off her lap in an un-Christian manner. She cast it upon the back of the pew in front of her.

The mouse bounced off the pew back and landed, momentarily stunned, on the kneeler. The woman's feet were beating on the floor beneath the kneeler. In a flash the mouse was off the kneeler and scurrying around among neighboring feet with such energy that shortly a large number of people were taking up the cry, "Aaaaaark! A mouse!"

People were scrambling without divine dignity. Some tripped over each other trying to get out of their pews. Others blocked the way by standing on the kneelers. Others—more tensile in joint—jumped up to stand on the seats.

Robby, popping from floor to pew seat to kneeler back to pew seat again, went against the general trend of his pew-mates and came out in the middle aisle—half a church away from Tony Savallo.

"Whup, whup."

Robby headed for the pulpit. Pastor Maple was peering through his grille, craning and straining to see what had so upset his congregation. What was the new panic? At the front of the auditorium, Robby crouched low, turned left and left again and scampered back down the aisle farthest from where he prayerfully hoped Tony Savallo was being stampeded to death by Christians thrown to a mouse.

In the church vestibule was a freckly boy Robby's age.

"Quick!" Robby demanded. "What newspapers do your parents read?"

The boy turned his head toward the central door to the auditorium. "What's going on in there?"

"I said, what newspapers do your parents read?"

Archly, the boy said, "*The New York Times*, of course, and *The Wall Street Journal*."

Robby didn't know how he had fared in *The Wall Street Journal*, but he did know *The New York Times* considered him an item for page thirty-six—and without photograph.

"Thank God," Robby said. "You're taking me to your house for lunch."

"Why should I do that?" the boy squeaked.

From the auditorium came the noise of bangs and bumps and shouts and shrieks. Someone even said "Jesus Christ!" prayerfully.

"Because I want lunch!" Robby exclaimed.

Something in the boy's eyes indicated to Robby that he considered Robby fallow ground upon which to cast even a single caraway seed.

Robby hissed into his freckles, "If you don't take me to your house for lunch I'll ram this"—he put his fist between the boy's face and his own—"so far down your throat, takin' your teeth with it, you'll get a chance to chew your breakfast twice!"

Such was the threat offered Robby at Wolsley School by an older boy who wanted the compass Robby's family chauffeur had given him. Robby had found the threat entirely effective. Now he hoped the freckle-faced boy was similarly intimidated.

He was.

"Okay," he said. "You stink."

"What's your name?"

"Roger vanWankle," the boy admitted, "the Third. You really stink."

"Okay, Roger. You tell your parents you know me from school, and that you invited me to your house for lunch. Or your last meal will be your own teeth."

"Okay, okay. But, you know, you really stink."

He tried to pick the smell out of his nose.

The vestibule was beginning to fill with red-faced, perturbed people.

"Tell your parents my name's Robby. Uh—Robby Burnes."

"They'll never believe it."

"Good."

"I won't have to tell 'em you stink."

"Come on, Roger. Let's wait for your parents in the car."

Robby took the boy by the elbow and headed for the front door of the church.

"Kids in my school," protested Roger vanWankle the Third, "don't stink."

18
The Odor of Sanctity

"How come you smell of garbage?" Roger vanWankle enquired reasonably after he and Robby had attained the backseat of the vanWankle Cadillac.

"I spent last night in a garbage barrel," Robby admitted.

Roger said, "Oh," as if spending the night in a garbage barrel is the way anyone might be expected to spend an odd night or two of his life. "Are you running from the police or something?" he asked, as if that, too, were within his purview of normal existential experience.

Robby reviewed his philological exercise of the night before: Thadeus Lowry, Will'um, Tony Savallo. That morning Robby had run through a surrealistic forest of his own photograph hanging from people's hands, staring up at him from the street, even hanging from lamp posts. He said mildly, "I feel pressed."

"You don't look pressed," said Roger, casting a critical glance over Robby's clothes.

The chauffeur opened the door again and Mr. and Mrs. vW stepped in.

"Why, Roger," said Mrs. vW, looking at Robby.

"This is Robby Burnes, Mummy," Roger recited through clenched teeth. "A kid from school. I invited him home for lunch."

"How perfectly delightful," said Mrs. vW, not sounding convinced. "But, Roger, darling, you know you should warn Cook before you invite anybody to lunch."

"I know," was barely audible through teeth clasped so tightly Robby doubted Roger would ever be able to get them separated again.

Mr. vW sat in a corner of the car and gathered his overcoat over his paunch. He had given Robby the merest glance, obviously consigning him quickly to that category of animate life to be seen little and not heard at all.

Mrs. vW scanned Robby's tailoring and smiled warmly.

"I know you boys like the winter air." Mrs. vW began to crank up the windows. "But we must think of Mummy's coiffure."

"I really like the winter air, Mummy," urged Roger, obviously thinking more of his mother's nose than her hair.

The long Cadillac embarked from the curb.

Through the rear window Robby saw Tony Savallo writing something on the cuff of his windbreaker.

"Really, Pastor Maple is such an inspiration," proposed Mrs. vW. "Such a pity his service was interrupted by a Communist conspiracy."

In his corner of the car, Mr. vW snorted.

"It was a Communist conspiracy, wasn't it, Ralph?" asked Mrs. vW of her husband. "Letting all those rats free during his sermon?"

"Of course it was," stated Mr. vW with no uncertainty at all. "Who else would do a thing like that? Can't let decent, law-abiding Americans have a moment's peace even in their churches Sunday mornings."

"Still," philosophied Mrs. vW, "I found the forces of good and evil, dear Pastor Maple and the Communists' rats, battling it out for the hearts and the minds of the congregation even more inspiring. I do hope you boys took a lesson from it."

"Yes, ma'am," said Roger, faithfully.

Robby said nothing. It was his opinion that Pastor Maple's entire *logos* had been routed by a mouse.

"Unfortunately our favorite Congressman, Representative Jerry Bradshaw, took a lesson from it," said Mr. vW bitterly. "It inspired Bradshaw to nick me for ten thousand dollars in the church aisle."

"Ralph! Whatever for?" Mrs. vW's nose rose in surprise. It sniffed and rose higher in repugnance.

"He's got to block a bill in Congress for me. He's made it a pretty expensive bill, I'll tell you."

"What bill?" Mrs. vW was twisting in her seat, looking out all sides of the car.

"A bill that stipulates that all blankets made for the United States military—Army, Navy, and Marines—must be manufactured in the United States of America."

"Seems reasonable," commented Mrs. vW, clearly distracted.

"Darling! You're not thinking! The vanWankle blanket which we sell on contract to the United States military—the Army, Navy, and Marines—is manufactured at the vanWankle Mills in Canada!"

"So they are," noted Mrs. vW.

"Such a bill would put our blanket operations out of business!"

"I would think so, yes."

"It would mean we would be producing a half a million blankets a year without a market!"

"A chilling thought," she said.

"We would have to shut down the Canadian mills," said Mr. vW. "Or retool them to begin making commercial, competitive blankets. Good God!"

"There must be lots of cold Canadians."

"They have their own blankets," Mr. vW said with dismay.

"Does something smell?" enquired Mrs. vW.

"Everything smells," offered Robby. "Roses smell nice, but noses smell better."

"Anton," Mrs. vW addressed the chauffeur. "Speed up. There must be a garbage truck somewhere in the area—although, for the life of me, I don't see it."

"Yes, ma'am."

"New York doesn't collect garbage on Sunday," said Mr. vW. "Or on any other day of the week."

"They don't collect garbage on Sunday?"

"I'm sure they don't collect garbage on Sunday."

"But, Ralph, I distinctly smell garbage. Don't you smell garbage?"

"I think I smell New York," said Mr. vW.

"I don't see a garbage truck anywhere," she repeated, looking through the car windows north, east, south and west.

"That's why you smell garbage," said Mr. vW. "Because you never see a garbage truck."

Mrs. vW relaxed against the Cadillac's leather seat and petted her mink.

"Ralph, that seems terribly unreasonable—introducing a bill in Congress the sole purpose of which is to put our blanket company out of business. Who would think of such a thing?"

"Pecuchet."

"Who's Pecuchet?"

"Pecuchet makes blankets in Cleveland."

"Oh, I see. He stands to make a lot of money if this bill is passed?"

"He does indeed. Which is why he got the bill introduced to Congress, through his friendly congressman."

"I'm so awful at practical business matters," said Mrs. vW.

"Pecuchet has given his representative to Congress a fortune." Mr. vW's nose had begun to twitch. "Anton, drive a little faster, will you?"

"Yes, sir."

The car was oozing up a lovely wide boulevard with a green mall. Robby was hoping to spot a pile of garbage somewhere.

"The smell is getting worse, Ralph."

"We'll be home soon."

"That's what I mean. Do you think Park Avenue has seen its better days?"

"If the smell of New York has gotten to Park Avenue, my dear, there's no place in the world left to go."

"Could the smell be in the car? Anton, is there something rotting in the car?"

"No, ma'am."

"Perhaps you left some groceries in the trunk."

"No, ma'am."

"Anton," Mr. vW charged: "Something smells."

"The car looks clean enough," said Mrs. vW.

"Anton," Mr. vW stated: "The car isn't clean enough."

"It can't be the car, Ralph. We didn't smell it going down to church service."

"Anton," Mr. vW questioned suspiciously: "Did you let something smelly into the car while we were at church service?"

"No, sir."

From his corner Roger's blue eyes glared at Robby. Roger's head was tipped. The palm of his hand covered both his nose and his teeth.

Mr. vW said: "Anton, did you watch the car every minute we were gone?"

"Yes, sir."

"I bet you did. I'll bet a Communist threw a pile of garbage or something in this car while we were at church service."

"Oh, Ralph!" Mrs. vW examined the area around her feet with distress. "Do you really think so?"

"Just the sort of thing those damned anarchists would do—put a pile of garbage in the car of decent people while they're at church. Anything to upset the fabric of society!"

"A pile of garbage!" echoed Mrs. vW to Roger and Robby, her eyes brimming with the distress of the insulted.

"I'll bet they planted it under one of the seats." Mr. vW bent down over his paunch and examined the floor between his feet.

"Oh, Ralph," protested Mrs. vW, looking increasingly uneasy. "They couldn't have!"

"Well, you don't see any garbage trucks around, do you?" said his head from between his thighs.

"No one would be so mean."

"That's what they do," said the red-faced but erect Mr. vW, re-settling his hat upon his head. "Instead of working for a living, driving garbage trucks around, picking up garbage, they plant garbage in the cars of decent people while they're at church!"

Mr. vW was settling into this conviction nicely. He looked to his family for support.

Roger knew his father was wrong, but said nothing. Mrs. vW already had said no one, not even Communists, could be that mean. Robby nodded with full assurance at Mr. vW and said, "I'm sure you're right, sir."

Robby didn't know what Communists were, but he had heard his father speak ill of them. If evil-doing could be attributed generally to Communists, Robby didn't mind his odor specifically being laid at their door as well—especially so close to lunch.

"Do hurry up, Anton!" ordered Mr. vW, his fingers pinching his nose.

19
Tempest in a Bathtub

When the limousine arrived at the apartment house a uniformed, epauleted, mustachioed, white-gloved doorman stepped out from under the canopy and opened the door. And from out of the car rushed three members of the vanWankle family, pale, breathless, and quivering from a lack of oxygen. Robby Burnes left the car with the equanimity of a person who knew some problems were inescapable.

"Give this car a cleaning!" Mr. vW shouted over the roof of the car to Anton, who had quickly escaped through his own door. "We'll not have the Communists thinking they can sabotage the car of decent people on a Sunday morning!"

A man dressed in formal clothes opened the apartment house's lobby door for them. Another piloted them up in the elevator.

"Ralph," said Mrs. vW, twitching her nose in the elevator with renewed alarm. "The smell! It's here, too!"

First Mr. vW gave the elevator man a suspicious look. Then he sighed. "The Communists are everywhere."

In the vestibule of the vanWankles' apartment was a statue twenty feet high of a naked lady. In her Venus mount was a clock. In time, Robby noticed it was twenty minutes to one.

"You boys go play in your room, Roger," said Mrs.vW as the butler helped her off with her coat. "Lunch at one-thirty. I'll tell Cook we have a guest."

The butler turned to take Robby's coat. The butler's eyes popped. The butler blanched. The butler stared.

Robby handed the butler his coat and gave the butler the smile Robby had long since learned to give servants, in which smile is acknowledged complicity in the universal conspiracy of servants and children against masters and mistresses, fathers and mothers, all adults and other guests. Only by so acknowledging and cultivating such a traditional conspiracy do children survive in well-run households.

The butler said nothing.

Robby followed Roger down a vast, tall and wide corridor to Roger's room.

Roger closed the door, about-faced on his heel, and pointed a finger at Robby. Two fingers of his other hand pinched his own nose.

"You're not coming to lunch smelling like a garbage truck," he said forcefully albeit nasally. "My father will fire all the servants as Communists and I've just got this bunch broken in!"

"I know, I know," conceded Robby. "How do I get my shoes polished?"

"Your shoes have nothing to do with it!" Roger insisted. "You stink! You've gotta have a bath!"

"I had a bath Wednesday."

"This is Sunday!" exclaimed Roger.

"At school we only get tubs once a week," said Robby, thinking he was scoring a good defensive point.

"Well, you don't go to my school," said Roger. He escaped through one of two matching doors.

Robby heard a bath being drawn. He had spent the night in a rubbish barrel. The real problem was not in his person; it was in his clothes. Robby's bathing wouldn't make his clothes smell a bit better. They, too, had spent the night in a rubbish barrel.

Roger's room was comparable to Robby's, at Pladroman House, except the furniture was newer and not at all broken. Robby's grandfather, when a boy, had punched up Robby's bed so unmercifully that ever after the occupant was inclined to tip out its left side. The grandfather had lived to sire an heir and numerous nasty rumors. The armchair by the fireplace in Robby's room had been sprung by Robby's father's nurse, who, tradition had it below stairs, was fat enough to be often spoken of as a possible stand-in for the Inns at Lincoln Court. Robby's own father, it was reported, had kicked a leg out from under the desk in the room upon receiving news he had flunked an examination in Greek. Ever after, that corner of the desk had been propped up by Volumes D through R of the *Encyclopaedia Britannica*. Looking around the room, Robby thought either Roger's ancestors had been far more careful with their furniture, or Roger hadn't any ancestors at all, which struck Robby as a funny thought.

Roger came through one door and the butler through the other simultaneously.

"Yes, Cabot?" said Roger.

Cabot said, "I thought your…guest…a friend from school, is he?…might be bathing before luncheon, and thought I might see what can be done about his clothes."

Robby smiled conspiratorially at the butler.

"There isn't time," said Roger. "What his clothes need is a match."

"We English perhaps know a bit more about brushing up…" The butler winked at Robby, and picked Robby's clothes up off the floor. "I'll just take these along and see what can be done with them."

The butler exited with Robby's clothes draped over his arm. He carried Robby's shoes between thumb and forefinger.

Roger sat on the closed toilet while Robby sat in the tub.

"So why did you spend last night in a garbage barrel?" asked Roger.

Robby said, "Because I was stuck in a backyard with fences all around it."

"Then how did you ever get out?"

"Oh, it was all right once the sun came up and I could see."

"What were you doing stuck in a backyard?"

"I got chased there. You see, I saw this man, Tony Savallo, shoot another man. Murder him. And Tony Savallo was chasing me. He wants to murder me, too. So I jumped over this high fence into a backyard, and then I couldn't get out."

"Tell me another," said Roger.

"It's true! I swear on a Bible! Last night I saw a murder."

"Yeah, sure," said Roger. "Tell it to the Marines."

Robby shrugged. Even in his short life, Robby had had this experience with truth before. The last thing people are wont to believe, sometimes, is the truth. Once Robby had told his nanny his mitten had been eaten by a guardsman's horse, when his mitten had been eaten by a guardsman's horse. Robby had been denied tea, not for having lost a mitten, but for lying.

Roger said, "It's okay you're coming to stink up my house instead of going home to face the music, but aren't your parents worried about you?"

Adhering strictly to the truth, Robby said, "They're not in New York this weekend."

In his heart Robby was saddened that his truth had not been believed. He had been thinking he might appeal to the vanWankle seniors during luncheon, tell them his whole terrible story, hope they would lay it all out as a Communist conspiracy and grant him their sympathy and aid. From Roger's reaction Robby knew now such a plan was hopeless. If a boy his own age wouldn't believe the story, Robby could not expect adults to believe. After all boys believe in many things—exercise, honesty and friendship, to name three—to which adults give lip-service but seldom practice. Seldom does one adult get up from the playing field and honestly admit his own error to save his friend a penalty. Even to his own ears, now having said it, Robby's story seemed more a nightmare than a true history. Children sometimes believe in nightmares, but adults, never.

"Are you a member of the Church of Jesus Christ Materialist?" Roger asked.

Again Robby shrugged. If truth did not serve him, he might as well lie. "Life-long."

"Then why weren't you at Sunday School? Why have I never seen you before?"

"We're new to this parish," said Robby. "I'm enrolling next week."

"In midyear?"

"Right after Christmas. Look for me."

"You'll never catch up. It's terribly hard."

"Is it?"

"I'm having to take private tutorials Wednesday afternoons. With Pastor Maple."

"Oh," Robby said, again observing American soap did not sink.

"I'm having trouble reading the stock tables," Roger continued. "The print's awfully small, you know, and when you have to read the par value, the year's high and low, as well as the asking and the bid prices, it gets damned confusing. And," he said significantly, "you have to add zeroes to the number of stocks traded every day, to arrive at the volume."

"Oh," Robby said. "I see."

"But, as Pastor Maple says, practical Christianity is worth it." Roger sighed. "And we're learning to read annual reports. I've read the car companies so far, airlines and the oils."

"Didn't Jesus throw the money-changers out of the temple?" asked Robby.

"Yeah," said Roger. "Pastor Maple says he doesn't want donations made to his church in change, either. He wants it in bills."

"Guess I'll need tutoring," said Robby.

"You're lucky. You'll probably get Tuesday afternoons with Pastor Maple. That's earlier in the financial week. Less to remember."

"Good."

"The thing that worries me," said Roger, picking a fingernail, "is my soul."

"Your soul?"

"Yeah. Whether I'm good enough, you know, as a person, to receive the Word of the Lord directly from Pastor Maple."

"Sure you are," Robby said. "Didn't you refuse me lunch until I threatened to shove your teeth down your throat?"

"That reminds me," said Roger. "How are you going to make it up to me? I mean, lunch. How are you going to pay me back?"

"That's easy," said Robby, thinking quickly. "Before I leave I'll give you a piece of advice."

"A stock tip?"

"A piece of advice."

Chin on hands, Roger thought. "Pastor Maple says good advice is very valuable. Is your advice good?"

"Is lunch?" Robby was beginning to get the hang of a life by trade.

Roger considered the proposition and apparently decided to suspend negotiation, at least until he saw what lunch was.

"But I keep having these impulses," he said. "Like, you know, I see a beggar on the street and, you know, it actually crosses my mind to give him a dime."

"Have you confessed this to Pastor Maple?" Robby asked solemnly.

"Yes," said Roger. "He says I must harden my heart against those who vouchsafe nothing."

"There, then," said Robby, meaning to console.

Robby ducked his head below the surface of the warm, soapy water. When he came up he found himself in a freezing downpour.

"We have a shower for that!" Roger shouted. He stood over Robby, his hands on a different set of knobs. The water was turning scalding.

"I'll fix the knobs!" Robby gasped. Instantly, he grasped the idea of a shower. He had never seen one before. Instantly he also concluded, finally, absolutely, irrevocably, after the collection of much evidence, that everything—absolutely everything about Americans, even their bath-taking—was violent. Only Americans, he decided in a flash, can turn a nice, warm leisurely bath into bad weather.

"If you wanted a shower, why didn't you say so?"

"Right," Robby said, fighting with the knobs while standing under the torrential spray. By the time he got the knobs set properly to provide a spray somewhat nearer his skin temperature, Roger had left the bathroom. "You'll be a bloomin' bishop!" shouted Robby, turning the squall off.

From the bedroom Roger said, solemnly, "Thank you."

Cabot was standing in the bedroom with clothes for Robby. The blazer and short trousers and tie and cap and overcoat were Robby's, beautifully brushed and pressed and smelling as if they had just come in from a walk in a greenhouse. The shoes were Robby's, looking as if they had never trod the earth. But the shirt and the underclothes and the kneesocks weren't Robby's at all. They were identical to Robby's but they were new.

Cabot winked at Robby.

He took the towel from Robby's shoulders and gave him a vigorous rubdown. Finishing, he said, "There you are, Your Grace."

It did not surprise Robby too much that Cabot recognized him. From Robby's experience with servants he knew they were apt to read more entertaining newspapers than were the householders. His father's newspapers were unrelievedly gray. The servants' newspapers had brightly colored comics, on Sundays, and big headlines about "LOVE NESTS." His father and mother never had anything to talk about except Churchill and Roosevelt and Hitler and Mussolini and Parliament and the Congress and the War. The servants were really up on the news of the world, and their conversation was much more interesting.

While Cabot was dressing him and Roger was fiddling around his desk Robby considered trying out the truth on Cabot. Whenever he'd had a problem servants had solved it. But what could a butler do? Sundays were busy days for butlers. There were always people in and out for tea and drinks and dinner, and Saturdays always tarnish at least one set of silverware. It isn't fair always to be running to servants with problems. Robby's father had told him so the night he spent three hours looking for his favorite pipe. *It's not a servant's job to locate missing pipes!* he had expostulated over and over again during the hunt. (Robby finally found the pipe in the left pocket of his father's smoking jacket.) Servants have their own work to do.

Cabot handed Robby the gold sovereign. "I believe your father gave this to you, Your Grace?"

Robby smiled. "Yes."

"I found it in your trousers. I think you'd better keep it, Your Grace." He slipped the sovereign into the handkerchief pocket of the blazer. "People in this household will relieve you of it as proof of their generosity."

While helping Robby on with the blazer the butler whispered in Robby's ear, "Is there anything I can do for you, Your Grace?"

Robby considered again. *It's not a servant's job to locate a missing...anything!* "Yes, please," he said. "Could you give me doubles for lunch?"

20
A Congressional Bill

Robby sat with the vanWankle family at lunch.

Roger, freshly inspired by Pastor Maple, ate greedily. The senior vanWankles, wanting nothing to go to waist, cast yearning glances at the food on their plates, and talked. Robby, having spent the previous night in a rubbish barrel and having other good reasons not to want food to go to waste, ate silently and heartily.

"My, how you boys eat!" trilled Mrs. vW. "I don't know where you put it all. Do you know where they put it all, Ralph?"

Ralph looked from boy to plate, to plate and to boy. "No matter how much money you give the government"—he shook his head sadly—"you don't know where it goes, either." He tasted his mock turtle soup, replaced his spoon, and concluded: "The government isn't a grown-up."

"Where do you live, Robby?" asked Mrs. vW.

"Mayfair, ma'am."

"Oh, that's nice. I think Clara Bow used to live at the Mayfair."

Even at his age Robby had learned that totally inadequate answers usually are grasped as entirely satisfactory—in polite conversation.

Robby was saying as little as possible.

He had a better use for his mouth, at the moment. He had discovered in the few days he had resided in this land of milk and honey that full-blown meals were as infrequent as tea shops in the North Atlantic. When one came across a proper meal one was wise to triple up on it, to make up for yesterday, do right by today, and conserve for tomorrow.

Cabot was most obliging. Like any well-trained butler he knew how to sidle food onto a plate (or off a plate—whichever was required, to avoid embarrassment) prestidigitatiously. As the main course was souffle, sausage and mustard pickle—each of which food is distinct in color and shape and therefore easily measureable—Cabot's genius shone.

Across the table from Robby, however, Roger noticed the frequency with which Robby was being served. Roger was not about to vouchsafe nothing. Each time Robby was served, Roger signalled Cabot, with his eyes or a wave of his hand, that he, too, would be served again. Cabot ignored half of Roger's signals, but could not ignore Roger's more blatant wavings with both hands. Roger, however, had been eating regularly and well. Competing with someone who had ceased to think of meals as a rightful and regular occurrence proved hard on Roger. During the courses of luncheon Roger's face broke into a sweat, his skin reddened, his cheeks puffed, his eyes protruded. His fingers yanked at his shirt collar as if his neck had grown noticeably between one-thirty and two. Clearly Roger was miserable in this eating competition, but he stuck to it with great fortitude.

Too, Robby spoke the minimum at luncheon because he did not want questions raised by what the vanWankles might think of as his accent. Robby knew he did not have an accent, but he had discovered so far in America that not only did everyone have an accent—everyone had an accent individual from that of every other American. Thadeus Lowry (Robby was to describe later) spoke Rhetorical-American. Words marched out of his mouth with huge strides as if the end of any sentence were The In Place for a word to be. His wife, his *chérie*, spoke a soft and sibilant Martini-American. Her words were pronounced deliberately through a spray which never reached beyond her gums. Marie Savallo spoke Devout-American. Every word lilted from her mouth reverentially as if aimed at only the ears of resting saints—even when that word might be *kidnap*, *ransom* or *murder*. Frankie Savallo spoke Exuberant-American. Words scrambled from his mouth in a great, loud hurry as if the right to speak freely were a new right, and one apt to be curtailed any moment. Pastor Maple spoke Pulpit, which Robby later would define as a universal language comprising two parts

GREGORY MCDONALD

Divinity, one part Wonder, three parts Exhortation, three parts
Pomposity, and five parts Collection Plate Indicative. Listening to
them at luncheon Robby heard from the vanWankles an accent he
would describe later as Business-American. Words sashayed from
the vanWankles' mouths with their eyelids fluttering and their
hips wiggling, so eager to be heard without being loud, so eager to
convince without argument that the listener might forget, or never
realize at all, that the principle behind seduction is not entirely
generous.

Robby remained as silent as possible throughout luncheon because he suspected that that which the vanWankles might think of
as an accent on his part would cause questions for which totally
inadequate answers would not be grasped as entirely satisfactory.
Talk might turn uncivil. The vanWankles might discover they were
feeding a homeless English boy at their table and quickly reason
there was no profit in doing that. They were sowing their mustard
pickle upon a destitute foreigner. Such a discovery on their part
would imperil his having dessert.

"That emblem you're wearing," Mr. vW said to Robby, referring
to the Wolsley School crest. "That bull is shaking all the leaves out
of that tree, right?"

"Yes, sir."

"And shaking down fruit and nuts, too, I'll bet," he said with a
good degree of spiritual satisfaction.

"Yes, sir."

"Doubtlessly," Mr. vW said respectfully, "that bull will make a
pile."

"Doubtlessly, sir."

"I find all this very disturbing," said Mrs. vW, properly introducing the main topic with the main course. "Representative Bradshaw actually came up to you in the main aisle of the church, as we
were leaving, and said he wanted you to give him ten thousand
dollars cash."

"He did," confirmed Mr. vW.

"To block passage of a bill forbidding us to sell blankets manufactured in Canada to the American military."

"Right."

She said, "It does seem corrupt of him. I mean, to want so much."

"You have to understand the figures," said her husband, counting his sausages off the platter. "Pecuchet paid his congressional representative in Ohio ten thousand dollars to introduce the bill into Congress. He paid Jerry Bradshaw, our representative, five thousand dollars not to oppose the bill."

"But why did Pecuchet do that? Why did he pay Jerry anything?"

"He knows I've been an active supporter of Jerry for years. Well, in fact, that Jerry's in my pocket. He had to pay off Jerry not to oppose the bill."

"It all seems wrong, somehow."

"Actually, I'm very grateful to Jerry for coming to me. He could have just pocketed the five thousand dollars and kept quiet. I wouldn't have known there was such a bill in Congress until it was too late to do anything about it."

"So telling you that he's accepted a five-thousand-dollar bribe from Pecuchet earns him another ten-thousand-dollar bribe from you?" Mrs. vW was frowning at her souffle.

Her husband shivered. "Don't use the word *bribe*! *Bribe* is entirely the wrong word for it." Mr. vW seemed entirely sure on that point. However, there was a long moment before he offered a word in substitute for *bribe*. "Political contribution," he said. "These guys have to run for office every two years, you know. That takes money."

"A political contribution for something in return…" Mrs. vW hesitated on the brink of spoiling luncheon, or a marriage, or both.

Mr. vW shook his knife at her. "A representative can't pay for a political campaign out of his own pocket every two years. He has to have the help of his friends. And if he can't help his friends be prosperous, then his friends can't help him!"

"Sounds perfectly reasonable, when you say it that way," Mrs. vW admitted.

"It's the American system," Mr. vW chortled. "How else could it work?"

"But, Ralph. Our representative to Congress, Jerry Bradshaw, is getting a total of fifteen thousand dollars, the net result of which is nothing at all—a bill introduced to Congress and not passed."

"Would you rather see the bill passed?"

"Of course not."

"Ten thousand dollars is cheap at the price. Pecuchet has spent fifteen thousand, and he gets nothing at all. See? Our representative is better than his representative."

"I'm so glad," she said.

"One of our most precious rights as Americans," Mr. vW lectured his son, Roger, whose eyes were beginning to bulge with an unwanted intake of food, "is our right to pursue happiness. Which, in a system of free enterprise, can mean only one thing—our right to make a buck." Roger's freckles were running together in digestive strain. "Does this mean that simply because a man becomes a public servant he must give up his right to pursue happiness, his right to be enterprising, his right to make a buck?" Sweat rolled from Roger's upper lip into his mouth. "It does not. When we vote a man into office, we are conferring upon him influence. And influence, like every other commodity—be it gold, silver, reputation, goodwill—has its value. Influence is the equity a politician develops during his career. Like any other equity, it can be sold, converted into cash, precisely as the politician sees fit." Mr. vW turned his attention back to his wife, having lectured her, obliquely. "That's all Jerry is doing."

Mrs. vW was impressed. Her eye shadow was stretched to the point of revealing pores. "Why, darling!" she sputtered. "That's beautiful! Never in my life have I heard the political system explained so...so...so poignantly."

Mr. vW shrugged modestly. "Those dudes who wrote the Constitution knew what they were doing, all right. They all had families to support." He laughed. "None of them ended up in the poorhouse!"

"I certainly hope you boys have been edified by what you just heard," Mrs. vW said.

Roger swallowed reluctantly. "Yes, Mummy."

Robby said, "Yes, ma'am."

"How are you going to make this contribution to Jerry?" Mrs. vW asked her husband. "Is there a hurry about it?"

Mr. vW looked at his watch. "He's leaving for Washington on the four o'clock train. He'll be standing outside the cocktail lounge in the Hotel Clemens at three-thirty."

"Ralph, you're not going yourself?"

"No," he drawled. "I never have yet. But it is Sunday. All my lawyers are at home with their families. I have the money in the safe, of course. I keep myself prepared for weekend emergencies like this."

"You can't go yourself. Someone might see you."

"Yeah." He scratched the back of his neck. "Someone might see me slip an envelope to a congressman in a hotel lobby the week before a bill important to my business comes up before Congress…"

"Not everyone understands the political system as well as you do."

"It would be just the time some nosy person would be passing by, recognize the two of us, put two and two together… Why," he said, "it would mean another bribe!"

"You can't send Cabot," she said. "I have the Ladies' Committee from the Church coming to tea, to discuss those buildings the Church owns in Harlem. You know how the residents there keep demanding light bulbs in the hallways, if you'd believe it, when they really ought not to go out at night!"

"I need a courier," admitted Mr. vW. "I'd sorely miss the opportunity to say hello to the Ladies' Committee. They do such good work."

"Maybe," speculated Mrs. vW, wriggling her eyebrows at Robby in such a way Robby wasn't supposed to notice, "we can think of someone who would be happy to run a little errand for us."

"Maybe so," agreed Mr. vW, immediately brightened by a solution which would permit him to say hello to the Ladies' Committee instead of his congressional representative.

"Robby, darling." Mrs. vW laid her forearm on the table in a supplicating manner. "Would you mind terribly doing us a little favor?"

"No, ma'am." Dessert hadn't appeared yet.

"We'll send you back to the Hotel Mayfair in the car with Anton if you'll stop off at the Hotel Clemens on the way and give an envelope to a man standing at the door of the cocktail lounge in the lobby. Will you do that for us?"

"Of course, ma'am." Robby knew that nothing was for nothing in the vanWankle household. He had attended their church.

Dessert was chocolate ice cream and vanilla wafers. Roger barely survived it.

The clock in the alabaster lady's Venus mount was striking three when Cabot helped Robby into his freshly brushed coat in the vestibule of the vanWankles' apartment.

Mr. vW had given Robby a sealed envelope and repeated his instructions again in the greatest detail. Robby was to be sure the man to whom he gave the envelope answered to the name *Bradshaw*.

Robby had left the senior vWs lurking in the living room.

Of the vanWankles, only Roger stood in the vestibule to say good-bye. And he did not stand well. His necktie was down, his shirt collar unbuttoned. His face was flushed from food. His legs bent just enough to indicate they no longer wanted to carry around such a big lunch.

"See you in church," Robby said to him.

"Wait a minute," Roger said. "You owe me something."

"Of course," Robby said. "What?"

"You promised to give me a stock tip."

"Not a stock tip," said Robby. "A piece of advice."

"Okay," Roger said impatiently. "A piece of advice. What is it?"

Robby looked up at Cabot, and then stepped nearer to Roger and whispered in Roger's ear, "Steer clear of becoming a duke."

Roger drew back. "*What?!*"

"'Bye. Thanks, Cabot!"

Anton awaited Robby on the curb with the back door of the

Cadillac limousine open. Robby crossed the sidewalk with dignity and got into the car.

Despite his seeing, halfway down the block, apparently studying the architecture on Park Avenue, Tony Savallo.

21
Pushing and Shoving

Oozing down Park Avenue in the back of the vanWankle limousine, Robby knew the slight peace of the moment and the heavy trepidation of the future. It had been only three meters from the door of the apartment house to the car and during that trudge Robby had been escorted, somewhat shielded, by the huge doorman. Tony Savallo could have shot Robby in the instant Robby crossed the sidewalk only if he had had his gun drawn and half-aimed while dawdling on the sidewalk admiring the architecture. Toying with a handgun while apparently engaged in esthetic pursuit would establish an irony anyone, such as a doorman or a chauffeur, might observe and question. Thus reasonably unprepared, Tony Savallo missed his chance to shoot Robby Burnes through the head outside the vanWankles' apartment house. Anton closed the back door on Robby the instant Robby scurried into the backseat.

Through the windows, as the limousine went in a U-turn around the mall to head downtown, Robby saw Tony Savallo getting into a taxi. Anton had his instructions, first to the Hotel Clemens to wait for Robby while he gave ten thousand dollars to a member of the House of Representatives, then to take Robby to the Hotel Mayfair, where Robby didn't live, but someone named Clara Bow might have, once. All the way down the avenue and through a cross street the silhouette of Tony Savallo's head remained steady in the backseat of the taxi behind them.

Robby didn't wait for Anton. He leapt out of the car as soon as it drew up to the curb in front of the Hotel Clemens. He brushed by the hotel doorman, who was dressed in the uniform of a riverboat captain. He threw himself at a door shaped like a vertical paddlewheel and flooded through it. He jumped up three or four stairs.

At the top of the stairs standing near the wall stood a man in a

Chesterfield coat. A Boston bag was on the floor at his feet. Near him was a door decorated with the outlines of champagne glasses and beer tankards. The sign over the door said THE BRIDGE. With glassy eyes the man was watching the revolving door as if it were a roulette wheel about to turn up his fortune.

Hand clutching the envelope in his pocket, Robby approached the man. "Please, sir?"

The man's eyes barely flickered from the entrance to the hotel. "Go along now, sonny. Your mother's looking for you."

"Please, sir, are you Mr. Bradshaw?"

"Yes, yes, but I can't do autographs now. I have a train to catch."

"Mr. vanWankle sent me, sir."

"vanWankle?" Bradshaw's glazed eyes popped fully surprised in Robby's face. "vanWankle sends children to do his dirty work now, does he?"

"Dirty work, sir?"

"Dirty enough. Either I take ten thousand dollars from him or he gives thirty thousand dollars to the scoundrel campaigning against me next election. Don't you call that dirty?"

"I don't know, sir."

"Well, I do. It's not the Congress of the United States that's corrupt, young man. It's the citizens of the United States. Won't let a politician do his job properly. Always threatening him this way and that."

"He said to say something about blankets, sir," Robby said, looking anxiously at the hotel entrance as the revolving door kept dispensing people toward the steps. "He said to say something about keeping you warm at night."

"Blankets!" huffed Bradshaw. "What do I care about blankets? Tell me that!"

Robby considered the question seriously. "We all like blankets, sir."

"What I care about are my constituents! The honest ones!" The Congressman belched. "The hard-working, God-fearing honest people of this district who elected me to represent them in Congress!"

"Yes, sir. I'm sure, sir."

"In order to serve the good people I have to put up with the pushing and shoving of the vanWankles and the Pecuchets of this land! Do you understand that?" Bradshaw looked over Robby's head, as if addressing more of an audience than a small boy. "Does anyone understand that?"

"I'm sure someone understands that, sir."

"Threats!" Bradshaw squeezed his eyes closed, wrinkled his nose and shook his head. "Some calls 'em bribes. I calls 'em threats!"

"Sir? I'm in somewhat of a hurry myself—"

"Either I play ball with those what got the money or I get thrown out of the ball park, retired for lack of funds, never again able to stand up at bat for issues important to me, vital to my constituents!"

"But you sleep warm at night, sir?"

"Bah!" Bradshaw swayed. "Blankets!"

"Yes, sir, blankets." Robby held the envelope out to Bradshaw but the man's eyes remained closed. The fingers of his right hand pressed the spot between his eyebrows as if to force individuation of the thoughts which swirled within. "Sir!"

In the revolving door Tony Savallo was behind a woman in a mammoth fur coat.

"Sir!"

"Blankets," moaned the people's representative to Congress. "Oh, my God—blankets!"

"Sir!" Robby tried to place the envelope in the pocket of Bradshaw's overcoat, but the pocket was too full. "Whup!" screamed Robby as Tony Savallo got through the crowd to the bottom of the stairs.

Stuffing the envelope back into his own pocket, Robby ran through the crowded hotel lobby. "Whup!"

From behind him he heard the bellow of an enraged man. Robby looked back as he ran. Bradshaw had picked up his Boston bag and was staggering with it into the crowd of the hotel lobby. Tony Savallo had passed Bradshaw and was much nearer Robby.

"Scamp!" the people's representative was bellowing in a well-practiced aggrieved voice. "Come back here! You have something of mine!"

✿

Hotels, at least those in the august class of the Hotel Clemens, by presenting thick carpets and thick drapes, heavy chairs and divans awkwardly placed, all decorated in amoebic patterns, attempt to impose standards of subdued behavior upon their guests, which imposition permits the hotel to present its guests with larger bills. One is not expected to be raucous in front of an oversized landscape of the Cathedral of St. John the Divine, or to perceive purple and yellow divans as common hurdles to be vaulted.

On that Sunday afternoon with Tony Savallo a few steps behind him, trying to yank something out of the pocket of his windbreaker as he ran, Robby abandoned dignity and presented the management of the Hotel Clemens with behavior shocking to any decor. When he looked back at the bellowing Bradshaw Robby bumped an end table, sending the lamp on it to crash on the rug. Two divans were back to back, holding two different sets of people who were holding two different sets of conversations under their hats. Robby jumped on one divan, over the backs of both, and down the other, bouncing the people on both divans and elevating their polite murmurs to angry shouts. He gave not a glance at the large painting of the Cathedral of St. John the Divine. Passing the hotel desk he knocked over several upright suitcases, scattered three overnight cases, and caused one agitated lady to knock her own hat off.

The dining room had only a few late lunchers in it. Forgetting for the moment the negotiations he'd had to endure, the concessions he'd had to make to secure his own lunch, Robby went under the table of two late lunchers, a man and a woman dawdling bored over their coffee as if waiting for a fashion magazine photographer to come by looking for just the right illustration for an article entitled "Weekend Fun in the City." Their table still had a long tablecloth. The bored couple became active immediately and began to kick at him with four feet. Her fashionable slipper got Robby on a cheekbone; his pliant black got Robby between two ribs. Deciding that under their table was not a good place to hide shortly after the feet began to kick, Robby scurried out and became upright again. He spotted a swing door to the kitchen and headed for it. A waiter carrying a tray on one hand came through the swing door. Gracefully he stood aside and held the door open for Robby, and said, "Yes, sir."

Halfway through the bright, white kitchen a salad cauldron on wheels was in Robby's path. It was not much of an obstacle for him. Hoping to make it more of an obstacle for Tony Savallo, Robby spun the cauldron around him with some energy. He then ran backwards. A cook, using a knife as long as his forearm, looked on with disinterest. Tony grabbed the cauldron by its rim and pushed it ahead of him as he ran. Robby turned again and made it through a door to a storeroom. He heard the rim of the cauldron clank against both sides of the door frame.

Robby tripped over one box in the dark storeroom, followed his nose to fresh air and found himself on a loading dock.

The alley was wide enough for two trucks to pass. After jumping off the loading dock Robby, who was beginning to think with the instinct of the hunted, realized that he had less cover than a quail four meters over a shooting blind. Signs every few feet read LOADING PLATFORM. Across the alley the signs read RAIL-ROAD LOADING PLATFORM. Robby crossed the alley at a trot. Getting onto the railroad loading platform required another great leap, but, as he had been practicing leaping in terror and therefore had some confidence in himself, Robby picked up his running pace to make the leap. He increased the pace even more when he heard a gunshot. At precisely the right instant a second gunshot caused all his muscles to leap and he found himself with both feet on the platform.

Through a wide door Robby found himself in a huge room. Many signs read LOST AND FOUND AREA. Many, many trunks, suitcases and wooden crates, stamped, stickered, stenciled, with labels dripping off them, all suggesting they shouldn't have been lost in the first place, were stacked on top of each other under thick layers of dust.

Hands on his knees, Robby grabbed breath. In the alley Tony Savallo had shot at him twice. Tony was getting careless. Tony was getting impatient. Tony was getting desperate.

Robby worked through Lost and Found and pushed through a door to the main concourse of the railroad station.

◦

Railroad stations are entirely different from hotel lobbies, Robby immediately realized. Whereas he had attracted great attention (which had done him no good) running through the hotel lobby, he attracted no attention whatsoever running through a railroad station. Of course railroad stations do not set up hurdles to subdue people. The main piece of art in that railroad station, Robby couldn't help noticing, was a huge, bright work of a young woman sitting in a most uncomfortable-looking position in a red bathing suit on a beach smoking a cigarette. Beneath her people looked and acted more excited than subdued. They hurried and jostled each other and yelled directions at each other. Those standing in groups, waiting with each other, saying hello, saying good-bye, spoke loudly, laughed openly, and did not hide their tears. Most of the men in the concourse were in military uniforms. One man, in fact, identical to any man in the Hotel Clemens who had shouted angrily at Robby for running, in the railroad station ran right into Robby, bowled him over and never stopped to observe any manners whatsoever.

Robby got up and looked in all directions through the crowd. For the moment he could spot Tony Savallo's green windbreaker nowhere. Which meant that for the moment, standing in the middle of the railroad station, Robby didn't know in which direction to run. He did not know in which directions Tony Savallo wasn't.

Robby went up to a group of men he recognized as naval officers. They wore blue uniforms with brass accoutrements, white hats with black visors. One or two of them glanced at Robby, but the conversation on the game at the Point continued. Robby did not like to interrupt naval officers, especially when it seemed they were discussing tactics. 'Round the left end was being debated with a slash through the middle. Robby trusted resolution of this question would end the war that much sooner, and thus remained silent as long as possible.

When he began to feel Tony Savallo's presence again, he plucked at the sleeve of the officer nearest him.

"Please, sir," he said.

"No shoe shines," said one of the officers.

In fact their shoes shone enough to make a good valet blush.

"He's not a shoe-shine kid," said another. "Look at his clothes. What's that insignia he's wearing?"

"You lost, kid?"

"Please, sir, I'm being chased by a murderer who kept me in a rubbish barrel all night."

"What? Where you from, kid?"

"England, sir. My name's Robby Burnes and just everybody's looking for me—except everybody who sees me, except nobody sees me, you see, sir, except Tony Savallo, who keeps chasing me because I saw him shoot a man dead in the streets, sir, and I know who he is, you see, sir—"

"He's English," said one.

"If he were any more English he couldn't talk at all," said another.

"Calm down, kid," said a third. "Tell us what's the matter?"

"He's been chasing me all night, sir, all day—"

"I didn't know an ox was powerful enough to uproot a big tree like that," said the officer, still studying the Wolsley School emblem.

"Who's been chasing you?"

"Tony Savallo, sir."

"I don't think you can train an ox like that."

"Ton-he Sa-va-lo. What does Sa-va-lo mean?"

"It was all right, sir, I had nowhere to go, and I understood that, all right. I made the best of it, honestly I did, but I've begun to upset people, sir, a naked lady in her kitchen this morning, she threw milk at me; I upset a whole churchful of people, I did, I put a mouse in a lady's lap; all the people at the Hotel Clemens, they yelled at me, and kicked at me, and I'm beginning to think less of myself for all that, I am. Honest, sir, I never raised trouble before, I haven't!"

"You put a mouse in the lap of a naked lady?"

"What naked lady? Where, where?" asked another officer.

"What's he talking about?"

"That kid's suffering from bad dreams."

"Only things are getting serious now, sir. Tony Savallo shot at me twice just now in the alley. He shot at me. Twice."

"Where's your momma, boy?"

"She's dead, sir. She died in the bomb. Thadeus Lowry took my picture of her."

"Is somebody shooting pictures?"

"Wouldn't you say, sir, things are getting serious?"

"Listen, son, I'll take you to Lost and Found."

"Oh, no, sir, not there. I've been there."

"You've been to Lost and Found?"

"It's all covered with dust, sir."

"What I think we have here, gentlemen," said the eldest officer, "is an escapee from Lost and Found."

"Yes, sir," said an officer.

"Bring him back, will you, Tom? Someone at the information desk should be able to help you."

"Yes, sir."

"Oh, no, sir, not that room! That room's no good at all, sir!"

The officer called Tom put his hand on Robby's shoulder. "It's all right, son."

When the officer moved his arm, Robby saw the green of Tony Savallo's jacket. Then he saw Tony Savallo.

"Oh, no, sir!" Robby ducked his shoulder from beneath the officer's hand.

Both Tony Savallo's hands were in his jacket pockets, but Tony was moving steadily toward Robby.

Robby ducked again as the officer was reaching for him, turned and ran.

"Oh, whup, whup, whup!"

Across the station Robby saw a gate closing on Track 19. He ran straighter for it than any bee ever made for a honeycomb. He skirted a man in a brown uniform so narrowly he left the man pirouetting in midconcourse. The momentum of the heavy pushed gate was such that the trainman pushing it tried to stop it as he saw Robby approaching at high speed but could not. Robby danced sideways through the narrow aperture.

Even on sneakered feet Tony Savallo skidded into the diamond-grilled gate.

From the other side of the gate Robby saw Tony's arm pull back and curve to reach into his jacket pocket.

"Whup!"

Robby ran down the station platform. The train was moving with him. Shortly the train was moving faster than he was. Train steps drew abreast of Robby. Remembering how Thadeus Lowry got into taxicabs, Robby ran a few steps sideways with the train and sat on its steps. He pulled his feet up.

He looked back along the train.

Still on the other side of the blurring gate was a patch of green.

"Ticket?"

"Oh, yes, sir!"

When Robby had caught his breath he found himself a seat in a coach car. He was near the front of the car. The old conductor came through the door, enquired of Robby, then proceeded on, punching tickets held out to him.

He turned back to Robby. "Ticket?"

"Yes, sir!" Robby answered agreeably.

The conductor continued down the aisle and did not turn back to Robby again.

The man in the seat next to Robby was in a sailor's uniform, smelled of beer, and was comfortably asleep. His ticket was in the holder in the seat in front of them and had been punched by the conductor.

Robby expected a nice, long train ride. He put his hands in his pockets and slumped in his seat. In his pocket he discovered he still had the envelope containing ten thousand dollars. *Scamp! Come back here! You have something of mine!* Robby had tried to give it to him. The politician had not stopped talking enough to listen. *Thief! You little thief!* had yelled the householder that morning from his front door, his naked, surprised wife behind him. Robby considered that he had been yelled at quite a lot for a Sunday.

He expected the train would carry him to some other place altogether, a place utterly without Tony Savallo. The trains he had taken from London had carried him long distances, to Edinburgh, once to Leeds, often to Wolmwold. The people in these places had never been the same people as those he'd left in London. Except for the people who travelled with him, different places had different sets of people in them altogether.

Robby was right in that he did have a nice train ride, and it did bring him to someplace altogether different. He was right about nothing else.

Very shortly the train stopped. He sat up straight. Another platform had appeared beside the train.

A sign over the platform read 125TH STREET.

No one in Robby's coach made a move to get off so Robby reasoned that wherever they were all going (including him) they hadn't gotten there yet. He settled back in his seat.

More people got on the train.

The train did not move for a longer time than it had taken the train to get there. It was dark out. Dim lights shone on the station platform. No one aboard seemed disturbed by the half-hour delay. Robby remembered the Lost and Found room at the main railroad station and understood that it took a lot of time for a railroad to lose that much luggage and freight. Beside him the sailor snored on every third inhale.

Finally there was a renewed banging of doors and cold drafts swept through the coach.

Through the train window Robby saw Tony Savallo's head appear in a stairwell. It rose at a reliable pace and below Tony Savallo's head, incredibly enough, was Tony Savallo's whole body. His right hand was in his jacket pocket.

Robby was so amazed, so incredulous, so doubting of his own eyes that he leaned over the sailor's inert body and stared through the window overlong.

Tony's face registered that he saw Robby. The train began to move. Tony headed for the steps at the rear of Robby's coach.

Robby bolted out of his seat, through the door at the front of the coach, and jumped down the steps to the platform. He caught his balance and stood still. If he crossed the platform he would be visible from the train windows. He stood as close to the train as possible as it pulled itself past him. He remained where he was, making the most of the blind spot until the train was 'way up the track.

Only then did he cross the platform and saunter down the long, iron stairs which Tony Savallo had climbed.

22
In the Lap of America

"Hey, boy. You lost?"

"No, sir."

"Whatcha doin'?"

"Nothing, sir."

The skinny young man crouched in front of Robby, his dark face looking at him through the dark. The whites of his eyes stood out like moons on a perfect night. "You need he'p?"

"Hep, sir?"

"You need he'p?"

"No, sir. I don't think so."

Robby didn't know what hep was, but he had been taught properly not to accept things he didn't know. So far, since coming down the stairs from the railroad station, standing on the sidewalk, he had been offered a drink from a brown bottle by a smelly, staggery old man who didn't speak at all understandably, and Robby had not accepted the drink. Now this young man had come along and noticed him and offered him hep.

"You sure you don't need he'p?" The young man looked at him as if he doubted him.

Robby looked back at him, not sure.

"You don' look to me as if you belong here, at all."

"Sir?"

"You belong downtown."

"Yes, sir."

"You goin' downtown?"

"Yes, sir. I guess so."

"You must be waitin' on someone, that it?"

Robby looked at his shoes. He wasn't *on* someone. He raised his eyes to the face of the man, who had stood up.

"All right, boy. You make up your mind you need he'p I'll be over there in that drugstore. You hear? I work behind the counter there."

"Yes, sir."

Robby watched the young man cross the street, walk to the corner and go into the drugstore. *Hep must be something you get in a drugstore.*

"Hey, Lilly! Hey, Lilly!" Across the street five boys, somewhat older than Robby, had stopped on the sidewalk. They were calling in his direction. "Hey, Lilly! Hey, Lilly! Hey, Lilly!"

Robby looked around himself in the dark. There was no one else to whom they could be calling.

"Lillypad!"

"Whatcha doin', Lillypad?"

Robby backed into the area under the stairs leading to the railroad station. He felt there was no light on him.

"You come over here, Lillypad, we'll cut your stem off!"

All the boys must have found that funny because they all laughed. They continued along the sidewalk. Three of the five had their hands in the back pockets of their trousers. One of the other two rolled over a rubbish barrel, spilling its contents into the street. That, too, must have been funny because they all laughed.

At the far corner one of them shouted, "Comin' to getcha, Lillypad. Cut yo' stem off!"

They turned the corner, and were gone.

It began to snow. There was little light in the street. In the windows in the brick buildings across from Robby there were only a few slits of light. There were no lights in the window of the drugstore at the corner. The sign saying STRON'S DRUGS was big and painted black against white so Robby could read it in the little light there was. When the drugstore door opened, as people went in and came out, a shaft of yellow light fell on the sidewalk. There were few cars going by and the headlights of all those were half-lidded to prevent their being seen from the air. It was in the headlights of a car that Robby first noticed it was snowing.

There had been several people walking the streets along the two sidewalks. There had been a few young men in uniform with girls; a few young men in uniform without girls, together; a few young men in uniform, alone. There had been the smelly, staggery old man with the brown bottle. There had been two women, each alone, both hurrying. One had worn a nurse's uniform and cape. There had been the young man in the reindeer sweater who offered Robby hep and asked if Robby were waitin' on someone. There were the boys who called Robby Lillypad.

Until Robby stepped into the shadow of the stairs everyone on the street seemed to notice him, look at him, *see* him, even those who had not spoken to him. For the most part, if their looks expressed anything they expressed mild curiosity. The woman who was not in a nurse's uniform looked as if she might speak, perhaps wanted to, but decided against it. In his days and nights so far on the streets of New York, America, Robby felt few had seen him until he came to this dark place. He had run right through a crowd of people looking at his picture in the Sunday newspapers, but none had seen him. He had sat stinking in a crowded church, and many had looked at him certainly; none had seen him. He had upset everyone in the lower floor of the Hotel Clemens (except the waiter who held the door open for him), and everyone had yelled at him, two had kicked him, but no none had seen him. Of course Marie Savallo had seen him and one thing had led to another. The vanWankles' butler, Cabot, had seen him and done his best for him. Robby marveled that in a world of people ordered by their newspapers to look for him so few had seen him.

Robby felt snowflakes on his cheeks. He looked up. The iron steps to the railroad station were latticed. Some snowflakes came right through them.

Of course Robby had seen black people before. There had always been some black people on the streets of London, and he had seen many black people on the streets of New York. Black diplomats and their wives had come to tea and dinner at Pladroman House. Robby had loved the long, graceful robes the men wore. His family had a special friend who was an English black man, who had married the Cullinan woman. They had stayed at the country house at Wolmwold a whole winter while the man wrote a book which everyone said was quite good and which was published in England and France. Robby had never been in a place before where all the people were black.

He supposed that was why people on this street were seeing him. They were all black, and he wasn't.

Or they all read newspapers, really read them, and no one else did.

It was snowing hard. Robby looked across the street to the drugstore and wondered again what hep was. The time might be coming when he wanted some of whatever it was.

On the opposite sidewalk a man hurried along clutching his coat collar to his throat.

Robby did not know what he was thinking. The aftertaste of marmalade was gone, even the stickiness; he was out of Resounding Rhetoric. There come times when one thinks nothing, and this was Robby's first. Resolve, Fortitude, Duty were made of the same alphabet as Fear, Cold, Hunger. He had followed Reason, he had followed Instinct, and he had no idea Where He Was. Literally and figuratively, Robby was freezing where he stood.

He had stamped down the snow in the patch where he stood but outside that patch the snow had accumulated to just over the soles of his shoes.

Then around the corner near the drugstore came the most marvelous, the shortest and the least tall parade he had ever seen. Flags flying, bands playing, horses prancing and pipes singing could not have struck Robby as half so marvelous.

First around the corner came a large, heavy woman who waddled like a duck. Cradled in each arm was a large, brown grocery bag, necessarily held out against her ample bosom as if even foodstuff, the growing things of this earth, potatoes and carrots and onions, whatever was in the grocery bags, needed to press against her vitality to improve, to take sustenance from her. As the bags were obviously heavy and the sidewalk was slippery her head bobbed between the bags with every step. Her feet were not webbed but even from where Robby was standing he could see they were large and flat. Despite their large size there was something extra about them that made them appear to flap. He was to see that she walked in the snow in red cloth bedroom slippers which were so variously torn it was a wonder she kept them on. The ripped sections of the slippers flapped as she walked.

Behind her came a giggle of little kids in two loose lines like ducklings. They jumped up and down and bowed to make snowballs and waddled backwards and detoured and returned and yelled and laughed and caught snowflakes on their tongues and held hands and stuck snow down each other's backs and punched and tickled. One doing a cartwheel slipped in the snow and landed hard on the sidewalk and yelled "Ow!" and even that did not impede the merry line. They punched and tickled. Last in line soberly walked a girl wearing glasses, reading an open book the bottom part of which was propped against her hip bones.

Robby's previous efforts to find a school not having been very successful, this new method presented itself to him. *Here*, he decided, *is a school going somewhere to happen.*

He crossed the road to them and ambled along beside them, joined their formlessness, and the various ducklings looked at him, and saw him of course, and in less than a moment Robby felt the friendly *splat* of a light snowball against his forehead and he said, "I say!" and he said, "Right!" and bent over to make his own snowball and was attacked from the rear, snow was tucked into his shirt collar and melted and slid all the way down his spine which gave Robby's snowball a worthy target, which it missed.

The children were dressed more in country wear, Robby thought, than city, and more in summerwear than winter. Their shoes were plimsoll sneakers, little good in the snow. Their trousers and skirts were light cotton, little good in the cold. And their pullover sweaters, those who had them, and windbreakers were too big and too small depending on who was wearing them.

The line turned a corner, frisking, and another. Then it turned up a long flight of cracked stairs leading to a tall, crumbling brown building.

Robby stopped on the bottom step.

At the top, still holding her bags, the woman held the door

GREGORY MCDONALD

open with her rear while the ducklings passed into the building.

The woman squinted down the steps at Robby. "What you doin', bo' weevil, out this late all by yourself? You want to get snatched up by them what makes dog food?"

"No, ma'am."

It was then Robby saw her red, torn cloth slippers. They were very wet.

"You been followin' me?"

"Yes, ma'am."

"Lordy Lord, you do make 'em."

The last in line, the girl who persisted in reading her book in the dark, stumbled through the doorway.

"You get yourself home, little bo' weevil," the woman said. "You don't belong 'round here."

She stepped farther into the vestibule of the house, letting the door go. The door swung shut.

A snowflake landed on Robby's nose.

He turned around. He sat on the step. He was warmer from having played with the children. He began to think again.

Frozen tundra. His nanny had read to him about both deepest jungle and frozen tundra and it was a good thing she had, as Headmaster had known about neither place. People in frozen tundra built houses of snow and lived in them although how they could had always been a puzzle to Robby as he couldn't figure out how they ever lit their fireplaces without turning their houses into bathwater. His shoe scuffed the snow on the lowest step. It seemed a poor building material but he could understand people in the frozen tundra building their houses of snow if that was all they had. It was all he had. Never again would he climb into the back of a truck thinking he had found shelter for the night. The once he'd done so the truck had moved and brought him to a place to see what he had not wanted to see. All the buildings he saw had doors on them and all the doors were closed. Surely this was not enough snow to commence construction. He looked at the sky. There seemed to be plenty of snow falling, more than enough, by the looks of it.

He reasoned that all he had to do was wait until there was

enough snow and then build himself a house. Snow would keep the snow out. He wouldn't worry about how to heat his snow house until after he had built it.

The door behind Robby opened.

A duckling stood in the doorway on one bare foot.

"Mrs. Clearwater said if you're such a dumb boll weevil you don't know where you belong you'd better come in out of the night."

"Oh," said Robby. "Right."

The building appeared to be nothing more than caked dust.

Robby followed the duckling up two flights of broken wooden stairs, down a short corridor and through an open door into a bright room.

A large, single, shaded light bulb hung from a cord in the center of the room. The walls were a bright yellow. In the room was a large brown rocking chair, with a curved back, curved arms, and a curved seat. In one corner was a sink with its pipes exposed; next to it was a brown wooden table with a hotplate, boxes of cereal, two bottles of milk, a few bowls, spoons, glasses. Next to the table a blue curtain hung in a narrow doorway. In the other far corner was a tall, neat stack of folded green blankets.

Otherwise on the floor—almost everywhere on the floor—were mattresses. Thin, gray, black-striped mattresses.

And on the mattresses, in various states of undress, was the full giggle of children. One girl, her back leaning against the stack of mattresses, read. In the nearest corner two boys wrestled. Four sat cross-legged playing cards. One boy lay propped on an elbow singing a song with the words "Don't trouble me, Harry/You've seen better days." Each looked up at Robby when he entered, even the reading girl, even the wrestling boys, and each saw him.

The boy who led Robby up the stairs went to the wrestling match and jumped on it.

Mrs. Clearwater was at the brown table mixing cereal and milk in a huge bowl. She, too, was barefooted.

"Lordy Lord, bo' weevil, don't you know where you belong?" she asked.

"No, ma'am."

Robby took off his wet shoes and crossed the mattresses to her.

"You ain't got no home?"

"No, ma'am."

"No mama, no papa, no one to take care of you?"

"Not right now, ma'am."

"What happen to your folks, bo' weevil? They up and leave you, or you up and left them?"

"They got killed in the war, ma'am."

Robby watched her crumb bread into the mix.

"There ain't no war 'round here."

"I'm not from around here, ma'am. I'm from England."

"'Cross the Land o' Goshen?" Mrs. Clearwater smiled at herself.

"Across the ocean, yes, ma'am."

"How'd you get here? Bo' weevils can't swim that far, usually."

"A terrible ship, ma'am. Called the Scarey-Much."

"Hunh! A ship called the Scarey-Much brought you to my door. I never heard such a story." With strong forearms and a thin tool she opened a tin can of peaches. She glanced at him sideways. "How come you're dressed that way?"

Robby looked down at his clothes.

"You been in a play?" She dumped the peaches into the mixing bowl. "Hunh! Overcoat and short pants. What folks dressed you that way?"

"Yes, ma'am. They were white."

Slowly she stirred the mixture in the bowl. "You got a shirt, jacket and coat coverin' up your elbows but your knees are stickin' out as if each one had an eyeball and the job of seein' where you're goin'."

"Yes, ma'am."

"Your knees are almost as blue as your eyes. Don't think they're supposed to be, though." In the bowl things were turning into a thick, yellowish paté. "That picture on your hat and on your coat. Doesn't seem a good enough picture to have sewn all over you. Why's that cow got her horns stuck in that tree?"

"It belongs to the school."

"What does, the cow?"

"No, ma'am. The cow doesn't have a school. I mean, the school doesn't have a cow."

"You sure talk funny, too. What folks taught you to speak that way?"

"Yes, ma'am. They were white."

"Never saw a worse-dressed bo' weevil than you. Whoever sends you out in this weather in those clothes is punishin' you, bo' weevil. Take off your coat, 'slong as your shoes are off." Robby took off his coat and cap and dropped them on a mattress. Mrs. Clearwater glanced at him again. "Lordy Lord there's another cow with her horns stuck in a tree. Must mean somethin' important where you come from. Likely your people aren't partial to cows. Or trees." She kept breaking up the mixture in the bowl with the edge of her spoon, and stirring again. "I know I haven't got a pair of pants for you. Maybe tomorrow in the Baptist poor box I'll find some. Franklin had a pair of pants, but Arthur's wearin' 'em, and I don't think he's done wearin' 'em yet, are you, Arthur?"

"Done wearin' Franklin's pants?" answered one of the wrestlers, the one momentarily on top. "This boy ain't never goin' to need to wear pants again! Ow!"

"Bo' weevils," said Mrs. Clearwater. "They're everywhere! Aren't they just?"

"Yes, sir, ma'am."

"Seein' your folks gave you so little, at least did they spring a name on you?"

"Oh, yes, ma'am. I got lots of those."

"Try a few on me."

"Robert James Saint James Burnes Farhall, I mean, Walter Farhall-Pladroman, ma'am."

"Phew-ie! Did I hear James twice in that string?"

"No, ma'am. James once and Saint James once."

"Like that cow all over your clothes. Once your folks decide on somethin', they sure do stick to it. What does anybody want with all those names?"

"My father once said they had to load me up with names to satisfy the families."

"Well, I hope they're satisfied. Bo' weevil, they set you out with near a dozen names and cold knees. I'd rather have one good name and a pair of pants, if I were you."

"I saw you out in the snow in slippers, ma'am."

"I got snowshoes. Somewhere. But an old woman's feet aren't impo'tant. No one's supposed to be responsible for an old lady, see?"

"No."

"Well, you are a nice boy. Did I hear Robert start that string of names you rattled off to me?"

"Robert James Saint James—"

"Robert will do just fine. More than fine. You ain't slept in a while, either, have you, bo' weevil?"

"I spent last night in a rubbish barrel."

" 'Course you did. You ain't the first, you ain't the last, and you ain't the only." She indicated the world with her spoon. "There are bo' weevils out there right now, in this snowy night, hunkerin' down in rubbish barrels. Hunh! Think of a world that can afford wars and can't feed the children. Hunh! Don't you never spend no night in no rubbish barrel while I'm alive, Robert. You hear me?"

"I certainly won't, ma'am."

"Say what?"

"I'll never spend no night in no rubbish barrel while you're alive, ma'am."

"You know what else I think, Robert?"

"What, ma'am?"

"I think it's been too long since I had a huggin'."

Robby looked at the bigness of her.

"Can't go too long without a huggin'," Mrs. Clearwater said. "Makes me worry." She put down her spoon and took Robby's hand. "You come he'p me out."

At the rocking chair, Robby hesitated.

"Now don' you worry 'bout the other bo' weevils," Mrs. Clearwater said. "I've about taken all the huggin's from them they can stand for just now."

Both her arms were out and when Robby climbed into her lap

they folded around him. He drew his knees up onto her. Through his right ear he could hear her heart beat. The skin of his face could feel her breath.

The chair began to rock, slightly.

Robby said, "It's snowin', ma'am."

"I hear you, bo' weevil."

"I was going to build a snow house."

"And I know you would have built a fine snow house, Robert. Just fine."

"You see, I was sent to America…"

"You're here, li'l bo' weevil. I'm America. Lordy Lord, I got black blood in me, and white blood, and yellow blood, and red-Indian blood, all in me. You're in the lap of America, bo' weevil. You go ahead and cry. I'm America; there ain't no mo': I'm just an ol' cow with my horns stuck in a tree."

23
The Charitable Lady

"Hunh! Look at that snow." In the morning Mrs. Clearwater stood, hands on her hips, looking out the window. "The charitable lady will never get here."

Breakfast was a more orderly procedure than supper had been. Blankets were folded and stacked in a corner of the room. Teeth were brushed at the sink with four toothbrushes. At the brown table Mrs. Clearwater put together another cereal mix. Heddy braided Ugly Mary's hair while Ugly Mary continued reading her book. Traffic to and fro the toilet alcove, behind the brown curtain, moved efficiently. The children pulled on their clothes and tied their laces. The bigger children helped the smaller children.

During supper the night before the games had continued. The card game changed players several times. Ugly Mary, cereal bowl in her lap, continued reading. Robby and Franklin and Arthur and Wellmet raced cockroaches along a narrow strip of floor, a raceway they made by separating two mattresses. After many races it was not established which cockroach was the fastest. Starting them over again and again and cheering them down a whole mattress-length wore the cockroaches out though, made them dizzy and stagger and try to escape under the mattresses. One cockroach clearly had more stamina than the others.

"Time to get the blankets, Franklin." Mrs. Clearwater had cleaned the bowls and glasses. "Hunh! We got nine mattresses and blankets and thirteen humans. Lordy Lord, if you're goin' to send me more children, please send me more mattresses and blankets with 'em!"

With the sole of a sneaker Franklin exterminated all the cockroaches except the one which had shown the most stamina. That one he told Arthur to put in a jar for safekeeping.

Then Franklin and Wellmet dealt out the blankets.

Ugly Mary finally put down her book. She looked at Robby and blinked. Her eyes shone with an extra vitality, an extra understanding. Robby knew that in touching her smooth, clear skin he would feel her vibrancy.

"That Mary," Mrs. Clearwater said to herself. "She has all the life there is or ever was or will be, all in that brain of hers. Hunh! Hasn't she, though?"

When they were all in their underwear Robby got a blanket and followed Ugly Mary to a mattress and they laid down together under it. All the while Ugly Mary's eyes were laughing. Under the blanket she punched Robby once, in the stomach, and giggled.

"Now you bo' weevils get under your blankets and pretend you're asleep, and soon you will be," said Mrs. Clearwater.

Under the blanket Ugly Mary smelled like the binding of a book.

Mrs. Clearwater turned off the overhead light. Robby fell asleep.

During the night, Robby felt something moving among them, and woke up. In a robe, Mrs. Clearwater stepped lightly among the bodies, stooping over again and again, tucking a blanket up to a chin, collecting an arm here, a leg there to replace it under the blanket.

She covered Ugly Mary's panties with the blanket.

"You awake, bo' weevil? You go to sleep, hear?"

"Yes, sir, ma'am."

"Your skin sure do show in the dark, bo' weevil."

"Yes, ma'am."

She covered Robby's legs, which he felt were cold.

Mrs. Clearwater continued through the room, stepping and stooping, like a gardener tending her flower bed.

Robby watched her settle down then, on her own mattress on the floor, a great mountain seen from any perspective, seen now over a considerable range of hillocks, only some of whose names Robby knew.

In the dark Robby put his hand on Ugly Mary's arm, then on her shoulder. Then he put his cheek on her shoulder. The weight of his head did not wake her. He felt the magic of her vitality. He breathed in the smell from her. He fell asleep again.

"Robert will come to help me clean the church today," Mrs.

Clearwater said during the busy breakfast. "Maybe we'll stop and register him at the school on the way home."

Some (Randolph, Franklin, Arthur and Wellmet) were insisting there was no school that day, because of the snow. They shouldn't even bother going down to the school to check, they said. Instead they should all go out and play in the snow before the plows came. Others (Heddy, Toby and Ugly Mary) disagreed strongly and said they should hurry up and leave for school earlier than usual, as the snow would slow them down. Mrs. Clearwater said, "You hurry up to school, and no playing in the snow on your way. You want to sit in wet skins all day?"

Through the window Robby watched them in the street. Some were hurrying to the school, not to be late. Others were playing in the snow schoolwards, to sit in wet skins all day.

Mrs. Clearwater was on her hands and knees looking in a corner cupboard. "Where are my snowshoes?"

Watching her, Robby was sure no snowshoes could fit in such a small cupboard. He knew no snowshoes which would fit Mrs. Clearwater could fit in such a small cupboard. He doubted snowshoes which would fit Mrs. Clearwater would need looking for at all.

"Here they are!"

Out of the closet she pulled a pair of floppy overshoes so holey, cracked and torn, Robby knew them incapable of either keeping snow out or her feet in. As galoshes they were as illusory as a Thadeus Lowry meal.

Mrs. Clearwater sat in the rocking chair to pull on her boots.

Watching her, Robby said, "You genuinely like children, ma'am?"

"Well, I love 'em," she said. "Why you ask?"

"A man I know once said if I ever meet an adult who genuinely likes children I should let him know and he'll build a statue to that person."

"Hunh!" said Mrs. Clearwater. "People do love to turn each other into stone statues. It's one more way of ignorin' the flesh and the blood of us."

There was a thump and a bump and a stamping from downstairs and a giggle all the way up the stairs.

Randolph was the first to burst into the room. "No school! I told you so! I told you no white teacher could make it through that snow to the school!"

"You'll catch your deaths!" exclaimed Mrs. Clearwater. "Get your clothes off and on the radiators to dry this minute, you hear?"

"White teachers can't get through the snow to school," said Franklin. "Us little black kids can!"

"White teachers aren't from around here," muttered Mrs. Clearwater. "They got a longer way to go."

It was then, while Mrs. Clearwater was taking off her galoshes again, while Ugly Mary (after she had placed her pants on the radiator to dry) crawled into her corner with her book, while Arthur, Franklin and Randolph were wringing out their clothes over the kitchen sink, while there were children playing inside the apartment and children playing outside in the street and children playing on the stairs between the inside and the outside, that a woman appeared in the apartment's door.

Invisible to those who zoomed past her and around her, in and out, up and down the stairs, she was the first person sensibly dressed for the frozen tundra Robby had seen. Her boots were tall and thick and encrusted with snow. Her skirt was a heavy tweed, hemmed with snow. Her coat was quilted and belted and ran from her knees to her throat. Her gloves were lined leather. An enormous scarf was wound twice around her neck; the ends hung below her waist. On her head, pulled down over her ears, was a knitted cap. Only her nose was exposed to the atmosphere, and it was red. She carried a briefcase.

Standing in the door, soundlessly her lips said, "Seven." Her eyes widened as she looked around the room. Red and white splotches appeared on her face. Her lips said, "Eight, nine, ten." Her look softened as she spotted Ugly Mary reading in the corner, yet still her lips said, "Eleven." Upon seeing Robby her face turned entirely red. Her eyes narrowed. Her lips said, "Twelve."

Mrs. Clearwater looked up from where she was bending over her boots in the chair. "Well, Miss Maisie! You made it through the snow after all! You're a credit to your race and as regular as the curse!"

"I'm glad to find you in," the woman said.

"In what?" asked Mrs. Clearwater. She got up and brought her boots to the cupboard, dropped them in, and closed the cupboard's door.

"At home." Miss Maisie sat in the rocking chair. "Obviously I have to talk to you." She pulled off her gloves. "This is an intolerable situation. It can't go on."

"But it do seem to," said Mrs. Clearwater. "It do."

Mrs. Clearwater's accent became more inflected, Robby noticed, more rhythmical, more mellifluous. And, Robby noticed, Mrs. Clearwater smiled at herself frequently, as if at hearing the way she was saying things, as she had the night before when she had referred to the Atlantic Ocean as the Land o' Goshen.

Miss Maisie took a large notebook and pen from her briefcase and opened both for use. Snow from her boots was making a puddle on the floor.

"Really," she said in disgust, indicating Arthur, Randolph and Franklin with the rear end of her pen. "Can't you make those boys stop that?"

"Here, you bo' weevils, stop that," Mrs. Clearwater said. "Can't you see the charitable lady's here? Your clothes are dry now. Go outdoors."

"Our clothes ain't dry yet," said Franklin. "We just put 'em on the radiator one minute ago."

"Then sit still, there."

"Disgusting," said Miss Maisie. "Three near-naked boys and there's a girl sitting right there in the corner." Miss Maisie made a note in her book. "She's near-naked, too."

Mrs. Clearwater laughed. "That's all right, Miss Maisie. You put this many people in a room small as this, and there ain't much they end up not knowin' 'bout each other."

"Those boys were wrestling near-naked."

"They just warmin' theyselves up. They ain't got no fine, quilted snow-coats. No, sir!"

"This certainly will go in the morals section of my report."

"Why, Miss Maisie, you makin' another report?"

"I certainly am."

"You know what, Miss Maisie? You make up reports and give 'em in somewhere downtown where they chew 'em up in some big machine and put 'em in boxes and next day I go to the store and buy 'em back as cornflakes."

"Perhaps if you had more respect for what we're trying to do for you, cooperate a little more, we could solve some of the problems you seem incapable of solving yourself."

"What problems I got, Miss Maisie? I got my children, my health and just enough money to keep goin' to the store and buyin' your reports as cornflakes."

Miss Maisie used the blunt end of her pen again. "You must tell those boys to cover up! If you don't find their nakedness objectionable in front of the little girl, I most certainly do!"

"The only clothes they got is wet."

"Have them do something! They're exposed!"

"Here, Franklin. Get a blanket and put yourselves under it. The charitable lady says she don't want to see so much of you until you're older."

"Mrs. Clearwater, I will not continue to put up with your insults."

"I hope not."

"And if you think by insulting me and abusing me you can get rid of me, you're badly mistaken. I am a trained social worker, a city employee, here to help you, and help you we will, even if our straightening out this intolerable situation means your ending up in jail. Do I make myself clear?"

"Jail! Hunh! Wouldn't that be somethin'. Mrs. Clearwater in jail. Anythin' else you can think to do for me, Miss Maisie?"

"It's not impossible. We have enough evidence to bring moral charges against you, charges for neglect, abuse, hampering a city official in the discharge of her duty—"

"And it's not impossible I'm gonna shut my door in your face! Think of you comin' here and talkin' that way in front of my children!"

"They're not your children, Mrs. Clearwater, and we will institutionalize them all, as soon as we can complete some paperwork. Then you'll see what we do to you."

"You're gonna institutionalize us all? Lordy Lord, we're goin' to jail, for makin' do. You keep doin' your paperwork, Miss Maisie, and we'll keep eatin' it up as cornflakes, and if anybody comes up with solutions better'n what we got, I'll go to jail quick enough to praise the Lord and get some rest."

"We'll begin by your addressing me by my proper name. I am Miss Caldwell, as you well know. Miss Carol Caldwell. I have reviewed reports about you going back years. Your penchant for calling your social worker, every one of us, *Miss Maisie*, has been noted with increasing irritation."

"That what your reports say? I've always wondered what you all spend the rest of the week writin' down about us."

"Whatever humor this appellation has had in your mind has been perceived by no one else, and must have worn thin in whatever mind you have."

"Lord, Miss Maisie, you've beaten me down." Mrs. Clearwater fluttered her hands in the air. "I'm cut and bleedin' on the groun'. You done put me in my place and stepped on my face. You're gonna take my children and put me in jail, and move on to make some other po' nigger wail!"

From under the blanket came giggles, and a very quiet cheer. "Yeah, Mrs. Clearwater!"

Contrary to her words, Mrs. Clearwater stood over Miss Maisie, hands on her hips, feet planted wide apart. "How come I never see no white people in Harlem except those what got jobs with the city? How come no black people got jobs with the city?"

Miss Maisie cleared her throat and looked down.

"How come they're no black social workers? You ever send me a black social worker, and I'll never call her Miss Maisie. That's a promise!"

"Jobs are available to black social workers. It's just that so few have the education—"

"So few have the education 'cause all the social workers is white! Ain't that right?"

"Mrs. Clearwater, you and I can't solve all the problems of the world—"

"Miss Maisie, you can't even solve your own problems!" Mrs. Clearwater pointed to the floor at Miss Maisie's feet. "You seem to be leakin' some."

Miss Maisie looked down at the puddle the snow from her boots had made.

Mrs. Clearwater said, "You expect me to clean that up? You expect me to come into your house and leave a puddle? You don't expect me to come into your house at all. My children might come into the house and take off their clothes to dry and wrassle around to get warm, but they take the snow off them before they come in and they don't leave no puddles for Mrs. Clearwater to clean up. They don't come in here and insult me and threaten me with no pen and leave no puddles on my floor. You hear me, Miss Maisie?"

"I hear you, Mrs. Clearwater," said Miss Maisie. "I realize I probably did insult you, and if I did I apologize heartily. If you'd just explain where all these children came from—"

"I've explained! Not once but one thousand times. The night I found Ambrose sleepin' in a packin' case I went to the police station and explained about it, and they said, 'It's late, now, you bring that boy home and somebody from the city will be in touch with you.'"

Miss Maisie flicked through her notebook to a list. "Ambrose?"

"That was years ago! Ambrose is now gone to the Army. Within a week, he brought home Billy and John."

"Billy and John?"

"Billy's already dead in the fightin' in North Africa. The world's full of bo' weevils, Miss Maisie."

"I see. I don't think I understand."

"I been explainin' all along! And once a month some Miss Maisie's been comin' along as if she had a right, comin' right in, sittin' in my chair, askin' me the same questions, gettin' the same answers, insultin' me, threatenin' me no matter what I say, makin' up reports and it never done no good. No truck full of food to feed my children never pulled up at my door. No car never come by with clothes and blankets and enough mattresses. Nobody never gave me no cash money this close to Christmas to buy no stockin's for my children. Nobody never found better homes for my children than the one they got. All you Miss Maisies ever done is come by regular like clockwork to insult what we got, to insult what we are, make up reports and go away leavin' puddles on the floor for me to clean up."

"*Burned*," said a voice from under the blanket.

"I see," said Miss Maisie. "I see how it can look from your perspective. With the war there really isn't much room in the orphanages—"

"There ain't no perspective to it. It's a fact. It's also a fact the city orphanages are a disgrace. My minister went and looked. He said they line naked boys who've acted up some against a wall and play fire hoses on them full force! That's lovin' 'em!"

"With so many children, there is a need for extraordinary measures of discipline."

"Some fine citizens they're makin'. Hunh!"

Miss Maisie's face, even her forehead, was entirely red. She looked up at Mrs. Clearwater. "It's also a fact, Mrs. Clearwater," Miss Maisie said, "that you are a prostitute."

"Yes, ma'am!" Mrs. Clearwater said joyously. "You better believe it!"

"You admit it."

"Never think otherwise, Miss Maisie."

Miss Maisie looked down at her notebook. "Our agency has had you on file for more than ten years now. No one has ever reported seeing a Mr. Clearwater. No record of your marriage has ever been found." Miss Maisie sighed. "Yet clearly you have children here, even now, who are only five and six years old."

"That's right."

Miss Maisie sighed much more deeply. "In fact, if I just counted correctly, you have twelve children here, all roughly between the ages of five and twelve."

Mrs. Clearwater laughed. "You figure it out, Miss Maisie. You think I got more'n my share of children."

"I think you have."

"But as long as you got me down in your book as a prostitute," chortled Mrs. Clearwater, "you can't figure out which are my *natural* children, can you?"

Miss Maisie asked tiredly, "Mrs. Clearwater, which are your natural children?"

"They're all natural children, sure enough."

Miss Maisie looked at Robby Burnes. "Are all these children your children, Mrs. Clearwater?"

"They ain't no one else's."

"When I visited you last month, I counted ten children."

"You must have counted wrong."

"As of last Friday you have eleven children enrolled in the local school—all under the name Clearwater."

"They must be slow in their paperwork down there."

"There are twelve children here, Mrs. Clearwater, and we can't find birth records for any of them."

"Well, Miss Maisie, they were all born, sure enough. It's just that slow paperwork. Terrible slow paperwork. No wonder the cornflakes is stale."

"I know you have a job cleaning the Baptist church, Mrs. Clearwater."

"Bowin' low before the Lord."

"You are willing to be thought a prostitute simply to obstruct the law...is that it?"

"You ain't goin' to find no partial solutions for us, Miss Maisie. You ain't goin' to take some of my children and throw 'em in front of no fire hose. I'd like to see these children well cared for. You find a solution for all of us, or none of us. I needs to help these children out, Miss Maisie. Not once a month, makin' out reports. I needs to help them out twenty-four hours a day. I'm doin' the best I can."

Miss Maisie laid tired eyes on Robby Burnes. "That white boy isn't your child."

"Robert? Sure enough, he's my bo' weevil."

"Mrs. Clearwater, he is blond, blue-eyed, and he wasn't here last month."

"I got white blood in me. I can have a white child. Why, you

should have seen the john who was that boy's father! He was extra-
white. Even whiter than you are, Miss Maisie! Last month while you
were here, Robert was 'round the corner buyin' up your cornflakes."

Miss Maisie said to Robby, "What is your name, son?"

"Robert, miss."

"Robert what?"

"Robert Clearwater, miss."

"How old are you?"

"Eight years old, miss."

"You look bigger than that. Do you go to school?"

"Yes, miss. I go to the local piss."

"What? What did you say?"

"I said, 'Yes, miss.'"

"How long have you been here, Robert, living with Mrs. Clearwater?"

"I was born here, miss."

"You don't talk like Mrs. Clearwater."

"I don't have much to say, miss."

"I mean, you seem to have an English accent."

"If I were any more English I couldn't talk at all, miss."

"What did you say?"

"I said, I have a toothache, miss."

"Why do you look so familiar to me, Robert?"

"You've seen me here before, miss."

"I've never seen you here before. But I've seen you someplace
before. I'll figure it out."

A new wrestling match was going on under Arthur's, Randolph's
and Franklin's blanket.

Miss Maisie pointed the blunt end of her pen at it. "Make those
boys stop that!"

Mrs. Clearwater said, "Here, you! Get dressed and go out in the
snow now. Before the plows come."

Happily they popped up from under the blanket and began to
pull on steaming clothes.

Miss Maisie screwed the cap on her fountain pen. "Well, at least,
Mrs. Clearwater, I think our little chat helped clear the air."

Mrs. Clearwater shrugged. "Air's never been smoky, in this room."

Miss Maisie picked the briefcase up from the puddle and put it in her lap. "I'll make my report and then we'll just see what shall be done."

"You won't do nothin', Miss Maisie. You Miss Maisies never have."

"Not me, precisely." Miss Maisie closed her notebook and put it in the briefcase and closed the briefcase and stood up. "I'm being reassigned—to another district. Out of Harlem, thank God. I've had just about all I can take of you black women and your unaccountable children."

"You're just earnin' a wage, Miss Maisie. I know that. We all have to earn a livin'."

Miss Maisie turned in the door and went through it and started down the stairs.

"Merry Christmas, Miss Maisie," said Mrs. Clearwater. "May all your Christmases be white."

Mrs. Clearwater chuckled and put her hand on Robby's head. "Robert Clearwater, eh?" Her hand slid down the back of his head to his neck. She gave him a gentle shake. "You like that name, Robert?"

"Yes, ma'am."

"It's a name you can remember, uh? You can say it without stumblin' over it, forgettin' parts of it."

"Yes, ma'am. You're America, ma'am. You said."

"I'm the melted pot, bo' weevil. Trouble with a pot, Robert, is that the melted part always sinks to the bottom." She laughed and shook him gently again. "Lordy Lord, I'm goin' to have much trouble explainin' you, bo' weevil. Why don't you go out and play with the other children?"

"Should I, ma'am?"

"There somethin' out there you afraid of, bo' weevil?" She turned him around to face her and looked into his eyes. "You go out and play. You have nothin' to fear with all the other bo' weevils around. Pretty soon I'll come out and see how you are."

"Yes, ma'am."

"Don't be afraid, bo' weevil."

"I won't, ma'am."

Mrs. Clearwater turned toward the sink. "I'll just get a rag, and wipe up this month's contribution from the social-workin' agency."

In the street Robby helped the others build snowmen until the snowplow came along and knocked them down. The giggle of kids pelted the back of the snowplow with snowballs. After the snowplow had gone by once each way they built snowforts on both sides of the street and had a long, wicked snowball fight.

As people came into the street from the buildings Robby noticed that many stopped and looked at him and walked along and looked back. *Lordy Lord, I'm goin' to have much trouble explainin' you, bo' weevil*, Mrs. Clearwater had said. Robby could not think about that just then. He was warm and happy and breathing hard and the cold felt good against his cheeks and even Ugly Mary came out to play. Robby busied himself protecting her in the snowball fight until he discovered her aim was much better than his and she could throw farther. It was simple, them against us/us against them, and the reality of play became the nearest and nicest and best and almost only reality. He lost his school cap in a tussle in the snow and reminded himself to look for it later.

Mrs. Clearwater, in her overshoes, left the house, went up the street, around the corner. In a while she came back, carrying a shopping bag so full the newspaper stuck out of the top of it like a flagpole.

They played Beat the Devil and dark fell on them as gently as snow had fallen the night before.

Just at full dark Mrs. Clearwater came out of the building again in her overshoes and again she walked up the street and turned the corner. When she returned she was carrying nothing.

A while later she called from the window that it was time all her bo' weevils came in. In they trooped, wet and warm and tired.

They tried to dry their clothes by wringing them over the sink and laying them on and near the radiator. Robby's knees and his cheeks were chapped and Mrs. Clearwater put some grease on them. During the long process of supper, using bowls and glasses one after the other, there were many laughs and wrestles. Francine stood on her head while others counted off the seconds for a full seven minutes. Pauley almost succeeded in teaching Blanchard, the youngest, how to wiggle his ears. Ugly Mary sat against the blankets with her skinny knees up, reading. Wellmet tried to get another cockroach race started but he could find only one cockroach. The cockroach Arthur had put in the jar the night before was dead.

They brushed their teeth and got under the blankets early because the radiators were working so hard at drying clothes the room grew cold. Under the blanket Robby kissed Ugly Mary and she kissed him back. When the light went off they put their arms and legs around each other and she went to sleep.

Robby was almost asleep when he remembered his school cap. Dark had fallen too soon and too fast for him to find it in the snow.

24
Trapped!

Robby saw his school cap first thing next morning, the instant he looked out the window. It was across the street in Tony Savallo's left hand.

Robby backed away from the window. The room was still cold but Robby was much colder.

Tony Savallo was on the sidewalk across the street, the other side of the farther snowfort. His arms were folded across his chest. Watching all the buildings at once he paced up and down the sidewalk, stepping lightly over the hunks of snow. He walked ten meters along the block one way, then ten meters back. Within two or three blocks of the railroad station, with the help of the school cap, Tony Savallo had located Robby Burnes.

"Curse my cap!" Robby said to himself.

The room was full of chatter, but Robby heard none of it. He picked his clothes off the radiator and dressed as quickly as he could, imagining terrible things. Robby was a danger to the Clearwater giggle of kids. He was a danger to Mrs. Clearwater. He had led a murderer to them. He imagined Tony Savallo bursting through the door of the little apartment and shooting everyone in sight. Robby's hands shook so much it took him forever to tie his shoelaces.

He put on his overcoat.

"Where you goin', bo' weevil?" asked Mrs. Clearwater. "You ain't had breakfast yet. Anyway, you're comin' with me today, to help me clean the Baptist church."

"Just cold, ma'am," said Robby. He shouldered his collars up around his neck and rubbed his hands together. "Just cold."

Doling out breakfast to the others she gave him a long look.

Robby went behind the brown curtain. It took forever for him to relieve himself. From his overcoat pocket he took the envelope. It was wet from yesterday's snowball battle. He tore it open. The one hundred one-hundred-dollar bills were held together by a wide elastic. He stuffed the bills back into his pocket. He tore the envelope into small pieces and flushed them down the toilet.

Back in the main room Mrs. Clearwater gave him another curious look. She was busy feeding the children. Heddy was arguing with Wellmet about Leonardo and the airplane and the Wright brothers.

Robby brushed his teeth. As he did so he moved so that his body concealed the little brown table from the rest of the room. With his left hand he took the ten thousand dollars out of his pocket and stuck it in a cereal box at the back of the table. He pushed the money down into the box so it was not visible. Then he moved back and spat into the sink and rinsed the toothbrush.

"You haven't eaten, bo' weevil," Mrs. Clearwater complained to him.

"Later, ma'am," he said.

He moved into the crowd of children around Mrs. Clearwater and vibrated with them there a moment. Heddy challenged him: "Who invented the airplane?"

"What?" Robby said. "I don't know."

Slowly he backed toward the wall near the door. He stumbled over a mattress. His fingers found the wall. Behind his back they danced along the wall until they found the doorknob. He waited until Mrs. Clearwater turned her back to help Willy put on his steam-stiffened mittens. With her back to the room, Ugly Mary was putting on her coat without dropping her books. Her movements were slow and dignified. Robby opened the door only wide enough to let himself through. Standing in the corridor he closed the door quietly.

He ran down the two flights of stairs lightly. He stood at the front door, looking through the thick window into the street. At first Tony Savallo was not in the window. Then he sauntered into view from the left. The uneven thick glass made his body seem to waver.

Robby went along the corridor to the back of the house. Under the staircase were bashed-in rubbish barrels. Newspapers and tin cans had spilled out of them onto the floor.

At the back of the corridor he found the door to the cellar open. The cellar stairs were blocked by cardboard boxes, some empty, some full of rubbish. He started down the stairs, hoping to wade through the mess. On the fifth stair down he was up to his shoulders in cardboard boxes. Some of them were not moving easily for him. With his foot he groped for a sixth stair and found none. Crouching on one bent knee, sinking in boxes, he felt for a seventh stair and found none.

Quickly, quietly, he ran up the five flights of stairs to the top of the building, and then up another half flight. At the top was a metal-sheathed trapdoor. The bolt was rusted. He took off his shoe and banged at the bolt until the door was unlocked. Robby pushed against the door with his hands and then with his hands and his head and then with his hands and his shoulders. He opened the trapdoor just enough for a few flakes of snow to fall through. On the roof the trapdoor was blocked with snow and ice.

He put back on his shoe and ran quietly down the stairs again to the front door. Tony Savallo was exactly centered in the window, facing the house. The window's distortion made him look very tall, his shoulders very wide.

From upstairs came the sound of a door opening. Arthur shouted, "No, no, Marconi invented macaroni!" There was a great clatter of feet as the children started down the stairs.

"The Wright brothers are not wrong," insisted Arthur. "They couldn't be!"

Robby dashed along the corridor again and squeezed himself in among the rubbish barrels under the staircase. He turned to face the corridor and sat cross-legged on the floor. Eleven pairs of feet thundered on the stairs over his head.

The front door opened and slammed, opened and slammed, opened and slammed as if it were waving the children good-bye. The last pair of feet down the stairs Robby knew were Ugly Mary's. They were slow, deliberate. Robby knew she was reading as she walked.

"Mr. Plane invented the airplane," said Francine. "Plain Mr. Plane!"

Behind Ugly Mary the front door closed quietly.

Robby heard another door open, somewhere up in the building. Then he heard Mrs. Clearwater's voice. "Bo' weevil? Robert? Where are you, Robert? Hunh! Must have forgot and gone to school with the others! Now what will happen…"

Upstairs the door closed.

Robby looked around at the rubbish under the stairwell. He was staring at himself. He stretched his legs out into the corridor and reached for the newspaper. It was the Monday *Evening Star*. The photograph of himself on the front page, albeit large, had been cropped. *The New York Star* had used less of his photograph, bigger, in each new edition. This version ran from the peak of his school cap to the bottom of his chin. His hand was missing from his chin, now, and his chin looked blotted. It was as if *The New York Star* were consuming him slowly while making his head balloon. He leaned his back against a rubbish barrel and smoothed the newspaper in his lap.

E X T R A

$100,000 RANSOM PAID
ROBBY'S RETURN IMMMENT

BY THADEUS LOWRY

Because of the heartwarming, fulsome and wonderful response of the readers of The New York Star, *the $100,000 ransom for the safe return of 10-year-old Robby Burnes has been paid.*

His return to safekeeping is expected imminently.

The kidnapping of the orphaned Duke of Pladroman has had the New York Police Department and the Federal Bureau of Investigation thoroughly baffled. Every telephone call to this reporter for The New York Star *from the kidnappers has been traced, but, because of electronic confusion, only traced back to the police station assigned the job of tracing the call.*

However, once it was reported in this morning's New York Star *that the ransom—every penny of the $100,000—had been raised successfully from the readers of* The New York Star, *this* *correspondent of* The New York Star *received a very special telephone call.*

In metallic, measured tones the heartless kidnapper gave this correspondent of The New York Star *precise instructions as to how to turn the money over to their criminal hands for the safe return of little Robby Burnes.*

Again efforts to trace the call (with the help of the New York Telephone Company) led back only to the police station administering the trace.

INTREPID

Dutifully, with no thought for personal safety, your correspondent followed the kidnappers' instructions precisely. The kidnapper ordered that this reporter, in delivering the ransom to them, was not to be accompanied or followed by any member of the police or F.B.I.

The kidnapper's precise words were: "If there's a cop anywhere in sight when you deliver the cash the kid's head will end up in the East River and his body in the Hudson."

Carrying $100,000 cash in a brown paper bag (the publisher of The New York Star *donated the first $5,000 to* The Robby Burnes Ransom Fund*) this correspondent made his way to Grand Central Station. Working through the commuters and the holiday throng this reporter reflected on how joyous an occasion is Christmas. If the joyous revellers in the railroad station only knew who passed among them, and what he carried in that brown paper bag! At what risk to himself! And for what purpose!*

Your intrepid correspondent crossed Grand Central Station attracting little or no attention, and, pretending to be an ordinary person going about routine business, placed the bag containing $100,000 in locker number 1313. He closed the door without locking it, and without taking the key.

His instructions were not to wait about, but to leave the station as quickly as possible.

NEWS

Police have just reported to your correspondent for The New York Star *that locker number 1313 of Grand Central Station was checked before noon.*

It was found empty!

The brown paper bag containing $100,000 ransom for Robby Burnes (age 10) has been taken.

Police efforts to apprehend the kidnappers of Robby Burnes have been to no avail.

The kidnappers have gotten the ransom money and have gotten away scot-free!

The nefarious voice on the telephone, dripping evil with every utterance, assured your correspondent for The New York Star *that if ransom was paid exactly in accordance with their instructions, 10-year-old Robby Burnes would be returned to safekeeping in some unannounced location today, Tuesday.*

Now we will see if there truly is honor among thieves…

The newspaper Robby read under the stairwell had darkened. A shadow had fallen across it. Robby realized he had left his legs and feet sticking out into the corridor. Robby inhaled. He took in as much breath as he could. A bulk, a person, a man was standing over him. In Robby's hands the newspaper began to shake.

"Robby?" a man's voice asked quietly. "Robby?"

25
Mort à Guerre

"Thadeus Lowry!"

"Perusing my deathless prose?"

Robby first had seen the two brown shoes near his own, then the ferule of a walking stick lower to the floor. His eyes snapped up over the vested belly, over the hanging overcoat and suit coat and over the double chins to the flushed face, bulbous nose and protruding eyes. He gulped. "No, sir. I'm reading your story in the *New York Star.*"

Robby felt as if he had screamed, when he hadn't. He was breathing as unevenly as if he had screamed.

"I'll have you know," announced Thadeus Lowry, "that you are reading the second-to-last Thadeus Lowry story for that rag, *The New York Star*. After a day of breathless waiting, a dramatic pause, an update by that hack, Ronald Jasper, reporting there is no news from the police on Robby Burnes, my last story about you shall appear in tomorrow morning's *Star*. The very last word."

"Oh?"

"I've already written it."

"What's it about?"

"Your safe return."

"Have I returned safe?"

"Of course," said Thadeus Lowry. "After a latish breakfast, which we call brunch here, dreadful word, of course, but an appetizing enough pastime—"

"But, sir, I haven't returned safe." Robby scrambled up from the rubbish and out from under the stairwell. "That man standing across the street—Tony Savallo—is going to shoot me. How did you find me, anyway, Thadeus Lowry? How did you know where I was?"

"Never mind about that now." Thadeus Lowry seemed as perturbed at the thought of Robby Burnes being shot as at the thought of having to rewrite his copy for the early edition. "What do you mean Tony Savallo is going to shoot you?"

"I saw him shoot a man Saturday night. In the street. I was in Tony Savallo's truck and I saw him through the window, and he saw me, and he's been chasing me, he shot at me twice—"

"Tony Savallo." Thadeus Lowry reflected. "So Tony Savallo shot Ginsy O'Brien."

"He shot *someone*, sir."

"He's shot lots of people. It's what he does."

Thadeus Lowry stepped to the front door and looked through the distorting glass. Robby peeped over the lower edge of the window frame.

"Odd I didn't notice him when I came in," said Thadeus Lowry. "Yet I did observe your legs sticking out from under the stairwell. It does go to prove," sighed Thadeus Lowry philosophically, "that one is inclined to see only what one is looking for." He turned away from the door. "That is Tony Savallo, all right."

"You know the Savallos, sir?"

"I've known Guido Savallo for years. We were both members of the 1928 crime commission. He had some remarkably instructive insights as to how crime is organized, I must say, but was extremely reticent about specific names and dates. A very theoretical fellow, he seemed. Tony Savallo I've been observing lurking about since he made his bones at the tender age of sixteen."

"Do you know him to speak to, sir?"

"I wouldn't speak to him."

"You wouldn't, sir? Nothing you might say—"

"He's a hit man for his Uncle Guido."

"A hit man?"

"He murders people."

"I know, sir."

"By the dozens."

"No one to talk to, sir? You talk to everyone."

"Conversations with Tony Savallo have a way of being short and terminating with a bang."

"He really wants to kill me, sir."

"He has every reason to." In the front hall of the apartment building Thadeus Lowry frowned for a long moment. "Young man?" he finally said. "You're in trouble."

"I know, sir. Is my return imminent?"

"Perhaps to your Maker."

"You see, Tony Savallo doesn't know which building I'm in. He found my school cap in the snow, so he knows I'm somewhere here."

"Playing cat to your mouse, eh? The minute you show your whiskers he grabs you by the neck and bangs you against the floor until you die? That it?"

Robby felt Thadeus Lowry's analogy in the back of his neck. "He has a gun, sir."

"Ah," said Thadeus Lowry. "So he simply blows your head off."

The simplicity outlined by Thadeus Lowry caused a stab of pain between Robby's eyes. "Yes, sir."

"Permit me to reconnoiter." Thadeus Lowry reconnoitered by walking a small circle in the front hall. "Is there a telephone in this building?"

"No, sir. I don't think so."

"But a Mrs. Clearwater called me last night, saying you could be picked up at this address."

Robby remembered Mrs. Clearwater leaving the building twice yesterday. The first time she returned with groceries and a newspaper. The second time she returned with nothing. "She went out, sir, to make the call."

"I see. Where's the back door?"

"There isn't one. There's a cellar door. It's stuffed with rubbish and the cellar stairs are missing."

Thadeus Lowry pointed up the stairs with his walking stick. "Door to the roof?"

"Blocked with snow and ice, sir."

"Fire escapes? Are there fire escapes?"

Robby recollected what he had seen from the front and back windows of Mrs. Clearwater's apartment. "No, sir. I haven't seen any fire escapes."

Thadeus Lowry's face was grim. "Some church owns these buildings," he said. "Doubtless they want their tenants to get a taste of hellfire before they perish. This place is a firetrap."

"A people trap, sir."

"Yes. More to the point: a people trap. Well, Robby, no point in our cowering under a stairway, as it were."

"No, sir."

"This is rather like how your father and I met. I think. We were both cowering under a stairway, so to speak. In France."

"Yes, sir."

"Makes a nice story, anyway. *Mort à guerre.*"

"Lovely story, sir. I enjoyed it."

"Never mind, Robby. I'm brave enough for both of us."

"That's good, sir."

"Now, I'll tell you what to do, Robby." Thadeus Lowry took Robby by the elbow. His voice became lower, somber, confidential. "I want you to go to the front door, open it, start out. Pretend you see Tony Savallo for the first time. Act surprised. Dash back in here. Slam the front door. Run and hide back here again, underneath the stairway."

Robby looked up at Thadeus Lowry. "And if he shoots me, sir, in the meantime?"

Thadeus Lowry nodded wisely. "Then we'll have to think of something else."

"Please, sir."

"I assure you, Robby. I've thought it all out. This is the best plan. It's called drawing the hare, or something."

"It's called putting me out for bait, sir."

"The only way. After all, it is you he wants to shoot. Who wants to shoot at a tired old journalist?"

"Almost everybody, sir."

"Now, now, Robby. It's our only way. Duty, Robby." Thadeus Lowry urged Robby forward by the elbow. He stood back, waiting for Robby to precede him down the corridor. "Duty," Thadeus Lowry admonished.

Robby's knees, despite all the healthful exercise and fresh air they'd had, didn't feel very strong to him at the moment. As articulately as thin, wobbly, clattering joints could, they wobbled Robby to the front door.

He put his hand on the knob. Robby remembered the last time

he had followed Thadeus Lowry's instructions. Not only had he not found a school, he had been kidnapped, threatened with dismemberment, pursued and shot at since. "Thadeus Lowry?"

"Right behind you, Robby."

"I'm awfully glad you're brave."

His hot hand twisted the doorknob. He opened the door a crack and felt the cold air against his perspiring face. He opened the door more.

There was something in Robby which absolutely prohibited his looking across the street. He could *feel* Tony Savallo; he didn't need to *see* him. If Robby were going to be shot, he felt the event would be bad enough without his being an actual witness to it.

Robby kept his eyes on his feet. He put his right shoe onto the packed snowy surface of the top step. He shrieked. He considered he had gone far enough. He pulled in his foot, stepped back into the hall, and slammed the front door.

He turned around in the hall.

Thadeus Lowry was nowhere in sight. He had disappeared. The large, fat man with his huge coat and his scarf and his walking stick had vanished from the front hall!

"Whup!" said Robby in a hoarse whisper.

He rattled down the corridor toward what he knew was a dead end. His feet moved more side-to-side than frontward, as if he were trying to run up a steep hill. His knees vibrated so that his teeth shook. His posterior felt that it was behind him, somewhere behind his knees, rather than where it should have been.

His forward motion was negligible. He was only halfway down the corridor when he heard the doorknob rattle again. Suddenly the roar and scrape of a snowplow filled the front hall.

Robby lost what little control he had over his legs. His knees shook and rattled him around so that he was facing the front door.

Tony Savallo was inside the open door of the building. His feet were spread apart and his knees were bent. His arms were in front of him, more or less straight. He was pointing his gun at Robby's chest. One of Tony Savallo's eyes was closed. The intensity of the look in his one open eye made his squint almost comical to observe.

"Oh!" said Robby.

Thadeus Lowry stood beside Tony Savallo.

Thadeus Lowry had stepped out from behind the open door. His side was to Robby. In Thadeus Lowry's hand was the gun he had taken from Tootsie's nephew, Minnie's boy, Richard. Thadeus Lowry's gun was only centimeters away from Tony Savallo's head.

"Oh!" said Robby.

One of the guns went off.

Robby said, "Oh!"

Tony Savallo's head went onto his right shoulder as if folded. His left foot left the floor as if scalded. His right knee buckled as if hit from behind. His body fell to his right, hard, as if smitten by the full weight and force of justice.

Subsequently, Robby believed the efficiency with which Tony Savallo was executed would have been appreciated by Tony Savallo. It did not make a mess.

But at the moment Robby looked down at his own chest. His own hands. His own feet. His skin was sweated as if he were in deepest jungle; his body shivered as if he were in frozen tundra. But there were no holes in him; he did not bleed. He was intact and standing.

"Oh!" he said.

He could hear doors opening throughout the building.

Thadeus Lowry was bending over Tony Savallo, who lay on his side in the front hall. Voices from upstairs and outside were beginning to shout. "What was that?" "A gunshot!" "No, no, the snowplow backfired!" "Call the police!" "What happened?" Thadeus Lowry took Tony Savallo's own pistol from his right hand and stuck it into the pocket of Tony's green windbreaker. Then Thadeus Lowry put the pistol he himself had used into Tony's left hand. Carefully he fed Tony's index finger through the trigger bracket. Without causing the gun to fire again, Thadeus Lowry squeezed Tony's hand around the gun.

The front steps of the apartment house were crowded with people, as were the steps leading to the second floor.

Thadeus Lowry stood over Tony Savallo's body.

"He shot himself!" Thadeus Lowry declared. "I was the first one here! The poor boy shot himself!"

"He shot himself," said the people on the top step of the apartment house. And the word was passed down the steps. "He shot himself," said the people on the bottom step of the staircase leading to the second floor of the apartment house. And the word was passed up the stairs.

Magisterially placing his walking stick at a dignified angle to himself, Thadeus Lowry again declared, as if he had *heard* the news and was merely confirming it: "He shot himself."

Mrs. Clearwater was coming down the stairs through the people. "Hunh! Hunh! Hunh!" People moved aside for her great girth, as it was descending and made weightier by gravity. "The po' bo' weevil! What happened to that bo' weevil?"

"Robby?" said Thadeus Lowry.

Robby stepped forward, but as he did so he watched Mrs. Clearwater kneel on the floor by Tony Savallo. She let herself down on one haunch. She picked up Tony Savallo's head and brought it into her own lap. Gristle spilled from Tony Savallo's head onto the floor, and onto her skirt.

Passing her, Robby saw her red, torn carpet slippers, their toes aspiring toward Lordy Lord, and he loved her.

"Lordy Lord," she said, cradling Tony Savallo's head in her lap. "What they done to you, bo' weevil?"

"Robby."

Robby Burnes stood with Thadeus Lowry in the door. "He shot himself," Thadeus Lowry said.

Robby wobbled down the front steps of the building, through the people.

"Yes, yes," Thadeus Lowry assured the people. "He shot himself."

On the sidewalk, Thadeus Lowry said, "This way. I have a taxi waiting at the corner."

Immediately he proceeded to stamp along the sidewalk. He used his walking stick through the chunks of snow in a perfect rhythm as if it were a lovely spring day, birds chirruped from every bush, and they had just been to see an exhibition of roses growing.

Robby wobbled along behind.

"Violent country," Thadeus Lowry proclaimed. "Violence everywhere. Never get used to it. Barely stick your nose out the door
and you're witness to untoward violence. Still..." Robby caught up
to him by sliding down a mound of snow Thadeus Lowry had had to
circumnavigate. Thadeus Lowry was smiling to himself: a retired
journalist who discovered there was one more story he must write.
"All grist for the mill."

They came to the corner where a taxi waited, its motor running.
The driver's face was wizened as it watched Thadeus Lowry. Robby
wondered if the driver's face was wizened before Thadeus Lowry
had first gotten into his cab.

Robby slithered over a snow pile and trudged into the backseat
of the taxi.

Thadeus Lowry made his lap in the street and backed into the
cab. He landed cater-cornered on the backseat.

"The Waldorf-Astoria," he instructed from that position.

The driver with the wizened face said, "Close the door, willya,
Mac?"

"My feet are still in the street."

Struggling, Thadeus Lowry collected his feet into the cab. He
constructed himself on the backseat, feet on the floor, hat firmly in
place, walking stick propped between his legs. He looked forward.
The taxi did not move. "Waldorf-Astoria," Thadeus Lowry repeated
to the driver. "We have an appointment."

The car slithered forward, not going by the building in which
Mrs. Clearwater and Heddy and Franklin and Wellmet and Arthur
and Ugly Mary lived. Through the window Robby saw down the
street that two police cars had drawn up in front of the building.

"Cheer up," Thadeus Lowry said. "No good looking green about
the gills. We'll have a brunch tucked away in some quiet corner of
the Waldorf-Astoria. Discuss old times. Compare notes. Celebrate
my retirement from the world of affairs."

"Will I get breakfast, sir?"

"How does kippered herring, bangers and strawberry marmalade
sound?"

"Like something you made up, sir."

Thadeus Lowry reached in his overcoat pocket and withdrew Robby's school cap. He handed it to Robby.

"Very careless of you," Thadeus Lowry said. "Losing that. What would your father say? My dear friend, your father, the Duke of Pladroman…"

26
"Allow Me to Explain."

"Allow me to explain," said Thadeus Lowry.

Thadeus Lowry and Robby Burnes were tucked away in a quiet corner of the mammoth Waldorf-Astoria. It was shy eleven o'clock in the morning. It was Tuesday. Robby had been in America a week shy one day.

A waiter craned over them.

"A double extra-dry martini," Thadeus Lowry said to the waiter. "I just shot a man through the head."

"Very good, sir," said the waiter.

"After you bring that," said Thadeus Lowry, "let the boy order. Although how he can eat anything, I don't know."

The waiter withdrew.

"But first," Thadeus Lowry said to Robby, "if you'll excuse me, I must phone in a story." Sitting forward in his chair, Thadeus Lowry pinched the skin on the bridge of his nose between index finger and thumb. "No rest for the weary. Thought I'd done my last story. Yet here I am, in a state of retirement, responding to journalistic duty…Let me see…*The murderer of Ginsy O'Brien was found dead before ten o'clock this morning in the vestibule of an apartment building in Harlem. The gun with which he shot himself was discovered in his hand. Ballistic tests will prove that a second gun, found in the pocket of his green windbreaker, is the very instrument of death which executed Ginsy O'Brien on West 26th Street last Saturday night.*" Thadeus Lowry opened his eyes and blinked at Robby. "How do you like that?"

"All right, sir, but—"

"No 'but' about it! *Apparently distraught by his recent foul deed, the crime of murder, Anthony Saxallo, age 23, apparently took his own life.*"

"There is a 'but,' sir."

"There is no 'but' that anyone will notice."

"You took one gun out of his right hand and put another gun in his left hand."

Thadeus Lowry stared at Robby. Thadeus Lowry stood up from the table.

"He was right-handed, sir. You put the gun in his left hand."

Thadeus Lowry's protuberant eyes protruded even more. "How many perfect crimes do you expect me to perpetrate in a week?" he demanded. "I shot him in the left side of the head! I had to! The door opened to his left!"

"Won't the police notice, sir? I mean, a right-handed person shooting himself with his left hand?"

"Not if I tell the story first!"

The waiter appeared with his tray. Thadeus Lowry sucked the martini off the tray as easily as a vacuum cleaner sucks up peanut shells.

"People always believe what they read in a newspaper," Thadeus Lowry said.

While Thadeus Lowry was at the telephone dictating his most recent pack of lies, Robby ordered kippered herring, bangers, eggs scrambled and fried, fried tomatoes and fried potatoes, toast, strawberry marmalade, orange juice, milk and tea. His order arrived with a double gin martini.

Robby was eating quietly when Thadeus Lowry returned.

"God love a goose," said Thadeus Lowry, eyeing the various plates in front of Robby. "Is eating all that good for you?" Thadeus Lowry did not slide into his place at the table. He drew his chair back, settled on it, more or less threw a line to his martini, and berthed. "Ah, well, we have to wait anyway. I've ordered a photographer to come around and take your picture. To run with my final story tomorrow. Concerning your return to safekeeping." Thadeus Lowry's eyebrows knotted in genuine concern. "You really shouldn't look too well fed," he said. "I mean, in the photograph."

"I won't, sir."

"I mean, the color is beginning to come back into your cheeks."

"I'll try to look pale, sir." Robby continued eating. "After breakfast."

Ignorant of the happy ending Thadeus Lowry already had written for Robby, nevertheless Robby thought there would be a happy ending, however fictitious. Hoping to glance a glimmer of his forthcoming glee, Robby thought he would try the gambit of polite conversation.

"You said you're retiring, sir?"

"Yes," said Thadeus Lowry. "Superannuation. After long, hard years of sterling service, I have quit the newspaper."

"I'm sure your work will be missed."

"But I've quit with a bang."

"I'd say so, sir."

"You've been reading me?"

"Yes, sir."

"What do you think?"

"I think I'm eight years old, sir."

"What did I write?"

"Ten, sir."

"A typographical error, my boy. A typographical error. Those damned printers can't get anything straight." Thadeus Lowry leaned forward over his elbows on the table. "Allow me to explain. Thursday night I didn't have a story. No one knew you were missing. *Chérie* thought you were out being a jubilant delinquent in some schoolyard. I had had an exhausting day out tramping around the city looking for a story to write. I was sitting at my desk at *The New York Star*, keeping my eye on that bastard who keeps shoving his desk up against mine, when the phone rang."

"The man with the 'icy, metallic voice,' sir?"

"As a matter of fact, it was William O'Riordan, one of New York's finest."

"Will'um the policeman, sir? You knew who it was?"

"Do you think I'd listen to anyone who hadn't identified himself properly?"

"Of course not, sir."

"Can't have just anybody calling the newspaper with a story, you know."

"Of course not, sir."

"One must always be sure of one's sources."

"Yes, sir."

"William told me you were at home with his sister, Marie, and his brother-in-law, Frankie Savallo, stuffing down lamb *Parmesan*, and that they'd all appreciate it if I would consider you kidnapped."

"You believed him because he was a policeman, sir?"

"Of course. If you can't trust the guardians of law and order, whom can you trust?"

"I wonder that myself."

"It was a moment before I grasped the full meaning of what he was saying. At first I worried that it was their intention to knock me, of all people, up for some cash, and you know that would have been impossible."

"Yes, sir."

"It would have been against my principles to pay ransom, even if I had the cash, which, of course, I didn't."

"I understand, sir."

"One must have one's principles. But then I grasped the pristine beauty of his idea—raise a subscription for your life from the public! Wring their hearts out, fleece them, all the while selling newspapers! Perfect! I wish I could take complete credit for the idea," clucked Thadeus Lowry. "But I can't." Thadeus Lowry drained the rest of his martini glass. "Ransom of one hundred thousand dollars: They were quite decided on that. It seemed a bit much to me, but I decided to take it on as a literary challenge worthy of my talents. How quickly could I raise one hundred thousand dollars from the public on a sentimental matter?" Victoriously, he smiled across the table at the matter of sentiment. "Four days! Would you believe that?"

"No, sir."

"Well, I did it! A fantastic testament to my literary ability! Do you realize how many dollars that comes out to per word?"

"I couldn't guess, sir."

Neither could he, apparently, as he next said, "Actually, yesterday morning, while the world thought I was going to Grand Central Station with my brown paper bag stuffed with cash, having made absolutely sure I was free of police observation, instead I sauntered around for my usual midmorning visit to The Three Balls."

"The Men Only, sir?"

"What? Yes. There I met Officer William O'Riordan."

"The man who had led 'a degenerate, degraded life far outside the law?' "

"We had a great laugh. So I gave him the fifty thousand dollars—"

"Fifty thousand dollars, sir?"

"Of course."

"Weren't there one hundred thousand dollars, sir?"

"Of course. I took half. That was the deal. We arranged that Thursday night."

"While I was 'cowering in some cold corner, starved and beaten, a knife at my throat?' "

"But that wasn't true," said Thadeus Lowry. "You should never believe your own press."

"But it became true! I spent the night in a rubbish barrel! I upset everybody in an hotel! Tony Savallo chased me all over the city. He shot at me twice!"

"Tush, tush, Robby. I daresay you saw parts of New York you'd never have seen otherwise."

"I saw underneath a lot of places."

"You survived. You're all right, aren't you?"

"I may be coming down with a nose cold, sir."

"From all that breakfast you're eating, I expect. Consider my retirement! Fifty thousand dollars. Why, Robby, this frees me to do all sorts of things! Perhaps I'll go into public service, run for Congress. Or I could buy a small country newspaper, build it into an empire!"

"Oh, no, sir."

"Why not?"

Robby looked through the window. On the sidewalk people were scurrying with Christmas packages. "I don't know, sir."

"Of course," said Thadeus Lowry, again apparently hearing some distant bell of duty, "what I really should do is write a book."

"Oh, yes, sir. You've hit upon it."

"I've hit what?"

"The answer, sir. Your writing a book. You type so fast, sir."

"The inside story of journalism," Thadeus Lowry mused. "How it really works, by the man who knows. The honesty, the integrity, the talent men and women bring to it, the long hours, the hard work, the sparse rewards. It would make a million."

Outside on the sidewalk, Santa Claus was setting up his money pot on a tripod. Robby was surprised. The last time he had seen Santa Claus he was on his back in a gutter being beaten by an enraged taxi driver. Looking more closely, however, perhaps more closely than he would have before, Robby observed that Santa's whiskers were not really a part of Santa's face. They were the whiskers of a fat man, slipping up and down a thin man's face. And in the sunlight, the snowy, flowing hair was a bit too gossamer to have been spun by time.

Robby Burnes said, "That Santa Claus is a fake."

Thadeus Lowry looked through the window. Quietly, he said, "Never believe anything, Robby. Including this."

Thadeus Lowry shifted uncomfortably in his chair, and signalled the waiter for another drink. "Yes, that's what I'll do. Write a book and make a million. I'll send you a copy."

"Send me a copy? Where am I going?"

"Oh, yes," said Thadeus Lowry. "I haven't told you that yet."

Robby waited to be told.

Thadeus Lowry said, "You have a grandaunt, in Scotland."

"I have?"

"You didn't know?"

"I was beginning to disbelieve it."

"You also have a lawyer living luxuriously in a suite upstairs— suite 1776—in full anticipation of your imminent arrival. Name of Carp. Firm of Pollack, Carp and Fish, London."

"I have, sir? I mean, he's here? In this hotel?"

"Who else can afford this hotel save an employed lawyer? The Waldorf-Astoria has floors and floors permanently reserved for other people's lawyers."

"Has he been here all the time?"

"Arrived Friday. By plane. Apparently your old grandaunt got wind of your family's current events belatedly, climbed aboard her escutcheon, whistled into London and pulled a lot of wigs. Raised all the circles of hell, according to Carp. Dispatched him on the next plane coming west to bring you back dead or alive."

"Dead or alive?"

"Just an expression, Robby. Anyway, he arrived Friday, bought a newspaper at the airport, saw you were among the missing, checked into a suite upstairs, and has been eating gloriously ever since."

"Eating! Was he no help at all?"

"Between meals he kept insisting things be done properly, phone calls traced, that sort of thing. That was all right, of course, as William O'Riordan would only call me from the police station."

"I'm going home!"

"By plane. This afternoon. Seems a very unsafe way to travel these days, but fly you shall. You'll be home in time for Christmas, Robby. Ah, here's the eminent picture-taker for *The New York Star*."

The entrance of the photographer caused a stir. He was stopped in the door and made to explain his camera to the headwaiter. He arrived at the table flanked by waiters.

"Hullo, Burnes," the photographer said. "How does it feel to be thadeuslowried?"

Robby stood up and shook hands with the photographer. Then he shook hands with the headwaiter and the other waiters.

As the photographer took pictures of Robby, other people crowded around, shook his hand, asked him to write his name on slips of paper. They congratulated him on his return to safekeeping, and several mentioned how glad they had been to send *The New York Star* a dollar or two toward his ransom.

On the slips of paper Robby wrote: *Robert Clearwater*.

The photographer left. The crowd thinned. Robby turned back to the table.

Thadeus Lowry was gone.

The headwaiter was speaking quietly to Robby. "I hate to bother you with this, Your Grace, but the gentleman who was with you left without paying the bill."

"What?" smiled Robby. "He didn't even tell you a story?"

"He didn't say anything, sir. He just left."

Robby took the gold sovereign his father had given him out of the breast pocket of his jacket. He looked at it before giving it to the headwaiter. "Will this be all right?"

"That will be fine." The headwaiter took the sovereign. "Sorry to bother you."

"Quite all right," said Robby. "You've just been thadeuslowried. One gets used to it."

A very, very thin man in a three-piece suit answered the door of suite 1776.

"Mr. Carp?" Robby asked. "I'm—"

"Yes, yes, my boy," the man said. "Have you had luncheon yet?"

"No," Robby beamed, "I haven't."